Zaynab's heart began to hammer against her ribs. What was it about this man's touch that could render her so confused? "Does a Love Slave always undress her master?" she asked him, trying to regain control of her own emotions.

"If it pleases him. She bathes him as you did me today, and both dresses and undresses him. Everything she does for him is meant to give him pleasure of some sort. She is not simply a concubine. She is more. She must learn how to release her own passions so that even if her master is not the best of lovers, he will believe that he is. His mere touch must send her into a swooning fit of pleasure." He tipped her face up to his. "Yet a Love Slave *never* loses command of the situation, even while in the throes of ecstasy. She is mistress of herself at all times, Zaynab. Do you understand me?"

"I am not certain," Zaynab said slowly.

THE
LOVE
SLAVE

Bertrice Small

FAWCETT CREST • NEW YORK

A Fawcett Crest Book
Published by Ballantine Books
Copyright © 1995 by Bertrice Small

All rights reserved under International and Pan-American Copyright Conventions. Published in the United States by Ballantine Books, a division of Random House, Inc., and simultaneously in Canada by Random House of Canada Limited, Toronto.

http://www.randomhouse.com

Library of Congress Catalog Card Number: 97–93374

ISBN 0-449-00213-6

Map by Mapping Specialists, Ltd.

Manufactured in the United States of America

First Trade Edition: March 1995
First Mass Market Edition: October 1997

10 9 8 7 6 5

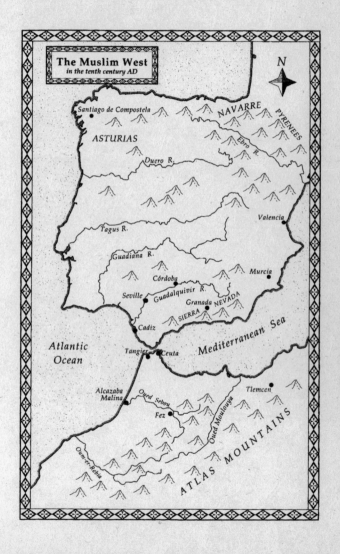

The Muslim West
in the tenth century AD

N

Santiago de Compostela

NAVARRE

PYRENEES

ASTURIAS

Ebro R.

Duero R.

Tagus R.

Valencia

Guadiana R.

Córdoba

Murcia

Seville

Guadalquivir R.

Granada NEVADA

SIERRA

Cadiz

Atlantic
Ocean

Tangier Ceuta

Mediterranean Sea

Alcazaba
Malina

Oued Sebou

Tlemcen

Fez

Oued Moulouya

Oum-er-Rebia

ATLAS MOUNTAINS

Prologue

SCOTLAND

A.D. 929

Sorcha MacDuff grunted sharply with her pain. Outside the gray stone keep, the early December winds keened mournfully, as if they shared her suffering. A grimace, almost a hard smile, touched her lips briefly as yet another pain tore through her frame. The room inside the keep was cold; so cold that its hard walls were lightly dusted with a thin overlay of frost despite the small fire in the fireplace. The tiny blaze struggled hard to maintain itself, crackling and sending small showers of sparks up the narrow chimney. Its energies were wasted, for the room was made no warmer by its presence.

The naked, straining woman did not feel the icy air creeping between the stones, or from beneath the closed door. She was far too intent upon bringing forth her child. It was her first childbirth, but there would be no others unless she remarried; and she had no intention of doing so. Her husband, Torcull MacDuff, the laird of Ben MacDui, was dead these three months past. Killed in a land dispute with Alasdair Ferguson, laird of Killieloch. Her child, *children*, she silently amended, for the midwife had said she would bear two bairns, would revenge their father upon the MacFhearghuis, and destroy all the Fergusons of Killieloch so that not a trace of them would remain in the history of the land hereabouts. She was exultant with the thought of her vengeance. "You will not have died in vain, my dear lord," she whispered to herself.

The midwife brought her back to the present. *"Push, lady!"* the crone urged her. Sorcha MacDuff pushed with all her strength while the midwife groped between her outstretched

3

legs, muttering and nodding. *"Again!"* the old woman commanded her.

Sorcha bore down with grim intensity. Then, to her amazement, she felt something bulky and slimy sliding from her wet body. She struggled to sit up more and see. The midwife grasped the bloody infant by its ankles, held it up and smacked its bottom. The child instantly began to howl loudly.

"Gie me my son!" Sorcha MacDuff growled menacingly. *"Gie him to me this instant!"* She held out eager arms.

" 'Tis a girlie ye've born, lady," the midwife said as she swiftly wiped the birthing blood from the wailing child. Then wrapping a shawl about the baby, she handed her to her mother.

A daughter? She had not even considered a daughter, but as the second child was certain to be a son, Sorcha decided that she was pleased to have a daughter as well. Two sons would have been difficult. They would have probably spent more time fighting each other than fighting the Fergusons of Killieloch. Nay. A daughter was a good thing. She could be used to cement an alliance with an ally. Sorcha looked down on the baby in her arms. "Gruoch," she said softly. "Ye'll be called Gruoch. 'Tis a family name."

The baby looked up at its mother with wonderful blue eyes. She was a very pretty creature with a tuft of gold down upon her head.

"Lady, ye've the other yet to birth," the midwife said, breaking her reverie. "Hae ye nae pains?"

"Aye," Sorcha MacDuff replied bluntly. "I hae pains, but I dinna mind them for I hae been too fascinated wi' my wee lassie."

"Ye hae best put yer mind to t'other one, lady," the midwife said sourly. "A laddie is more important to the MacDuffs than the lassie yer cradling. Gie her to me now. I'll put her in her cot where she belongs." The midwife almost snatched the infant from her mother, tucking her into the carved cradle by the struggling fire so that Sorcha MacDuff could put her mind to the business of bearing the MacDuff son now striving to be released from her womb.

The second child, its passage unblocked by the birth of its

sibling, was born far more quickly. It pushed impatiently into the world, crying loudly as it came.

"Gie me my lad!" Sorcha MacDuff cried excitedly.

The midwife wiped the blood from the twin, peering carefully down at it as she did so. Then she shook her head sadly. " 'Tis another lass," she told the pale-faced woman. "The Mac-Duffs of Ben MacDui hae died wi' out a laird." She wrapped a shawl about the second squalling infant, sighing mournfully even as she did so. Then she handed her to her mother, but Sorcha MacDuff recoiled angrily.

"I dinna want her," she hissed. "What guid is a second daughter to me? *I wanted a son!*"

"Will ye question the will of God above, lady?" the midwife demanded. The children were both girls, and there was no help for it. "God hae seen fit to gie ye twin daughters, lady. Both are healthy bairns. Surely ye canna deny them. Thank God for your guid fortune. Many a childless lass would envy ye."

"I'll nae deny my wee Gruoch," Sorcha MacDuff said, "but the other is naught but a burden to me. Gruoch is the heiress of Ben MacDui now, but what good is the other? *I needed a son!*"

" 'Tis a harsh land and time in which we live, lady," the midwife reminded her. "The bairns are both strong now, but what if one took sick and died? Wi'out the other, there would be nae MacDuff at all to inherit. The secondborn has her place as well, I'm thinking. Ye hae best gie her a name too."

"Call her Regan, then," said the disappointed woman.

" 'Tis a laddie's name," the midwife said, shocked.

"She should hae been a lad," Sorcha MacDuff replied stonily. " 'Tis the price she must pay for disappointing me." Then she grunted as a final pain swept over her and she birthed the placenta.

Shaking her head, the midwife placed Regan MacDuff in the second cradle waiting by the little fire. Then she turned back to attend to her mistress. She had hardly finished this final task when the door to the room burst open with a bang. Several armed men strode boldly in, having pushed their way past the feeble and frightened MacDuff clansmen guarding the keep.

The midwife shrieked, recognizing the green Ferguson plaid wrapped about the intruders. She cowered by her mistress.

A tall, hard-eyed man grasped the terrified woman by the arm, and gazing fiercely down into her face, demanded, "Where are the bairns?" The midwife was speechless with fear, but Alasdair Ferguson followed her gaze to the two cradles by the fire. *"Kill them!"* he ordered his men fiercely. "I'll hae nae more MacDuffs threatening my lands."

Naked, and still bloodied, the new mother struggled to arise from the birthing table, her hands reaching out to grasp at the MacFhearghuis's dagger. Without even looking at her, he slapped her hands away. "Bastard!" she shrieked at him.

"They are lasses, my lord!" the midwife finally managed to gasp in defense of the helpless babies. "Lasses canna harm ye!"

"Lasses? Both bairns?" His look was incredulous. Then his eyes swung to the naked woman on the birthing table. "So," he said mockingly, "Torcull MacDuff could only get lasses on ye, Sorcha. I'd hae gie ye sons, and yet will, my hot-eyed bitch. Ye should hae wed wi' me instead of MacDuff."

"Is three wives not enough for ye, MacFhearghuis?" she demanded scornfully. "I wed wi' the man I loved. Though ye hae killed him, I dinna regret my decision." She made no effort to cover herself before him, or before his men, who were wise enough not to stare.

"I could kill yer bairns, Sorcha MacDuff," he said coldly, his eyes narrowing to contemplate her. Even naked and bloody with the efforts of her childbirth, she was still a handsome woman to be desired, and desire her he did. She had refused to marry him almost two years ago this very month, choosing his enemy instead. Torcull the Fair, the MacDuff had been called. He was a tall young man with shining gold hair and an easy smile. Well, thought the MacFhearghuis, he would not be so handsome now that the worms were feasting on him; and his widow would regret her previous actions toward the laird of Killieloch. To protect her bairns she would do exactly what he wanted her to do. Her maternal instincts would far outweigh her pride and her outrage when he made her his leman. He had once sworn to her that she would suffer for refusing him and choosing the MacDuff instead. Now he would have her, and he would dispose of her as he saw fit.

Alasdair Ferguson released his iron grip on the midwife's arm, shoving her toward the cradles. "Unwrap both bairns," he said. "I would see for myself if ye both speak the truth. Unwrap them, and lay them on their mam's belly so I may see them together. Quickly, old crone! I hae nae any more time to waste this day."

The midwife scurried to do his bidding, unwrapping the protective covering from each of the babies and laying them atop their mother's now shivering body. "There they be, my lord," she quavered. "Two wee lassies as ye can plainly see."

The laird of Killieloch stared down at the infants. With a single finger he gently examined each one's genitals, seeking for a tiny manhood, but there was none. Both were lasses, without a doubt. He grinned briefly, pleased, and then an idea came to him. "Which of them is the firstborn?" he demanded.

"This one," the midwife said, pointing. "Her name is Gruoch."

"How can ye tell?" he asked her. "They seem to be identical in both features and form to me. How can ye separate them, old woman?"

"The firstborn has clear, bright blue eyes, my lord," the midwife said. "Look and see. The secondborn's eyes, though blue now, hint of possibly another hue to come in time. Nae the firstborn. Her eyes are wi'out a doubt blue. Can ye nae see it?"

He peered down at the children. "Aye," he said impatiently, although he really could see no difference between the twin girls. "Wrap them up and put them back in their cradles." He turned to the woman lying on the birthing table. She was pale, but defiant. "I'll spare yer bairns, Sorcha MacDuff. The old woman is right. Lasses are nae a danger to me and mine. But I'll hae yer firstborn, Gruoch, for my heir, Ian. The feud between our clans is now settled, for the lands in dispute between us will be Ferguson lands wi' this match."

Sorcha glared at him. She knew she had no choice in the matter. He would have her precious Gruoch for his lout of a son, whatever she said. In that moment Sorcha MacDuff hated

Alasdair Ferguson with every fiber of her being, but she would have to accept his terms. She was a clever woman, and despite her ire she could see the good side to the situation. The stronger Fergusons would consider the lands of Ben MacDui theirs from the moment the betrothal agreement was signed and sealed. They would aid the weaker MacDuff clansmen to defend those lands. Gruoch would grow up in peace and safety. *And I will have my leisure in which to consider my revenge upon the Fergusons of Killieloch,* she thought craftily. They had killed her Torcull. Now they were annexing his lands. They would pay dearly for their treachery one day.

"What if Gruoch dies? Children are fragile," she said practically.

"Ye've two daughters, and if Ian should perish of some childish complaint, I've half a dozen sons to take his place. If both yer lasses die, however, these lands are forfeit to me and mine. But ye need nae fear, Sorcha MacDuff, yer lasses face nae danger from me. It is better to be united by our blood than by conquest, I think. It will ensure a real peace between our peoples. Then I can turn my attentions to yer Robertson relations," he mocked her.

"What of my other lass?" Sorcha asked him. "She must have a respectable portion for a dowry, for she'll want a husband one day."

"She goes to the Church," the MacFhearghuis answered firmly. "I will hae nae other clan laying claim to these lands through the other wee wench. But she'll nae go until Gruoch and Ian are properly wedded, and bedded, Sorcha MacDuff. If, God forfend, we lose the firstborn, we'll hae the secondborn in reserve." Then seeing her shiver, Alasdair Ferguson took his own plaid and put it over her. "I'll fetch the priest and hae him make all the arrangements. Ye'll be informed when all is in readiness. Ye and yer lassies are now under my protection, Sorcha MacDuff. Ye nae fear any longer." So saying, he turned, and signaling to his men to follow him, the MacFhearghuis departed.

As the door slammed behind him, Sorcha struggled to climb from the birthing table. Stumbling across the room, she tore the dark green and blue plaid with its narrow red and white stripes from her body and flung it into the fire. "Fetch me water, old woman!" she snarled at the midwife. "I would wash the Ferguson stench from my person!"

The midwife scuttled to obey her mistress, quickly bringing a basin of warm water from the kettle over the fire, along with a clean rag. "Here ye be," she said, a little afraid of the look on the lady's face.

Sorcha MacDuff scrubbed at her body almost violently. Dark thoughts swirled about in her head. She was not certain yet how she would revenge herself upon the Fergusons and their ilk; but she would do it! The MacFhearghuis had foolishly given her all the time she would need to effect her plan, whatever it was to be. In his great arrogance he had decided that all was settled, but it would not be settled between them until she had taken her vengeance for Torcull's death and the robbery of his lands. No Ferguson would ever hold sway over Ben MacDui. She would let them protect her, and protect her bairns, but in the end she would find a way to triumph over Alasdair Ferguson and his clan. Suddenly a wave of weakness swept over her, and she staggered slightly.

"Lady, ye should be in yer bed," the midwife said, coming to her aid. "Ye'll need all yer strength if yer to nurse both those sweet bairns. They'll be hungry soon enough, I'm thinking."

"I cannot nurse them both," Sorcha said. "Find someone to nurse Regan. She can take the lass to her cottage as soon as possible." The new mother climbed into her bed. A bed empty of a husband now, she considered bitterly, yanking the fox robe over herself.

The midwife pursed her lips in condemnation. "There is nae reason ye canna nurse both yer bairns, lady," she said sternly. "Yer a strapping lass, and I can see the milk is already rising in yer breasts. There's more than enough for two."

"My milk is for Gruoch only, old witch," Sorcha snapped irritably. "Find a wet nurse for the other." Then she turned her face to the wall.

Shaking her head with disapproval, the midwife moved to the

cradles to look down on the two infants, who slumbered peacefully now, unaware of the fates they faced: one to be a bride for the Fergusons, the MacDuffs of Ben MacDui's bitterest enemies, and the other little lass for the Church, whether she would or no. The heiress, and the abbess, the midwife thought wryly with a soft chuckle. Then she slipped from the room quietly, closing the door silently behind her.

Part I

SCOTLAND

A.D. 943

❧ *Chapter 1*

*T*he little hall at Ben MacDui was blue with smoke, for the chimney drew poorly. Sorcha MacDuff, seated at the high board, gazed down upon her numerous offspring tumbling about the room. Six little bastards, and a seventh in her fertile womb. Five were boys, the fourth born a girl. She felt nothing for them. They were Fergusons. Her mother love, at least that which she possessed, was for Gruoch MacDuff, her firstborn. For Gruoch's twin, Regan, she allowed a small bit of affection. Regan had grown to be much like her father, Torcull, of sainted memory. The girl had his daring, and was brave to the point of foolishness. Sorcha could not help but admire her second-born twin.

In the spring after her MacDuff daughters had been born, Alasdair Ferguson had returned to Ben MacDui. The betrothal contracts, drawn up by the Fergusons, had been signed then in the presence of a priest. They could have said anything and Sorcha would have known no different, for she could neither read nor write. The priest told her that Gruoch would be Ian Ferguson's wife as soon as her womanly flow began. Regan would then go to a convent on the west coast of Scotland to devote her life to God. The matter settled, the MacFhearghuis dismissed the cleric and raped the widow MacDuff, keeping her locked with him in her bedchamber for three days while he had his way with her. Nine months later she birthed him a son.

In the years that followed, Alasdair Ferguson visited his leman on a regular basis, as her growing family attested to, but he would not marry her, nor would she have had him if he had asked. Three times Sorcha MacDuff had gone in secret to the old witch woman in the glen, paid an exorbitant fee, drunk a disgusting potion, and aborted her violator's offspring. When he learned of her deeds, he had sought out the witch, hung her from a tree, burned her cottage, then returned to Ben MacDui and beaten Sorcha MacDuff so badly she'd been unable to arise from her bed for a week. After that she bore his bastards without complaint, but she could not love them. *They were Fergusons.*

Outside, she heard the blare of a hunting horn, and then the hall door burst open to admit Alasdair Ferguson in the company of his two eldest sons, Ian and Cellach. Sorcha MacDuff arose slowly. Her time was quite near. "My lord," she greeted him quietly, signaling the servants to bring food for the men.

"I've brought a stag," Alasdair Ferguson said by way of greeting, and kissing her mouth in a show of proprietorship, he seated himself at the board.

The servants scurried to bring him wine, bread, and meat. They knew he was not a patient man.

Ian and Cellach Ferguson seated themselves next to their father and began to stuff their handsome faces. They had not bothered to greet Sorcha MacDuff. Reaching out, Alasdair cuffed the nearest of the pair.

"Hae ye the decency to greet the lady Sorcha properly before you eat her food, ye pair of uncouth cubs," Alasdair growled at them. " 'Tis her home yer in and her table at which ye sit."

" 'Tis Ferguson property," Cellach said surlily, rubbing the spot where his father's hand had made contact with his skull.

With a roar, the MacFhearghuis leapt to his feet and knocked his second son onto the floor. " 'Tis Ferguson land because I made it so," he said, "but before it was Ferguson land it was MacDuff land, and Ferguson or MacDuff, it is this lady's home. Ye'll mind yer manners in her presence whether I'm here or nae." He gave the young man a kick. "Get up, and go eat in the stables where ye belong."

Cellach scrambled to his feet. "I dinna know why ye dinna gie me Gruoch to wife instead of Ian. Then I would hae had my own lands," he said.

"Aye," his father rejoined, "and ye'd be looking to *my* lands, ye would, ye greedy little beggar!" He aimed another blow at the boy, who this time skillfully ducked it, running out of the hall. Then he turned to his eldest, but Ian was quickly on his feet, bowing to Sorcha MacDuff and thanking her for her hospitality.

Reseating himself, Ian said, "And how are the bairns, lady? They all appear to look well. My sister Sine grows prettier every day, I'm thinking. 'Tis nice to hae a sweet wee sister." He took up a joint of meat and bit into it.

"Yer father's bastards seem to thrive," Sorcha MacDuff answered him pleasantly. "All my bairns do, thanks be to God."

"About my lass," Alasdair Ferguson said, "I want to take her back home wi' me. I've nae a woman in the house but the servants. Sine's a Ferguson, my only daughter. 'Tis time she took her place. There's nae shame to any of our bairns for I've acknowledged them all."

"Take her, then," Sorcha MacDuff said. "Take all yer other bastards too, my lord. They're nothing to me. I've my Gruoch."

He shook his head at her words. "Yer a hard woman, Sorcha MacDuff," he told her. "Very well, I'll take Donald, Aed, and Giric as well. They're all old enough to be separated from ye. Ye'll keep Indulf, Culen, and the new bairn for the time being." He quaffed down the wine in his cup, and the servant by his side hurriedly refilled it. " 'Tis about Gruoch I've come, Sorcha. Surely her flow has come upon her by now. She celebrated her thirteenth birthday last December, and 'tis now April. We hae a marriage to consummate. Ian is twenty-three, and more than ready for a mate. He's populating the whole damned district wi' his bastards, woman. He needs his wife!"

"Ye'd take my lass away so soon?" Sorcha began to weep in a genuine show of emotion. "Dinna take her, my lord. *Not yet.*"

"In the name of all the saints, woman," he said angrily, for he hated a crying woman, "she's nae going away from ye! She and Ian will live here at Ben MacDui for the time being. That way ye'll be wi' her when she spawns her first bairn nine months after the wedding. I may nae hae experience wi' daughters, but

I know a lass needs her mam at a time like that. Hush yer howling, Sorcha, and answer me. Is Gruoch's flow upon her now, or nae?"

"Only just this month," she said slowly, although both Gruoch and her sister had begun their woman's flow the previous autumn. They had kept it a secret in order to have more time, but now it mattered no longer, Sorcha thought to herself. She was to finally have her revenge after all these years.

"Then let us hae the wedding!" the MacFhearghuis replied with enthusiasm. " 'Tis what I've waited for all these years, woman!"

"Ye canna hae a wedding just because ye want a wedding," Sorcha told him coyly. "We hae preparations to make, my lord."

"Ye've had thirteen years for those preparations, Sorcha MacDuff," he answered. "Today be the twentieth day of the month of April. Our children will wed in seven days' time." He turned to his son. "Ian! What think ye? Ye'll be a married man in another few days at long last. She's grown into a pretty wench. Yer a lucky young fellow!"

"Aye, Da," Ian Ferguson answered his father dutifully. He was an attractive man with russet hair and blue eyes.

"Where is Gruoch?" Alasdair Ferguson demanded. He peered about the hall, but only his children were in evidence.

Sorcha shrugged. " 'Tis spring," she said by way of explanation.

"Donald Ferguson!" the MacFhearghuis called to the eldest of his and Sorcha MacDuff's sons. "To me, laddie!"

The boy, who had been wrestling with his younger brothers, Aed and Giric, scrambled to his feet and ran to stand before his sire. Like all of Alasdair MacDuff's sons, he was russet-haired. "Aye, Da?"

"Ye and Sine and the other two will come home wi' me today," the older man said. "Does that please ye, laddie?"

The boy's face broke into a broad smile. "Aye, Da!"

"Do ye know where yer sister Gruoch is?" the MacFhearghuis continued. "I would speak wi' her."

"Aye, Da, I know where Gruoch is," Donald replied with a

sly glance at his mother, but Sorcha's threatening look was enough to guarantee his silence. "Shall I run and fetch her for ye, Da?"

"Aye, laddie, go and do that," his father told him. As Donald ran off, he turned to Sorcha MacDuff. "He's a good laddie, woman. Ye hae done well wi' him and the others, even if ye hae no mother love for any of my offspring. Yer a foolish woman, I'm thinking."

"Think what ye will, my lord," she answered him calmly. "From the first moment I saw her, Gruoch became my sole reason for being. I need none other. I want no other."

He shook his head at her. He knew he was a hard man, but he dearly loved all of his children. How could he not? They were his flesh. Well, from now on all the bairns Sorcha bore him would come to his house as soon as they were weaned. Indulf, who was two and a half, and Culen, who was one, were still nursing, but he'd have them as soon as they were not. He realized he should have taken the elder children three years ago. Their mother was a cold woman. For a brief moment his thoughts turned to Regan MacDuff. She had no one, poor lassie. Her mother's passion was for Gruoch alone. Regan would be better off in the convent to which he was sending her. His cousin Una was the abbess there. Regan would find kindness and companionship within the walls of St. Maire's.

Young Donald Ferguson ran from the hall of the tower house and up the hill where the sheep were pastured. To his surprise, he found both of the twins, but Jamie MacDuff was there as well, as Donald had known he would be. "Gruoch!" he called. "The MacFhearghuis is in the hall, and he would see ye! I've come to fetch ye. Yer to be married next week, sister! My brother, Ian, is eager for his bride!" Donald grinned.

Gruoch MacDuff turned from the young man with whom she had been in conversation. "Dinna speak so intimately to me, whelp," she chided Donald. Then she asked, "When did they decide the wedding date?"

"Just now," he said. "My father asked the she-wolf who is our mother if yer flow wasn't finally upon ye. She said it was just this month, but I know that to be a lie." He grinned again at her.

Gruoch paled. "Ye canna prove it," she said low.

"And if ye tell yer father," Regan interjected, "ye'll nae live long enough to join the MacFhearghuis's household, Donald." She smiled sweetly at him, all the while fingering the dirk in her waistband. "Think very carefully, whelp, before you decide what you will do."

"Yer as mean as our mam," he told her sourly, and turned back to the tower house.

"They say I'm like my sire, Torcull MacDuff," Regan called after him, laughing.

"Are ye afraid of nothing at all?" Gruoch asked her twin. "I dinna think ye'll make a good nun, Regan mine."

"I hae no desire to be a nun, but a nun I'll be," her sister answered. "There is no other choice open to me."

"Ye could take a man, and hae a bairn," Jamie MacDuff spoke.

"And be hunted down and killed wi' my babe because I am in line to inherit Ben MacDui? I thank ye for yer suggestion, Jamie MacDuff, but 'tis nae a good one, I fear. The Mac-Fhearghuis is a fierce man, and a bad enemy to hae, as our father found out."

"If ye switched places wi' Gruoch and pretended to be her, then ye'd be Ian Ferguson's bride. If ye did, Gruoch and I could flee away to some other part of Alba, or Daldriada, or Strathclyde, to live our lives in peace, free of the Fergusons." His brown eyes were serious.

Gruoch gasped with his words. "Ye might at least ask me before ye decide to change my life," she said sharply, and Regan hid a smile. "I am the heiress to Ben MacDui, not Regan!"

"Do ye nae want to wed wi' me then, Gruoch?" He looked hurt.

"I'm betrothed to another, Jamie MacDuff, and besides,

how would ye support me and the bairns we would hae? Yer no lord."

"The MacFhearghuis will be wondering where ye are," Regan reminded her twin. "Come, we must go." She looked at the crestfallen young man. "Yer a fool, Jamie MacDuff," she said to him. Then taking Gruoch by the hand, she led her back to the tower house.

"Why do ye lead him on so?" Regan demanded as they hurried along.

Gruoch shrugged wordlessly, and Regan knew she would get no more from her unless her sister wanted to tell her. Doted on by their mother, Gruoch was but a younger version of Sorcha MacDuff. Much of what she thought, she kept to herself. She had a passion for vengeance against those who she believed had done her wrong. Still, there was an odd bond between the twins, for Regan sensed a fragility beneath Gruoch's hard veneer. Perhaps that was why she was always jumping to her sister's defense, protecting her, watching over her. Who will keep Gruoch from herself when I am gone? Regan wondered.

"How do I look?" Gruoch demanded as they reached the doorway of the tower house. She brushed imagined dust from her woolen gown and smoothed down her fair hair.

"Every bit as good as I do," Regan said with a chuckle, and Gruoch laughed with her. It was a longtime jest between them.

They were, as they had been at birth, identical in both face and form but for one difference. Gruoch's eyes were a rich azure color. Regan's, however, were an aquamarine with tiny gold flecks. It was not often that people were able to tell them apart, for they were so stunned by the girls' beauty, they did not look into their eyes. They saw only the exquisite faces of the twins, and hair like molten gold silk. No one could ever recall having seen hair so fair.

They entered the hall together, greeting their mother and her guests politely. Then they stood dutifully before the high board.

"Though I've known them all their lives, I still canna tell

them apart," grumbled the MacFhearghuis. "Gruoch, come up here!"

The girl stepped daintily up onto the dais, and coming to the laird's side, kissed his rough cheek. "My lord."

He pulled her down into his lap and pinched her cheek. "Yer a pretty lass. Ye'll gie me strong Ferguson grandsons to inherit my lands, will ye nae, Gruoch?"

Gruoch blushed and giggled. "Donald says ye've set the date of the wedding, my lord. Is it so, then?"

"Aye," he confirmed. "In seven days, lass, ye'll wed wi' my Ian and become a wife. It is past time."

"Dinna send Regan to the convent, my lord," Gruoch said suddenly. "We've ne'er been apart. I dinna like to think of my life wi'out her."

"Ye'll hae nae time for Regan," Alasdair Ferguson told the girl. "Ye must concentrate on gieing the Fergusons another generation of sons and daughters. Ye'll nae miss yer sister."

"Aye, I will," Gruoch replied stubbornly. Her blue eyes were both angry and sad at the same time. She wanted very much to defy him, but being young, she wasn't quite certain how to go about it.

Still standing below the high board, Regan heard, and was touched by, her twin sister's plea. Despite their mother's obvious preference for Gruoch, the two girls had always been close. Gruoch, however, could never make up for the neglectful atmosphere in which the secondborn of the twins had grown up. Gruoch had always been cuddled and fussed over. Regan was always an afterthought. Even now she was being ignored. It was as if she were not even there. With a soft little sigh, Regan slipped from the hall. She would not be missed, she knew. The focus of everyone's attention was Gruoch, as it always had been.

The MacFhearghuis tipped Gruoch from his lap. "Go and gie yer intended a wee kiss, lassie," he ordered her.

"Ohh, nay!" she said, cowering against her mother's chair. " 'Tis nae proper until we are wed. 'Tis what my mother hae always taught me, my lord. A man will nae respect a woman who is loose, or free wi' her affections."

Ian Ferguson grinned. She was a virgin, of course, and he very much liked taking a girl's maidenhead. Each was different. Some were eager for a strong cock. Some were shy, but could be coaxed with patience. Best of all he liked those girls who fought him. He could not explain it even to himself, but he liked forcing a maiden to his will. They always ended up enjoying themselves in the end. He peered closely at Gruoch. He wasn't certain if she could be coaxed or if she would fight him. Either way, he would have her maidenhead in just seven days' time. She would be his wife, and certainly could not refuse him.

Later, when the Fergusons had gone from Ben MacDui, Gruoch sat alone with her mother. Sorcha said to her eldest daughter, "That was nicely done today, my darling. I can see that the MacFhearghuis is well pleased wi' ye. Jesu!" She rubbed her distended belly. "I can only pray this is the last of his bastards I'll be forced to bear."

"Did you see how Ian looked at me?" Gruoch said quietly. "I am told he likes it best when a woman struggles against him. He is fair of face, but black of heart, I fear."

"Yer a lass of my ilk, Gruoch. Ye'll tame him, my daughter," Sorcha assured her. "As soon as he learns he is to be a father, he will worship ye, even as will his father." She shifted uncomfortably, and then swore, "Jesu! Maria! My waters have broken. My time is here again."

"Let me help you, Mother," Gruoch said, and with the aid of a servant, got Sorcha MacDuff to her chamber and onto the well-worn birthing table. "Fetch old Bridie, and find my sister," Gruoch ordered the serving woman.

Sorcha groaned as the first of the spasms tore through her.

"What will you call this one?" Gruoch asked her mother in an effort to distract her from the pain of her labor.

"Malcolm, after the new king," Sorcha said through gritted teeth. "And if 'tis a lass, I'll call her Maire. Ahh, Jesu! The pain is fierce."

Old Bridie, the midwife, arrived and said sharply, "Hush yer complaints, Sorcha MacDuff. This is your eighth labor, yer ninth child. Yer nae a lass haeing her firstborn."

"Yer an evil old crone," Sorcha said irritably, "and canna remember yerself the pain of bringing a bairn into this world. Ahhhhhh! Damn Alasdair Ferguson and his hot lust to hell and back!" she cried as Regan came into the room.

"I dinna know why the MacFhearghuis continues to climb into her bed," the midwife said to no one in particular. "Surely he can find someone younger and prettier than yer mam. Twenty-eight is too old to be hae'ing bairns!"

Gruoch and Regan looked at each other and chuckled low. They agreed with old Bridie. The MacFhearghuis, however, could not seem to resist Sorcha MacDuff, despite her bitterness and vicious tongue. And though neither of the twins would admit it to another living soul, they had heard their mother crying out with pleasure and encouraging her enemy lover onward when he came into her bed. Those cries had been a part of their life from earliest childhood.

Sorcha MacDuff's labors had always been relatively simple, but this time it was different. The hours went by, and still the child was not born. Finally, as a second day began to dawn, she bore a healthy son, but he was an enormous child, the largest baby they had ever seen. He fought his way into the world, red-faced and squalling with anger, his small fists flailing furiously. Upon the top of his head was a thick tuft of carrot-red hair.

Old Bridie placed the bloody infant upon his mother's belly, cutting the cord neatly as she did so, knotting it tightly. "He's a braw laddie, lady. Yer labors are well rewarded."

Sorcha looked down at the howling child. Another Ferguson, she thought wearily. Another damned Ferguson! Jesu, she was tired. More tired than she had ever been before. She closed her eyes with a sigh of relief, barely feeling the last pains as the placenta slipped from her exhausted body.

The midwife set about her tasks, but she looked worried. When Sorcha had been cleaned up and tucked into her bed—

and raging Malcolm, as the infant was quickly dubbed, quieted and settled in his cradle—she motioned to the twins to follow her, and moved out of the lady's chamber to the stairway landing.

"I dinna like the looks of yer mam," she told them bluntly. " 'Tis a look I've seen before. I think she is going to die. She is too old for such a hard birth. Ye hae best tell the MacFhearghuis."

"But I am to be wed in five days' time," Gruoch protested.

"She might live that long," Bridie said, "but then again, she might not. If 'twere me, and I wanted my mam there to see me take my vows, I'd marry in the next day or two." Then the midwife shuffled off down the stairs, her duty done.

"She canna die!" Gruoch whispered, almost to herself. *"Nae now!* Nae when we are so close to haeing our revenge on the Fergusons!"

"What are you saying?" Regan asked, confused. She had never seen Gruoch like this before: so intense, so determined, so very much like Sorcha.

"I canna tell ye," Gruoch replied. "Only our mam can tell ye. That damned old Bridie is lying! She'll nae attend me at my births."

"Bridie has nae reason to lie to us," Regan answered quietly.

Gruoch took her twin by the hand and drew her back into the bedchamber. "Mam must rest first. Then she will tell ye. We must wait for her to awaken. Yer right, sister. Bridie has nae reason to lie to us. We must be here when our mother first stirs from her slumbers, before any others come to her."

"Should we nae advise the MacFhearghuis as Bridie suggested?" Regan questioned her sister. "He will be angry wi' us if anything happens and he was nae informed. Let me go to the hall and send a man for him."

"Nay!" Gruoch said, her tone more vehement than Regan had ever known it to be. "If ye send for him," her sister continued, "he will come at once. We will hae nae private time wi' our mam, *and we must*!"

The sisters drew a small bench up by their mother's bedside, waiting in the deep silence. There was no noise from the hall

below. Donald and the three next eldest of their Ferguson siblings had departed with their father and half brothers back to
MacFhearghuis's keep. The two younger boys would be with
their nursemaids. Occasionally the new baby made little snuf-
fling noises in his cradle. His mother lay as pale and silent
as death. The twins sat biding the time away until suddenly
Sorcha MacDuff opened her blue eyes, staring directly at her
daughters.

"I am dying," she said matter-of-factly.

"Aye," Gruoch answered honestly. "So the old hag of a midwife says."

"Ye must wed wi' Ian Ferguson tomorrow," Sorcha said
slowly.

"Aye, and Regan must be told now of our revenge, of the
part she will play in avenging our sire. There is nae more time
to waste, Mam. How do you feel?"

"Weak, but I will live to see ye marry and avenge my Torcull," Sorcha replied fiercely. Then she smiled at Gruoch. "Tell
Regan."

"Tell me what?" Regan asked.

"I am wi' child," Gruoch said calmly.

"Jesu! I dinna know that ye and Ian had . . . well, ye seem to
be so shy of him. What a sly creature ye are, Gruoch. I would
hae nae guessed! Does he know?"

" 'Tis nae the get of Ian Ferguson, Regan mine," her twin
said in hard tones. " 'Tis Jamie MacDuff's bairn growing in
my belly."

"Ohhh, Gruoch!" Regan's eyes were wide with shock.

"Did ye think I would let a Ferguson inherit MacDuff lands?"
Sorcha growled low. "Did ye really believe that, Regan Mac-
Duff? *Never!* 'Tis a MacDuff who will inherit, and nae only
MacDuff lands, but Ferguson lands as well! And the best part
of it all is that the Fergusons will ne'er know it. They will
believe the child Gruoch delivers in a few months is one of
theirs! When that devil Alasdair Ferguson dies, Gruoch will
whisper the secret in his ear at the moment of his death. He'll
go to hell knowing it, and unable to do a damned thing about

it!" She began to laugh, but her laughter grew into a fit of coughing.

Gruoch ran to fetch her mother a cup of strong wine, but Regan could not move for a moment, so overcome with consternation was she. It was a stunning revenge her mother had devised. It was subtle, yet complete. It had required a great deal of patience. Regan realized that her mother must be devastated to know she would not be here to witness the final culmination of her skillful planning. Then a thought struck her.

"Will Ian Ferguson nae know that Gruoch is nae a virgin when he first attempts her?" she asked. Sorcha had long ago explained the ways of men and women to the twins, although Regan had always wondered why she had bothered in her case, since she was to be a nun.

Gruoch put an arm about her mother and helped her to drink. When Sorcha had satisfied her thirst and quieted her cough, she said, "Ian Ferguson will hae a virgin in his bed on his wedding night, Regan. Ye will take yer sister's place, although Ian will nae know it."

"You canna ask such a thing of me!" Regan cried. "I am to be a nun. I must come to the convent of St. Maire's chaste. How can I swear chastity before God when I am nae chaste, lady? 'Tis true I dinna wish this life before me, but I hae nae choice. Will ye take away my honor before I leave Ben MacDui?"

"Yer honor? *Yer honor?*" Sorcha MacDuff mocked her daughter. "The Fergusons took away the honor of the MacDuffs before yer birth. They slaughtered yer father and many other good men in their rapacious greed for our lands. I never told ye exactly how yer da died. What did it matter how? He was dead to us, and could nae return. But I think ye must know, Regan MacDuff—ye who are so like him. The MacFhearghuis ambushed yer da and his men as they returned from a cattle fair. Yer sire was the last man standing, I was told, the last to be slain. The MacFhearghuis and his bandits brought my Torcull's body back to me as a final insult. They hae carved F's in each of his cheeks and upon his forehead. He was still the bonniest man who ever lived! Then Alasdair Ferguson gie me a wee box. Inside it were three bluidy bits he said were yer da's manhood. The bastard hae personally castrated my Torcull! It 'twas a wonder I dinna miscarry ye both in that moment, but I knew my duty was to bear the MacDuff heir and revenge my Torcull.

"I hae been patient," Sorcha continued. "For thirteen years I hae been forced to take Alasdair Ferguson into my bed, between my thighs. I hae been made to bear seven of his bastards, and this last one hae killed me! Now when I lie upon my deathbed, within the hour of my revenge, ye would defy me, prattling childishly of yer honor? Well, Regan MacDuff, there is more involved than just the honor of our clan. Yer sister's very life, and that of her child, are at risk. How do ye think the MacFhearghuis will react if he learns that Gruoch is nae the pure lass he believes her to be? He will kill Gruoch wi'out a single thought if he learns of it. Ye are yer sister's only hope, Regan MacDuff. If ye dinna take her place in her marriage bed on her wedding night . . ." Her voice trailed off weakly, and she fell back upon her pillows.

"What if his seed takes root in my belly?" Regan demanded. "How will I explain that to the abbess at St. Maire's?"

"Our mam has convinced the MacFhearghuis to let you remain wi' her and wi' me for at least a month," Gruoch told her sister. "If ye show any signs of being wi' child, there is a potion that will bring on yer flow." She caught her twin's hands and looked up into the mirror of her own face. *"Please, Regan,"* she pleaded. "No one will ever know of this but you and I. 'Twill only be once. I know ye dinna want to do it, so surely God will forgie ye. Besides, in doing it ye save my life, and that of the bairn I will bear, *and* the MacDuffs will be revenged upon the Fergusons. *Please, Regan! Please!"*

Regan looked coldly at their mother. "All my life ye hae ignored me, and now ye ask this of me. Were it nae for the love I bear Gruoch, I would refuse ye," she said bitterly, "but I will nae hae her blood upon my conscience. Ye knew that, lady. I curse ye for it!" Then Regan stood up and stalked from the room.

Gruoch felt the relief pouring through her entire being. "I knew she would nae fail us, Mam. Regan is a true MacDuff. She will sacrifice herself that our father be avenged."

"She doesna gie a thought to my Torcull," Sorcha said weakly. "She does it for love of ye, my Gruoch. I am glad that when I am gone, ye will hae her. Dinna let the Mac-Fhearghuis send her away until ye are certain she is nae wi' Ian Ferguson's bairn. I will nae live the week out, I fear. Do what ye must, but keep Regan by yer side long enough to be certain she is not wi' Ian's bairn. No one must know of our revenge. It is enough that we know." Then she closed her eyes and fell asleep again.

Gruoch MacDuff looked upon her mother. She was worn with her years of childbearing. I will nae let that happen to me, Gruoch thought to herself. Let Ian Ferguson populate the district wi' his bastards. I will nae care, for I will be his wife, and my MacDuff son will inherit everything they stole from us, plus everything the Fergusons own as well. I shall be meek and mild, but I shall bear only the bairns I choose to bear. I shall keep Jamie MacDuff for my lover. If this child I am to have dies, then I shall hae another by my Jamie. If a Ferguson stands in its way, I shall see it sickens and dies. Nothing and no one shall prevent the MacDuffs from regaining their own, and more!

Gruoch's twin sister would have been very surprised to see the look upon her usually lovely face. Sorcha MacDuff had trained her beloved daughter well. She might die in the next day or two, but Gruoch would not fail her mother. She would exact their secret vengeance upon the Fergusons because she believed in it, fiercely.

Regan had fled the tower house and gone down to the loch. The water was always soothing, but today even it could not bring her the peace she needed. That she had grown up without bitterness was a miracle and testimony to the strength of the human spirit. She knew nothing of love, or real kindness, and had therefore not missed them.

Regan had known from the time understanding came upon her that Gruoch was the heiress, the favored one, and she was to be a nun. But there had not been a priest at Ben MacDui since she was five. She knew little of her faith, or indeed if she even had a faith. She had heard various explanations of the life she was to lead. It did not seem particularly appealing.

She would live in a place with other women. They would pray a great deal, and do good works. Men were forbidden. When it was deemed she was fit, she would swear before this God she wasn't even certain she believed in to lead a life of poverty, chastity, and obedience, before the head of the convent and all the other nuns. Regan sighed deeply. Lying was foreign to her, yet to protect her sister, Gruoch, she would have to live the greatest lie of all. Nuns were supposed to be virgins, and she would not be a virgin after she took Gruoch's place in her twin sister's marriage bed. Still, if she did not, Ian Ferguson would learn his bride was not untouched. The MacFhearghuis would, as her mother had said, kill Gruoch without another thought. Regan knew well the story of their birth and how old Bridie had saved their lives by promising the Fergusons that lasses could not harm them.

Regan sighed, and bent down to pick up a small flat stone, skimming it expertly across the ruffled surface of the water. She walked slowly along the shoreline, contemplating her future. She had never been more than a mile or two from Ben MacDui in her entire life, yet the place to which she was to be sent was across the width of her homeland, Alba, on the farthest coast of Strathclyde. She would never see Ben MacDui or her twin again. Tears flooded her eyes. Despite the difference in their stations, Gruoch had always been loving to her. As for the others, none but Sorcha could tell the twins apart, and so everyone had been pleasant to her, never certain who was Gruoch, the heiress, and who was Regan, the unimportant child. Now she would have nothing but her fragile memories. Yet was there really a great deal more to life? Would she ever know if there was?

A drop of rain fell upon her cheek. Looking up, Regan saw

the spring storm clouds gathering beyond the hills about the loch. She hurried back to the house to find Gruoch sitting by the fire. "Hae ye sent for the MacFhearghuis yet?" Regan asked her twin. "He will want to know of Malcolm's birth and our mam's condition."

"Nay, I hae sent no one," Gruoch replied. "I hae been sitting here thinking how odd it will be to nae hae our mother wi' me. I shall be alone when yer gone, Regan mine. I cannot bear to think on it."

"You will hae a husband and children to fill yer days, Gruoch," Regan answered her. "I am the one who will hae nothing. I dinna think I particularly like the sound of this convent, but then what other choice do we hae than accept the fates decided at our birth by the MacFhearghuis? We will be warm, and dry, and fed, but is that enough, I wonder?"

"There is love," Gruoch said softly.

"I dinna know what love is," Regan admitted. "No one hae ever loved me, Gruoch, except perhaps you. Our mam has nae loved me. The lads will nae even smile at me for fear I am you, or for fear I am me, and to be a holy nun." She laughed almost sadly. "What is love? It is naught to me, Gruoch, but if it is a good thing, then I wish it for ye, my sister. May you hae it in abundance!"

"I may nae get the opportunity to say it once the MacFhearghuis comes, but I thank ye for yer sacrifice, Regan MacDuff," Gruoch said.

"I would nae do it, but that it is for you," Regan replied seriously. "Yet you are a part of me, Gruoch. I canna deny it. There is a bond between us, and if it is in my power, I will nae let any harm come to you. I think our mam wrong to have convinced you to do this thing. It will nae bring back our father. Yer marriage will unite the MacDuffs of Ben MacDui and the Fergusons of Killieloch. Hae ye ever thought if our sire had lived, he might hae ended the feuding between our families with such a marriage?"

"But he dinna live. He was murdered by the Fergusons," Gruoch said harshly. "I will revenge him and our poor mam who lies dying now because of the Fergusons. And what of ye, Regan MacDuff? The Fergusons hae condemned ye to a barren life wi'out love. How can I nae revenge *that*?"

■ *Chapter 2*

The MacFhearghuis was finally sent for, and he came quickly. He admired his latest son, raging Malcolm; observed Sorcha's deteriorating condition; and ordered that the wedding be held that same evening.

"She's a strong woman, but I canna be certain she'll last the night," he told the twins. "I want her to see ye wed to my laddie, Gruoch MacDuff." His glance swung to Regan. "Prepare yer sister, lass, as yer mam canna now. I'll fetch the priest myself."

"Bring water for bathing," Regan commanded the servants, and when they had obeyed her, she sent them away, saying, "I will tend to my sister alone. Come for us when the MacFhearghuis returns wi' the priest and the bridegroom, but do not disturb us before then."

"Why did ye send them away?" Gruoch asked her sister curiously when they were alone.

"I dinna want anyone to see ye naked lest yer belly, small though it may be, arouse suspicion," Regan told her. Then she smiled. "See," she said, holding out her hand to show Gruoch. "I made a wee cake of soap for this day, and scented it wi' lavender for ye."

The two girls stripped off their clothing, and then each in her turn bathed, Gruoch first, and then Regan, washing not just their bodies, but their long golden hair as well, which they dried by the fire. Regan went to the storage chest and removed clean clothing for them both: first, fine soft linen chemises, and then high, round-necked tunics, both under and over. The bride was garbed in an undertunic woven of light wool, green in color, and a shorter outertunic of rich purple silk belted in gilded leather with an enamel buckle. Her sister wore the same colors, but reversed. Neither wore shoes, as they would be indoors.

Gruoch fitted a narrow gold band studded with small sparkling stones about her forehead to hold her hair. Neither she nor Regan knew what the little jewels were, but Sorcha had always said the band was to be worn by the bride on her wedding day. It had been part of her own dowry. Gruoch's hair was loose, befitting a bride. Regan's single braid was bound with a piece of transparent fabric topped with a silver band. Each girl had attached to her shoulder a small sprig of red whortleberry, the badge of Clan MacDuff.

"How will we switch places later?" Regan asked her sister.

"Ye will prepare me for the bedding in Mam's place," Gruoch answered her. " 'Tis then we will change identities."

"And afterward?" Regan pressed her.

"I dinna know. Perhaps ye'll be forced to spend the entire night wi' Ian, but if he sleeps, and ye can slip out of the chamber, I will be waiting to take my rightful place back. If nae in the night, 'twill be in the morning," Gruoch told Regan, patting her twin's hand comfortingly. "I canna thank ye enough, Regan mine. Remember, though, dinna show Ian any fear even if ye feel it. He can be cruel, I am told, if a woman is weak. Ye must be strong. Just do what he tells ye, and try nae to weep."

When they were finally called into the hall, they found that Sorcha had already been brought down from her chamber on a cot, carried by two of the MacFhearghuis's sons from one of his earlier marriages. Everyone was assembled: the Fergusons of Killieloch and their clansmen, the surviving MacDuffs of Ben MacDui and their clansmen, and the priest.

"Come forward! Come forward!" The MacFhearghuis beckoned them with a bony finger. And when they did so, he took Gruoch by the arm, drawing her next to his son Ian.

He never even looked at her, Regan thought. Were it not for the jeweled gold band she wears, he would not really know which of us is which. *None of them would.* For some reason she didn't even understand, it made the deception they were going to play on the Fergusons all right. Regan's eyes met those of her mother in the first direct gaze that either of them had ever shared. A tiny smile of acknowledgment touched Sorcha's lips only briefly. Then her attention was once again all Gruoch's.

Oh, bitch, Regan said silently to herself. You have sacrificed both of us to your vengeance, and will leave us now to fend for ourselves separately, we who have always had each other. I wonder what my father really would have thought of what you have done, Sorcha MacDuff?

Regan's thoughts so absorbed her that she had paid scant attention to what was going on about her. Suddenly she saw that her mother was showing relief. The MacFhearghuis was slapping his eldest son upon the back. Gruoch was pretending to look the blushing bride. The marriage ceremony was over, and the pipes had begun to play. As the servants passed about wine to the assembled guests, the sisters joined their weakening mother and the MacFhearghuis at the high board while the groom and his brothers danced for them.

Whatever Sorcha MacDuff might think of the Fergusons, Regan had to admit that they were handsome men, with their russet hair and bright blue eyes. They were all dressed alike, with lengths of Ferguson plaid wrapped about their waists, the dark blue, green, white, and red fabric held in place with wide leather belts. White linen shirts, open at the neck, revealed for all to see the mat of chest hair that all but the youngest sported. Their footwear followed the line of their feet and were laced halfway up their shapely legs. The bridegroom wore leather, but his brothers wore shoes of heavy waterproof cloth. They noisily drank toast after toast to their sibling and his new wife, even while dancing for the guests.

A fit of coughing overtook Sorcha, and when her daughters had eased her pain, she managed to gasp, "*The bedding.* I must know Gruoch has been properly bedded before I die! Take your sister, Regan, and prepare her for her husband as I cannot."

The two young women slipped from the high board unnoticed by the MacFhearghuis and the other guests, who were quite busy helping the bridegroom and his brothers with the creation of a particularly bawdy toast. The twins ran as quickly as they could up the tower stairs to the bedchamber that had been prepared during the ceremony for the newlyweds. Hurriedly, Gruoch stripped off her bridal garments, replacing them with Regan's clothing, and hastily braided her hair.

"Am I to be naked?" Regan asked her sister, standing in her linen chemise, combing swift fingers through her own golden locks.

"Aye," her sister told her. "It saves on the clothing, Regan mine. He'll only tear it off ye if yer wearing it, I fear."

"Gruoch," her twin corrected her. "I am Gruoch, and yer now Regan," her sibling warned her.

"Get into the bed," the false Regan told her. "I can hear them coming up the stairs from the hall already. Mam dinna gie us much time, did she? She'll die before the night is out, I think."

The counterfeit bride had no sooner climbed into the bed when the door to the small room was slammed open, and almost broken off its hinges, by the Fergusons. A naked Ian Ferguson was thrust into the chamber by his family.

"Do yer duty by the wench, Ian," his father said loudly. Then reaching out, he pulled the substitute from the room. " 'Tis no longer any place for ye, my little nun," he told her.

Gruoch was astounded. She had never imagined that Ian Ferguson would be so . . . so . . . *well proportioned.* Jamie MacDuff was a fine lover, but Ian Ferguson's ample manhood portended many pleasurable hours. Perhaps Regan was correct. Their mam would shortly be dead. The feud was over. Her MacDuff child would inherit, ensuring the MacDuffs' revenge; but she, Gruoch, would be content to let peace grow between their two clans as the MacFhearghuis had intended all along. As for her twin, once Gruoch was certain nothing had come of whatever attentions Ian might lavish on Regan, she would be sent with all haste to St. Maire's to live out her life.

"Attend to yer mam, Regan MacDuff," the MacFhearghuis ordered her. "I will wait here outside the bridal chamber to make certain that my son does what he should, *and* to ensure that yer sister is the virgin she is purported to be. If I find the MacDuffs hae played us false . . ." He made a slicing motion with his forefinger across his throat.

"My lord," she asked him, "why would ye think Gruoch is nae a virgin and would play ye false?" Who had put such an idea into his head?

"Yer brother Donald says she had been verra friendly wi' young Jamie MacDuff," the older man answered her.

"Ye must beware of our brother Donald," she told him. "He tells terrible lies, and seems to gain pleasure from causing trouble between us. Mam hae beaten him for it many times, sir. Both Gruoch and I hae always been fond of our cousin Jamie, but there hae been nae naughtiness between any of us, I swear it. I was always wi' them, for Mam was insistent upon the proprieties being observed."

"Yer a good lassie, Regan MacDuff," he told her. "Go to yer mam now, and ease her final moments upon this earth."

"Will ye nae see her again, sir?" she importuned him.

"Yer mam and I hae said our farewells," he said, and gently pushed her toward the stairs, turning his full attention back to the bridal chamber and its inhabitants.

Within, a single candle burned. Ian Ferguson paraded for the girl who awaited him within the bed. "Well?" he demanded of her.

"Well, what?" she replied. Regan's heart was beating violently, but her fear was invisible to the man before her.

"Do ye not think I've a fine lance, Gruoch? 'Tis nae even half roused, but the little nun's eyes grew as round as twin moons when she saw me. She'll ne'er see its like, or any other for that matter, e'er again, puir wee lassie. 'Tis a shame I canna be like the infidels and hae both of ye to wife. Our ancestors took more than one wife, I'm told; and the pagan Saxons still do it now as well. Would ye like to share me wi' another, my wee wifie?"

"I hear that I already do," Regan answered him, amused. "They say ye hae a dozen or more of yer bastards scattered about the countryside, Ian Ferguson. The bairns ye get on me, howe'er, will end a feud, and be yer legitimate heirs, *husband mine.*"

"Yer bold," he said, not knowing if he should hit her for her impudence or let it be. He decided he liked her fearlessness. "Donald says ye hae played me false wi' Jamie MacDuff, Gruoch. If it is so, I shall kill ye, and the wee nun will be my new wife."

"Donald is a liar," she answered him calmly. "Come, my lord, and see for yerself if I am a virgin or nae." Donald will suffer for his mischief, Regan decided, even as she was holding out her arms to Ian.

He pulled back the coverlet that had obscured his view of her young body. She had sweet small breasts and a long torso. Her skin was creamy-looking. He reached out to touch it. It was soft, and very smooth. He fingered a lock of her golden hair. It was like thistledown. Bending, he kissed her mouth for the second time this day, and immediately his lust was engaged. He climbed into the bed with her, wrapping his arms about her tightly.

Regan wrinkled her nose. Ian Ferguson smelled of horses and sweat. He had obviously not bathed in some time. While she was curious to know what transpired between man and woman, she did not envy her sister this man. His hand pushed between her thighs, seeking, touching her where she had certainly never thought to be touched. He pinioned her down with his body, his other hand fumbling at her breasts. Regan bit her lip to keep from crying out, for his rough manner was beginning to frighten her. She remembered Gruoch's warning. *Dinna let him see yer fear.*

She squirmed away from him, and he grunted with irritation. "What should I do, Ian?" she asked him. Surely she should be doing something in all of this.

He looked at her, surprised. "Why lassie, ye need nae do anything. I'll fuck ye soon enough. Just lie there for me like a good lass. The man does the work in the lovemaking." He mashed his lips against hers once more, forcing her mouth open, thrusting his tongue down her throat.

Regan gagged, surprised, as he continued his assault. If all a woman did was lie still, why did so many of them enjoy this thing called making love? she wondered. Maybe when he got to the fucking it would be easier. She was certainly not enjoying any of it now. It was rough and sweaty, and not pleasant at all.

"Spread yer legs, lassie," he ordered her, settling himself between them when she did. Her confusion certainly indicates that she is a virgin, Ian thought. Donald was going to get a fine beating if he was lying. Ian Ferguson positioned himself and thrust hard, only to find himself blocked by something. *Her maidenhead,* he silently exulted, and pulling back a bit, drove himself even harder into her.

Regan shrieked with surprise as the pain of his entry radiated throughout her entire torso. Gruoch's advice forgotten, she fought him with all her strength, pummeling his hairy chest with small fists as, ignoring her, he continued his onslaught. "Yer hurting me, Ian!" she sobbed. "Stop it! *Stop it!*"

It was as if he did not hear her. Pushing himself in and out of her now-widening passage with increasing rapidity, he groaned and he sweated until finally, with a triumphant cry, he collapsed atop her. "Jesu, ye were tight, lassie, but we've taken care of that, the braw laddie and I," he said hotly in her ear. Then climbing off of her, he took the candle and, holding it up, grinned down on her, pleased by the blood of her innocence staining her thighs, the bedding, and now his limp member. Walking to the door, he opened it and said, "Come in, Da, and see for yerself. My wee wifie was indeed a virgin, were ye nae, Gruoch?"

It had hurt less as he continued, Regan considered. Still, she had not enjoyed the coupling between them at all. The Mac-Fhearghuis stared down at her and nodded, satisfied. She felt no embarrassment—only a deep coldness suffusing her entire body. If this was lovemaking, her twin was more than welcome to it. Nothing about it appealed to her.

"Gie Donald a beating for me," Ian told his father. "The bastard lied to us."

"So the little nun suggested when I questioned her earlier," Alasdair Ferguson replied. "Well, then, I'm satisfied the lassie was pure. I'll leave ye to yer pleasures, lad. Hae a good night."

Regan thought that Ian would never sleep. Twice more he probed her sore body. Then at last he fell to snoring deeply, to her everlasting relief. When she was certain he would not awaken, she slipped from the bed and crept to the door, taking a moment to gather up her chemise. Putting it on, she carefully slipped the bolt and fled the room. Hurrying down the stairs, she entered the room below, where her twin sat watching over their mother.

Gruoch rose quickly to her feet as her sister slipped into the chamber. "Are ye all right?" she whispered.

"Barely," Regan answered. "He hurt me dreadfully," she told Gruoch, swiftly recounting the past two hours in the nuptial bed with Ian Ferguson. "Ye'd best hurry back upstairs before he awakens. I hae nae doubt he'll want to rut wi' his *wee wifie* yet again. He seems to be as lusty as a stallion, sister mine."

The twins quickly exchanged clothing once more, Gruoch smearing chicken's blood upon the insides of her thighs before pulling her chemise down over them. "Thank ye," she said simply, and then was gone.

Regan quietly washed away the evidence of her lost virtue and pulled her own clothing back on. She sat down, wincing as her small bottom made contact with the wooden bench. She yet ached.

"Regan." Her mother's voice cut into her thoughts.

Regan leaned over, looking into Sorcha's face. "Aye?"

Her mother reached out and took the girl's hand in hers. "Yer a good lassie," she said. Then Sorcha MacDuff died.

Regan was astounded, but by what, she was not certain. Her mother's death had been so simple. Her last words had not been. She had longed her whole life for a kind word from Sorcha MacDuff, but all of her mother's thoughts and dreams and kind words had always been for Gruoch. Yet the last words she had spoken had been for her.

"Ahh, Mam," was all she could say, "God speed yer poor soul home."

Then freeing herself from her mother's death grip, Regan MacDuff went downstairs into the hall to tell the MacFhearghuis that her mother was dead. He nodded, and she thought she saw the glitter of a tear in his blue eyes.

"I'll get old Bridie to help me prepare her, my lord," Regan said. "Let Gruoch and her bridegroom sleep in peace tonight."

"Aye," he agreed. Nothing more.

They buried Sorcha MacDuff the following day next to her husband on the hillside overlooking the loch. The day was gray and rainy. The pipes wailed MacDuff's Lament as the shrouded body was lowered into its grave. After Torcull MacDuff's death, Sorcha had become the heart of the clan. Now that heart had ceased to beat. The heiress of Ben MacDui was wed to a Ferguson, and within a month's time her sister would be sent south and across the breadth of Scotland into a convent, never more to be seen. The mourning cries of the MacDuffs were prolonged, and genuine.

Jamie MacDuff sought out Regan. "And how did Ian Ferguson find his bride?" he demanded slyly.

"*A virgin,*" she responded softly, "and should any say otherwise, they would invite a dirk to the heart, *cousin,*" she warned him.

"Marry me," he said, surprising her.

"Why? So ye can pretend I'm Gruoch, Jamie? Nay, I think ye insult me. Dinna be a fool, laddie. Let it be now," she advised.

"Yer Torcull MacDuff's daughter," he said. "There are many who would hae a MacDuff chief for Ben MacDui, nae a Ferguson."

"Then they are fools too, Jamie MacDuff," Regan responded. "I ne'er knew my sire, for he was killed in the feuding before our birth. For all these years we hae had peace. The Fergusons outnumber us, which is why they triumphed in the first place. To what purpose would ye start the warring all over again? That our young men be killed for the glory of Ben MacDui? I would nae hae such a thing on my soul."

"Yer mam would nae hae fled a fight," he said.

"Our mam is dead," she told him harshly. "Now if ye canna be content wi' the way things are, Jamie MacDuff, then get ye gone from Ben MacDui! I will nae let ye spoil my sister's happiness."

"Happiness? Wi' Ian Ferguson?" he said incredulously.

"She told me just this morning that Ian is a fine lover," Regan said, and then added cruelly, "the best she hae ever known."

With a look of pained disbelief he flung himself away from her. It was the last time she would see him. She learned to her great relief several days later that Jamie MacDuff had gone soldiering to a place called Byzantium. To Regan's amazement, Gruoch was equally glad to be free of her former lover. Her bridegroom's style of lovemaking seemed to appeal to her, and she was very content with him.

Regan remained at Ben MacDui, but to her surprise, she found that without her mother, her home now seemed a foreign place. Gruoch was fast becoming jealous of any attention Ian gave her sister, and seemed openly eager for her departure. She greeted with great relief the news that Regan's flow had come upon her.

"Ye'll be going, then," she said almost too bluntly.

"Aye," Regan replied. "Ye'll gie me time to recover, will ye nae, sister? Ye know how motion affects me during this time."

"Aye," Gruoch grudgingly allowed. "Ye will nae hae an easy journey as it is. I would nae make it harder for ye."

"We will ne'er see each other ever again once I am gone," Regan said, "yet I will always love ye, Gruoch."

"And I, ye," Gruoch said, her manner softening. "I truly wish ye dinna hae to go, but the old man is firm. He says yer but a temptation to the MacDuff clansmen, Regan mine."

"He is correct," her twin told her. "Jamie MacDuff suggested we wed and defy the Fergusons, before I sent him away. I told him ye said Ian was a better lover."

"He is." Gruoch giggled. "Ye were right when ye said he was a stallion, Regan mine. I am almost sorry to be wi' bairn now, for I shall nae be able to satisfy him when my belly gets too big. He'll run off to one of his mistresses then, I fear."

"Hae ye told him yet, Gruoch?"

"Nae, but I will soon," Gruoch said with a smile. "He'll boast like a peacock, and the old man will be pleased too," she concluded.

She is content, Regan thought. The revenge our mam planned will soon be complete, but Gruoch does not really care about that now, I think. She is simply happy to be Ian Ferguson's wife, although why, I cannot understand. He's a pleasant enough fellow, but a lout at heart. He'll grow more like his da with every passing year. I wonder what their children will be like, but I'll ne'er know that. Soon I'll be gone from Ben MacDui. Once I thought I would care, but now I dinna think I will. Gruoch has her place in the world, but I dinna seem to hae mine.

Regan MacDuff left the only home she had ever known on an early summer's morning. The trip, which would take at least two weeks, would see her travel from the hills of eastern Alba to a place called Strathclyde in the southwest corner of the land. She would be escorted on her journey by a mixed troupe of both Ferguson and MacDuff men. The old MacFhearghuis showed her a small but weighty bag, which he then gave to the captain of her escort.

" 'Tis yer dowry, lass," he said. "Andrew will gie it to Mother Una." Then somehow understanding her fears, he continued, "St. Maire's is on the Mull of Galloway, facing the North Channel. 'Tis the sea. Ye've nae seen the sea, I know, lass. It can be beautiful, and it can be fierce. On a clear day ye'll be able to look all the way to Eire, the land of the Celts, which is across the waters. My kinswoman, Una, is the abbess there, or at least she was when ye were born. She is a good woman, as I remember,

Regan. But no matter if she is there no longer, yer name will be in the book of those expected to take the veil. Ye'll hae a home there, and a place of yer own."

"And I've none here now, hae I, my lord?" Regan asked boldly.

He sighed. "Ye'll nae make a good nun, I fear, but what else can I do wi' ye, lassie? There can only be one heiress to Ben MacDui, and she's now my son's wife. There is to be a bairn. Yer a danger to us all, Regan MacDuff. Wi'out a word ye can set MacDuff against Ferguson again, and I will nae hae it! Yer nae a stupid lass. Ye understand."

Regan nodded. "Aye," she replied, "but I dinna hae to like it, my lord. Could I just nae go away? I would nae bother anyone here at Ben MacDui again! I canna bear the thought of being locked up!"

"I will tell ye the secret to yer survival, lassie," Alasdair Ferguson said to the girl. "First ye must learn patience. That is hard for the young, I know. Then, lass, seek power wi'in yer own wee world. Dinna be satisfied just to be a nun. When ye hae power, ye will find a measure of peace. Now come, and bid yer sister farewell."

Gruoch was both eager and reluctant to see her twin sister depart. Part of her was relieved to see Regan go. Ian delighted in teasing her about being unable to tell them apart. What if he bedded the wee nun, as he called the other twin, by mistake? The suggestion was too close to the uncomfortable truth. Then, too, Regan shared her secret. With both Regan and their mam gone, Gruoch could pretend to herself that the child she was carrying was indeed Ian's. There would be no one here who knew the truth once Regan had departed. Yet Regan was as much a part of her as her right hand. They had never been separated in their entire lives, and this separation was to be such an ultimate one. It was highly unlikely that they would ever see each other again.

The sisters hugged almost desperately. There were no more words left for them to say. Then Regan was helped upon her small palfrey. She turned only once as they went down the road that bordered the loch, but Gruoch was sobbing against her husband's shoulder. She did not see her twin's final wave.

They traveled a bit faster than Regan would have expected. The weather was good, and her escorts eager to have their task over and done with, that they might return home. The clansmen were uncomfortable in unfamiliar territory. They traveled west, then finally turned south. Had the journey been for any other reason, Regan might have enjoyed it. She was astounded by the beauty of the countryside. Most nights they camped by the roadside, but sometimes they were fortunate enough to find accommodation in the guest house of some isolated religious order. None of the men escorting her, either MacDuff or Ferguson, were anything but respectful of her. She was relieved not to be tempted again by a dissatisfied clansman seeking to revive old times.

They finally reached the coast road, and Regan's first glimpse of the sea amazed her. It seemed to stretch forever. "Does it nae end?" she wondered aloud.

"I imagine there's a lass on the other side asking the same question," the captain of their troupe said in reply, a small smile touching his lips. He was a MacDuff, and while he felt sorry for Regan, he was not anxious to renew the hostilities between the MacDuffs and the Fergusons. Peace was a good thing for a man with a family.

The weather turned, coming gray and wet from the ocean, so the little convent of St. Maire did not look particularly inviting when they knocked upon its gates late one afternoon. It was a gray stone building, with high walls around it, which sat upon the edge of the sea. The porteress, a small, nervous woman, admitted Regan and the captain.

"Please wait," she said in a soft, almost shy voice. "I will tell Mother Eubh that we have visitors."

"Is Mother Una no longer in charge, then?" Regan queried the nun. "Perhaps I am not expected after all," she said hopefully.

"Mother Una is very old and lives in retirement within the convent," the little nun explained, "but she could no longer attend to the responsibilities of such an establishment." The porteress scurried off.

"It doesna seem to me there would be many responsibilities in such a wee place as this," the captain said, but as he looked about, he could see that the convent was richly appointed. There were fine gold and silver candlesticks on an oak sideboard, behind which hung a beautiful tapestry. The room in which they waited had an enclosed fireplace that drew well, leaving the room smoke-free. "Ye'll be safe and comfortable here, my lady," the captain said in an effort to comfort the glum young girl.

"There are walls," Regan said. "There were no walls about Ben MacDui. I was free to come and go as I pleased. I do not like walls." I shall run away, she thought. Once my escort has gone so that there is no one to tell, I shall run away. No one will care.

"Perhaps if there had been walls at Ben MacDui," the captain said, "yer father would be alive, and ye a bride like yer sister, lady."

The chamber door opened and a tall, attractive woman entered. She was garbed all in black, but upon her chest was an exquisite jeweled cross, and the hand she held out was beringed. "I am Mother Eubh," she said in a husky, sensuous voice. Her dark eyes swept appraisingly over the MacDuff captain.

"This be the lady, Regan MacDuff," the captain said, certain he had mistaken the look in the nun's eyes. "She is sent by the laird of Killieloch to enter this order. The arrangements were made many years ago wi' the Mother Una, the laird's kinswoman. Here is her dowry, holy lady."

Regan's eyes met those of the nun, and to her surprise she saw amusement. Was the woman mocking her?

"She hae nae a calling to this life, hae she?" Mother Eubh said. "Why then is she here?" She weighed the purse in her palm. It was not the heaviest she had ever been given, but neither was it light. The girl obviously was valued to some extent.

"She is one of the two heiresses to Ben MacDui," the captain explained. "Twin sisters were born to the late laird, Torcull MacDuff, and his wife. There were nae sons. The laird of Kil-lieloch, Mother Una's kinsman, betrothed the elder of the twins to his heir. This be the younger. He will nae hae two heiresses for Ben MacDui, and now her sister, the bride, is already wi' bairn. It was planned from the lass's birth that she come here, holy lady," the captain finished.

"And where is Ben MacDui?" Mother Eubh asked him.

"In the hills of Alba, almost to the other sea, holy lady," the captain explained. "We hae been on the road fifteen days."

"I see," Mother Eubh said thoughtfully. The lass had, in effect, been sent to the other side of the world that her clans-men not be tempted to rebel against this laird of Killieloch, who clearly had taken over her inheritance through a marriage between his son and the girl's sister. "What is your lord's name, good captain?"

"Alasdair Ferguson, holy lady," the captain replied.

"Then ye may tell Alasdair Ferguson that he need nae worry about the lady Regan. He hae my word that neither he nor any at Ben MacDui will ever see this lass again. She is now in my keeping." Mother Eubh smiled. "Ye may go, Captain," she dis-missed him.

To her great surprise, the captain knelt before Regan and kissed her hand. "God keep ye safe, lady," he said, and then rising, departed. The porteress scurried after him to see him out.

"Come wi' me," Mother Eubh said abruptly, her dark skirts swirling about her ankles as she hurried from the small chamber.

Regan followed the tall nun, almost running to keep up. The building, she discovered, was built around a quadrangle. They crossed the courtyard, which was planted with a small rose garden. It was very quiet, but Regan could see other women praying, each in her individual cell on the ground floor. On the far side of the quadrangle, Mother Eubh entered a door and climbed a narrow flight of stairs. Regan followed close behind her. At the top of the staircase a doorway opened into a large, bright room.

Reaching up, the nun pulled off her wimple, and black hair

cascaded down her back. Turning about, she ordered the girl, "Remove your mantle, lass. I want a better look at ye."

Stunned, Regan slowly obeyed. Beneath her dark cloak she wore a tunic dress of dark blue.

Mother Eubh pulled the veil from Regan's head. "Jesu!" she swore softly. "Your hair is wonderful!" She turned, and said to a man Regan had not realized was also in the room, "What do you think, Gunnar? Nae corn-colored hair like yer Danish wenches, but a rich silvery gold!" She turned back to Regan. "Take yer clothes off, lass."

"Lady!" Regan was shocked.

Mother Eubh slapped Regan lightly on her cheek. "Dinna disobey me, lass," she said. "Yer in my charge now. I rule here at St. Maire's."

"What kind of a nun keeps a man in her rooms, and demands that lasses strip themselves before her?" Regan demanded. "Where is Mother Una? I dinna think she would approve of what ye are doing. I will nae remain here!"

The man arose from his seat. He was of medium height with a thickset body, and was hard-looking. His skull was smooth, and a single ponytail of dark blond hair bound in brass-studded leather sprang from its center. Walking over to Regan, he looked her directly in the eye, but she did not quail before him as so many others had. He smiled coldly. Then reaching out, he grasped her by her hair with one hand, while the other fastened on the neck of her tunic dress and tore the garment from her in a single, swift motion. Spinning her about, he pulled the rest of the material off her body and then stood back.

"A blond virgin," he said appraisingly. His voice was harsh. "She'll bring us a pretty sum. Donal Righ says the Moors will pay a fortune for a blond virgin. She's young, too."

"I am nae a virgin," Regan spat at him. *There!* That would spoil his plans, whatever they are.

"Nae a virgin, and ye came here?" Mother Eubh screeched. "What kind of a dishonest creature are ye to come here, and nae a virgin?"

The man burst out laughing. "Eubh, calm yerself," he said

between chortles. "The lass is obviously lying to protect herself, are ye nae, my pretty?"

"I dinna lie!" Regan said angrily.

"I will know if yer lying," he told her, his hand fastening itself in her hair again.

"I dinna lie," Regan repeated stubbornly.

"Ye hae a lover?" he asked.

"My sister's husband," she told him.

"So that is why ye were sent here," Mother Eubh said indignantly. "Ye bold vixen!"

"And what are ye, lady?" Regan demanded angrily. "I dinna know what ye be about, but 'tis nae a nun's business, and ye should be ashamed!" She was not afraid, although she suspected that perhaps she should be. She could almost smell the danger about her.

The man called Gunnar, still holding her tightly by her hair, turned her about and shoved her toward a table facing the window. Changing his grip to her neck, he forced her to bend over. "Stay submissive," he snarled, "or I'll kill ye, lass." Then she felt his hands grip her about her hips. His hard body was pushing against hers. The last thing she remembered before she shut it all out was that he was invading her body.

"Bastard!" Mother Eubh hissed at him. "Ye are an awful man, Gunnar Bloodaxe! To take the lass in front of me! I hate ye!"

"She doesna lie," he responded to her umbrage. "She's nae a virgin, but she's tight, and hasna been well used. Her sister's husband was probably her only lover." His buttocks contracted and expanded with his efforts as he ground himself into her. "Donal Righ will hae her, Eubh, and he will pay well. Considering all the others we hae for this voyage are nae of the quality of this wench, 'twill be well worth the trip now." For a moment his eyes closed, he groaned, and relaxing, withdrew his now limp member from Regan's body. "She's nae afraid, and that is to the good." Releasing Regan, he said, "Put yer gown back on, girl."

Regan bent and picked up her torn garments. "Ye've ruined them," she said quietly, refusing to acknowledge what had just happened to her. He was just another man like Ian. Their encounter meant nothing. "Either I must mend them or hae something else, lady," she told Mother Eubh.

There was a calm about her that frightened the nun. The lass had just been violated in a particularly cruel manner. She should be hysterical, and broken, but she was not. "There is nae time for ye to mend anything," Mother Eubh said nervously. "I'll gie ye a gown to wear." She went to a chest set against the wall and, opening it, drew forth a dark tunic dress and a single threadbare chemise of rough flax. "Here, lass," she said grudgingly.

Regan took the proffered garments. They were nowhere near the quality of those that had been destroyed. How strange, she thought, that she should notice such a thing at a moment like this. Pulling on the clothing, she said to the nun, "Gie me needle and thread, lady. I will mend my own garments, and return these to ye afterward. I dinna like waste." She picked up her mantle and pulled it about her. The familiar scent of her own clothing was comforting.

Gunnar Bloodaxe nodded. " 'Twill keep her busy during the voyage," he said to Mother Eubh.

Regan looked up from the clothing she had gathered. "Where are ye taking me?" she asked him.

"Dublin," he said.

"Where is that?" Regan wondered aloud.

"Yer too full of questions to suit me," Mother Eubh snapped, angry again.

"It's across the sea in Eire," Gunnar Bloodaxe answered her.

"What if the MacFhearghuis sends after me?" Regan said.

"He'll nae send after ye, lass," the nun said nastily. "Ye were sent far away because he does nae want to see ye ever again. But should any ask after ye, I will say yer dead!"

Gunnar Bloodaxe laughed. "Yer a mean bitch, Eubh," he told the woman. Then, "We will sail on the afternoon tide. See that the other cargo is ready for me to load on board immediately."

"When will ye return to me?" she asked him cloyingly.

"Ye'll not have another cargo for me for several months at

least, Eubh," Gunnar Bloodaxe said. "I'm sailing home to Daneland when I've finished in Dublin. Perhaps I'll see ye early next spring."

"What of my share of the profits?" Mother Eubh said in a hard voice. "Do ye think I trust ye to remember them next spring? Either pay me my share before you take this cargo, or return to gie me what is owed before ye go home, Gunnar Bloodaxe."

He scowled at her, but answered, "I'll bring ye yer silver, ye greedy bitch, before I sail north. Now, gather up the wenches else I lose the tide. I'm not of a mind to wait another twelve hours." Reaching out, he took Regan in a firm grip. "I'll take this prize myself."

"First my needle and thread," Regan insisted, and the nun angrily gave her what she asked for before storming from the chamber.

"Yer hard as rock, girl," Gunnar Bloodaxe told her. "Were ye not worth more to me in Dublin, I'd take ye for a wife. What is yer name?"

"Regan," she told him.

" 'Tis a lad's name," he said.

"My mam wanted a son," Regan replied. "The firstborn was a daughter, my twin sister, Gruoch."

"There's another like ye?" He whistled softly. "If I had ye both I could triple my fortune, girl." Then, without another word, he led her away.

They retraced her earlier steps, but when they reached the bottom of Mother Eubh's private staircase, he led her not across the quadrangle, but out a small door in the wall nearby. There, a narrow path wandered down the rocky hill to a beach below. Upon the sandy shore was drawn up the first real sailing ship that Regan had ever seen. The little cockles that had plied the loch below Ben MacDui were all that she had ever known, but she knew immediately that this ship could sail the sea well beyond sight of the beach.

"What is it made of?" she asked Gunnar Bloodaxe.

"Oak," he answered. "The mast is pine. We use the wind when we can, but the boat can take thirty-two oars, although I have but twenty men with me on this trip. The summer seas are easier to traverse."

"It will float upon these waters?"

"Aye."

"How long? How long will it take us to get to this Dublin?"

"Three, four days, depending on the winds," Gunnar answered, and then he said, "Are ye not curious as to what I mean to do with you, Regan? Do ye have no fear at all?"

She turned her aquamarine eyes on him and said, "Would my curiosity as to my fate change it, Gunnar Bloodaxe? And why would I fear ye? Ye obviously mean nae to kill me. I dinna choose to come to St. Maire's. I dinna desire to be a nun. Whatever ye hae in store for me canna be any worse than what was previously planned for me."

"I have never met a woman who could reason before," he said admiringly. "Ye are not bound by foolish emotions, Regan, which is to the good. Well, I will tell ye what I plan to do with ye. I am going to sell ye to a slave merchant in Dublin who is called Donal Righ. You are very beautiful, and Donal Righ deals only in the finest slaves. There is a market for women like ye in the land of the Moors. Ye will end up living a far more glorious life than yer sister, for ye will be the cherished possession of a rich man. If ye give him children, sons, your fortune will be made."

Regan nodded. "It is a better fate than the one I thought I must endure," she told him.

She was so calm. So accepting. He asked, "Is there no one you leave behind whom you love, Regan?" What of her lover, her sister's husband? he wondered.

"There is no one," she said, and seeing the question in his eyes, she explained to him about Ian Ferguson. "My virginity was sacrificed to protect Gruoch and ensure my mother's revenge on the Fergusons," she finished. "There was nothing more to it than that."

"You have never loved a man?" he asked her.

"I have never loved anyone, except perhaps Gruoch," she told him honestly. "I am not even certain I understand what the word really means. *What is love?* My mother's love for my father seems to have become naught but a desire for vengeance. What was it before that? Her love for Gruoch was equally flawed. Gruoch was nae more than a means to her revenge. She cosseted and cajoled my sister into believing what she believed. I was nothing to our mother. Only in the end, when I could be of use to her, did she speak with kindness to me. On her deathbed. Until that moment it was as if I dinna really matter. She never nursed me at her breast, nor bound up my wounds when I was a wee bairn. Gruoch was all I had, and then only when our mam dinna want her. *Love?* I dinna even know what it means, or if it even exists, Gunnar Bloodaxe."

Now he understood why she had not cried out when he had raped her earlier. She was like a legendary ice maiden. He could almost envy the man who would finally awaken her spirit, her passions, *her love.* She was the most beautiful woman he had ever seen. Despite everything, she had an untouched, flawless perfection about her. She was clever, and would learn to bend, but no man would ever break her. There was no other like her.

His men began descending the hill, driving a small group of weeping women before them. When they had reached the beach, the men pushed the vessel from the sand into the shallows, some of them clambering aboard as they did so. One by one the women were lifted into the boat and herded into its stern beneath a small canvas awning, where they were told to sit down upon the deck. The remaining sailors boarded, the sail was raised, and the ship began to move away from the land. Almost immediately the women set up a loud wail, some even tearing at their hair.

"Why do you weep?" Regan demanded of a young girl next to her. She was a scrawny creature with a freckled face and big brown eyes.

"Why lady," the girl sobbed, recognizing quality when she saw it, "we are leaving our homeland forever."

"What did any of you hae here that was so wonderful you are loath to part wi' it?" Regan demanded of them.

"They mean to sell us as slaves, lady," one woman said.

"And were ye nae little else to those who raised ye, or to those who sent ye to Mother Eubh at St. Maire's?" she demanded of them. "A woman is but chattel to her family. Ye but exchange one master for another," Regan said in practical tones.

"But the Celts are said to be pagans!" a woman cried.

Regan shrugged. "All men are the same," she told them, and then wrapping her mantle about her, she closed her eyes.

Around her the other women chattered in amazement, and then a small voice said, "Ye are verra wise, lady. I am nae so frightened now."

Regan opened her eyes. "What is yer name?" she asked the freckle-faced girl. "I am Regan MacDuff of Ben MacDui."

"Morag is my name," the girl said. "I dinna know my parents. I was sent to Mother Una eleven years ago by the Kennedys, when I was just a wee bairn."

"What happened to Mother Una?" Regan asked, curious.

"One day she had a fit and fell into a swoon. When she awoke," Morag said, "she could nae speak. At first the nuns dinna know what to do, for Mother Una was so strong and always did for everyone else. Then Sister Eubh said that as none of them could decide what was to be done, she would take over for Mother Una. None of the others dared tell her nay. At first everything was the same as it had been. Then Gunnar Bloodaxe came. Mother Eubh said he was her kinsman. Some of the younger nuns, and then the novices, began disappearing.

"At first we did nae know what was happening. Then one day I overheard Mother Eubh and Gunnar Bloodaxe planning who next would disappear from St. Maire's. I listened further and learned that they were selling women for profit. And I learned that Gunnar Bloodaxe was Mother Eubh's lover! I ran to Mother Una to tell her what I had found out, but Mother Eubh overheard me and my own fate was sealed," Morag finished.

"What did ye think a woman who could nae speak could do to help ye, foolish lass?" Regan wondered aloud.

"Aye, yer right," Morag agreed cheerfully, "but I dinna

know what else to do. The convent dinna suit me anyhow," she admitted.

Regan laughed. "It dinna suit me either," she told Morag.

The voyage to Ireland was an uneventful one. While the other women alternately wept and prayed the time away, Regan MacDuff and Morag became friends. Both of them thought their companions foolish creatures to bewail a fate that could not be changed.

The ship upon which they sailed was a sturdy vessel. Because the light summer winds could not fill its sails, the twenty men at the oars were kept busy. The women were fed bread and dried smoked fish, and given water to drink from a large barrel that stood by the main mast. During the day they huddled nervously together in the stern, whispering, while at night they slept restlessly beneath the canvas awning. A single bucket was provided as a necessary, and emptied into the sea each time it was used.

Regan had certainly never considered her life at Ben MacDui a luxurious one, but by comparison to her current circumstances it seemed sumptuous. The other women were peasants. They knew no better. What would Gruoch think of this? Regan wondered. Did Gruoch even consider what might be happening to her twin any longer? Or was her life as Ian Ferguson's wife all she wanted or needed now? She would never know.

The afternoon of the fourth day out from Strathclyde they sailed across Dublin Bay and into the mouth of the Liffey River, where they anchored for a short time awaiting the tide. Regan had never seen a town before, but the ragtag cluster of wooden buildings that made up the settlement called Dublin didn't particularly impress her. Gunnar Bloodaxe strode to the stern, sending the fearful women scuttling into a whimpering knot, but for Regan and Morag.

"I want ye with me now," he addressed her harshly.

"Morag too," she told him boldly.

"I canna sell her to Donal Righ," he said impatiently. *Why was he even arguing with her?* "Yer the prize in this batch, wench." Gunnar Bloodaxe gestured impatiently.

"Do ye think only my beauty will affect this Donal Righ?" she asked him. "I think he will be even more impressed if I have my servant wi' me. I am, after all, a laird's daughter, Gunnar Bloodaxe."

He silently debated her contention, and decided that she was absolutely correct. A nobleman's daughter and her servant. Donal Righ would pay well for such a purchase, *and* he would be affected by its elegance. Donal Righ was a man who appreciated style. "Very well," Gunnar Bloodaxe agreed, "your servant comes too." He turned about, and hearing the obedient footsteps behind him, smiled, satisfied.

Regan grinned conspiratorily at Morag. They had planned this together the previous night while the other women slept. Neither of them had ever had a friend before, and they did not want to lose one another.

The ship's anchor was finally pulled aboard. The vessel moved slowly under oar power up the river to a long wooden dock where it was made fast. The women in the stern of the boat began to wail again.

Gunnar Bloodaxe looked thoroughly disgusted. He turned to his first mate, Thor Strongbow, and said, "Dispose of them in the usual manner while I take this prize and her servant to Donal Righ. Don't let Lars Silversmith cheat you. You have ten women. All are in their prime, and none is ill or weak. They're excellent slaves. I will expect a goodly weight in silver for them." Then he looked at Regan and Morag, who were close by his side. "Come then," he said, and hurried off the ship, the two young women behind him.

They followed him down the long wooden dock, gazing with interest at the other vessels tied up there. Some were smaller than the boat they had traveled on, but others were much larger and more elaborate. The men upon the decks were equally interesting to the two girls. Some were fair, others darker-skinned, and to their amazement, there were a few who were actually black in color. They were fascinated, and a bit afraid, as they hurried along after Gunnar Bloodaxe.

Dublin was the first of the Viking settlements of any note in Eire. It had been founded over a hundred years ago upon the site of two earlier Celtic settlements. The Vikings called their town Dubh linn, meaning *dark pool*, after the place where the river Liffey and a smaller stream called the Poodle met and joined. The Norwegians and Danes had battled for supremacy in the town over the past century. It had been destroyed once by the Celtic tribes, but within twenty years was flourishing once again. It was in Dublin that the Vikings had introduced the lucrative slave trade to the Irish. It now flourished along with other commerce. Until recently cattle had been the currency of exchange, but of late the Norsemen of Dublin had taken to coinage of gold and silver. It had made trade far more interesting, and easy.

Upon a rise within the town they stopped before a structure erected from both stone and wood. Gunnar Bloodaxe rapped sharply upon the large oak doors of the building with the hilt of his sword. Within moments the door was opened a crack and a small dark face peered out curiously. Then the visitor was recognized, and the door opened wider to admit him and the two girls.

"Greetings, Abu!" Gunnar Bloodaxe boomed in his rasping tones. "I see the Gods still allow you to live on in the house of Donal Righ."

"I survive, Gunnar Bloodaxe," a high, piping voice responded.

"I never saw anyone so small," Morag whispered to Regan.

"What kind of a man is he?" Regan asked Gunnar.

"He's a pygmy," came the answer.

Regan did not understand, and she shrugged at Morag, who was equally confused. They were in a courtyard enclosed by the building's walls. It seemed overcrowded with goods and bales of all sorts and shapes. Gunnar turned about, gesturing to them to keep up as they followed Abu into a separate section of the building.

"Wait here," Abu ordered them, then hurried on short legs through a door. But a brief moment later he popped back out and called, "Come! My master will see you, Gunnar Bloodaxe."

They entered the room. Both girls were astounded by what they saw. The walls were of polished wood, hung with silk tapestries. The floor was of polished stone. There were no windows in the room, but a neat fire pit burned applewood, lightly scenting the air, and taking the chill out of the cloudy day. Lights such as they had never seen—tall, of metal, and footed—lit the room. There was a dais. Seated upon it in an armed chair with a leather seat was a man with light brown skin. He was a very round man, from his body to his smooth polished pate, and his hairless face resembled nothing more than a benign full moon. He was the most foreign-looking creature either of them had ever laid eyes on, yet when he spoke, his accent was familiar.

"What have ye brought me, Gunnar Bloodaxe?" he demanded, wasting no time on amenities. He wore a wonderful robe of silk, striped in purple, red, blue, and yellow, and his pudgy fingers were richly beringed.

"A nobleman's daughter, Donal Righ. Plucked from her convent on the Scots coast of Strathclyde," Gunnar Blood-axe replied. Reaching out, he pulled Regan's mantle from her, revealing her face and long pale gold hair, which was loose. "This maid is worth a fortune. The other girl is her servant."

"She is a virgin?" Donal Righ demanded.

"Alas, my lord, she is not," Gunnar answered him. "She was sent to the convent for taking her sister's husband for a lover."

"And you tried to be certain her virtue was indeed lost," Donal Righ said dryly. He shook his head. "Half her value is gone, Gunnar Bloodaxe. You know that."

"If she were any other girl, perhaps," Gunnar argued. He gestured at Regan to remove her tunic, pulling at it to hurry her along. *"Look at her, Donal Righ!"*

Regan now stood naked before the man, her long golden hair her only covering. Her belly was flat. Her breasts, though small, were mounds of snowy flesh, each topped by a deep pink berry of a nipple. Her legs were slender, tapering to slim ankles and high-arched, narrow feet. At the impatient prodding of Gunnar

Bloodaxe's thick finger, she turned slowly, revealing the graceful sweep of her back, leading into the firm, rounded twin moons of her buttocks.

"Hmmmmmm," Donal Righ considered, his gaze carefully assessing the woman before him. She might not be a virgin, but there was a delicious freshness about her.

"She is a jewel beyond price!" Gunnar Bloodaxe enthused.

"What is your name, girl?" Donal Righ asked her.

"Regan MacDuff, my lord," she told him.

"How many men have you known, Regan MacDuff?" he said.

"I lay wi' Ian Ferguson one time, my lord; and Gunnar Bloodaxe forced me once when I said I was nae a virgin," she explained to him.

"Why are you not afraid, girl?" His black eyes bored into her.

"I am afraid, my lord, but what can I possibly do to alter my circumstances? To weep and wail would be useless, would it nae?" she said.

He nodded. She had distinct possibilities. Her beauty would have been enough for most men, but he had a very special man in mind to master this girl. A man who would be as intrigued by the girl's intellect as he would be by her beauty. "She is very outspoken," he complained to Gunnar Bloodaxe nevertheless. "A slave should be humble."

"The boldness can be beaten out of her, Donal Righ," Gunnar Bloodaxe replied. "There are some men who might even enjoy such an exercise in discipline," he suggested with a smirk.

"Give the girl back her gown," Donal Righ ordered the Norseman. "I have seen enough. She is fair, but not a virgin. She is too forward, but perhaps with proper training I can eke out a small profit on her. *Mayhap.*" He appeared to consider a moment, and then he said, "What do you want for the girl, Gunnar Bloodaxe, bearing in mind, of course, that her fairness does not make up for her many deficiencies?"

Gunnar Bloodaxe named his price, and Donal Righ winced delicately. He counteroffered, saying as he did, "The serving wench is to be included in the price as well. I cannot have the girl parted from her companion, lest it sadden her and she sicken and die. Too many of these girls will do that, you know, and then the entire investment is lost."

"If you would have the servant, Donal Righ, you will have to better yer offer," Gunnar Bloodaxe told him. He was not fooled. The slave merchant wanted his fair captive, as he had known that he would.

Donal Righ's short, stubby fingers worried the fabric of his sleeve. Properly trained, and he knew what she could be, the girl was perfect for what he had in mind. The Norseman was a wily, stubborn fellow fully capable of selling her as a whore to some Celtic brothel keeper just to get what he felt was a fair price. Donal Righ upped his offer by half again, and Gunnar Bloodaxe, who had not expected to get that good a price for Regan, was stunned. He nodded mutely.

"Abu, take the women to the baths, and see that they are made comfortable," Donal Righ instructed his servant quickly, before the Northman could change his mind. "Then bring me my strongbox, and send Gerda for wine, that Gunnar Bloodaxe and I may toast this sale between us."

"It is a good bargain," the Norseman said slowly, still amazed by his incredible good fortune. Eubh would certainly be surprised . . . *if he told her.* He looked up to discover that the two girls had been shepherded from the room by the tiny Abu. "What will you do with her?" he asked Donal Righ. "You must have some purpose in mind, I know."

"I owe a debt to a certain lord in my mother's homeland," Donal Righ answered him. "I shall send the girl to him in gratitude for his patronage. Fair-skinned and fair-haired girls are greatly prized amongst the Moors. He is a man who enjoys a variety of women. She will undoubtedly please him, furthering the lord's gratitude to me." He smiled broadly at Gunnar Bloodaxe. "I have paid you too much for the girl, my friend, but it pleases me to do so, knowing the advantage the girl will give me with my lord."

"Yer a sly old fox." The Northman chuckled, feeling expansive now that he believed he had gotten the upper hand with Donal Righ.

"Will you be back in Dublin before year's end?" Donal Righ asked Gunnar Bloodaxe.

"I think not. I would be home in time for the midsummer festivities. I'm taking another wife then, and my oldest two sons cannot get in the harvest without me. Besides, my cousin, Eubh, the abbess, will not have another shipment of slaves readied for me until next spring. Her convent is where I got this beauty. Mostly they are just peasant girls with small dowries sent to be nuns. Their families never expect to see them again. It makes it easy for us. If I ever get another like this one I've just sold ye, I'll bring her to ye, Donal Righ." He chuckled good-naturedly.

Abu returned, his little legs almost buckling beneath the weight of his master's strongbox. He was accompanied by a tall, spare woman carrying a tray with wine and goblets. Gunnar Bloodaxe watched, astounded, as Donal Righ removed small bars of silver from the brimming chest. The Norseman was a simple man with a single ship, a farmstead in Daneland, and two wives. In his entire life he had never seen so many riches. He wondered if there was some way in which he could steal the money box, but then decided there was not. Donal Righ's house was too well fortified.

Donal Righ shoved the bars of silver across the table to Gunnar Bloodaxe. "The price agreed upon," he said, closing the chest. He signaled to Abu, who picked it up and tottered from the chamber.

The serving woman had already poured them goblets of wine, and now stood deferentially by, awaiting her master's further orders.

Donal Righ picked up his goblet, nodding to his companion to do the same. *"Skaal!"* he said, and drank the wine down in a single gulp.

"Skaal!" Gunnar Bloodaxe returned, doing the same even as he pocketed the silver.

"May ye have good seas for yer return home," Donal Righ said, dismissing the Viking, who, realizing there was nothing left to say, thanked his host and departed. As he walked back through the town toward the docks, he wondered a moment

about the beauteous Regan MacDuff. Then seeing Thor
Strongbow coming toward him, Gunnar Bloodaxe hailed
his mate and together they continued on their way back to
the ship.

◼ *Chapter 3*

"What manner of place is this?" Regan asked the old woman called Erda.

"Why, child, it is a bathhouse," she replied. "Have ye ne'er seen a bathhouse before? This is my domain. I am mistress here. It is my task to see that all of Donal Righ's expensive slaves are washed and cosseted so that they may be shown to their best advantage."

"At home we washed in the loch," Regan replied.

"Ye will like this," Erda promised. She turned to Morag. "Ye'll wash too, lassie, but watch what I do for 'twill be yer task in the future to see to yer mistress's bath. Slaves such as the lady Regan are sold into the eastern countries, and there bathing is an art."

Abu had brought them from Donal Righ's chamber to this square stone building, where he had left them in the care of the plump old lady now attending them. At her direction they removed their clothes, a trifle surprised to see Erda removing hers as well. They were shocked to discover that she had no hair upon her body.

She saw them exchange looks, and chuckled. "The Moors like their ladies, both young and old, as smooth as silk," she told them. "The master's mother was a Moorish lady. I served her as a girl. In practices conducive to cleanliness, Donal Righ prefers the eastern ways. He says they are healthier."

"Why has *Righ* been added to his name?" Regan asked. "He is not a real king, is he?" The room in which they were now standing was filled with steam, and very hot. She had never been so warm in her entire life.

"He was the only child, alas, that my mistress ever bore her good lord. She called him the king of her heart when he was a babe and small lad. Eventually everyone began to call him Donal Righ." Erda ladled some water from a bucket over a pit of steaming stones, and immediately a foggy vapor arose with a sizzle and a hiss.

"I am going to die in this heat," Morag complained.

"Ye'll get used to it, lassie," Erda said with a chuckle.

"Why do we do this?" Regan asked her.

"The steam makes yer body sweat, aiding in the removal of dirt and poisons from yer skin, lady," Erda explained. Once the girls were oozing sweat, she took up a silver scraping tool and drew it lightly down their bodies in a steady motion. "See," she finally said, "the dirt is swept away. Now if ye will follow me, we will go to the bathing chamber itself."

In the next room they found a square pool filled with scented water. Erda took them into a corner where a small fountain flowed. There, upon a shelf, were several alabaster jars. The old lady scooped a handful of soap from one and rubbed it briskly over Regan's body. The soft soap lathered and gave off a fragrance of lavender. She next washed Regan's hair while encouraging Morag to wash herself in the same manner. When both girls were soaped, she filled a basin with water from the fountain, pouring it over them until they were free of the scented cleaning substance.

"Now," she told them, "yer ready to be denuded of all that unsightly hair upon yer pretty bodies." Her hand sought another jar upon the shelf, and dipping into it, she smeared a pink paste over Regan's legs and pubic area. "Go on, lassie," she said to Morag, and held out the jar. "Though ye'll ne'er be the beauty yer mistress is, yer a pretty girl, and will catch the eye of some guardsman, I'm certain."

Morag giggled, and following the old lady's instructions, smeared the pink paste over her own haired body parts.

After a few minutes Erda took a cloth and began removing the paste. As it disappeared, Regan's fair skin beneath was revealed smooth and flawless. Erda nodded, satisfied. She resoaped and rinsed the girl; Morag followed her lead. When both girls had been washed once again, she led them to the bathing pool and instructed them to enter it.

"Why?" Regan questioned her once more even as she stepped down into the warm, fragrant waters of the pool.

"Because, lady, it is pleasant and relaxing," Erda explained. Then she turned away to see to her own ablutions.

"I could get used to this," Morag admitted to Regan as they moved about the pool. "I nae knew such lovely things existed."

"Aye," Regan agreed with her friend. "'Tis verra pleasing indeed."

Overhearing them, Erda chuckled as she entered the pool herself. "This is just the beginning, lassies," she told them as she paddled about. "The world ye will enter is beyond yer imaginings."

"How would ye know?" Regan said.

"Did I not say I was a servant to the master's mother? Twice I went with her to her homeland. It is a city called Cordoba, in a place the Moors call al-Andalus. Never have I seen such a magnificent city! Nor such a wondrous place!"

"How can you know that we will go there?" Regan questioned.

Erda grinned, showing toothless gums. "I know everything that goes on in this household, and everything that is going to happen," she boasted to them. "For over a year now my master has been looking for a particularly beautiful slave woman whom he plans to send to the ruler of Cordoba. Ye see, he is in the caliph's debt." She climbed slowly up the steps from the pool, shaking herself free of water.

"What is a caliph?" Regan demanded.

"The caliph is the title of the ruler of Cordoba," Erda explained to them. "Ye are, my beauty, the very one Donal Righ has waited to find. Ye'll see Cordoba before the year is gone, mark my words. Come now, and let us attend to the rest of your grooming."

She led the two young women from the bathing room into another chamber, which was furnished with marble benches. There she instructed Morag in the art of massage, showing her the proper oils to use. She taught the girl how to carefully pare Regan's finger- and toenails. Lastly they dried Regan's long golden hair, combing just the tiniest bit of scented oil through it, and finally polishing it with a pure silk rag until it positively gleamed in the flickering lamps. While Morag had dried her own hair, Erda went to a chest, drawing forth fresh, clean garments for the two girls to wear. For Morag there was a soft, cotton chemise, a navy-blue undertunic, and a scarlet outertunic of fine linen. For Regan there was a silk chemise coupled with a natural-colored undertunic topped with an outertunic of pale blue satin embroidered in gold-thread windflowers.

Regan's hand fingered the embroidery atop the silk. "I hae nae anything so fine," she said in a soft voice.

" 'Tis just the beginning, lassie," Erda counseled her. "Yer a beautiful young girl. Once yer properly trained, ye'll please the caliph well. He'll surely fall in love with ye. If ye have his sons, yer fortune will be made. Of course, ye'll have to watch out for the other women in his favor. They'll be a fierce lot, each trying to retain the caliph's attention, devotion, and favor. The harem is a cruel place. My mistress said it many times, and was grateful to be wed to my lord Fergus. She did not like the climate here, but she said it was worth it to escape the harem. Still, the harem is a grand place to be for a beautiful young thing such as yerself," Erda continued. Then she led the two speechless girls back to Donal Righ's chamber.

He sat at his supper, but seeing them, he smiled and beckoned them forward. "Ahhh," he said, pleasure written all over his round face, "Erda has done well by ye, I can see. She's a treasure, are ye not, old woman? Were she not, I should have found her a husband long ago. Some randy young sailor who'd keep her up all night, eh, eh?" His laughter boomed.

Erda cackled toothlessly. "Ye'll ne'er get rid of me, master," she said. "I love ye much too much."

He grinned, pleased. She was a relic from his youth, but for his late mother's sake he kept her. "Take the serving wench, what's yer name, lass?" She told him and he nodded, saying, "Take Morag to the cook house and see she is fed, Erda. I'll call ye both when I need ye. Sit down, Regan, and join me at my supper. Pour yerself some wine, girl!" He passed her a platter of broiled rabbit.

Regan took a trencher of fresh bread, a joint from the rabbit, and a silver goblet of wine. She ate delicately, desperately trying to remember what little manners she had been taught. The wine, however, she could not help but quaff lustily. It was sweet and potent, and seemed to breathe new life into her veins.

"Cheese?" He offered her a wedge upon the end of his knife.

"Thank you, my lord," she replied, taking it and biting into it, chewing more slowly now. As she finished she was startled to find Abu at her elbow. She hadn't even noticed that he was in the room. He held out a basin of warm, perfumed water to her. She looked to Donal Righ.

"Wash yer hands in it," he instructed her. "Ye don't want to ruin that pretty tunic dress of yers, do ye? 'Tis a custom of the Moors."

" 'Tis a custom I like," she answered him, rinsing her fingers free of the greasy rabbit and cheese crumbs.

"I suppose old Erda has told ye that I intend to send ye to my friend the Caliph of Cordoba, and don't deny it. The old woman knows things in this house even before I do. She's not loath to share her information with any who'll listen."

Regan laughed. "I like the old lady. She's kind, my lord, in a world where few are. Aye, she told me, and then she explained what a caliph was; but what I dinna understand is what a harem is, and why I must be *trained* properly. What is wrong wi' me?"

"A harem," he said, "is a place where a Moor keeps all his women—his wives, his daughters, his female relations, his concubines."

"Wives, daughters, and female relations I comprehend, but I hae nae heard the word *concubine* before. What manner of creature is it, my lord?" Her puzzlement was honest.

"A concubine," he said, phrasing it carefully, "is a woman who pleases her master both physically and in a variety of other ways, Regan. He may enjoy her music, or dancing, or even discussing matters with her that trouble him. She can become his friend, and if she gives him children, her value is increased in his sight."

"I see," she said softly, now fully understanding.

"The Caliph of Cordoba is a powerful man," Donal Righ went on. "His household is large. In order to attract his interest, *and* to retain it, Regan, you must be trained to both give and receive pleasure as no other woman can. I would not just send Abd-al Rahman a beautiful woman for his harem, I would send him a Love Slave. To become a Love Slave, you will have to study the erotic arts and the craft of seduction with a man who is a master of those arts.

"There is only one such man to whom I would entrust you. He is the younger son of a friend of mine. He captains a vessel that sails between Eire, al-Andalus, and his own home in the city of al-Malina on the North African coast. He will be arriving in Dublin shortly on his summer visit. I intend that you go with him when he leaves. When he feels you have attained the highest level that a Love Slave can, he will present you to the caliph in my name. Until he comes, I would have you rest and regain yer strength. Ye have not had an easy time of it, Regan MacDuff, but know now that ye are prized and ye are valued above all women," he concluded with a warm smile that extended all the way to his eyes.

"I dinna know if I can become what ye want me to, my lord," she said slowly. "I dinna know how to give, or if it is even possible for me to receive this pleasure ye speak of with such certainty. I hae found no pleasure in coupling wi' a man, yet ye say I must find pleasure in it, and make the man find pleasure as well. I dinna understand how it can be done, Donal Righ. Perhaps ye would be better served to sell me to some Celtic chieftain for a servant. I can work hard, I promise ye, and my Morag too. If I disappoint ye, then it would reflect badly upon ye, and ye hae been good to me."

Reaching out, Donal Righ gently patted her hand in what he hoped was a reassuring gesture. "I do not want ye to fret over this, Regan MacDuff," he told her. "Yer experience with the physical side of passion has been very limited, and of the worst kind. Yer sister's husband was obviously not a man who knew how to make love to a woman. His own pleasure was his only concern. A clever man knows that the more the woman enjoys her pleasure, the greater his own will be. He therefore strives to give her that delight. As for Gunnar Bloodaxe, he too sought only to take his own enjoyment, and to ascertain that you did not lie to him. He did not care how you felt. No man has yet touched your heart and spirit. You have no idea how sweet love can be, but trust me, my beauty, you soon will."

She did not believe him, of course. She knew he but sought to ease her terrible fears. She was surprised by his kindness. She had never received such patient indulgence from anyone. She could only hope it would continue, at least until he realized that she could not be made to enjoy lovemaking. She sighed sadly, for the first time in her life feeling truly heavyhearted. What would become of her? Of little Morag?

Her depression, however, could not sustain itself. She was clean, warm, and better fed than she had ever been in her entire life. She had a real friend in Morag, who would forever be grateful that Regan had saved her from the common slave market. Morag had learned from listening to the other women aboard ship that the slave market in Dublin could lead at best to a household position, and at the worst to one of the waterfront brothels where most women died within a year or two.

Donal Righ kindly allowed them a measure of freedom within his house. He did not lock them away. They strolled in his private garden, a carefully tended enclosure with two neatly raked gravel paths in the shape of a cross, interspersed with small marble benches. There was a wonderful rose of Damascus, its many pink blossoms now in bloom, their heady fragrance filling the air. The old rosebush climbed up the stones and over the wall into the street below. There was a fountain at the center of the cross that bubbled up from a little round stone pool.

The girls walked atop the house's walls, watching the harbor traffic as the many and varied ships came and went. They saw small coastal freighters, larger freighters of all descriptions,

passenger vessels and fishing boats, and little cockles that
bobbed dangerously across the waters of the Liffey. Each day
old Erda shepherded them to her domain, and they bathed.
Regan had never realized that her skin could be so clean, or so
very soft. Sometimes she thought about Gruoch, and wished
that her twin sister could know so delicious a luxury, but
Gruoch, she sensed, was not thinking of her. Gruoch was lost to
her forever.

One day as they walked upon the walls of Donal Righ's house,
looking toward the sea, they saw a large, beautiful ship entering
the harbor of Dublin town. It was a graceful vessel, fully two
hundred ten feet in length. It was lateen-rigged, and its sail was
striped in cloth-of-gold and bright green silk. It swept up the
river to the main dock, nestling alongside the wooden pier, its
weathered lines binding it fast to the wharf. Both girls were
goggle-eyed.

"I hae nae seen anything so beautiful before," Regan said.

Morag echoed her sentiment. " 'Tis a braw ship to be sure."

Old Erda had joined them, and saw the direction in which
their interest lay. " 'Tis *I'timad*, the ship of Karim al Malina,
the master's good friend. We have been told to expect him."

"What does *I'timad* mean?" Regan asked Erda.

"Reliance," came the answer. Then she said, "I had best
see my baths are ready for the lord. He is a man who likes
the baths, a true Moor. He will have been at sea for many
weeks now, and be eager for sweet water and fragrant oils.
Stay upon the walls, my chicks. You will see Karim al Malina
as he comes up the street. More than likely he will be in the
company of his first mate and best friend, Alaeddin." She
chuckled. "There's a right charming devil, that Alaeddin!"
Then she hurried off to see to her duties, for Erda took pride in
her office.

They sat upon the wall, watching the street below, chattering
about nothing in particular, enjoying the early summer's day.
Then the two men, garbed in long white robes, came walking up
from the harbor. As they reached Donal Righ's house, one of
them looked up and grinned raffishly at the two girls. Regan

turned away shyly, but Morag grinned back at the black-bearded man with the twinkling dark eyes. Then she giggled as he blew a kiss at her.

"Ohh, he's a bold one," she said to Regan. "And a wicked one wi' the ladies, I can tell."

"How can ye tell?" Regan asked. "Ye've spent all yer life behind the convent walls. What would ye know of men?"

"Mother Una said she thought me more suited to marriage than the convent," Morag said frankly. "She was going to make a match for me wi' one of the local shepherd's sons. I was to hae a silver coin for every three years of my life for a dowry, and linens too. Mother Una said fifteen was a good time for me to wed, but then she grew ill, and Mother Eubh would nae hear of it. She said that the five silver pieces could be better spent, the old bitch!"

"Mother Una spoke to ye of what transpires between a man and a woman?" Regan probed.

"Aye, she said 'twas no mystery, for if God made it so, where was the evil in it?" Morag explained. "She let me roam outside the convent walls on pretty days. I met several young lads who took my eye, but I nae strayed from virtue's path, though once or twice I will admit to being tempted," she finished with a chuckle.

Regan was amazed. Morag could be no older than thirteen, and yet she had no fears about being with a man. Of course she was still a virgin. She could not know the degradation and pain involved in experiencing a man's lust, or the feelings of total helplessness a woman suffered. Regan wondered if she should tell her. Nay. Why frighten the lass? It was unlikely she would ever have to know the humiliation of submitting to a man's perverted desires. As the servant of a slave of high rank, she would be protected from such debauchery and brutality. She need never know, Regan decided.

They were called to the baths in the late afternoon, and it seemed to Regan that Erda was fussing over her even more than usual. On her knees, the old woman carefully inspected Regan for any sign of superfluous body hair. Struggling to her feet, she peered at the girl, turning her about, then finally gave her a small dish of parsley and mint leaves.

"Chew them slowly, and carefully," she instructed Regan. " 'Twill sweeten yer breath, my chick. Yer teeth are good, and I see no sign of rot. Yer fortunate. Too many have pretty faces but bad teeth."

"What is this all about?" Regan demanded of her.

"Why, child, yer to be presented to Karim al Malina in a little while. The master has ordered that ye be brought to him. He has chosen Karim al Malina to train ye in the erotic arts."

Regan felt suddenly cold. These last few days had been so pleasant that for a brief time she had forgotten what was to come. Donal Righ, to be fair, had warned her.

"Come along, come along," Erda said, bustling from the baths, the two girls behind her. She brought them to a large rectangular room that was filled with chests. "This is the master's personal storeroom, my chicks. He has said I may dress ye as I see fit, and I know just what I want for ye. Morag, child, open that chest there." She pointed.

Morag lifted the lid of the coffer up and gasped with delight. Within it were a variety of fabrics, each one more beautiful than the other. Erda bent over and drew out first a length of white silk, which she handed to Morag.

" 'Tis a tunic," she explained. "Take off yer garments, both of ye, and then garb yerself, Morag. Don't be shocked, for it has no sleeves." She helped the girl pull the garment over her head. It fell in graceful folds to Morag's ankles, the neckline revealing the girl's collarbone. Erda opened a small box and drew out several jeweled pins. She looped Morag's dark braids against the side of her head and affixed them firmly. Then reaching into the chest, she drew forth a length of silver cord, which she tied about the young girl's slender waist. "There!" she said, satisfied. "Ye look the perfect attendant for yer mistress, my chick."

Morag couldn't, it seemed, stop smiling. "Ohh, lady," she said to Regan, "is it nae lovely?"

"Aye," Regan told her, smiling back. " 'Tis indeed lovely. Ye look verra fair, Morag. 'Tis sorry I am ye canna wed wi' yer shepherd."

"Shepherd, indeed," Erda sniffed. "She's fit for better than that, lady. Now let us see what I have for ye." Reaching into the storage unit again, she drew forth a sheer, glimmering fabric, narrowly pleated. Its color was neither silver nor gold, but a blend of the two, and it was diaphanous. Erda helped Regan into the garment. It had long, flowing sleeves that came to her wrists, and it was open from the round neckline to the ankle. Erda pinned the gown closed with a golden pin upon the girl's right shoulder. She stood back, eyeing her charge critically, making small noises as she looked. "Ummmmm. Hmmmmm. Aye!" Moving behind Regan, she took her long hair and fastened it back with a small length of jeweled silk. "When the master tells ye," she instructed Morag, "just pull it here, and her hair will fan out." Then she fastened a silk band sewn in pearls around Regan's forehead.

"Ye can see my nakedness beneath this fabric," Regan said.

"Aye," Erda agreed, "but not quite. The gown is intended to tantalize. It is exactly what the master would want." She turned to Morag again. "Now, child, when Donal Righ instructs ye, unfasten the pin at the shoulder and help yer mistress out of the gown. Ye must be graceful, not clumsy. The catch is simple. Come here and try it. Aye, that's it! Yer a quick girl, and will be of great value to yer lady. Now go behind her and draw the gown away from her body. Lady, raise both of yer arms as they are freed of the fabric, and put them behind yer head. It lifts the breasts for better viewing."

Regan gritted her teeth, but she obeyed the old lady. This was not Erda's fault. She was doing what she was instructed to do. This was Donal Righ's doing, and he would regret it. When they tried to display her like some animal at a fair, she would rebel. Then this Karim al Malina would see that she was not at all suited to being a Love Slave. Donal Righ would have to sell her to some householder, and she could live at least with dignity, even if she was worked to death.

"Very nice, my chick," Erda hummed her approval. "Ye've a talent for this sort of thing, and ye'll go far, I warrant. The master will be very pleased with ye this night. Now ye may rest until it is time for ye to redress and be presented. Come, and we'll go to yer wee chamber. Morag, child, carry yer mistress's gown."

The hum of conversation emanated from the chamber where Donal Righ took his meals. Inside, the fire pit burned merrily, and seated about the table on the dais were three men. The man in the center was Donal Righ. To his left sat the first mate of the *I'timad*, Alaeddin ben Omar. He was a large bear of a man, with a beard as black as night and eyes to match. Those who were ill-advised enough to believe that his marvelous good nature made him a fool, usually ended up at the business end of his scimitar. He was a loyal friend and a ferocious fighter. On Donal Righ's right sat the son of his old friend, Habib ibn Malik, who was called Karim.

The three men had eaten and drunk well. They would discuss business at another time, for the *I'timad* was a freighter. It brought luxury goods to Eire from al-Andalus and other ports, and carried back raw wool, hides, Celtic metalwork, and jewelry, as well as slaves. Donal Righ had already indicated to his friend's son that there was another reason for his summoning him this night, his first in port in some weeks. Now the older man sat back, stretched, and spoke.

"Ye know I owe an obligation to the caliph in Cordoba, Karim. I have long been in his debt. Were it not for his patronage, ye would not bring me the goods that have made me a rich man. I shall never be able to fully repay our great lord, Abd-al Rahman, but I would send him a token of my respect and gratitude. For some months I have sought for the perfect gift. Knowing the caliph's penchant for beautiful females, I decided to see if I could find a woman who might be trained as a Love Slave. A mere slave girl is simply not a good enough offering to show my gratitude to our master. Several days ago, by merest chance, a magnificent creature came into my possession. She is young, a Scot, a nobleman's daughter."

"A virgin who will cry to her God in heaven for death before she accepts the embrace of the infidel," Karim al Malina said dryly.

"She is not a virgin," Donal Righ said, surprising both men.

Then he went on to explain Regan's history. When he had finished, he said, "I want to put her in your care, Karim, son of my old friend. Ye are a Passion Master. It is known that ye trained in the erotic arts at the secret school in Samarkand. Ye can take this girl and mold her into the perfect Love Slave for the caliph. *My gratitude will be boundless.*"

Karim al Malina considered, and then he said, "I do not like to refuse ye, Donal Righ, but I cannot help but remember the last girl I trained. The foolish creature fell in love with me and committed suicide rather than go to her true master. It was very embarrassing, and I had to compensate the man double for the loss. No Passion Master has ever had such a thing happen. I obviously did not do my duty properly. I am loath to take another maiden in my charge."

"It has been five years since that unfortunate incident, my young friend. The girl was unstable. This girl is not. She is proud and fierce. She will bend, but never break beneath your tutelage. Regan is a strong lass, Karim. She needs ye if she is to succeed in truly attracting Abd-al Rahman. Even sending him a Love Slave is not enough. She must enthrall him, and bear him children."

Karim sighed. "I do not know," he said slowly.

"Let me show ye the girl," Donal Righ suggested slyly. "Do not refuse me until ye have seen her and tested her mettle. Abu!" He called to the pygmy. "Fetch the lady Regan and her servant quickly."

His two companions laughed at Donal Righ's eagerness.

"Ye must be very certain Karim will acquiesce, Donal Righ," Alaeddin ben Omar said. "Is the girl *that* beautiful?"

"She is as the sun and the moon," the older man replied.

"Now ye speak with the tongue of a Moor," Karim told him, amused. "I promise ye nothing, friend of my father."

"Wait and see," Donal Righ advised him. "Ye are not the man I have always believed ye to be if ye are not ravished by her."

Alaeddin ben Omar chuckled deep in his barrel-like chest. The old devil had thrown down a gauntlet Karim al Malina could not fail to pick up. He had pricked the young captain's pride with a sharp thorn.

The door to the chamber opened. Abu returned, bringing two women with him. The first mate's eyes lit up at the sight of Morag. He had thought her a toothsome little creature when he first saw her this afternoon. The other girl kept her face in shadow, obviously instructed to do so. Neither man could at first quite make out her features, but then she raised her head and looked directly at them. Alaeddin ben Omar whistled softly through his teeth in admiration. Donal Righ had not lied. The girl was probably the most beautiful female he had ever beheld. He looked to Karim, but as usual his captain's face was unreadable.

Though Regan appeared to be looking at both of the two strangers on the dais, she was in reality staring only at Karim al Malina. She had never seen so handsome a man. His face was an oval, the forehead and the sculpted cheekbones high, but the chin was squared. His nose was long and narrow, but the nostrils flared sensuously. His mouth was also long, but more narrow than full. Unlike his companion, he was clean-shaven. His dark eyebrows were winged, and the eyes beneath them an azure blue. His hair was a deep brown, almost black. It was pulled back from his forehead. She could not tell how long it was.

"Remove her robe, Morag." Donal Righ's voice broke her reverie.

"No." Karim al Malina spoke. "Let me do it." He arose and stepped from the dais to stand in front of Regan. His eyes held hers in thrall as he reached up with a big hand to unfasten the pin holding her garment together. His nails, she noticed, were round, but there was absolutely no expression upon his handsome face to give any indication of his thoughts. He nodded to Morag, who drew the robe from Regan's body slowly, as she'd been instructed. Just the faintest smile touched the corners of Karim's mouth. It had been artfully done. He turned to Donal Righ. "Who is this girl?" he asked.

"Morag is the lady Regan's servant," the older man replied. "She is skilled," the captain noted, and then turned his full attention back to Regan. His voice was low when he spoke again. "I see rebellion in those aquamarine eyes, Zaynab," he said softly. "You will obey me, for if you do not, you will embarrass Donal Righ. Now put your arms behind your head. I wish to view your breasts better."

"No," she replied as softly. "I will force Donal Righ to sell me as a household slave to some Celtic chieftain."

"He will sell you to the most infamous brothel keeper in Dublin, who will pay a far better price for you," Karim told her. "You will have some sailor between your legs before Donal Righ has left the establishment, *and* you will be dead of overwork and disease within a year. Is that the life you would choose?"

Both she and Morag looked shocked at his words. "Donal Righ would not do that to me," Regan protested nervously. "He is kind."

"Only because you are of value to him, Zaynab," he told her. "Now raise your arms and put them behind your head as I have commanded you."

For a long moment their gazes locked in a silent battle of wills, and then Regan obeyed him, albeit reluctantly. Morag let out an audible sigh of relief, and Karim chuckled. He stepped back a pace and let his eyes sweep in leisurely fashion over Regan's body. His look was assessing, never lewd. Reaching out with his hands, he molded her breasts, causing a soft flush to rise in her cheeks. Her top teeth caught her lower lip and worried at it as he fondled her, but again there was nothing lascivious in his touch.

"Do you want me to open my mouth that you may inspect my teeth?" she muttered darkly.

"Shortly," he said quietly, "but for now I would like you to turn about. You may lower your arms to your sides. Slowly, Zaynab. Anticipation is an art you must practice, I can see."

Regan turned as he had ordered her. "What is it you call me, my lord? Zaynab?"

"In the tongue of the Moors it means *the beautiful one*," he told her. "You must have a Moorish name, and so I shall call you." His eyes traveled from her pretty shoulders down the delicate line of her backbone to her buttocks, which, he decided, were like the twin halves of a firm young peach. She was tall for a woman, but not too tall, and her length was in her torso, not her legs with their graceful calves. Kneeling, he lifted up a foot. It was slender, and the arch was high. Her bones were small. She was finely made. Donal Righ had not lied. She was like the sun and the moon.

Karim stood and unfastened the clasp on her hair. The silvery gold tresses spread themselves like a fan across her shoulders, reaching just to the tip of her tailbone. He fingered a lock. It was like the finest silk.

"You may turn back to face me now," he said, and when she had, he ordered her to open her mouth.

Regan was outraged. She thought he had been mocking her when she snapped at him a moment ago. She thought of refusing him, but then saw Morag's pleading eyes and obeyed.

He peered in, noting, "Her teeth are all there, and they are free of rot. Her breath is sweet. It's a good sign." He took Regan's chin between his thumb and his forefinger, turning her head this way and that as he peered again, this time at her skin. "The skin is translucent, and healthy," he said. "The nose is pretty, the mouth tempting, and the eyes a fine color, like a first quality aquamarine." Releasing Regan, he turned abruptly away from her, rejoining the two men on the dais. "She has definite possibilities, Donal Righ, and as you say, she is strong-willed."

"Then ye will take her and train her for me, Karim? I would entrust her to no one else. I know two lords in al-Andalus who have Love Slaves schooled by ye. These girls have brought their masters so much happiness that they prize them above all other women. The girls are called Aiysha and Subh. You educated them about seven years ago."

"I remember the maidens involved," Karim said. "Aiysha was sent to a rich lord in Seville, and Subh went to the king of Granada. I received magnificent gifts from both men in gratitude. It was after those successes that I was sent that poor girl who later killed herself. I have not trained another girl since, Donal Righ."

"But ye will train this one, won't ye, Karim?" the older man said with a sly grin.

The younger man laughed, resigned. "Aye, old friend of my father, I will school Zaynab for you. When she is ready, I will take her to the caliph's court myself and present her to Abd-al Rahman for you. Be warned, however, she will not be easy. She has as strong a streak of independence as ever I have seen in anyone, man or woman."

"Ye have named her!" he chortled. *"Zaynab.* I like it! It suits ye, Regan MacDuff, and that's the last time I shall call ye by the name yer mam gave ye. Morag, reclothe yer mistress and take her to the special chamber that has been prepared for her. Erda will show ye, girl." He turned back to Karim. "This girl is now in yer charge. Ye will stay with me, and Alaeddin too."

"Not until tomorrow, Donal Righ," the captain told him. "I have been at sea for several weeks. I both need and want the company of a skilled courtesan. Alaeddin and I have made other arrangements for tonight, but I will begin Zaynab's education tomorrow, I promise you, old friend of my father's. It is agreed, then?" He held out his hand, and Donal Righ grasped it gratefully.

"It is agreed, Karim al Malina," he assented. "Abu, take the women back to Erda."

Regan and Morag were escorted out, and when they had gone, Alaeddin asked Donal Righ, "Would you object if I paid a bit of court to the little one with braids? She sets my heart to racing. How old is she?"

"Old enough," Donal Righ answered with a chuckle. "Erda says she has her woman's flow, but be advised that she is a virgin."

"I'd like to be her first," Alaeddin ben Omar admitted.

"Ye'll spoil her for other men." Donal Righ chuckled again, and his companions laughed as well.

Regan and Morag could hear the men's laughter as they followed Abu back to the women's quarters, where old Erda resided. When he had left them in her charge and departed, Regan exploded with anger.

"Ye would hae thought I was a mare or a cow for sale," she fumed, outraged. "I hate that man! He is horrible and awful! He actually dared to look in my mouth! He sniffed at my breath, Morag!"

"I thought him rather gentle, and nice," Morag ventured.

"Nice?" Regan hissed.

"He wasna cruel, mistress," the girl said quietly, "and nae once did he look at ye wi' lecherous eyes."

"How could ye tell, lassie? Ye were much too busy flirting wi' the black-bearded companion of his," Regan snapped.

Morag giggled, admitting her guilt. "He's verra handsome, mistress, and he flirted back wi' me."

"Did he put his hands between yer thighs?" Erda demanded.

"What?" Regan shrieked, horrified.

"Did he put his hands between yer legs?" Erda repeated. "Did he investigate yer private parts?"

"Nay!" she answered, outraged by the very thought.

"Then why do ye carry on so, my chick?" the old woman wondered. "The man has but looked at ye. 'Tis no crime to admire a beautiful maid."

"He felt my breasts!" Regan told her.

"To test the mettle of yer flesh," she answered calmly.

"I am nae someone's possession," Regan exclaimed angrily.

"Aye, my chick, ye are," Erda said quietly. "When Gunnar Bloodaxe sold ye to Donal Righ, ye became my master's possession."

"But that damned Viking had no authority to sell me to anyone!" Regan protested. "I was sent by my family to the convent of St. Maire."

"Which," Erda countered, "put ye under the rule of the abbess, Mother Eubh, who sold ye to Gunnar Bloodaxe, who brought ye to Donal Righ. He will put ye in Karim al Malina's charge, and when ye are considered properly trained, Karim al Malina will present ye to the caliph in Cordoba, in the name of Donal Righ. Ye will be the caliph's possession, child. Ye had best set yer mind to accepting yer fate. Ye'll be happier if ye do. 'Tis a good future, Zaynab. Would that I had had yer beauty when I was yer age. I would have become a queen!"

"My name is Regan MacDuff," she said stubbornly.

"Ye have been renamed, my chick, and ye must answer to Zaynab from now on," Erda told her.

"Never!" Regan swore. If she accepted this name, then she would lose her very self. She was Regan MacDuff of Ben MacDui, and nothing would ever change that. *Nothing!* Zaynab indeed! It was a heathenish name, and she would never answer to it. *Never! Never! Never!*

The next day she fought a battle of wills with everyone around her. Try as they would, she absolutely refused to answer to her new name.

"What are we to do with her, master?" Erda complained to Donal Righ. "Morag has willingly accepted her new name of Oma, but this stubborn Zaynab will not answer to anything but her birth name. Even Oma cannot get around her, and she is usually good with her mistress. Should I beat her, master? I know not what else to do."

"Do not beat her," Donal Righ said expansively. "It would only bruise her fine white skin. Karim will handle the matter when he returns this evening. Take Zaynab to the special room that has been prepared for her. Karim has suggested that you use oil of gardenia in her bath today. He thinks that fragrance will suit her." The slave merchant was in an excellent mood. Everything was proceeding exactly as he had hoped it would.

Regan was bathed that day as Donal Righ had requested. She sniffed suspiciously at the lush scent. "What is it?" she demanded. "It is neither rose nor lavender. I am not certain I like it."

"It is gardenia," Erda told her.

"I do not know the flower," Regan replied.

"Of course ye do not," Erda said. "It is a beautiful creamy white flower that blooms in the pots and the gardens of al-Andalus."

Regan said nothing more. Actually, she liked the new fragrance, but she would not give them the satisfaction of knowing it. It was an exotic aroma, and its heaviness suited her mood. "Where are you taking me?" she demanded of Erda as they left the baths. They were not turned in the direction of the women's quarters of the house.

"Ye have been given a new chamber to yerself, Zaynab," the old lady said. "Oma will have her own little room nearby ye. She's waiting for ye now, my chick. Come along, and do not be so sullen."

The room to which she was escorted was not a large room, but it was light and airy. Located at the top of the house, and on a corner, it had two windows with heavy shutters, one facing the river, the other, Donal Righ's garden. The walls were white-washed, the furnishings simple. There was a brass brazier that could be used to heat the room, a chest for storage, a single chair with a slung leather seat, and a small oak table. Upon an almost-square raised dais lay a mattress covered in pale blue satin and stuffed with down and fresh herbs. Upon the mattress were several large pillows in striped fabrics and cloth-of-gold. Regan had never seen such a fine room, and as she walked about it, her mood began to lighten somewhat. "Where is Morag?" she asked.

"Oma has a small room next to this one. There is a con-necting door, and ye have but to call her," Erda said. "I will leave ye now to rest. Karim al Malina will be returning soon to begin yer tutelage." The old lady then retreated with a speed that Regan would not have believed her capable of, locking the door loudly behind her as she went.

At first Regan was outraged, but then she laughed. Where did they think she would go? she wondered. "Morag!" she called.

The connecting door opened and the girl came through. She sniffed delicately. "What is that wonderful fragrance, mistress?"

"The new scent that hae been chosen for me," Regan told her. "It is called gardenia. Erda says that they are white flowers that grow in al-Andalus. I must admit to liking it, but dinna tell them."

"This is a fine chamber," Oma said. "Come and see mine."

Regan stepped through the door into a narrow little room with a single window. There was a storage chest and a well-stuffed pallet. "Ye'll need a brazier for heat," she noted. "Is yer door locked too?"

Oma nodded. "Aye," she said. "I suppose we're nae to go anywhere, nae even the garden below. Well, 'tis almost dusk now. I love these long summer's days!"

Erda brought them an evening meal of bread, hard-boiled eggs, cheese, and two round, greenish fruits. "They are called oranges," she told them. "You peel the skin away and eat the sweet flesh inside. They are grown in al-Andalus. The captain brought them for Donal Righ." She set a small decanter of watered wine on the table and left them, locking the door behind her again as she departed.

The two girls sat together on the edge of the dais and ate the food. Saving the oranges for last, they giggled as the juice from the tangy fruit ran down their chins and all over their hands. They agreed with each other that oranges were very good, if just a trifle messy. When they had finished, Oma poured some water in the washbasin and they bathed their hands and faces. The servant then gathered up the dishes and goblets, setting them neatly upon the tray. They had eaten everything. Only the orange peels remained as evidence that they had dined.

Outside the windows, the sky was pinkish-lavender with the long summer twilight. The air was cool but soft, and Regan decided to leave the windows unshuttered for the moment. A blackbird began to sing its sweet song in the garden below. The crescent moon shone down, while near it a bright blue star glittered.

Both girls turned as the door to the room was unlocked and Karim al Malina entered, closing and relocking the door behind him.

He looked to Oma. "You may go to your chamber now, Oma. Your mistress will not need you again until morning."

"Yes, my lord," Oma said softly, bowing, and then she went through the connecting door to her own room.

"How dare ye instruct my servant!" Regan said in a tight voice.

"If I have offended you, Zaynab, I ask your forgiveness, but the time has come for your lessons to begin. If you would like

Oma here to watch, I will call her back," he said in a quiet voice.

"I am Regan MacDuff of Ben MacDui," she said stonily. "I will nae answer to such an odd and foreign name as Zaynab." Crossing her arms over her chest, she looked directly at him, eyes blazing defiantly.

She is marvelous, he thought. What spirit! His calm return gaze, however, gave no indication of his admiration. "Regan MacDuff of Ben MacDui is foreign-sounding to my ears," Karim al Malina told her. "What does Regan mean? MacDuff, I comprehend, is your family name."

"It means *king*," the girl replied proudly.

"You are no king, my beauty, but a lovely woman whom I shall teach to be magnificent. You may think of yourself however you wish, Zaynab, but you are no longer in your world. You are in mine, and you will answer to your new name very soon, if not today, then tomorrow or the next day."

He began to remove his clothing: first his long white cape, then the wide belt about his narrow waist and his white shirt. Seating himself, he drew off his boots, then standing up again, he began to pull off his white pantaloons.

Regan gasped, shocked. "What are ye doing?" she squeaked.

"Is it not evident?" His azure eyes were twinkling, although his countenance was very grave. "Have you ever seen a man's naked body, Zaynab?"

"I am no virgin," she muttered, trying desperately to avoid looking directly at him, but it was just too tempting. He had a broad chest, lightly furred toward the top with a narrow band of dark hair sliding down directly in the middle of his navel, traveling to his groin. She stared at his manhood. It lay very white, and limp. His legs were long and, like his upper chest, were covered with dark down.

"Remove your chemise for me, Zaynab," he told her.

"No!" she snapped sharply.

Eliminating the small distance between them, he grasped the round neck of her chemise and tore it to the hem. "When I tell you to do something, Zaynab, you must obey me," he said as he pulled the ripped fabric off her and tossed it aside. Then taking her by the hand, he led her to the dais, drawing her down upon the mattress. When he turned her face to his, he was shocked to see that her eyes had gone blank. There was absolutely no expression in them at all. It was as if her spirit had flown her body, leaving only the empty shell. "Why are you afraid of me?" he asked her gently, still holding her hand in his. "There is no need for you to fear me, Zaynab."

She struggled within herself to find the words, and then finally said, "Ye will hurt me. I dinna want ye to hurt me!" She arose from the bed and stood nervously by it.

"I will not hurt you, Zaynab. Tell me of the two who hurt you, my beauty. Sometimes the retelling helps ease the pain," he said.

"Ian Ferguson hurt me," Regan whispered so low that he was forced to bend his head to hear her. "He stank of horses, and paraded himself before me, bragging of his attributes. He squeezed my breasts and pushed his hands between my legs, all the while wriggling against me and making strange noises. Then he ordered me to spread my legs, and he climbed atop me. Ohhh, it was so big, and it hurt me so. He dinna care. *He dinna care!* He kept pushing himself in and out of me, groaning and sweating. I hae nae known such pain. And after the first time, he did it to me twice more that night. I hated it! I hated him!" She began to weep.

"And Gunnar Bloodaxe?" he asked her. "Did he hurt you?"

"It did nae hurt when he pushed himself wi'in me," she said softly, "but I hated it nonetheless. He bent me over a table and forced me to accept him, grunting like a hog until he spilled his seed."

"I will never force you," Karim al Malina promised her.

"Then ye will never hae me, my lord, for I shall never surrender my body willingly to any man," Regan told him.

"You will surrender to me, Zaynab," he told her gently. "Not tonight, and perhaps not for many nights, but in the end you will give yourself to me both body and soul. I shall not have to force you." He tenderly brushed the tears from her cheeks with the fingers of one hand. "Do not cry. What is past cannot be changed, but I will help to make you a fine future, I promise. You have but to trust me."

"I trust nae man," she answered, and he understood. Then she looked at him, her eyes once more alive. "What is it ye are supposed to do with me to make me presentable to this caliph?"

"Teach you the erotic arts," he said with a small smile, "but you do not really know what I mean, do you?"

Regan shook her head.

"To make love is an art, Zaynab. The two men who so cruelly used you knew nothing of the real pleasure that can be attained between a man and a woman. They were rough, and selfish, and thoughtless. They couple with their women like dogs couple with bitches. They are little better than the animals they emulate. It does not have to be like that, my beauty." He slipped an arm about her and pressed a kiss to her forehead. "In time I will teach you all I know. You will go to your new master, the caliph, and ravish him with your beauty and skill."

She did not look as if she believed him. Coupling, a pleasure? Frankly, she could not see how, but he had piqued her curiosity. "Where did ye learn these arts of yers, my lord?" she asked him.

"In a city called Samarkand," he told her.

"Why did ye learn them?"

"I am my father's youngest son," he began. "Like many second sons, I was, in my youth, a wild young fellow. After I had impregnated three of my father's slave girls, he lost patience with me. My brother Ja'far interceded for me with our parent. He told Father that since I seemed to be best at making the beast with two backs, perhaps I should go to the School of the Passion Masters in Samarkand. Then, at least, my desires would have a practical usage. The men who studied with the Passion Masters were few, for they accepted few, but those lucky enough to have learned from them are in great demand to train Love Slaves. I was received by them, tested for my prowess, and only then did they agree to take me into their school. When I had finished my course of study, I began to use my skills to earn my living. That is how I was able to purchase *I'timad*, my ship." Karim al Malina smiled at Regan. "I am very good at what I do," he told her mischievously. "I have taken you into my charge as a favor to Donal Righ, but when I am finished with you, Zaynab, you will be my finest creation, I promise you."

"Why must I be a Love Slave? Why canna Donal Righ be content to sell me for a servant? I dinna want to yield myself to a man."

"You are too beautiful to be a servant," he said. "You know it, Zaynab. Do not be coy for it does not suit you. You must always speak honestly. It is true that I will teach you how to yield yourself to a man, but I will also teach you how to make that same man yield himself to you."

" 'Tis nae possible!" she declared. "Nae man would ever yield to a woman. I dinna believe it for a minute, my lord."

He laughed. " 'Tis true, Zaynab. A beautiful woman has great power over the strongest man, and can defeat him in the battle of love."

"I am cold," she said, shivering.

He rose from the dais, and crossing the chamber, closed the wooden shutters. Then going to the storage chest, he drew forth a light woolen coverlet and brought it to her. "When you are beneath it, and next to me, you will regain your warmth," he said. "Come, let us lie together." He lay down, drawing the cover over him, then held his hand out to her.

"You mean to share my bed?" Regan's eyes were filled with fear again, although her voice was strong.

"This is our chamber," he told her calmly. "Come under the coverlet, Zaynab. I told you I would not force you. I do not lie."

She could not help but remember Ian Ferguson and his braggadocio. Ian, who had ripped cruelly into her innocent flesh, taking his pleasure, wounding her spirit. Gunnar Bloodaxe had been little better, although at least she had not had to look at his leering face as he violated her. She turned to gaze at Karim al Malina. He lay on his back, his blue eyes closed, but he was not asleep, she sensed. Could she trust him? Dare she trust him? With trembling hands she reached for the coverlet, and lifting it, slipped beneath its soft warmth.

Almost immediately he put an arm about her, and Regan

jumped. "What are ye doing?" she demanded in a frightened voice.

"You'll warm yourself faster," he said calmly, "if you come closer to me, but if you would prefer not to, I will understand."

She felt the arm about her shoulders. She felt the length of him against her body. His presence, to her surprise, was comforting. "Nae more than this," she warned him in a hard voice.

She did not see his smile in the gloaming. "Not tonight," he told her. "Good night, my sweet Zaynab. Good night."

Chapter 4

"Well?" Donal Righ demanded on the following morning of Karim al Malina. "Will Zaynab be worth the silver I expended on her purchase?"

"In time, old friend," came the answer. "The girl has been terrorized by two clumsy men. It will take time to gain her trust, but I shall. I have never had a woman like this to school. She is innocent, in truth, but wise beyond her years. Still, she knows absolutely nothing about love, or passion. It will be at least a full year before she is presentable, perhaps more." He sipped a mixture of hot mulled wine and spices from a silver goblet studded with onyx. "Are you willing to give me that time, or would you prefer to sell her, at a good slave market in al-Andalus, and take your profit now while you have expended little on her training?"

"Nay! Nay! The girl is worth the effort. I saw it when she first came into my presence with that oaf, Gunnar Bloodaxe. She easily outfoxed him. Erda told me that Zaynab and Oma became friends aboard Gunnar Bloodaxe's vessel. Then Zaynab told the Viking that I would be more impressed by a woman with her servant than just a woman alone. Heh! Heh!" he chortled. "She is a clever wench, Karim, for indeed I was! Heh! Heh! Heh!" Then he grew serious. "How long do ye intend to remain here in Dublin? Where will ye go from here?"

"My vessel is already unloaded, Donal Righ," Karim told him. "It will take another week to fill her holds, and then I will set sail for al-Malina. The summer is half over, and I sense an early autumn in the air. I would be off these northern seas of

yours before the seasons change once again. Besides, I believe
Zaynab will be easier to teach once she is totally removed from
her former life."

Donal Righ nodded. "Yer wise," he said, agreeing with the
younger man. "Where will ye take her?"

"I have a villa outside al-Malina. I will take her there. It is
where I have trained all of the maidens brought to me. It is an
elegant and sensuous place, and my servants are well disci-
plined in my ways. Zaynab will be less fearful at Paradise."

"Paradise?" Donal Righ looked puzzled.

Karim laughed. " 'Tis what I call my home, old man, for
to me it is paradise. The house sits on the edge of the sea, and
is surrounded by gardens and fountains. It is a place of peace."

"And your father?" Donal Righ asked.

"He prefers the city, and leaves me to my own devices. In a
sense I have become exactly what he wanted me to become. I
am loyal to my family, independently wealthy, and not only
respectable, but respected. In only one sense have I failed him,
and that is my failure to take a wife and sire sons. I leave those
duties to my elder brothers, Ja'far and Ayyub. My father is
very disappointed, however."

"You owe it to him to marry, my boy. A man as passionate
as yourself would no doubt sire only male children. Surely
Habib ibn Malik's youngest son would be considered a fine
marital catch," Donal Righ finished with a smile.

"I am not ready to wed yet," Karim replied. "I enjoy my life
as it is now. Perhaps if my time with Zaynab is successful, I
shall take another maiden or two to train."

"How large is your harem?" Donal Righ asked.

"I have none," Karim answered him. "I am not home enough,
and left to themselves, women grow restless and treacherous.
They need a man's strong hand to guide them constantly. When
I marry, I will build a harem."

"Ye are probably wise," Donal Righ agreed, and then he
chuckled. "Ye have too old a head for such a young man,
Karim."

"Let Zaynab and Oma have the privacy of your gardens,

Donal Righ," Karim requested. "The journey home to al-Malina will take several weeks, and they will be confined upon my vessel. I cannot allow them the freedom of the decks, lest they inflame my men."

Donal Righ nodded. "Aye, the voyage will be hard for the lasses. They are used to the land. The trip from Strathclyde took but a few days, and they were rarely out of sight of land."

"They will not see land for many days," Karim said.

Regan and Morag were informed by Erda that they would once again be permitted the freedom of Donal Righ's small garden. Delighted, they hurried downstairs to spend the day in the sunshine, sitting upon one of the little marble benches, chattering and speculating about the mysterious al-Andalus to which they would soon travel.

In mid-afternoon Alaeddin ben Omar appeared, telling Regan, "My lady Zaynab, Karim al Malina desires your presence. He awaits you upstairs." The black-bearded sailor bowed politely.

Regan thanked him and departed the garden.

Alaeddin ben Omar grinned at Morag. Reaching out, he tweaked one of her braids, and she giggled. Taking her hand in his, he began to stroll the garden with her. "You're a pretty girl," he said to her.

"And yer a bold rogue," she answered pertly. "I may be convent raised, but I know a rascal when I meet one."

He chuckled, the sound a warm rumble, and in that instant Morag lost her heart to him. "Aye, Oma, I am indeed a rascal, but one with a warm heart. You seem to have stolen it away from me, my pretty one. I do not think I want it back."

"Ye've a silver tongue, Alaeddin ben Omar," she told him with an inviting smile, and then she bent to sniff a rose.

When she stood straight again, he was directly before her. "Are you aware, my pretty one, that yer name, Oma, is the female of Omar?" Reaching out, he stroked her cheek, and Morag's eyes grew wide.

Nervously she stepped back a pace. His touch had been

tender, yet it had sent a small shock through her. Her heart beat faster as she gazed into his black eyes. He reached out again, but this time it was to draw her into the shelter of his arm. Morag came perilously close to swooning. The shepherd lads on the hillside outside the convent had never been this daring or bold with her. "Ohhhhh," she exclaimed as his mouth touched hers in an exploratory kiss, but she did not struggle or draw away from him. She was curious about what would happen next, and she felt safe with this big man.

From the windows above the garden, Karim al Malina watched his first mate as he began his seduction of the young girl. He had never seen Alaeddin so gentle, so patient with a woman. He suspected his old friend was possibly biting off more than he could chew this time. The adoring look on Oma's pretty face portended something more than just a quick passion.

The sound of the door opening behind him caused him to turn. A smile lit his handsome features. "Zaynab," he said. "Did you sleep well?"

"Aye, I did," she admitted. The truth was, she had never felt so well rested as she had this morning when she awoke to find him gone from her side. She smiled slightly.

"Shall we continue our lessons then?" he said. "Remove your garments for me. I would begin to teach you the art of touch. The skin is a very sensitive instrument of the amatory arts, Zaynab. To learn how to properly caress it is important. You must learn to touch yourself, as well as your master, in such a way as to inflame the other senses."

Regan was slightly taken aback. He spoke in an everyday voice. There was absolutely nothing suggestive in his tone. Slowly she drew her garments off. To refuse would be ridiculous, she knew. He had shown her last night that he expected immediate obedience from her. She had spent part of the morning trying to mend the chemise he had torn from her last night, but the garment was ruined, and she was embarrassed to have been so wasteful. As she drew her undertunic off she sneaked a peek at him from beneath her thick golden lashes. He wore only white pantaloons, and in the daylight his body was very beautiful. She blushed at the thought. Could a man be considered beautiful?

He watched her disrobe through dispassionate eyes. She was absolutely exquisite, but he believed that all of his old training had reasserted itself once he had decided to take on the task of training this girl in the erotic arts. The first thing he had been taught by the Passion Masters in Samarkand was that you absolutely did not become emotionally entangled with a student. The woman being trained must be completely and thoroughly dominated, but tenderly, not harshly. As for the man training her, he must always be patient, kind, and firm, but never must his heart become involved.

"My lord?" She was completely nude now.

He focused his attention upon her once again. "Making love," he began, "can be done at any time of the day or night, although there are some who are overly prudish and think passion can be attained only in the dark. Because you are fearful, I have decided that if I begin your lessons in the daylight, and you can fully see what is happening, you will lose half of your fears. Do you understand?"

Regan nodded.

"Good," he told her. "Now, before we begin your experiences with touch, you must accept the name that has been given you. You cannot retain what is to us a foreign name."

"I will lose myself if ye take my birth name from me," she said desperately. "I dinna want to lose myself, my lord!"

"You are far more than just a name," he said quietly. "A name does not make you who you are, Zaynab. You will never return to your homeland. Your memories will always be with you, but you cannot live your life through those memories. You must leave that life behind, and with it the name your mother gave you at birth. Your new name indicates your new life, a better life, I believe, than the one you lived before. Now say your name, my beauty. Say, my name is Zaynab. *Say it!*"

For a moment her beautiful blue-green eyes filled with tears that threatened to spill over onto her cheeks. Her mouth was mutinous, her look defiant. But finally she swallowed hard, and said, "My name is Zaynab. It means *the beautiful one*."

"Again," he encouraged her.

"I am Zaynab!" Her voice was stronger now.

"Good!" He gave her his approval, pleased that she had obeyed him without further ado. He fully understood the difficulties for her in putting aside her past, but he was pleased she had shown the wisdom to understand that only by putting herself in his hands could she hope to survive in this new world into which she was being sent. "Come here to me now," he commanded her. "Remember that I will not force you, but I am going to touch you. You need not fear me, Zaynab. Do you understand?"

"Yes, my lord." She would not be afraid, and if she was, he would not see it in any gesture, or in her eyes. I am Zaynab, she thought, beginning to forge this new identity for herself. I am a creature to be cherished and admired. My survival depends upon what this man can teach me. I do not regret the life I have left behind. I would not want a man like Ian Ferguson for a husband. Nor did I wish to spend my life in a convent praying to a God I do not even know or understand. *I am Zaynab, the beautiful one*. She caught the shudder about to overtake her as he put an arm about her and drew her close.

He felt her suppress her distaste and was silently pleased. He tipped her face up to his, the back of one hand brushing along her jawbone and across her cheekbones. A single digit ran down the bridge of her straight little nose, then played across her lips, teasing at them until they parted slightly. He smiled into her eyes, and Zaynab felt her breath catch in her throat. "You see the power of touch," he said matter-of-factly.

"Aye." She nodded. " 'Tis a strong thing, my lord."

"When done properly," he corrected her. "Now, to continue." He pushed her head aside with the back of his hand, and his lips found the tender spot just below her ear. "The mouth may be used in touch as well as the hands," he explained, "and the tongue." He licked the gardenia-perfumed flesh of her neck in a long, sensuous stroke.

Zaynab shivered, unable to help herself.

"You are beginning to experience arousal," he told her.

"Am I?" She wasn't quite certain what he meant.

"What caused you to shiver?" he asked her.

"I am nae certain," she answered him honestly.

"Look at your nipples," he said.

She did, and was surprised to find they were small and tight like frosted flower buds.

"What did you feel when my mouth touched you?"

"I tingle, I think?" She struggled to recall.

"Where?" His azure eyes bored into her.

"A-All over," she admitted.

"Arousal," he said in plain tones. Then, to her surprise, he picked her up and carried her across the chamber to the bed, where he gently laid her down. "We will continue our lesson for today here," he said. "I wish to get you used to a more intimate kind of touch, and it will be easier if we are here, and not standing."

He is not going to harm me, she forced herself to remember.

"I am going to touch your breasts," he warned her, immediately caressing a small round orb with his long fingers. His hand closed over it, tenderly kneading the soft flesh, and she murmured, a faint sound of nervousness. He released his hold upon her and began to stroke her bosom with light, almost tickling touches. He put a single finger into his mouth, his eyes never leaving her as he sucked upon it; and then he began to encircle a nipple with the wet digit, around and around and around until finally the nipple was slick with his saliva. Then bending his head low, he blew softly upon the wet nipple.

This is really very pleasant, Zaynab thought to herself, and then she asked him, "Can I do the same thing to ye? Will it gie ye pleasure, my lord?"

"Did I give you pleasure, Zaynab?" he asked her.

"I think so," she admitted.

"In time I will allow you the freedom of my body, but not quite yet, my flower. We will take your lesson a tiny bit further today, however." He lowered his dark head again, but this time his mouth closed over her nipple, and she gasped loudly.

There *was* pleasure! she thought, startled. The mouth that tugged so insistently upon her breast was stirring up feelings she had not even known existed, nor would have even considered she possessed. "Ohhhh!" The sound escaped her before she might contain it.

He recognized her tone as one of enjoyment, and not fear. Immediately he transferred his attentions to her other breast, and within moments her young body was arching against him, against his mouth. He was pleased. She was quickly losing her fear. The damage was not as severe as he had previously believed. Finally, when he determined she had had enough teasing, he raised his head from her pretty breasts and kissed her mouth lightly. "I am pleased with you, Zaynab," he said with a warm smile. "You have done well this afternoon. If you wish to dress and join Oma back in the gardens, you have my permission."

"Ye dinna wish to continue?" Her whole demeanor was one of disappointment.

"We will practice again tonight," he said calmly.

"Ohh." She arose from the bed, and dressing quickly, left him.

Karim al Malina chuckled. It had been a long time since he had schooled a maiden. He had truly believed himself in complete control. And indeed he had been, until she evinced pleasure at his homage to her charming breasts and pressed against him. His manhood had in that single instant gone from well behaved to a raging hunger. It had been all he could do in that moment not to take her there and then. She did not realize it, but she would have been willing.

Instead he had continued suckling upon her perfumed flesh almost as a self-discipline for himself. Then he'd dismissed her as her master would one day dismiss her when he had taken his pleasure of her lovely body. It had not been easy. He realized now that he'd been foolish to stop training Love Slaves simply because Leila had killed herself over him. It had unnerved him, true, but he should have taken another maiden to school immediately.

His education with the Passion Masters in Samarkand had been a valuable source of income, permitting him to purchase his freighter, *I'timad*, and sail it where and when he wanted. It allowed him to pay his crew in the periods he chose to remain ashore, so that they would not sail with another vessel. In the years since he purchased his vessel, he'd assembled a band of sailors whose temperaments suited his and each other's. Without his other source of income, he had had to spend more time at sea in the past few years. Donal Righ had not discussed what he would pay him for training Zaynab, but he knew his father's old friend would be very generous.

As Zaynab reentered the little garden, Alaeddin ben Omar was just leaving it. She nodded to him, but said nothing. She found her servant upon a marble bench, flushed and breathless. "He seeks to seduce ye," she said by way of admonishment.

"Aye, he does," the other girl admitted, "but he'll nae succeed, my lady Regan, until I wish to be seduced."

"I have accepted the name of Zaynab," her mistress told her then. "It is foolish to oppose these Moors, as we are being taken to their al-Andalus to live out our lives. I shall nae call ye Morag again, my good Oma. Dinna think me cowardly for giving in to them."

"I dinna think ye craven, my lady Zaynab. I think ye verra wise," Oma told her. "Alaeddin says we shall also hae to learn their language if we are to get on. It is called Romance."

"I shall request of Karim al Malina that we be taught together," Zaynab replied, "but we shall speak our own tongue from time to time, lest we forget it. Besides, it is unlikely anyone else will know it, and we may communicate in secret when we need to do so, Oma."

In early evening the two girls went to the baths, where Erda was awaiting them. "Have ye heard?" she asked them. "Ye're to set sail in just seven days' time for al-Andalus. I heard the master speaking with the handsome Moorish captain, Karim al Malina, this afternoon." She peered at Zaynab closely. "Is he the magnificent lover he is reputed to be, my girl? Ye should certainly know by now." She chuckled.

"My lord Karim hae nae made love to me, ye nosy old woman," she told Erda. "There is more to the art of seduction than a man's member nesting itself within a woman's secret garden. That is the final outcome. One must begin at the beginning," she finished loftily.

Oma's jaw dropped with surprise at Zaynab's words.

Erda, however, rolled her faded brown eyes. "Listen to the wench," she said in outraged tones. "Three weeks ago she did not know what a bath was, and now she thinks she's a houri! Well, ye've got a lot to learn, lassie! A wee bit of humility might be a good first lesson."

"Ohh, Erda," Zaynab relented, "I dinna mean to offend ye. Will ye forgive me, old woman? *Please?*"

"Well, perhaps I might," Erda allowed, mollified. Then she said brightly, "Don't be disappointed, lassie. He'll make love to ye soon enough."

Oma burst out laughing at the look on Zaynab's face, and even Zaynab was unable to withhold her own amusement.

"Yer a dreadful old thing, Erda," she scolded the bath mistress, who cackled in toothless appreciation.

They bathed and then ate a simple supper with Erda in the women's quarters. When they returned to the chamber at the top of the house, Oma said, "I hae been told yer to remove yer garments and go to sleep. Erda says those were her orders for ye."

"Will the lord Karim come tonight?" Zaynab wondered aloud.

"I dinna know that," Oma replied, helping her mistress off with her clothing and into her bed. "Sleep well, my lady." The door between their chambers closed.

Zaynab lay quietly. The house seemed very quiet tonight. In the garden below she could hear the soft chirping of the summer insects. If she closed her eyes, she might be back at Ben MacDui. For the first time in weeks there was no sadness in the memory. Her fate had not lain in the land of her birth, she now realized clearly. "Farewell, dear Gruoch," she whispered to herself. "May yer life be a happy one, my sister." Then she closed her eyes again and drifted into a light sleep.

* * *

He stood over the bed, upon the dais, looking down upon her. He had seen many beautiful women in his time and in his travels, but this girl was probably the most beautiful of them all. He wondered if all the maidens from Alba were as fair as she was, for he had never before seen a girl from that land.

She had told Donal Righ the story of her life, and Donal Righ, in his turn, had passed it on to him. It was amazing that her mind was whole, he thought. He was not surprised by her fear of men or her inability to feel love. She had never really known any. Now he would teach her all the skills of passion at his command, that she might gain favor with the Caliph of Cordoba. He wondered if Abd-al Rahman would appreciate Zaynab. He was a respected ruler, and a patron of the arts, but now, in his later years, there were rumors that it took more than just a beautiful woman to please him. He knew this was why Donal Righ had besought him to train Zaynab as a Love Slave.

Karim quietly drew off his clothing and lay on his side facing the girl. She stirred restlessly. He ran a single finger from the pulse in the base of her throat down to her sweet cleft. She murmured, and he drew the finger back up her body. Her eyes opened and she recognized him. Leaning over, he began kissing the nipples of her breasts, each in turn. He then began to bathe her with his hot tongue, moving from her breasts to her chest; gently forcing her head back as his tongue swept in long, leisurely strokes up her slender neck and back down again to her breasts.

Zaynab shivered, but the feeling, she quickly realized, was one of delight, not fear. Neither of them spoke a word as he licked her torso and her abdomen. Poor Gruoch, she thought, amazed. She'll know only the grunting and sweating of Ian Ferguson, never this wondrous pleasure of just touching. He pushed his tongue into her navel and wiggled it about. "Ahhhh!" she sighed, a delicious tingle suffusing her lower body. She stiffened, but only momentarily, as he came near her smooth Venus mont, but his attention seemed more diverted by her

shapely thighs. He kissed her slender feet and then, to her surprise, sucked each of her toes in turn before revolving her from
her back onto her stomach.

He seated himself upon her buttocks, his big hands with
their supple fingers smoothing in lazy movements over her
shoulders and back. She was practically purring. Bending,
he lapped his tongue easily across her shoulders, and then, as
he swung off her again, down the graceful line of her backbone. He kneaded the perfectly matched halves of her posterior, but when his fingers pushed between those halves, she
stiffened.

"Do not be frightened," he said, speaking for the first time.
"You are going to learn to take a man's member in a variety of
ways, Zaynab. You've never been touched here?" His fingers
explored her gently, but did not press within her.

"Nay," she replied tightly.

The offending digits withdrew themselves, and he continued his slow tasting of her flesh, nibbling at her calves until
she could not refrain from giggling. Suddenly his body was atop
hers, covering it, and she felt a momentary panic, but he did
nothing but nuzzle the nape of her neck and nip gently at it.
Then the weight of him was gone and he was turning her over
onto her back again.

"Why do ye nae kiss me?" she wondered.

"Kissing is inflammatory, Zaynab. I do not think you are
ready for kissing *and* touching," he told her.

"Could ye nae just kiss me?" she asked him.

"If I kiss you, I'll want to touch you, flower," he warned her.

Her brow furrowed a moment, and then she said, "Very well,
my lord, I gie ye my permission. I trust ye, and I believe ye hae
the strength to cease should I beg ye to do so."

"The touching would be different, more passionate," he said.

"I am ready," she insisted, and then she pouted adorably. "I
want ye to kiss me!"

"Zaynab," he said sternly to her, "you must accept that I
know what is best for you. Yesterday you were fearful of passion. Three little lessons, and suddenly you think you are ready
for anything."

"*I am!* I want to know more of this passion! It is lovely, my lord. 'Tis nae at all like with Ian, or Gunnar Bloodaxe," she pleaded.

"The lesson is concluded," he told her sternly. "It is time for us to sleep." He rolled onto his back and closed his eyes.

Zaynab was outraged. He had aroused her once again, more this time than the two times before, and now he would sleep? She wanted to feel his mouth upon hers. Despite her lack of experience with all of this *passion*, she felt a desperate need to have her lips touching his lips. Raising herself quietly upon an elbow, she swiftly lowered her head down and kissed him firmly. She squealed with surprise as his arms wrapped themselves tightly about her and his azure eyes blazed furiously into her own. Rolling her beneath him, he brought his mouth down hard upon hers, silencing the gasp she barely managed, before breathing became almost impossible between the tightness of his grasp and the pressure of his lips fused hotly to her own.

This wasn't quite what she had wanted when she asked him to kiss her. She thought his kisses would be sweet and tender. They were instead wild and fierce. She attempted to struggle from his embrace, but even as she flung her head back, his mouth was scorching a blazing trail down her straining throat. Suddenly, she didn't want to escape him. She moaned low, her hands tangling themselves in his shoulder-length hair. With an instinct she hadn't known she had, she returned his kisses. She could feel his hands, fingers splayed across her back, almost burning into her skin. She molded her length to his, whispering hungrily into his ear.

"*Take me! I am not afraid! Take me!*"

He was quickly losing control of the situation. If he did not regain the upper hand, Zaynab would be impossible to train. *He wanted her.* He wanted her suddenly as he had never wanted any woman, but it would be in his time, and not hers. A Love Slave must give her master immediate and perfect obedience. Releasing her from his embrace, he pulled her across his lap and spanked her bottom hard, several times. "You are disobedient, Zaynab!" he scolded her. "If you belonged to me, I should have you bound between the punishment pillars at my villa and whipped. You will not sleep by my side tonight. Go to the foot of the bed at once, you hot-blooded vixen!"

"Ye kissed me back!" she hissed at him angrily. His hand had hurt her, but she would not cry like some silly child.

"Obey me, Zaynab." His voice was menacing.

"I will sleep on the floor," she said furiously.

"You will sleep where I told you! *At my feet!* There is a punishment room in this house, I am certain. The lash's tip can be plied so as not to damage your skin. Have you ever been tied between two posts and whipped, Zaynab? The pain of such punishment is exquisitely cruel, I am told. If you defy me a moment longer, I shall request that Donal Righ have you beaten. Twenty lashes, I believe, would be a good beginning. You must be taught to obey. Instant obedience is the hallmark of a well-trained Love Slave. Badly trained Love Slaves do not go forth from my house, Zaynab. *Now go to the foot of the bed."*

Had there been a knife at hand in that instant, she would have used it on him. Instead, his threats ringing in her ears, she crept to the foot of the bed. The hard look in his eyes told her that he was not bluffing. He would have her beaten if she did not obey. "I hate ye!" she snarled at him, eyes blazing her frustration.

"Good," he told her. "I do not want your love, Zaynab. Love the man who will be your master, but do not love me. You will respect me for what I can teach you. Learn your lessons well, and you will be beloved by a powerful man. If that should come to pass, my flower, your life will be perfect. You will remember me with gratitude then. Go to sleep now. You have quickly overcome your initial fears. In the morning we will begin in earnest to train you."

Within minutes he was snoring lightly, but Zaynab lay at the foot of the bed seething with anger. Afraid? Nay, she was not afraid of him. He had shown her that passion actually existed, that a man need not be cruel to a woman when they made love.

For that she was grateful, but he had pricked her pride when he spanked her. She had begun to believe that he liked her. Obviously she was no more than a special commission for Donal Righ. Well, she would show Karim al Malina. She would become the finest Love Slave he had ever schooled, and when she was, she would have her revenge! She would make him fall in love with her! Then she would leave him to go gladly to this caliph in Cordoba. The Passion Master's heart, if indeed he even had a heart, would be broken! She would never think of him again except to imagine him pining away, knowing that his special skills had made her the caliph's favorite. Zaynab smiled grimly in the darkness. There was obviously a bit of Sorcha MacDuff in her after all. It was a revenge worthy of a Celt.

When the morning came, Zaynab behaved as if nothing untoward had happened between them the previous night. "Good morning, my lord," she greeted him sweetly.

He responded in kind. "You should begin to learn a man's body with your hands today," he told her. "Let us go to the baths. Erda and I will teach you how to bathe your master."

"As my lord commands," she replied.

He looked sharply at her. "You are amazingly amenable."

"I dinna sleep well at the foot of the bed," she said. "It gave me the time to think on what ye had told me. I want to succeed wi' the caliph, my lord. Donal Righ has been kind to me. I would bring honor to his gift. If I behave badly, it would reflect upon him."

She sounded very reasonable. Still, he was suspicious. It was too great a change from her attitude last night. Then he relented. She was intelligent, he knew. She just lacked any experience, and obviously had had no discipline growing up. She was used to being willful, but perhaps his strong actions last night had made her realize that she could not continue to behave mulishly.

They went to the baths, where Erda awaited them. The old woman was an expert bath mistress, and Zaynab an excellent pupil. She mimicked each of Erda's actions perfectly, scraping

away the sweat on Karim al Malina's body and rinsing him
with warm water. Her fingers imitated Erda's, dipping into
the alabaster soap jar, smoothing the creamy substance over his
chest, working it into a fragrant foam. Her hands smoothed
over his upper body; his long, lean back.

"My bones are all of an ache today, Zaynab," Erda told her.
"Kneel down and wash Karim al Malina's legs, then his feet,
being certain to do each toe separately, my chick."

When Zaynab had finished this task, he surprised her by
turning quickly about. She suddenly found herself facing his
manhood. Startled, she looked up at him questioningly.

"Be gentle," were his only words of instruction, said in a
monotone, but his azure eyes were dancing devilishly.

"Aye, my lord," she answered meekly. " 'Tis a verra small
thing, and shouldna take long," she finished.

Erda cackled with appreciation at the jibe. Something was
going on between these two, although she could not quite
decide what it was.

Zaynab soaped Karim al Malina's manhood and his pouch
of life with tender fingers. Gently she smoothed and rubbed
him, watching, fascinated, as he grew in breadth and length. It
was really quite amazing, but she gave no indication of either
admiration or fear. When he was hard, his male member thrusting itself straight forward, Zaynab stood and, reaching for the
nearest basin of fresh water, said, "Let me rinse ye, my lord,
lest the soap burn ye."

"Zaynab!" Old Erda's voice cried out urgently even as the
girl splashed the water upon Karim al Malina. " 'Tis cold . . ."
Erda's voice faded away. For a long moment there was only
the sound of dripping water from the corner fountain and the
lapping of the water in the bathing pool.

"Oh dear," Zaynab said in a small, innocent-sounding voice.
The icy dousing had all but sent his magnificent display of
manhood into hiding.

Had she done it deliberately? he wondered. Of course she
had! It was her revenge for the spanking he had given her.

"My lord, my apologies," Zaynab said. "I believed the basin

filled with warm water. Erda always adds a pitcher of warm water from the pool to the cold water. I thought she had done it."

"My chick, I told *ye* to do it," Erda said, pointing to the full pitcher by the basin. "Ye forgot, I fear."

"My eyes were blinded by my lord's exhibition of his manhood. Remember that I am but an innocent maid with little experience." Then, without another word, she rinsed the rest of his big body, but this time with more tepid water from a separate basin.

Oh, yes! It had been deliberate. She would drive him to the whip yet, he feared, but when he finished with her, she would be the most perfect Love Slave he had ever trained.

With a sweet smile, she led him by the hand down into the bathing pool. "Is it better now, my lord?" she queried him solicitously.

"You're a vixen," he told her softly.

"Aye, my lord," she replied in equally low tones.

"You learn quickly," he said. "You bathed me well, but for that one mistake. Do not make such a mistake again, Zaynab, or you will indeed feel the sting of my lash. I will not warn you further, my flower."

"As my lord commands," she murmured humbly, but he sensed absolutely no humility at all in her modest demeanor.

It was to be war between them, then. He recognized it in that moment. She would be outwardly obedient, but never truly so. What a challenge she presented to him, he thought. His excitement rose. To tame her, yet not to break her spirit. Without that spirit, she would be just another beautiful creature, and she would certainly not survive in the harem of the caliph. She must be strong, but she must also learn when to bend. Was such a thing even possible?

They returned to their chamber and he dressed. "I must go to the docks, to ascertain that *I'timad* is being loaded properly and on schedule. Have Oma bring you something to eat. Rest, for I shall return by mid-afternoon to resume your lessons." Then he was gone. Zaynab opened the storage chest to draw out fresh garments, but the chest was empty. "Oma!" she called.

The girl came through the door wearing a foreign-looking garment and carrying another. "Donal Righ has had his woman alter some of his mother's clothing for us. This garment is called a caftan, and worn by the women of al-Andalus. He says we must get used to Moorish garments. Here is yours. Is it not lovely?"

The caftan was the pale blue of a summer sky. It was made of silk. The neckline was high, yet had a keyhole opening embroidered in silver thread that matched the embroidery on the edges of the long, wide sleeves. Zaynab slipped it over her head, delighted by the softness of the fabric. "It's verra beautiful," she said, almost to herself.

"Now let me bring ye some food," Oma replied briskly.

"Let us eat in the garden," her mistress suggested, and the servant agreed.

While the two girls ate their meal, Karim al Malina sat in his cabin aboard *I'timad* and pondered his next move, much to the amusement of Alaeddin ben Omar.

"I have never seen you so perplexed over a woman," the first mate said with a chuckle. "I will admit these northern girls are different. That little Oma may be a virgin, but she is no fool."

"They are too independent," Karim said slowly. "I wonder if such a woman can truly become a good Love Slave. I have never dealt with such a woman before. What if she cannot be properly trained?"

"Does she fight you?" Alaeddin asked curiously.

"Aye, and at the same time nay," came the answer. "She has overcome her initial fear of passion, but she finds it difficult, nay almost impossible, to be obedient. I am not certain what to do with her, my friend. Were she another girl, I would beat her. I have indeed threatened to do so, but she will not be quelled."

"What does she want of you?" the first mate asked intuitively.

Karim was startled by the question at first, and then he said, "She wants me to make love to her, and she is not yet ready."

"Why?" Alaeddin queried. "This is no virgin, Karim, but a girl who has been cruelly treated. Now you have shown her that a man need not be cruel; that a man can give pleasure while being gentle. She is aroused and curious to know more. You cannot treat her as you would a dewy-eyed virgin whom you are training for some rich master. With such a virgin, you would spend weeks gently leading her up to that moment when you would remove the impediment of her virginity for her master, initiating her into the joys of love. This girl does not understand love. She has already been brutally used. She only knows that when a man couples with a woman, it brings her pain, and shame.

"Now you have suggested by your actions that this may not be so. Before you can continue on with her, she needs to have the reassurance that only your full passion can give her. You must erase from her memory the previous cruelties done her if you are to have her full cooperation. I will wager if you make complete and sweet love to her, she will become as obedient as any woman mastered by a loving and skillful cock." He chuckled again. "Surely the Passion Masters did not teach you to be so rigid in your methods, Karim. You know better than even I that all women are certainly not the same. Each is different in her own way, my friend. Each must be approached differently."

"Perhaps I am afraid," Karim told his friend.

"Afraid? You? Never!" came the sure reply.

"I cannot help but remember Leila," Karim said.

"I remember Leila too," Alaeddin ben Omar replied. "She was a beautiful girl, but as finely drawn and as high-strung as a Berber chieftain's brood mare ready to be mated by a powerful desert stallion. Any sensible man could have seen she was not suitable to be trained as a Love Slave. Any man except that fool, who in his lust purchased her. Then he was not satisfied by her extraordinary beauty. He had to have a Love Slave. He was a friend of your father's, as I recall, wasn't he?

"You would have never taken the girl into your charge except that he was. Perhaps you do not recall it clearly, but I do. You did not think her suitable for training at the time, but your father pleaded with you to do this favor for his old friend. So you did, and of course the girl fell in love with you when her only other choice was that aging fool who owned her. It was never your fault, Karim. This girl is not the same. She is sound of mind and strong of heart. Give her a taste of true passion, and she will come to heel, I guarantee it."

"Perhaps you are right," the captain said thoughtfully. "Mayhap when the mystery is over for her, and she is reassured, she will settle down, paying heed to her instructions. Her success with the caliph will not only bring honor to Donal Righ, but to me as well. That would please my father."

Alaeddin ben Omar grinned wickedly. "Then why are you yet here, my captain? Go back to the house and give the stubborn wench the pleasure she craves. I will see to the ship."

"And what of you, Alaeddin? Will you continue in your seduction of the little Oma? She is a toothsome creature," Karim remarked.

"She will have taken my lance into her virgin sheath before we sail, my captain," the first mate bragged. "I mean to be the first with her, and I'll teach her well, I promise."

Karim al Malina picked up his cape and drew it about his broad shoulders. "Be gentle with the girl," he advised. "I do not want her unhappy, lest she distress Zaynab. The two are close, and I want them both content, my friend. Remember, you are a man of vast experience, and I do not remember that you have ever had a virgin. They must be treated in a kindly fashion, not taken harshly."

"I will not harm the little wench," Alaeddin promised. "I will just widen her world as I widen her sweet passage," he finished with a grin. "I'll not force her, my captain."

"Good!" The captain exited his cabin with his mate. "Be certain that all the hides are aboard today, and see each is whole, not damaged. Check them individually. Accept none that are ripped or spoiled. I do not expect I shall be back until sometime tomorrow."

The first mate nodded. "I wish you joy of your conquest," he said, a twinkle in his dark eyes.

"We shall see," came the reply. "These girls from Alba seem unpredictable at best, and totally wild at the worst. We shall see." Then he went down the gangplank and up the street to the house of Donal Righ, where Regan MacDuff, now called Zaynab, awaited his coming.

Chapter 5

Karim al Malina found both girls in Donal Righ's garden upon his return from the harbor. Oma bowed and discreetly attempted to depart so that her mistress might have privacy, but Karim stopped her, gently taking her arm. As fond as he was of his first mate, he did not want Oma believing that unless she succumbed to Alaeddin's wiles she would displease everyone.

"Alaeddin ben Omar pays you court, Oma," he began. "If he should at any time displease you, or frighten you, you have but to tell him to cease. He will. He is no barbarian. You will anger no one by refusing him or his attentions."

"Thank ye, my lord," Oma replied, "but I am nae afeared of yer big bear of a mate. He hae a soft heart, for all his bluster." Then, with a mischievous little smile, she bowed again and went from the garden, leaving the two together.

" 'Twas kind of ye, Karim al Malina," Zaynab said quietly, glad that her friend would not be forced into an unpleasant situation.

He chuckled. "At first I feared for the little wench, but now I think I should fear for my old friend, Alaeddin ben Omar."

Zaynab laughed. "Oma is strong-minded, yet she is also a kind girl. She longs to taste passion, I think. I believe your mate will eventually succeed with her because she wants him to; though perhaps not in his good time, but rather hers."

"Passion should indeed come in the woman's time, and not the man's," he agreed, his gaze locking onto hers. Then he took her hand in his, raising it up to his lips to first kiss the upturned palm, and next the tender inside of her perfumed wrist. "Last night you insisted most vehemently that you were ready for a deeper passion than I was willing to share with you. Are you still certain that you desire that passion, or have you changed your mind, my flower?"

"I dinna know now," she told him. "Last night ye inflamed my senses with yer touch, and I longed to learn more. Now, however, I canna be certain. I dinna feel the same now as then." She made to remove her hand from his, but he would not let her go.

"Come," he said firmly, leading her from the garden. "Let us see if when I inflame your senses again, you feel the same way."

"Perhaps ye will nae inflame me again," she responded coolly, still a little angry with him.

He forced back a chuckle at her tart retort. "I have considered this day upon your history, my beautiful Zaynab," he said as he led her upstairs to their chamber. "I think, perhaps, that you will not successfully learn what I can teach you if you are not settled in your own thoughts with regard to the act of making love. Maidens brought to me for training as Love Slaves are usually virgins. Their knowledge is either limited or nonexistent regarding what transpires between men and women. You, however, are different. You have suffered badly at the hands of two men. You know not how lovely the joining of lovers can be.

"When you finally desire it, my flower, I shall show you that the act of love is both sweet and hot, and wonderful. If you understand that, Zaynab, then we may make better progress in your education."

"Possibly, my lord," she allowed him.

"Now remove your garments for me," he said when they were in the chamber. "The caftan is lovely. Where did you obtain it?"

"Donal Righ," she told him, drawing the silk garment slowly off. "He told Oma that it is Moorish garb, and that we should get used to it. I like it. The feel of silk against my skin is most pleasurable, and far nicer than the linen and wool I am used to wearing."

He nodded in agreement, saying, "Now disrobe me, Zaynab."

"Yes, my lord," she answered, attempting to be obedient. She took the long cloak from his shoulders, laying it carefully across the single chair. Next she unlaced the white silk shirt that he wore, opening it and drawing it off. She felt the temptation to smooth her hands over his muscular chest, but fought it back, instead placing the shirt with the cloak, and turning back to him. Her slender fingers fumbled clumsily with the large buckle on his wide leather belt.

"Let me," he said, his hands covering hers for a moment, causing a wave of heat to wash over her. He pulled the belt off and laid it too upon the chair. *"Touch me,"* he commanded, and she raised startled eyes to him. "If my touch gave you pleasure last night, so can your touch give me pleasure. A man likes the feel of a beautiful woman's hands on his skin, Zaynab," he told her. Then he took her two hands in his and drew them up to his chest.

Tentatively, she began to move her fingers in little circular motions across the expanse of his skin, brushing lightly over the dark down upon his chest. To her surprise, it was not wiry when dry, but soft. Growing a bit bolder, she molded her palms over his broad shoulders, sliding them up and over, then down his long back. "Yer very strong, are ye nae?" she asked him, feeling the muscles beneath her fingertips. His body was hard and gave the impression of great strength. She moved her hands to clasp his narrow waist, and without being asked, she began to draw off his pantaloons, carefully loosening the drawstring, tugging at the waistband, which for some reason would not budge.

"It would be easier if you knelt," he told her.

She obeyed, slipping to her knees before him, careful to keep her eyes averted from his manhood. She did not think she was quite ready to stare it in the eye yet. She let her gaze wander elsewhere. He had wonderful, firm thighs. They were well shaped, and hard to her touch, she discovered as she drew his final garment completely off. As he stepped away, she quickly rose, gathering up the pantaloons, smoothing the fabric neatly, and laying them with his other garments.

" 'Twas not so hard now, was it?" he said with a small smile. Then he drew her into his arms, his lips brushing her pale hair.

Zaynab's heart began to hammer against her ribs. What was it about this man's touch that could render her so confused? "Does a Love Slave always undress her master?" she asked him, trying to regain control of her own emotions.

"If it pleases him. She bathes him as you did me today, and both dresses and undresses him. Everything she does for him is meant to give him pleasure of some sort. She is not simply a concubine. She is more. She must learn how to release her own passions so that even if her master is not the best of lovers, he will believe that he is. His mere touch must send her into a swooning fit of pleasure." He tipped her face up to his. "Yet a Love Slave *never* loses command of the situation, even while in the throes of ecstasy. She is mistress of herself at all times, Zaynab. Do you understand me?"

"I am nae certain," Zaynab said slowly.

"In time you will understand," he told her.

"I must learn to separate my thoughts from my emotions," she said thoughtfully. "Is that the secret to it, Karim al Malina?" She looked up at him questioningly. She really did want to learn. She never again wanted to find herself a victim of any man, even one who called himself her lord and her master. She must control her own destiny as best she could. It was obviously the key to her survival and success.

He nodded in answer to her inquiry, pleased that she had grasped the significance and the subtlety of his words, but then looking into her face, he said, "Have you any idea of how absolutely beautiful you are, Zaynab?"

"I know what I look like," she told him slowly, "for Gruoch, my sister, was said to be identical to me in face and form. Only our eyes were different blues in their shading, but few ever looked. I hae also seen my face in the waters of the loch when it was still. Gruoch often bewailed our lack of a looking glass. We never saw one, but we were told that they were clear,

smooth surfaces where one might look upon oneself. I know I
am prettier than most, *but beautiful?*"

"Aye, very beautiful," he assured her, touching her cheek
with just a single finger. "There are many kinds of beauty, Zaynab, but yours is superior. I do not think there is a single
woman like you in all of Abd-al Rahman's harem." He pulled
her hard against him, his hands reaching down to cup her
buttocks, feeling the soft give of her thighs as they touched
his own.

She put her palms against his chest to steady herself, struggling to draw a breath, for she found herself breathless. Then
he smiled down into her eyes, his look enveloping her with its
warmth. Zaynab's legs gave way beneath her. Lifting the girl
up, he placed her upon the bed. Then kneeling by her side, he
looked into her face, saying, "A thoughtless man snatched your
maidenhead. Another violated you. But in your heart and soul,
Zaynab, you are yet a virgin. This night I shall make love to
you as if that maidenhead were yet intact."

His lips touched hers with a gentleness she had never imagined a man capable of. Her heart hammered wildly. Both his
words and his actions thrilled her. When he lay next to her, the
feather mattress giving way beneath his weight, the mere touch
of his naked body against hers almost did set her to swooning.
Karim took her hand in his as she lay trembling, waiting for his
next move. His words were burning into her brain. *You are yet
a virgin in your heart and soul.* Aye, she was! How had he
known it? How could he feel her pain when she herself
declined to feel it, hiding it deep inside herself, refusing to
acknowledge it? To admit to any weakness just gave others
power over you, Zaynab thought bitterly. She had learned that
lesson early in her life, when she was but Regan MacDuff, the
unwanted daughter.

"A virgin," he said softly, "should be approached with tenderness, never haste." He raised her hand to his mouth, kissing
the palm with a lingering kiss that seemed to score her skin.
Then he kissed each finger in turn.

Those fingers tarried against his lips. Then, slowly, boldly,

Zaynab explored his long, narrow mouth, feeling the faint yielding of the smooth flesh. She pulled away, startled, when he teasingly nibbled upon the curious digits.

Laughing low, he rolled over upon his side to face her. "It is good that you are inquisitive, Zaynab. A virgin always is. It is how she learns both to please and to receive pleasure." His lips found hers again, and his kiss was slow and gentle at first.

Zaynab allowed herself to relax for a brief moment, stiffening only when the kiss became more intense. She sensed his desire, although never before had she truly known it. Her lips parted, allowing him to insert his tongue into her mouth. She felt him seeking, and shyly touched the probing tongue with her own. The sensuous contact sent a great shudder through her body. Her sensibilities reeled as hot flesh stroked hot flesh. She knew that she didn't want the communion between them to end. She was breathless when he finally ceased kissing her, smiling down into her eyes as he did so.

"Did you like it?" he asked, knowing what she would answer, for he had divined her enjoyment.

Zaynab nodded, wide-eyed. "Aye!"

He bent over her again, kissing the tip of her nose, her chin, her forehead, her fluttering eyelids. "Now you do the same," he told her, combining a lesson with her desire to be made love to by him. He lay back.

Raising herself upon her elbow, Zaynab leaned forward, touching his face with her lips; first the high cheekbones, the corners of his mouth, and then, unable to resist, his lips. She could feel a pounding heat beginning to suffuse her body. Her pulses leapt when he wrapped his arms tightly about her, drawing her down so that her round little breasts pressed against his chest.

"You're too quick, my flower. Ye have absolutely no self-control," he chided her gently.

"Nay, none," she admitted. "Something drives me, but I dinna know what it is, my lord. Am I very bad?"

"Aye." He grinned. "Totally incorrigible, my jewel. You

must be patient. You want too much, too soon. Making love is
a fine act. It should be done slowly in order to give and to
receive the most pleasure." He rolled her over onto her back,
lowering his head to kiss her breasts. "Such pretty, saucy little
tits," he told her. "They beg for a caress."

"Aye, they do," she responded boldly.

He fondled her, feeling the soft flesh give beneath his touch.
He cupped a single breast within his palm, gently pinching
the nipple with his thumb and forefinger. She stirred restlessly
beneath his touch. He transferred his attentions to the other
breast, then bent his head to suckle upon her nipples. His
tongue flattened, and smoothed along the valley between her
breasts. Then it began to tease at the already tight buds of her
nipples, flicking back and forth until she moaned low with
the pleasure he was giving her. He bit gently upon a nipple,
and she cried out. His kisses soothed where he had given her
tender pain.

The touch of his mouth upon her body left Zaynab almost
mindless with pleasure. His big hands caressing her flesh caused
the most wonderful of sensations. Enfolding her in his embrace,
he raised her body up and began covering it with hot kisses.
She lay weak with pleasure within his arms as he began to lick
at her perfumed skin.

"Ohh, yes, my lord!" her gasp of delight came, telling him
that he was pleasing her.

He laid her back and pushed a pillow beneath her hips.
Parting her legs, he slid between them, slowly drawing them
up over his shoulders. "Now," he whispered, "I will show you
a sweet and secret pleasure, my fair Zaynab." Leaning forward, he gently parted the soft pink flesh of her nether lips. The
flesh within was already pearly with her love juices, although
she was not even aware of them. He gazed spellbound a
moment, for she was so perfectly formed. Then his tongue
sought the tiny badge of her sex and he began to caress it
fervently.

For a short moment Zaynab was not certain what it was he
was doing, and then the knowledge burst upon her. She opened

her mouth to gasp with her shock, but no sound would come out. She could not even draw a breath. She wanted to protest this incredible invasion of her body, yet . . . yet . . . The tongue worked fervently against her flesh, and the faint heat she had felt earlier flared suddenly into an all-consuming flame. A husky sound rose up from her throat and echoed about the chamber. She was gasping for air. Stars exploded in her head and she cried out to him.

In answer, he drew her legs down from his shoulders, and taking his manhood in one hand, began to rub it against her tiny jewel. He was hard, and eager for her. She saw it in his eyes when she managed to open them to gaze spellbound at him. "Take me," she begged him. *"Take me now!"*

"A man should enter a virgin slowly, with tenderness," he said through gritted teeth as he pushed himself into her. She felt him filling her with his warmth, his length, his bigness. Instinctively, Zaynab wrapped her shapely legs about his torso, that he might drive himself deeper into her. She needed him deep inside of her. He groaned at her action, his full length sinking into her like a man drowning in quicksand. She shuddered when he was finally sheathed. She could actually feel him throbbing within her. She sensed that at this moment he was as helpless as she was. The realization gave her a new strength.

He began to move upon her, slowly at first, then with increasing urgency. His handsome face was tense with passion. She could look no longer! Her aquamarine eyes closed as the pleasure began to claim her as well. The stars that had earlier exploded within her head returned, joined by another galaxy. Neither of the two men who had previously used her had prepared her for this . . . this . . . wonderment. She was swept away upon a tide of rapture so great that she thought she might die from it. The ecstasy reached its magnificent crescendo, and Zaynab was lost amid the splendor of her starry passion.

Her returning awareness was marked by his kisses upon her wet cheeks. Zaynab realized that she was weeping. Slowly, she opened her eyes, gazing into his, amazed. No words were needed between them now. He had moved off her, and now he enfolded her in his embrace, saying but one word, "Sleep." She willingly obeyed, realizing to her surprise that she was exhausted.

He watched her as she tumbled into unconsciousness. He had had so many women in his twenty-eight years. Each, in her own fashion, had been different. Each had presented him with a challenge. Making love was not just a physical act. It was sensing your partner's needs, fathoming their vulnerabilities, filling their lives for the time that you were with them. None of those women had ever moved him. None of those whom he had taken, had trained in the erotic arts, not one of them had ever touched his heart. It had been impregnable. *Until now.* Why had this barbaric little infidel from a cold, wet, northern land affected him? It wasn't simply her beauty. He wasn't even certain what it was about the girl that reached out to him.

He lifted a lock of her silvery gold hair to his lips, sniffing at the lush gardenia fragrance, tenderly kissing the silken tresses between his fingers. It was utter madness! In even thinking such thoughts he was breaking the cardinal rule of a Passion Master. One did not fall in love with his pupil, *and* one made certain that his pupil did not fall in love with him. Had he not learned anything from his previous disaster? This was not just any slave girl. This girl belonged to his father's friend. She was intended for the harem of the Caliph of Cordoba. *Utter madness.*

How fair she was in all aspects of her person. The thought slipped by him before he might stop it. He let his eyes wander over her voluptuous young body. He had surely named her well. Abd-al Rahman would be ravished by this girl, and indebted to him for having schooled her to become the finest Love Slave ever created. The caliph would be equally grateful to his loyal friend, Donal Righ of Eire, who would then owe him, Karim al Malina, a debt that mere gold could not satisfy. Having a man like Donal Righ in one's debt was not such a bad thing. Yet how much more he would have rather had Zaynab for his own.

"My days as a Passion Master are over," he said softly to himself. "I cannot allow a thing like this to happen. I must be getting old, for I am helpless to control my emotions any longer."

Reaching out, he stroked Zaynab's satiny skin. He must teach her more than just erotic arts. He would have to teach her how to survive in the harem of her master. Abd-al Rahman's favorite wife, Zahra, was a powerful woman known to be vindictive, even to use poison. It was her grown son who was his father's heir. She guarded her son's fate jealously and fiercely. Zahra would not welcome this young, beauteous rival. Indeed, she would do all in her power to remove Zaynab should she please the caliph too much, and Karim al Malina would see to it that Zaynab did indeed please Abd-al Rahman. It was his duty.

"It was wonderful!"

The girl's breathless words reached out to pierce his own thoughts. Looking down into her eyes, he smiled a slow smile. "You're no longer frightened? You understand how sweet passion can be?" he queried.

"Aye! I want to do it again, my lord! *Please!*"

His warm laughter waved over her. "You are simply too impatient, my flower," he chided her. "Have I not counseled you to patience? There is so much to teach you. So much for you to learn. First we must bathe each other with the love cloths. Go, and fetch the basin on the windowsill. The cloths are with it, my beauty. Then we will discuss your request further."

She scrambled from the mattress, hurrying to do his bidding. When she had brought the basin to him, she asked, "What should I do, my dear lord?" She knelt by his side expectantly.

She is a most adorable pupil, he thought. He wanted to take her in his arms, to smother her upturned face with kisses. Instead he said in a pedantic tone, "The water in the basin should always be warmed. In the future it must be scented with your fragrance. The cloths with the water should be of the finest, softest linen. Take one up now, Zaynab, and refresh my manhood. I will then do the same for you. Remember, I have tasted the most intimate portion of your body. I may want to do it again. Eventually I will teach you to accept a manhood within your mouth to give it a different kind of pleasure than it receives sheathed within your body."

She raised her startled eyes to his at this new information, but said nothing to him, instead wringing out one of the cloths and bathing his member. Her touch was gentle, and she was quite thorough. She was surprised that something now so small could have offered her such rapture. Then she noted that his manhood was disfigured. "Ohhh," she cried softly. "When were you so grievously injured, my lord?"

"Injured?" For a moment he was puzzled, and then realizing her confusion, said, "I am not deformed, Zaynab. I am circumcised. All Moors, Jews, and other men of the East are. I was seven when it was done. My brothers were also. I was given a special sherbet to drink that had a small amount of narcotic in it to dull my pain. Then the foreskin of my member was drawn up hard, and cut. My father is a charitable man. When each of his sons was circumcised, poor boys of our city who were seven were invited to be circumcised with us, thereby sharing in all festivities at my father's expense. It does not harm a man, or as you can certainly attest, his ability to give pleasure. It is a health measure. In hot climates it is sometimes difficult if not impossible to find enough water to drink, let alone bathe. We men of al-Andalus are clean people. We love our baths. Removing the foreskin of the male simply makes it easier for him to keep his manhood clean and disease free."

"I thought ye had been hurt," she answered. "I feel most foolish now."

"How could you know?" he told her. "Do not be afraid to ask questions, Zaynab, my jewel. You cannot learn unless you do. A woman's body pleasures a man in many ways, but a wise man also enjoys more of her than just her body. In a few days we shall sail for my home. Once there, I shall undertake to educate you, not simply in the amatory arts, but you shall learn to dance, to sing, and to play at least one instrument. You shall be taught poetry, the history of my people, and any other intellectual pursuit for which you appear to have a talent. You must learn Arabic and Romance, our two most important languages. You will study all manner of things that you cannot imagine, but when I finally deem you fit for the caliph's harem, you will be neither ashamed nor afraid of who you are. You will rise above all other women known to Abd-al Rahman, even as the sun shines brighter than the moon. I shall, however, teach you discretion, that you not offend the lady Zahra, the mother of the caliph's heir. Good manners are the hallmark of a Love Slave."

He took up the other cloth from his basin. "Now, let me bathe you, my jewel. Lie back amid the pillows and open yourself to me, Zaynab."

She repressed a small shiver as he began his task. This fine art of lovemaking was so intimate a thing. His touch was very delicate; very, very sensual against her sensitive flesh. Slowly, with great care, he gently erased all evidence of their bout with Eros. At the same time, however, he was skillfully arousing her once more. She could feel a single finger, wrapped in the soft cloth, teasing subtly at her. Her eyes closed for the briefest moment as she dared to enjoy the delectable sensations he was awakening in her. Why could other men not be like Karim al Malina? Or were all the men of al-Andalus like him? Perhaps it was only the men of the north who were so crude and brutal.

Placing the cloth back in the basin, he said to her, "Now, take but a single finger, Zaynab, and touch that sentient little jewel of yours." He watched as she obeyed him, shyly at first, and then, as she discovered what she herself was capable of, more boldly. When her flesh had become moist and pearlescent to his eyes, he grasped her wrist. Drawing her hand to his mouth he took the finger into his mouth, sucking hard upon it. "You're like pungent, wild honey," he told her, releasing his grip.

She was breathless for the moment as he smiled that slow

smile of his that always set her heart to racing. For a moment she thought she might swoon.

He swung his body over hers, seating himself lightly upon her chest. "Put your hands behind your head," he commanded her.

"Why?" she countered, all efforts at obedience gone. She wanted to trust him completely, but her ignorance caused her to be afraid.

"It is the position a woman takes for this particular exercise in sensuality, my jewel. You need not be afraid," he explained patiently. Leaning forward, he propped her shoulders up with the pillows. Then raising up his manhood, which, she now noted, had enlarged a bit, he said, "Open your mouth, Zaynab, and take it in. You will use your tongue to tantalize it, but your teeth must *never* harm your master. When you are comfortable with this new sensation, you will suckle on me. I will tell you when to cease."

She shook her head. *"I canna,"* she whispered, shocked yet at the same time fascinated by his directive.

"You can," he told her quietly.

"Nay!" she declared vehemently. *"Nay!"*

He did not argue further with her. Instead he reached out and pinched her nostrils shut with his two fingers. Deprived of air, Zaynab gasped, and Karim pushed his manhood firmly between her lips, releasing his grip on her nose as he did. "Now, gently begin to tongue me, my flower. Nay, do not take your hands from behind your head, or I shall have Donal Righ beat you. Remember, obedience to your master at all times."

For what seemed like a very long time she lay frozen, her mouth filled with him, not quite certain what to do with *it*. Then, curious, she slipped her tongue, which she had drawn far back in her mouth, forward to make contact with his flesh. He watched her through half-closed eyes, barely breathing. This was a hard test. Tentatively she licked at him. Then again. Her eyes met his.

He nodded encouragingly. "That's it, my jewel. Do not be afraid. Your tongue will not hurt me. Run it around the knob now."

The taste of him was not unpleasant. It was slightly saline. Her fear was beginning to wane away. Slowly she lapped at him, her tongue swirling over his smooth flesh, feeling him begin to swell within the warm cave of her mouth.

"Suckle upon me," he commanded in a tight, hard voice.

Obeying him, she found the action to be exciting. He groaned low as Zaynab stared up at him, amazed. His eyes were closed, his face tense with a mixture of rising desire and utter pleasure. She realized to her surprise that it was she who was in control of the situation, not Karim. Suckling hard on him, her own excitement soared with this newly discovered power.

"*Cease!*" his voice ground out harshly, as, pinching her nostrils shut again, he forced her mouth open and withdrew his swollen manhood.

Her eyes widened at its new size. "Hae I displeased ye?" she whispered, half afraid again.

"Nay," he told her, sliding off of her, his head dropping to plant kisses on her naked body. She murmured, reassured, her body arching as he fastened his mouth upon a nipple. He suckled, nipped, and then kissed it. One hand traveled down her silken torso, slipping between her legs, seeking out the little pearl of her sex, finding it, teasing at it. "I want you," he told her. His fingers pushed themselves into her. "You're young, and ill-trained, my flower, but you were born to be a Love Slave."

His touch was setting her afire with a hunger to be possessed by him again. He taunted her, drawing down her love juices to bedew his digits. His mouth covered hers in a burning kiss to which there seemed to be no end. Their tongues entwined in a sensual dance. His other hand played with her until she thought she would scream. Her flesh grew taut with her desire. Both her belly and her breasts felt heavy, as if they would burst and pour forth a rich sweetness.

"*Please!*" she whimpered to him.

"*Please, what?*" he demanded.

"*Please!*" she pleaded again.

"A Love Slave never begs, though it is flattering to her master to know that she wants him," he advised. Then he swung his body over hers and drove himself deep within her, his groan of pleasure punctuating the room.

Her cry of delight encouraged his lusty efforts. He felt enormous within her. The hot, hard throbbing pulse of him almost took her breath away. "Ohhh, my lord, ye will kill me wi' this pleasure!" she half sobbed.

"Very good, my jewel," he lauded her, his buttocks contracting and releasing as he thrust rhythmically into her tight sheath.

She wrapped her legs tightly about him. Her slender arms wound themselves around his neck. "Dinna stop!" she begged him. "It is too sweet! *Ahh, I die!*" She shuddered lightly.

"Not yet, Zaynab," he told her. "You're too quick. You must give yourself again, for I am not yet satisfied. Remember, your master must first know delight. Only then can you take yours."

"I dinna think I can," her voice came weakly to him.

"Aye, you can!" he insisted, and began to thrust hard into her.

"Nay! Nay!" She half struggled against him, but then her body arched, her breasts pressing against him. *"Ahhhh! Ahhhh!"* she sobbed. It was happening once more, to her utter amazement. The feeling was even stronger than it had been but a moment ago. How could she have been so easily satisfied? Her nails raked down his back as her own lust rose, almost overwhelming her in its intensity.

"Little bitch!" he growled fiercely in her ear, and bending, sucked hard upon a breast. He could feel himself almost to the point of shattering, but now she would not let him go, encouraging him on in this overwhelming desire that she had aroused in him. Farther and farther he pushed himself within her until he could go no deeper, his hunger for this girl mushrooming until it erupted wildly in a hot explosion of fiery, staccato bursts.

For several long minutes they lay entwined. They were both wet and sticky with their exertions. Their hearts hammered wildly at first, then slowed. Karim finally said, "Call Oma.

Instruct her to bring us a fresh basin of water, love cloths, and wine. We both need to regain our strength."

"Ye would hae my servant see us like this?" Zaynab was shocked.

"She must learn to serve you in all situations," he responded. "Have you not seen each other naked in the baths?"

"But ye are naked!" Zaynab persisted.

"Aye," he answered her calmly.

The girl shook her head wonderingly. "This world to which ye are taking me is so different from the one in which I was born into, my lord," she told him. Then she called to Oma, instructing her while the blushing girl listened; struggling, not without difficulty, to keep her eyes from Karim al Malina's attractive body.

"I hae heard that all men from yer land were dark-eyed," Zaynab said while they waited for Oma to return. "Why are yer eyes blue?"

"My mother is a Norsewoman," he told her. "She was captured in a raid, and given to my father as a gift. He made her his second wife. My two brothers are dark-eyed, as is my sister."

"Second wife? How many wives does yer sire hae?" Zaynab was not certain whether or not to be shocked. Were Moors like the Saxons in Angleland? Saxons were known to take several wives.

"My father has only two wives. He is a very romantic man, and will but marry for love. He has a harem of concubines, however, to keep himself from becoming bored. There are perhaps a dozen women in it. 'Tis considered a small harem. The caliph has a hundred or more women for his personal pleasure," Karim told her, "and there are several thousand ladies living in the caliph's harem."

"Several thousand?" Zaynab was astounded. "How do ye expect that I shall attract the attention of this mighty ruler amongst all those others, my lord? He shall nae see me. I will die friendless and alone!"

"The women in Abd-al Rahman's harem are not all concubines," he reassured her. "Many are serving women like your own Oma. Some are family members: aunts, cousins, daughters. Only those hundred or more women are for the caliph's delectation. Besides, you are a Love Slave, a rare creature. You will be presented in a charming spectacle to your new master, along with the other gifts Donal Righ is sending. Abd-al Rahman will but see you once to desire you forever, I promise."

"Is the caliph a young man?" she asked.

"Nay, but neither is he an old man, Zaynab. He is a man of great experience in sensual matters. He is yet vigorous as a lover, having fathered three children in the last two years. He is also a wise and great ruler, both beloved and respected by his people. Ahh, here is Oma." He turned to the girl. "Did you scent the water as your mistress instructed you?"

"Aye, my lord," she replied. Then placing the silver basin by the bed, she hurried from the chamber.

Zaynab did not need tutelage a second time. Taking up one of the love cloths, she bathed his manhood. Then lying back, she allowed him to do the same for her.

When he had finished, he said, "Are you hungry, my jewel?"

She nodded vigorously. "Are ye?"

"Aye, I am! Instructing you is hard work," he teased.

"Learning is equally tiring," she countered. "I will call Oma again and hae her bring us food."

"If you are tired, perhaps you should rest first," he suggested.

"Oh, nay, my lord," she said. "I would regain my strength, and then continue learning everything that you can teach me."

He chuckled. "Tell Oma I would have a bowl of oysters. They are an excellent restorative."

"Then I will hae them too," she replied, laughing. "Yer a hard master, my lord, but I will keep up wi' ye, I promise."

"Aye, I think you will," he told her, thinking as he did that the months to come would not be easy ones for him. The feelings this girl engendered in him were far different from those he had ever felt for any other woman. Was he falling in love with her? Because if he was, he must not. She could never really be his. He reminded himself that his possession of her body was but in order to train her, as one would train an animal, so that she would know how to give another man supreme pleasure. To love her, or to encourage her to love him, would be dishonorable. Such behavior would bring shame on them all.

The School of Passion Masters in Samarkand no longer existed. He had been one of its last pupils, for the masters in his day had been ancient in years, and were now all dead. There had been none left to take their places. Mankind in general did not appreciate the arts of love any longer. Most cared little for the niceties. They knew naught of the supreme pleasures of love. They had passed on their knowledge to their last few pupils, then vanished from the face of the earth as if they had never even existed.

No one knew when the Passion Masters had come into existence. At the school there had been vague tales of the priests and priestesses of some ancient love goddess, but whatever the truth, the school was gone. He was one of the last Passion Masters remaining. He knew of no more than half a dozen scattered about the world. The others of his kind were in the Far East. That was why Love Slaves were so highly prized by connoisseurs in al-Andalus; why they were so few in number at all.

The disaster with the girl, Leila; his feelings for Zaynab; all served to convince him that he was no longer capable of practicing his art. He would settle down as a merchant of rare goods. When he had thoroughly schooled Zaynab for Donal Righ and presented her to the caliph, he would take a wife, as his family wanted him to do. The bride would naturally be a virgin. He could amuse himself teaching her, and those other women who would people his harem; *but never again would he school a Love Slave.*

Zaynab was clever, intelligent for a woman, and quick to learn. A year, no more. In that time he would have taught her what she needed to know to please the caliph; to survive in the world of the harem. He would present her to Abd-al Rahman, and that would be the end of it. He would never think of Zaynab again. *Never!*

Part II

IFRIQIYA

A.D. 943–944

✺ Chapter 6

I'timad rode low at her berth. The dark waters of the river Liffey lapped about her sleek body like a lover caressing his beloved. She was a beautiful ship, some two hundred ten feet in length, with a width of thirty feet. Her cargo capacity was one hundred twenty tons. This day her hold was filled to capacity with the gifts Donal Righ intended to send to the caliph along with Zaynab. They would be presented to Abd-al Rahman in a demonstrative spectacle of almost theatrical proportions.

Three of the items would be purchased for the Celtic merchant by Karim al Malina in Ifriqiya, thereby saving their transport from Eire. It was also impossible to obtain those particular gifts in Eire. Donal Righ had paid for the hire of the Moor's entire vessel, including a generous stipend to Karim al Malina's crew, who would have otherwise shared in the profits of a cargo sold.

Toward the stern of the ship was the galley, located below the deck and accessible by a ladder from above or below. It was a small room with a tiled roof. For cooking there was a tiled firebox, open in front and set upon a bed of clay and clay fragments. Small iron bars formed a grill. The galley also held a cupboard for tableware. Cooking utensils, cheese in netting, strings of onions and garlic, a bag of apples, and another of flour hung from the narrow rafters. Above the grill was a small shelf holding a bowl of salt and a bowl of saffron. In a small, tight corner was a pen with half a dozen squawking chickens and three ducks.

There were two stern decks. Upon the forward one had been

129

built the captain's cabin. It was a simple room with a double
bunk, a single bunk, a table, and several chairs. It had only one
entrance, and a window that could be shuttered at night or in
poor weather.

Behind the cabin was a smaller deck half shaded by an awning, with chairs that had been set up to give the two women
their privacy while allowing them to get fresh air. It would be
a small escape from the narrow confines of the little cabin
when the weather was good.

The helm deck was just forward of the galley roof. There
were forward and main hatches where the crew might hang their
rope hammocks amid the cargo. In the main hatch there was a
large table with two benches, so the sailors would have a place
to bring their food and eat. Usually Alaeddin ben Omar shared
the captain's cabin, but this voyage both men would sleep with
the crew, leaving the single shelter to the two women, who
would be under guard at night for their protection.

Karim al Malina had decided that his ship was no place to
practice the arts of a Passion Master. As long as Zaynab and
Oma remained segregated from the men, and the crew was
aware that the proprieties were being observed, there would be
no difficulties. Women were not favored passengers.

They had a last hour in the baths, and old Erda wept copious
tears as she bid the two girls farewell. "What a wonderful future
ye have before ye," she sobbed. "Ahh, to be young and ripe
again!"

"I'm an old man," Donal Righ said on hearing her words,
"and I cannot remember a time when ye were either young or
ripe, my faithful Erda."

She glowered darkly at her master, and then hugging the
girls a final time, said, "God protect ye both, my chicks, and
may yer fates be happy ones." Then Erda shuffled off, muttering about the harshness of her lot in such a household.

"I'd send her with ye just to be rid of the old crone, except
she couldn't bear to be separated from me," Donal Righ said
gruffly.

"She is too ancient a soul to make such a change in her life
now," Zaynab said. "If she were nae, I should want her wi'

us. Nae one hae ever treated me wi' more kindness, Donal Righ, except perhaps yerself."

"Humph," he said, flushing. "Do not flatter yerself, wench. 'Tis yer rare beauty that attracted me to ye. Were ye not the fairest of God's creatures, I would have sold ye off quick as a wink to some chieftain from the north. Now remember, don't trust anyone, Zaynab, but yerself and yer own instincts. And don't disgrace me before the caliph. Yer being trained as a Love Slave, and sent to Abd-al Rahman to bring me more of his favor here at the end of the world. Remember that!"

"I will, Donal Righ," she promised him. Then she kissed his cheek quickly before turning away and hurrying from the room with Oma.

Donal Righ touched the place where her soft lips had rested but momentarily, then, all business, he turned back to Karim al Malina. "Ye've the gold to buy the horses and the camels as well as enough to outfit her like a princess. She is not to go to the caliph in beggarly fashion, but rather like a bride from a wealthy family. What I have set aside for ye, son of my old friend, is not enough to repay ye for what ye are doing, but now I am in yer debt, Karim al Malina. Ye know that I shall expend all my resources, if necessary, to repay that debt. May the seas be kind to ye, and the winds swiftly take ye home."

The two men shook hands and went their separate ways.

I'timad sailed from Dublin on the morning tide, gliding down the river Liffey and out into the open sea, where she was met with gentle swells and a good wind that filled her lateen rigging with deep breaths. For a while the misty hills of Eire remained in their view. No ship strayed far out to sea for any extended period of time, fearing storms or sea serpents. Only the Norsemen were that daring. No Moor wanted to be caught far from land, for they were originally men of the desert, and it was yet strong in their blood.

I'timad sailed south from Dublin, then around the place the Britons called Land's End. Across the open water she tacked, slipping between the island of Ushant and the coast of Brittany. The late summer days remained remarkably fair. As the weather gave no indication of changing, Karim al Malina charted a course directly across the Bay of Biscay, a large body of water not usually noted for its benign seas. They tracked from Pont de Penmarc'h on the southern coast of Brittany around to Cape Finistère.

Carefully, they skirted the busy shipping lanes along a coastline belonging to the Christian kingdom of Leon, passed the coast that formed a frontier zone between Leon and the Muslim south, and finally sailed into the waters belonging to the land of al-Andalus. Still, amazingly, the weather held. So once again Karim routed his vessel across the stretch of open sea known as the Gulf of Cadiz to the city-state of Alcazaba Malina on the Atlantic coast of Ifriqiya, fifty miles south of Tanja, which was located on the Straits of Jibal Tarik. Zaynab had asked him about his name as they voyaged. His full name, he had explained, was Karim ibn Habib al-Malina. "Ibn Habib, son of Habib," he said.

The voyage had been filled with lessons of a different kind than she had been used to receiving from him. Each day he had spent two hours with both young women, teaching them to speak Arabic. To everyone's surprise, it was Oma who seemed to have the knack for learning another language. Zaynab struggled with the intricacies of the foreign tongue, and with Oma's help finally mastered it. She found Romance, the second of the new idioms she must learn, far easier.

It was the dawn of a new day when they finally reached Alcazaba Malina. The wind had practically died away entirely, and the seas about the vessel were dark and calm. The rising sun gilded the pure white marble city, slipping across the buildings, banishing the dark shadows with pure light. Alcazaba Malina was surrounded entirely by walls, including its harbor area, a natural deep-water port in the shape of a crescent moon. On each side of the bay there were lighthouses. It was the job of the keepers not only to indicate the entrance to the harbor with their lights but also to raise and lower the chain-mail net that was stretched across its entry as a first line of defense.

Zaynab and Oma stood openmouthed at the ship's rail. They had been at sea for several long weeks, but nothing, not even what

Karim al Malina and Alaeddin ben Omar had told them, prepared them for the sight that now appeared before their eyes.

"If Dublin was a city, then what be this?" Zaynab asked, awed. She spoke in Arabic now. Both girls did, for it was, they had discovered, the only way to really learn the difficult language. Only one hour each day did they revert to their own Celtic tongue, in order not to forget it. Zaynab felt it would be a way of communicating in the harem impossible for anyone else to understand. Such an asset would be invaluable.

"It is a magic place, I think," Oma answered her mistress, eyes wide. "I never thought to see such a place."

"I never even imagined such a place existed," Zaynab rejoined. "They surely would not believe it back at Ben MacDui."

Karim al Malina came to stand between them. "The city was founded over one hundred and fifty years ago by an Arab warrior, Karim ibn Malik, who was loyal to the Umayyad caliph in Damascus. Sixty-five years afterward, the Umayyads were driven out of Syria, the family massacred, exterminated in a wholesale slaughter but for one prince who escaped. He was Abd-al Rahman, the first of that name," Karim told them. "The rulers of this city have always been loyal to the Umayyads, but I shall teach you their history later on, Zaynab."

"Will we live in this beautiful place?" she asked him, her face turned up to his.

Tonight, he thought. Tonight I shall possess her again. It has been too long. "Nay. My father has a home in the city, but my home is out in the countryside. I prefer it to the city."

"May Oma and I see the wonders of this place, for surely it is wondrous?" she queried him.

"When you are rested from your journey I will bring you both to see the sights. I can well imagine how exciting Alcazaba Malina must seem to you. Still, it is but a tiny town when compared to Cordoba, where you will eventually make your home, my flower."

She was astounded. "Cordoba is larger?" It was difficult to even envision such a thing.

"Alcazaba Malina is like an olive is to Cordoba's melon," he told her with a smile.

"What is an olive? What is a melon?" she demanded of him.

He laughed aloud, realizing what was ordinary in his life was unknown to this girl from her barbaric northern land. "I will show you both when we reach our destination," he promised her. "First, however, I must see to the docking of *I'timad*. You will remain on board, in the cabin, while I first pay my respects to my father, and arrange for a litter to take you to my villa."

"Yes, my lord," she said in a dutiful little voice. He was so handsome. She had missed his passion. Would he share it with her tonight, or would he expect her to rest from their long journey? I am not that tired, she thought rebelliously. I want him to make love to me! Then she was struck by a sudden, unpleasant thought. "Are you married, Karim al Malina?" she asked him.

He was startled. "Nay," he replied. Then seeing a look in her eyes that made him uncomfortable, he continued, "But I will have my father arrange a marriage for me, to take place after I have delivered you to the caliph in Cordoba. It is past time I settled down."

She smiled up at him with her small, even, white teeth. "But you have no wife now? Or a harem?"

"Nay," he said nervously.

"Gooood," she almost purred, her blue eyes glittering.

"A Love Slave," he said sternly, "does not allow her emotions to become entangled with *any* man, Zaynab. Remember, you are not my property, but rather the property of the Caliph of Cordoba. My interest in you will never be more than that of pupil and teacher."

She turned quickly away from him, but not before he had seen the glint of tears in her eyes. "He hae no heart," Zaynab murmured softly to 'Oma as he walked away from them.

"He be a man of honor, my lady," the younger girl replied. There was nothing else she could say that would comfort her mistress. She had seen Zaynab's gaze soften at the sound of Karim al Malina's voice. She had noted how Zaynab's eyes followed him secretively when he came into her view. Her poor mistress was falling in love with Karim al Malina, and she must not. There was no future for Zaynab with the captain, Oma thought sadly, and therefore she herself had no future with Alaeddin ben Omar. She sighed deeply.

I'timad was made fast to her dock and the gangplank run up. The ship's master debarked, disappearing quickly into the early morning crowds upon the wharf, even as Alaeddin ben Omar shepherded the two women back to the privacy of the cabin, away from prying eyes.

"What is a melon?" Zaynab asked him. She must put her mind on other things, she realized, not Karim al Malina.

"It is a large, round, sweet fruit," Alaeddin answered.

"And an olive, please?"

"A small fruit, black, purple, sometimes green, and very salty because they are preserved in brine," he explained.

"Karim says this city is like an olive to Cordoba's melon," Zaynab said. "I did not know what olives and melons were."

The first mate smiled, his white teeth flashing in his bronzed face. " 'Tis a good description. Aye, Cordoba's a big place compared to Alcazaba Malina, but I prefer the smaller town myself. Besides it's unlikely, lady, that you will live in Cordoba itself. It's true, there is a royal palace in the city, next to the Grand Mosque, where the caliph used to live much of the year. In the summer months he would decamp to al-Rusafa, his summer palace to the northeast of the city, but now he has built Madinat al-Zahra, northwest of Cordoba."

"The city of Zahra? That is his wife, isn't it?" Zaynab asked.

"His favorite wife, mother of his heir," came the answer.

"And I am supposed to attract the affections of a man who has built a city for this woman? She must be a marvelous lady. 'Tis impossible!" the girl declared.

Alaeddin ben Omar laughed heartily. It was a deep, booming laugh. "We Moors are not like you northerners," he told her. "We enjoy everything of beauty that Allah has created for us. We do not limit ourselves to simply one woman. The caliph may respect and admire the lady Zahra. He may even build a city for her. But it does not mean he cannot admire, respect, and love other women too. You are the most beautiful woman I have ever seen, my lady Zaynab. If you are clever, and I believe you can be, the caliph will fall madly in love with you."

"Am *I* beautiful?" Oma said coyly.

He chuckled. "You, my pigeon, do not have to be beautiful," he replied, "but," he amended, seeing her black look, "you are beautiful enough for me. If you were any fairer, the caliph might want you for himself too. Then poor old Alaeddin's heart would be broken." He pinched her cheek, chortling as she smacked his hand. What a girl! he thought. What a fine wife she would make a man.

"I must go, and begin giving orders," he told them. "Open the shutters if you wish, but do not go out upon the decks."

When he had gone, the two girls opened the shutters and gazed out upon the harbor. The day was bright and sunny, the air hotter than they had ever known. There was a gentle breeze blowing in from the sea. Its salty tang tickled their nostrils. They could not see the town now, for the stern of the vessel faced the water, not the land; but they could smell its smells.

"I wonder how long we will have to remain in this stuffy old cabin," Oma said. "I have only been able to bear the voyage because we were not completely penned up in here. Sometimes I miss the hills and fields outside the convent where I used to play as a child. Do you miss Alba, my lady?"

Zaynab shook her head. "Nay," she said. "The only thing I miss is my sister Gruoch, but she was lost to me the day she wed. There is nothing for me at Ben MacDui any longer. I like the warmth of this place. I wonder if the sun shines all the time, Oma. We've seen no rain since we left Eire. Do you think it ever rains here?"

"It must," her servant replied. "I saw trees as we came into the harbor this morning, and flowers. They need rain to grow."

"Aye, they do." Zaynab's countenance was thoughtful. She wondered when Karim would return to the ship; when they would be allowed to leave it; if they would see Alcazaba Malina today, or another time. Where had he gone? Ahh, yes. To see his father, he had said. She imagined his father was a merchant too. Karim had obviously gone to report to him on the voyage just completed. She wondered what Karim's family was like. He always spoke of them so lovingly. How different, she thought, from her own family.

* * *

Karim al Malina made his way through the winding streets of his city. Finally he stopped before a small gate in a long white wall. Reaching into the voluminous white robes he was wearing, he drew out a small brass key with a round head, fitted it into the gate's lock, opened it, and entered a fine, large garden. The gate swung shut behind him with an audible click, causing a gardener working amid the rosebushes to look up.

"My lord Karim! Welcome home," the gardener said, smiling.

"Thank you, Yussef," the captain replied, and hurried toward the building on the far side of the garden. As he went, servants seeing him smiled and added their voices to Yussef's welcome. He greeted them all by name, with courtesy. Finally he entered the building, going directly to his father's apartments.

The old man was already awake. Coming forward, he embraced his son and smiled broadly. "*I'timad* rides low in the water, my son. You have obviously brought home a fine cargo. Welcome!" He was a tall man with piercing dark eyes and snow-white hair.

"I have brought home a fine profit, Father, but not necessarily a cargo," Karim told him, drawing a heavy pouch from his robes and placing it on the table before them. "The cargo I carry is not for sale. Donal Righ hired the ship to bring gifts to the caliph in Cordoba."

"Why did you not go to Cordoba first?" his father inquired.

"Because one of those gifts is the most beautiful girl you have ever seen in all of your life. I am schooling her to be a Love Slave for the caliph. When I have delivered her, and all of the other gifts that Donal Righ has packed my ship with, I shall come home to Alcazaba Malina for good, as you have always wanted. You will find me a pretty wife, and I will endeavor to add to your cache of grandchildren."

A broad smile lit up Habib ibn Malik's handsome old face, and he once again embraced his youngest son. "Praise be to Allah the most merciful, for He has answered the prayer nearest to my heart," the father cried. He brushed away the tears that had sprung into his eyes. "I am becoming an old fool," he said, "but I love you, Karim, and I enjoy having my family about me. Your mother will be equally delighted."

"Why will I be delighted?" A tall, slender woman entered the room. *"Karim!"* She hurried toward him, arms outstretched. "When did you arrive, my son?" She hugged him hard. "I had feared that you meant to winter in Eire with that old reprobate Donal Righ."

"That old reprobate has sent you a fine strand of pearls, my mother, and one for the lady Muzna too," Karim told her with a smile. "I have only just arrived, lest you scold me for not coming to see you."

The lady Alimah turned and said to an attending slave, "Why do you stand there, fool? Bring food for us! Hurry!" Then she sat down upon a small chair. "Now, Karim, tell us of this voyage. Habib, seat yourself, my love." Her azure eyes caught those of another attending slave. "Wait, Karim." Then she said to the slave, "Fetch the lady Muzna and the lords Ja'far and Ayyub, and my daughter, Iniga." She turned back to her son. "Muzna always asks questions I can't answer, and your brothers too. You might as well tell us all at once."

The two men laughed at her. She once was a captive his father had seen in the slave market in Cordoba many years ago. She was Norse, and it was from her Karim had inherited his blue eyes and fair skin. Habib ibn Malik had fallen hopelessly in love with the captive girl. With the permission of his first wife, Muzna, he had taken Alimah, as she was called, to be his second wife. She had borne him first Ja'far, Karim's older brother, then Karim, and finally a daughter, Iniga. The oldest of Habib ibn Malik's children was his son, Ayyub, the lady Muzna's only child. By kind fortune the two women were good friends.

The lady Muzna was an Arab of good family. Neither the house nor the children interested her in the least. She was sweet-natured and kind, and she preferred writing exquisite poetry to other, more mundane pursuits. She was delighted to welcome Alimah, who quickly took over the household, the slaves, and the major burden of childbearing while Muzna wrote her beautiful verses, accepting her place as Habib ibn

Malik's first wife. It was, she thought, a most satisfactory situation.

The family arrived before the food. Muzna entered the room, her black hair liberally silvered, her brown eyes bright with excitement. Kissing her smooth soft cheek, Karim thought to himself that she did not ever appear to age, although she was past fifty. His sister, Iniga, her hair as sunshine-blond as his mother's had once been, threw herself at him with a shriek of delight.

"What have you brought me?" she immediately demanded of him.

"Why should I bring you anything?" he teased her.

"*Karim!* You had best treat me with more respect. I am going to be married," Iniga told him. "Now, what did you bring me?"

"A gold ring studded with rubies and pearls, greedy one," he told her, "and what man was foolish enough to offer for you? It couldn't be Ahmed now, could it?" Allah! Iniga couldn't be old enough to marry, could she?

"She is sixteen, almost past a good marriage," his mother said softly, answering his unspoken question.

"I keep forgetting that she is growing up, for I was half grown when you bore her, my mother," he answered as quietly.

Alimah patted his hand. Then as the servants began entering his father's apartments with food, she directed them to the terrace overlooking the sea, where there was a table upon which they might place the food. There was fresh bread, a platter of peeled green figs, bowls of newly made yogurt, grapes and oranges, and a steaming platter of rice with small chunks of grilled lamb. The beverage maker came with his brazier, charcoal, and kettles. Mint and rose-petal teas were brewed and passed about. Couches were brought, and the family sprawled upon them, eating and listening to Karim's adventures.

"I thought you swore never to train another maid in the erotic arts again," Ja'far ibn Habib said to his younger brother. Then he chuckled knowingly, and winked at their eldest sibling, Ayyub.

"It was not a commission I sought," Karim answered him honestly, "but Donal Righ played upon his friendship with our father. How could I refuse him under those circumstances?"

"This is not a discussion I wish you to have in Iniga's presence," the lady Alimah said sternly to her sons.

"Oh, Mother! I know that Karim is a Passion Master," Iniga said, laughing. "Everyone does. It has given me quite a status among my friends to have such a brother. All the girls want to know just what it is that he does to train a maiden. Unfortunately, I have been unable to enlighten them much."

"You should not be able to enlighten them at all," her mother said sharply, turning to her husband for aid. *"Habib!"*

"She is to be married soon, Alimah. I am certain neither Karim nor Ja'far will be indelicate in their speech," he answered her.

Alimah sighed dramatically and rolled her eyes with displeasure. "You have always spoiled Iniga, Habib," she complained.

"She is his baby, and the only girl," the lady Muzna interjected softly, her dark eyes twinkling. The truth was, they had all spoiled Iniga, for they all adored her.

The discussion no longer totally forbidden, Ayyub asked, "Is the girl beautiful?"

"She is the most beautiful girl I have ever seen," Karim told them. "Eyes the color of the finest aquamarines, hair like thistledown, pale gold in color. Skin like a gardenia petal."

"Is she a good pupil?" Ja'far said mischievously.

"An excellent one," Karim replied. "She is the finest Love Slave I have ever trained. Never have I known a girl like this one."

"And when he has delivered her to Cordoba," their father told them all, "he will come home for good, and marry a girl of my choice."

"Ahhhh," Alimah and Muzna breathed as one, both women very pleased by their lord's words, for Ja'far and Ayyub had both been long wed.

"I have a niece," the lady Muzna began.

"Not your brother Abdul's daughter?" her husband said. "She is not at all suitable, my dear. She has already outlived one husband, and is sharp-tongued as well. Besides, she was married three years, and never once gave sign of being with child."

"Perhaps that was her husband's fault," Lady Muzna replied with uncustomary spirit. "He had two other wives, and they had no children either. It was never my niece's fault."

"Be that as it may," Habib ibn Malik answered his first wife, "she is too old for Karim, and besides, she has a squint."

"I think we shall find a fair young virgin for my son," Lady Alimah interjected quietly. "An innocent girl will be easier for him to mold into the kind of wife that he desires."

"And we all know how good Karim is at *molding* women," Ja'far laughed, winking at both of his brothers. Then he said boldly, "Do we get to meet this fairest of Love Slaves, little brother?"

"Can I meet her too?" Iniga asked.

"*Iniga!*" her mother gasped, shocked, and even Muzna paled.

"Well, why can't I meet her, Mother? You were once a captive like she is. Is she nice, Karim? What is her name?" his sister demanded.

"Her name is Zaynab, and yes, Iniga, she is a very nice young woman, younger than you by a year, but unless Mother will allow it, you may not meet her. I will bow to her wishes in this matter."

Alimah was shaken by her daughter's reference to her own captivity. Of course Iniga was correct in one sense, but Alimah had not been a slave for close to thirty years. She had forgotten about it. Habib had freed her upon Ja'far's birth. Those brief years spent as a slave had easily faded in the light of her husband's love. Still, a Love Slave . . . Iniga was so innocent.

"*Please, Mother!*" Iniga put forth her most bewitching smile.

Alimah, however, could not be moved as easily as the rest of her family by her daughter's charms. "I must first meet Zaynab myself," she said firmly. "When I have assessed her character, I will decide if she is the type of young girl I wish you to know, Iniga."

"A fair and equitable solution to the problem," Habib ibn Malik said with a broad smile. "As always, my dear, you are just."

Karim arose from his couch, washing his hands in a basin of perfumed water and drying them upon a linen towel supplied by an attending slave. "I must return to *I'timad*," he said. "Zaynab and her servant, Oma, will need to be transported by litter to my villa."

"And Donal Righ's cargo?" his father asked.

"I will store it in my warehouse. I must purchase some Arabians and a few racing camels for the trip to Cordoba. Alaeddin will see to the unloading of my vessel."

"*I'timad* rides low in the water, my son. What cargo do you carry that is so heavy? Will there be room for the additional load?" his father wondered aloud.

"Donal Righ is sending, among other things, a dozen columns of green Irish agate," Karim explained. "That has been my ballast this return voyage. They will not be easy to present in procession."

"Must Donal Righ give the caliph racing camels, Karim? Everyone gives Abd-al Rahman racing camels. He has a huge herd of them. The Hall of the Caliphate at Madinat al-Zahra is huge. I saw it last year, it's a wonder! Why not let us seek out two dozen elephants. We will sling the twelve columns between the twenty-four great beasts. It will be quite a spectacle for both you and Donal Righ if you make such a presentation in the new hall."

"You have always been the cleverest of us all, Ayyub," Karim told his eldest brother admiringly. "Elephants it shall be! I shall have to have another vessel built to carry it all, but then I shall need a second ship once I become a respectable married man."

"Will you have time to build a ship?" his mother asked him.

"Aye, I will. Zaynab will need a full year's tutelage before she is ready to go to Cordoba. She is talented, but she must be perfect if she is to bring honor to Donal Righ, and to me."

"Is she Norse?" his mother asked softly.

"No," he said as quietly. "She is from Alba. She was brought to Eire by a Norseman who raided the convent in which she was installed. If you ask her, Mother, she will tell you her history. She is not ashamed of it."

"She has pride?" Alimah queried.

"She was a nobleman's daughter," he replied.

His mother nodded. A nobleman's child, and one who did not go to pieces in her greatly altered circumstances. Her own father had been a wealthy farmer. She understood this Zaynab's strength, for she had it herself. She was now curious to meet the girl. "I will give your guest several days to recover from her voyage," Alimah said. "Then I shall come and meet her."

"And then I shall come and meet her," Iniga said brightly.

"If I permit it," her mother responded swiftly, and the others laughed. They all knew that unless Zaynab was totally unsuitable, Iniga would have her way in the matter.

Karim borrowed a litter, and bearers from among his father's household. Instructing them to go to his vessel, he crossed the garden again, letting himself out by the little gate into the street, which now bustled with the daily traffic. Small vendors carrying their wares moved through the streets, calling to their customers. Respectable women and their servants, properly veiled, moved gracefully along toward the main market square to shop for the variety of goods, both luxury and everyday, displayed beneath the gaily colored awnings shading the open stalls from the hot sun. Seeing a fruit seller, Karim stopped and purchased a large round melon, then hurried along to the harbor.

Alaeddin ben Omar had already begun overseeing the unloading of *I'timad*. The bales and bundles were being carried from the ship, down the gangway, and directly into the warehouse by a steady stream of black slaves. A winch and tackle was slowly lifting one of the heavy agate columns from the forward hold. Karim watched as it was carefully lowered to an open wagon, which was then hauled the short distance into the warehouse by three teams of sturdy mules. Once inside, another winch and tackle would remove it from its transport and lay it upon the floor in a pile of hay that had been placed there for each of the columns, to prevent their being scratched.

Karim boarded the vessel and spoke to his first mate. "Have the more portable valuables transported to my villa, the gold and jewels, and set a guard round-the-clock both there and inside and outside the warehouse, Alaeddin. Call me when the litter arrives."

"How is your father?" the first mate asked.

"Well! The whole family is well. Iniga informs me that she is preparing to wed, but I didn't get the details from her. There will be time for that, but Allah! Is she *that* old already?"

The mate grinned. "Aye, it just seems like yesterday she was a little girl with her golden pigtails flying about her, begging to come on a voyage with us. I remember carrying her on my shoulder. Who is the lucky man? Your father's rich, and could have his pick of husbands for her."

"He is allowing her to marry for love," Karim answered. "Iniga is the baby, the only daughter, and doted upon by us all. None of us would see her unhappy. She is a fortunate girl." He clapped his first mate on the back. "You have done a good job with the unloading, my friend."

Entering the cabin, he held up the fruit for Zaynab and Oma to see. "This," he told them, "is a melon. I bought it in the market for you on my return from my father's house." He plunked it down upon the table and, removing his knife from his sash, began to slice it for them. After handing them pieces of the juicy fruit, he looked for comment.

Zaynab bit into the melon and chewed. Another bite followed, and then another. "Ummmm," she said approvingly. "It's delicious!"

Oma nodded in agreement. Her little tongue caught at a droplet of juice.

"Do you have other fruits like this melon?" Zaynab asked him, placing the rind upon the table and reaching for another piece.

"Oranges, bananas, pomegranates, apricots, figs, and grapes," he told her. "I will see you get to taste them all, my flower."

"I thought grapes were for making wine," she answered him.

"And for eating, my adorable little savage." Reaching out, he pulled her into his arms and kissed her mouth swiftly. She sighed, and he laughed. "You are hot for a wench from such a cold clime," he teased her, and nibbled upon her earlobe.

Oma turned away blushing, but Zaynab said, "Such a deduction, my lord, would lead one to believe that you, being from a warm clime, would therefore be of an opposite nature, but you are not, I think."

"Nay," he murmured, pressing his length against her so she might feel his rising desire. "I am every bit as hot as you, Zaynab, my flower." His hands cupped her buttocks, drawing her even harder against his body. *"Now!"* he whispered in her ear. "Send Oma away, for I want to make love to you now." He buried his face in her soft neck.

To his great surprise, she squirmed from his embrace and stepped away from him. "How unseemly of you, my lord," she said in cool tones. " 'Tis neither the time nor the place for such love sport. Is not the litter here to transport us to your villa? How I long for a bath," she concluded with a feigned sigh.

Astounded, he could only gape at her for a moment, and then yanking her back toward him, he forced his hand into her caftan. "Your heart is thundering wildly," he said, and then releasing her, he began to laugh. "Magnificent, Zaynab! A truly incredible performance! I am proud of you, my beauty. 'Twas well done! Allah help the caliph in the presence of a woman who can practice such wiles. Your look is calm and elegant. No one would ever know you are as filled with lust as I am at this very moment." A knock sounded upon the cabin door, and Karim called, "Enter," though his manhood was still throbbing with his desire for her.

The door swung wide and Alaeddin said, "The litter is here, Karim. Your father also sent a horse for you to ride."

"Oma," Karim said, "you will find streetwear for both you and your mistress in that small chest at the foot of your bed."

The young girl drew forth two black, all-enveloping garments. She helped Zaynab into one, and drew the other over her own form. Then looking at her mistress, she began to giggle. "We look like a fine pair of old crows, lady. Why, only our eyes are visible."

"Which is as it should be for respectable women," Karim said. "Only women of questionable virtue and easy morals walk the streets showing their faces, their bodies, and their hair. In these robes every woman is like another, rich or poor. No man will ever approach a woman so garbed, or even attempt to attract her attention. In fact, it is a crime punishable by death. These robes offer you total safety."

"Must they be black? They are so ugly," Zaynab said.

"Black is modest," he answered. "Come now. The day is growing hotter, and the bearers are waiting in the sun. Even the most menial slave should be treated with courtesy if he is obedient and works hard."

The two girls followed Karim al Malina from the ship's cabin.

"Keep your eyes lowered," he ordered them softly. "No reputable female makes eye contact with a man not her master, Zaynab. Male slaves, and eunuchs, of course, are not considered men."

His words absolutely amazed her. *And what was a eunuch?* Coming from what now seemed a plain and simple world into this new and complicated one made her feel like a small child in many ways. There was so much she didn't know. There was so much to learn. She wanted to learn it! Her previous life as the unwanted twin had not offered her any perquisites of note. She had been tolerated mainly because few could tell the difference between her and Gruoch; because there was always the terrible chance that Gruoch might die young, and she would then be needed to take her sister's place.

Now, suddenly, life had placed amazing choices before her. She was a slave, true, but she was young, beautiful, and fairhaired. That was, she knew, the most valuable sort of slave in al-Andalus. Alaeddin ben Omar had told them this morning that often dishonest slave merchants would kidnap simple country girls and bleach their hair in an effort to palm them off as northern captives. The ruse was generally discovered, but by then more often than not the slaver had disappeared. And woe

betide the poor maid who, unless she had had the time to ingra-
tiate herself into her master's affections, found herself back on
the block, her value greatly reduced.

Zaynab, however, would not have that problem. She had
already accepted her fate. Now she must strive to become the
most fascinating, the most seductive, the most desirable Love
Slave ever trained in the erotic arts. The caliph was, she had
reasoned, a very powerful man. Even this wonderful city of
Alcazaba Malina owed him fealty and paid him homage, she
had learned. To capture the affections of such a man would
assure her a wonderful life. Could she do it? She wanted to, yet
how could she love another man when she loved Karim al
Malina? *There!* She had admitted to herself what she would
admit to no other. She was in love with him. Yet he could never
know. It would only anger him. He would send her away
from him, perhaps to another Passion Master. It was a horrific
thought.

A year. He had said he would keep her for a year before
taking her to Cordoba, to the man who would become her
master. Who knew what could happen in a year? Perhaps the
caliph would die. Then Karim al Malina would not be bound
by honor to send her away. Then perhaps he would keep her.
He had said he wanted to take a wife and settle down. Had he
not told her during the voyage that his own mother had been a
captive? And Oma. Oma might have a chance to wed with her
black-bearded Alaeddin, whom she had neatly kept at bay all
this time. How different their lives would be were it not for this
Abd-al Rahman.

Neither Zaynab nor Oma had ever seen a litter before. It was
a wonderful vehicle, more than large enough for the two girls.
It was built of fragrant camphor wood, gilded, and painted with
a delicate floral motif. The interior was upholstered in soft,
honey-colored leather, and filled with brightly colored silk
cushions. The litter was hung with diaphanous silk curtains,
pale apricot in color. Twelve coal-black male slaves of identical height, in simple white loincloths, their skulls shaven,

their necks encircled with solid silver collars studded with turquoise, stood waiting patiently.

The girls were helped into their transport. The slaves picked it up as if it and its occupants weighed naught. They padded off out of the harbor area, but did not go through the city. Instead they hurried with their burden along a road bordering the harbor that led out into the countryside. The road they traveled was paved in smooth stone and bordered by tall elegant trees, which Karim told them were called palms as he rode by their side on the horse his father had sent.

The countryside about them was a broad green coastal plain that seemed to stretch for miles. It was framed by mountains on two sides; the Er Rif to the southeast, and the Atlas range to the northwest. There was snow visible on the high purple peaks even from a distance. A river, the Oued Sebou, opened into the harbor. The river, Karim explained, was used to irrigate the plain, which was planted with neat fields of barley and wheat.

They followed the road several miles from the city, finally turning down a dirt road. Rounding a curve in the path, they saw Karim al Malina's villa, a beautiful white marble building set amid a magnificent garden. Beyond, the blue sea gleamed in the sunlight. The bearers moved through the open gates into an inner courtyard and set the litter down.

Karim dismounted from his horse and drew the litter's curtains open, handing out the two girls. "Do you like it?" he asked them.

They looked about them, and Zaynab said, "It's wonderful!" Her eyes lit upon a fountain in the courtyard's center: a pale pink basin resting upon the backs of six silver gazelles set in a circle. It was filled with creamy water lilies. "How marvelous, my lord," she said softly. "Is it all like this?"

"You will judge for yourself, my flower," he replied, leading them into the house.

A tall light-skinned black man came forward as they entered. "Welcome home, my lord Karim," he said.

"It's good to be home, Mustafa," his master replied. "This is the lady Zaynab, and her servant, Oma. In a year's time the lady will be presented to Abd-al Rahman. She is a gift from Donal Righ, the merchant with whom I trade in Eire."

Mustafa immediately understood. He was surprised that his master had taken another student after the tragic Leila. Still, his smooth face remained impassive. "I will see the lady is made comfortable, my lord."

"Go with Mustafa, my jewel. He will take you to the women's quarters. I will join you later, after I have bathed."

They followed Mustafa from the entry hall down a light-filled corridor that led into another wing. Passing through double ebony doors, they entered the women's quarters, which Mustafa explained were smaller than those usually found in a well-to-do man's home. This was because Karim al Malina used this villa for one purpose alone. He could deal with only one woman at a time in such circumstances. The two girls looked at each other and swallowed back their laughter.

"You will have the services of a masseuse, bath attendants, and seamstresses at your disposal, my lady. Some evenings you will take your meal with the master. If he wishes to see you, you will be brought to him. If he does not, you will eat here in your quarters with your servant. Do you understand?"

"Of course my mistress understands you," Oma said sharply as Zaynab turned silently away from Mustafa to explore their new surroundings.

"Do these quarters have their own bath?" Oma demanded.

"Naturally," he responded haughtily.

"Then send the bath attendants and the masseuse at once, Mustafa. My mistress and I have not had the opportunity to bathe in all our weeks at sea. I am certain we must reek of sweat. The master has ordered that my lady wear gardenia fragrance, for it suits her."

"At once," Mustafa said, recognizing in Oma an upper servant of the first degree. He was impressed that this Love Slave had her own servant. She was obviously a girl of noble blood, and not some insignificant little peasant's get. He inclined his head slightly in Oma's direction, acknowledging her position, and departed.

When the door had closed behind him, Oma giggled softly as Zaynab said, " 'Twas nicely done, my girl."

"I but took my direction from you, my lady. I think I see how to get on with the other servants. You have status, and therefore I do too. I must be mannerly and proper, but I must never let any of the others lord it over me, else you lose stature."

"You must be deferential to the slaves serving persons of higher rank than mine, however," her mistress counseled. "We cannot give anyone an excuse to harm us. There may even be those who will help us. Come now, Oma, and let us investigate our new home."

The room in which they stood was square. Its walls were a blush-colored marble, as was its floor. Upon the floor were coverings they later discovered were called carpets. They were blue and red, and soft beneath the feet. In the center of the room was a small square pool of pink and blue marble in which several gold and silver fish were swimming. In the middle of the pool a crystal spray of water thrust upward, sprinkling clear droplets back onto the surface of the water. There were chairs, and several pieces of furniture that Mustafa told Oma were called couches, as well as tables and standing brass lamps that in the evening burned scented oil. The room opened out into a small walled garden.

There was a hallway off the main room, leading to several other rooms: one large bedchamber, two smaller bedchambers, and the bath. The main bedchamber also opened into the garden. It had a beautiful bed set upon a dais, its feather mattress upholstered in turquoise-blue cotton of the best quality, its coverlet of turquoise silk and cloth-of-gold stripes, and it was strewn with coral and gold-colored silk pillows. The floor was covered with several small rugs scattered about. There was a couch for napping by the doorway to the garden, which could be shuttered in inclement weather. The tables were made from camphor wood, polished, their carved legs lightly gilded. The walls were plain marble; the room was elegant yet simple.

As they stood admiring it, slaves began arriving with their chests. The two girls moved on to the baths, but not before

Oma had seen that her chest was put in the smaller chamber across the hallway from her mistress. Arriving at the bath, they found the attendants ready and waiting for them. Gratefully, they let the slaves do their work; allowing their garments to be taken, their bodies rinsed with clean warm water, soaped, scrubbed, and rinsed once again. They rested in a scented pool for several minutes, and then the bath mistress asked to be permitted to wash their hair.

"Do Oma first," Zaynab told her. "I am enjoying the water too much. It has been so long."

The bath mistress nodded sympathetically, signaling Oma to come. When the girl's brown hair had been washed, she called to Zaynab, who reluctantly came, rising gracefully from the pool to walk across the bath. The other slaves gazed admiringly at the girl.

"You are the most beautiful Love Slave our master has ever trained," the bath mistress said frankly as she washed Zaynab's hair. "Aiyee! Look at these tresses," she enthused, finishing with a lemon rinse to bring out the highlights in the girl's hair. "Never have I seen such a color! It is gold, yet silvery as well. Gilt! Your hair is the color of gilt! What a lucky girl you are, my lady Zaynab. Do you know who your master will be yet?"

"The caliph," was the quiet reply.

"The caliph?" There was awe and admiration in the bath mistress's voice, and the bath attendants were wide-eyed at Zaynab's words. "Aiyee! The caliph! Of course, the caliph," she continued. "You are fit for him and no one else, lady. Allah has blessed you greatly that you are to go to Cordoba and become a Love Slave of the caliph." She brushed the girl's hair over and over and over again, until it was finally almost dry. Then she rubbed it with silk in the same manner until it gleamed. Affixing Zaynab's hair atop her head with tortoise-shell pins, she said, "You are ready for the masseuse, lady."

A cotton mat was laid atop a low table, and Zaynab lay upon it facedown. The masseuse, a tall Slavic girl, began to lave gardenia oil in great, sweeping strokes over Zaynab's body. Her supple fingers kneaded the girl's pliant flesh, soothing it and removing all signs of tension.

"You have good skin, lady," the masseuse remarked, her thumbs pressing into Zaynab's flesh. "It is firm, yet soft. By the time you go to the caliph, I will make it even finer for you. I will also teach you how to make certain the masseuse in the caliph's harem cares for you properly. Favored women in the royal harem are always bribing the slaves to help them destroy a rival, or to get better treatment for themselves. That must not happen to you." She pummeled Zaynab's flesh, the sides of her hands drubbing swiftly up and down her body. "This stroke brings the blood to the skin's surface, which is good, lady," she explained. "Roll over, please."

The masseuse worked Zaynab's shoulders and neck, her clever hands seeming to find the sore spots as if by magic. Her arms, her hands, her legs, each finger and each toe, were skillfully manipulated, until the girl was so relaxed she was close to falling asleep. She started at the sound of the bath mistress's voice, her eyes flying open.

"Now, you are ready for a nice nap, lady. Your servants will escort you to your chamber. You are a pleasure to serve, lady." She bowed politely from the waist.

Zaynab thanked them all, complimenting them upon the excellence of their service. Then she asked, "I will need a fresh caftan."

"There is no need," the bath mistress told her. "You are but going to your bed to nap, lady. There is no one here in the women's quarters but us. Your Oma will need time to see to your garments, for they have spent so many weeks at sea in a tiny chest."

"But what if Mustafa should enter these rooms?" Zaynab queried nervously.

The bath attendants giggled behind their hands, silenced only by a stern look from the bath mistress. "Why, lady, Mustafa is a eunuch. We could all run naked beneath his very nose and he would not care at all."

Zaynab took a deep breath. Ask questions, Karim had counseled her. "I do not know what a eunuch is," she told the bath mistress. "In my land no such creature exists; at least to my knowledge there is no such thing. Please enlighten me, I beg you."

Although the attendants looked surprised, the bath mistress was not. This girl was a northerner from a far land. "A eunuch, lady, is a male being who has been castrated. He has had his testes removed. He cannot reproduce as normal men do, nor does he even feel desire for any woman. The operation is done when the eunuchs are boys, or very young men. Some physicians even remove the manhood, and then the poor fellow must pee through a reed the rest of his life. Most, however, just remove the testicles," she explained. "Your nudity would have absolutely no effect upon Mustafa. Your beauty to him is like that of a lovely vase or jade carving," she concluded.

"Thank you," Zaynab said. "I have so much to learn." Then, in Oma's company, she returned to her own chamber, and naked, lay down to sleep in the afternoon heat.

"She will go far," the bath mistress predicted to the others.

"Because she is beautiful?" the youngest among them asked.

"In part," the bath mistress answered, "but mostly because she is wise, and kind, and has the breeding to thank those lower in rank than she herself. She is not puffed up, nor overweening proud as so many women of high rank are. This, as well as her beauty, will set her apart from the others and catch the caliph's eye. Our lord, Abd-al Rahman, it is said, is a man of good judgment. He cannot help but love Zaynab. Aiiiyeee! What a bright future this Love Slave has. She will be the greatest of all those our master has ever trained."

The object of their discussion fell into a deep, comfortable sleep. For a time she was without thought, and then she began to dream. Hands caressed her slowly until she was all a-tingle. Warm lips pressed kisses all over her body, sending a flush of heat racing through her veins. Zaynab sighed deeply, turning from her side to her back. Half awake now, her legs fell apart. *Warm. Wet and oh so warm.* She was being overwhelmed with pleasure. Her half-conscious body shuddered, and suddenly she was awake!

His dark head was buried between her splayed thighs. He was teasing at the badge of her womanhood. She whimpered, and raising his head up for a brief moment, he gazed on her with lust-filled eyes before bending once more to complete his sweet work. Reaching out, Zaynab dug her fingers into his dark hair, encouraging him onward. Within moments he was raising his body up and sliding between her legs, his engorged manhood delving deeply into her flesh. *Seeking. Seeking. Seeking.*

It was wonderful! She was dying! "Ohhh, God!" she moaned, "Yesss, my lord! *Yessssss!*" How she had missed this co-joining of their bodies in their time at sea. Yet abstention had, if anything else, brought her this incredible heaven. "Please," she begged him. *"Please!"* She wrapped her legs about him, and he slid deeper within her eager, hot sheath.

"Allah! Allah!" he groaned, lost in the sweetness of her. How could he have gone so long a time without her? How would he survive after she was gone? After he had given her into the keeping of another man? Deeper and deeper he drove himself into her. They were one. There was nothing else but this raging hunger. *This all-consuming passion!*

Together they attained paradise; reaching it in a simultaneous burst of pleasure that left them breathless and eager for more. Still joined, he pulled them into a seated position, wrapping his arms about her, covering her face with kisses. They were both trembling with the force of their desire.

"You are magnificent," he finally said. "You were born to be loved and to love, Zaynab, my flower."

He was still within her, throbbing softly with his first satisfaction. "I cannot love you, can I?" she said low. The hair on his chest tickled her sensitive breasts.

"No," he replied sadly, "you cannot. You must not."

"Could you love me?" Her eyes searched his face.

"What man possessed of a healthy manhood, two good eyes, and common sense, could not love you?" he replied, skillfully evading her, keeping his face emotionless, his eyes blank and without feeling. Could he love her? He would never, Allah help him, love anyone else! He cradled her gently, all desire suddenly gone, and withdrawing from her, he laid her back. "I have disturbed your rest," he said with a small smile.

"I did not mind, my lord," she answered him, and drawing him down, she kissed his mouth tenderly. She could not ever remember praying in her entire life, but she prayed now. Prayed for the demise of the caliph, Abd-al Rahman, so that she would not have to go to him. That she could remain with Karim forever. She would rather be the lowest of the low in his house than the favorite of this great prince. If only it could be!

His head now rested upon her breasts. She stroked his dark hair. He loved her. She sensed it even if he could not, would not, say the words. She understood. He was a man of honor, as she was a woman of honor. She would not burden him with the knowledge that she loved him; and if there was no other choice, she would go to this caliph gracefully. She would make Karim proud. She would bring additional glory to the name of Karim al Malina, the great Passion Master, even if it broke her heart. *And it would.*

❧ *Chapter 7*

*T*here was so much to learn! Zaynab had had absolutely no idea what Karim had meant when he'd promised to make her the most accomplished Love Slave ever created. Now she knew. She had simply assumed being beautiful and accomplished in bed sport would be really all that was required of her, but it was not. Men, it would appear, liked interesting women. Karim assured her that there were even schools in cities called Mecca and Medina for educating women in intellectual and artistic pursuits. *Lessons! Lessons! Lessons!* Her day was filled with lessons. The learning of any kind that she had previously had was only in household matters, but even there she had not been greatly encouraged, for her fate was to have been the convent, not the castle.

A tiny old woman came each day to teach her the fine art of calligraphy. At first she thought she would never learn to use her bamboo pen, but she did. One day what had appeared as chicken scratches became exquisite script, much to her delight. Although Zaynab soon excelled in the rounded cursive style of writing, she also practiced the angular kufic form as well. At the same time, she was learning to read. Once she had accomplished that, her tutor began to teach her how to compose poetry.

Karim taught her the history of al-Andalus, the rest of the known world, and its geography. An elderly eunuch was brought in to teach Zaynab music, for which she had quite a talent. Her voice was exquisite, and she learned to accompany herself upon three instruments: the rebec, which was played with a bow; a pear-shaped lute; and lastly, a qanun, a stringed instrument that was played by plucking.

156

Another old eunuch instructed her in Logic and Philosophy. A third educated her in the intricacies of Mathematics, Astronomy, and Astrology. A second woman of indeterminable age came to explain perfumes and their application, cosmetics, and the art of dress. Lastly, a stern young imam, the fiery light of religious dedication in his eyes, arrived to instruct her in Islam.

"You do not have to convert," Karim told her, "but it will be easier for you if you do so, or like many, pretend to."

"I have no beliefs," Zaynab told him quietly.

"Are you not a Christian?" She had once again surprised him.

She thought a moment, and then said, "I know that I was baptized, but the priest at Ben MacDui died when I was very little. Sometimes a priest would come seeking shelter, and shrive us. The MacFhearghuis did have a priest, who drew up my sister's marriage contracts and performed the marriage, but at Ben MacDui we went without the sacraments from one year to the next. I do not think it did us any harm. Do you believe in one God?"

"Yes, we do," he told her.

She shrugged. "I am happy to learn about Islam. Surely it cannot harm me, my lord."

"Then you will convert?"

"I will listen," she responded, "and consider well on what the imam teaches me; but what is in my heart is mine alone. The small bit of religion I have is all that is left of what I once was. I am not certain I wish to relinquish it now, or ever, my lord Karim."

He nodded his understanding. Just when he believed he had learned everything he might about her, she surprised him once again. What heights she might have attained if the caliph had been ten years younger than he was. The best she could hope for would be a child to cement her relationship with Abd-al Rahman and his family. The caliph was already the father of seven sons and eleven daughters, a relatively modest total considering his antecedents, most of whom had had between twenty-five and sixty children.

The autumn came, and with it the rains. They would fall

throughout the winter months, Karim explained. The rest of the
year was dry, which was why they needed irrigation from the
river. The weather grew cool in comparison to the summer
months, but it was still not nearly as cold as Alba had been.

Two months after Zaynab arrived, she had a visitor. The lady
Alimah had promised her son that she would visit, but she had
chosen her time carefully. Karim had departed on a short trip
into the mountains to buy the horses he would take to Cordoba
in Donal Righ's name. He wanted several months to make certain that the beasts he purchased were sound of limb. It would
not do for them to arrive at the caliph's court only to be discovered to be broken-winded.

Karim's mother arrived in the same litter that had brought
Zaynab and Oma to the villa. Mustafa hurried to greet his
master's mother.

"Welcome, gracious lady! You should have sent word of
your coming. My lord Karim is away at this time seeking fine
horses."

Alimah alighted from the litter. Her blond hair had darkened
somewhat over the years. She wore it in a small coronet of
braids atop her head, topped by a veil of deep blue shot through
with silver. Her warm gown was of quilted silk of a matching
color. Its neckline was modestly round, its sleeves wide and
long, trimmed in soft white fur. Beneath her gown she wore
crimson silk pantaloons, the ankles of which were trimmed in
bands of silver thread and gold beads. About her neck she wore
a gold chain with a single round medallion studded with diamonds. Diamonds also hung from her ears, and upon her hands
were several beautiful gold rings dotted with precious gem-
stones. Upon her feet were gold and silver kid slippers.

"I know where my son is, Mustafa. It is the Love Slave I
have come to see. Tell me now, what kind of a girl is she?"
Alimah's blue eyes filled with curiosity. "The truth now!"

"She is different, lady, from any of the others, but I like her,"
Mustafa responded slowly, considering his words.

"*Different?* How is she different, Mustafa?" Alimah's interest
was even more piqued. Mustafa, unlike so many of these

eunuchs, was usually a straight-spoken individual. It was not like him to beat about the bush like this. "Speak up!" she commanded him.

"She is obedient, lady, and yet I believe what she does is because she chooses to do it," he told her. He shook his head. "I cannot quite explain it, lady, any better than that."

"Will she bring honor to my son, and to Donal Righ, who is sending her to the caliph?" Alimah questioned him. Her gaze was sharp.

"Oh, yes, lady! The lady Zaynab is mannerly, and clever. She is probably the finest Love Slave my lord Karim has ever trained," Mustafa enthused. "And her beauty! It is as the sun itself!"

"Very well then," Alimah replied. "Take me to this paragon, my good Mustafa. Tell me, how does she amuse herself in Karim's absence?"

"She studies, lady."

"She is proficient in her studies?"

"Yes, lady. All her teachers are satisfied with her, even Imam Harun," Mustafa responded as he led Alimah into the women's quarters.

They found Zaynab seated by the pool in the day room, her qanun in her lap, plucking a tune and singing sweetly. Alimah waved the eunuch away and stood listening. The girl had a pure, sweet voice that would certainly please the caliph. She played her instrument nicely, and her voice was not simply adequate, it was excellent. Here was a piece of good luck. The caliph's concubines were expected to be more than just beautiful and skilled in the erotic arts. They were expected to be clever in other ways. This girl had an outstanding talent that would stand her in good stead at the court.

"What song is it you sing?" Alimah asked Zaynab as she concluded her solitary recital.

The girl started, and almost dropped her qanun. "It is a song of my homeland," Zaynab answered, rising politely, bowing to the handsome woman and putting her instrument aside. "It speaks of the beauties of the hills, the lakes, and the sky, lady. I like to practice some songs in my own language, for they will be unique at the caliph's court, and hopefully will please him. It also helps me to recall my own tongue, which I wish to do."

"I am the lady Alimah, Karim al Malina's mother," she told the young girl. Allah, this Zaynab was beautiful! The gilt hair, the aquamarine eyes, the pale skin. She would bring a fortune in the open market. Why, she was fairer than a Galacian!

"Would you take some mint tea with me, lady?" Zaynab inquired politely, offering her honored guest a chair. How beautiful Karim's mother was!

"I would, child," Alimah answered. "And some of those delightful little honey cakes with the chopped almonds, if they are available."

Zaynab's eyes twinkled. "I believe we do have them, lady. Oma, to me!" When the young girl answered her call, she instructed her in their wants.

Oma bowed politely. "Yes, my lady, I shall see to it at once." She hurried from the apartments.

"You have your own servant?" Alimah was impressed in spite of herself. Well, Karim had said she was a noble's child.

"Oma came with me from our homeland. We are from Alba, which is peopled by both Picts and those Celts called Scots," Zaynab replied.

"My son says your history is an interesting one. Would you tell it to me, Zaynab?"

For a quick moment a shadow crossed Zaynab's face, but then she began to speak, and Alimah was fascinated by the tale she told. "I far prefer this life to the one I led," Zaynab finished.

"I too was once a captive," Alimah told the younger woman. "My father was a wealthy farmer. One day the Danes came a-Viking up our fjord. They killed my parents and two older brothers. They carried off my three sisters, my two little brothers, and me. How I fought them! I was taken, like you, to Dublin. There, a Moorish slaver bought me and one of my sisters. We were resold in the great market in Cordoba. I do not know what happened to Karen, for I was purchased first. In al-Andalus it is the custom of the slave merchants to exhibit one girl at a time for sale. The others are kept behind a curtain. I was very fortunate, for my dear Habib, Karim's father, bought me, took me for his second wife. I have borne him three children. I wish you such good fortune, my child, when you go to Cordoba. May you catch the caliph's eye, keep it, and give him a fine son."

"You are kind, lady. I thank you for your good wishes," Zaynab replied. "Ahh, here are the refreshments!"

"What think you of Ifriqiya?" Alimah asked, biting into a small honey-nut cake. The sweetness trickled down her throat, tickling it, and she coughed delicately.

"I have seen little of it, lady, for I am kept busy with my lessons. I must be accomplished if I am to succeed in Cordoba, and succeed I will, bringing honor to both Donal Righ, who has sent me, and my lord Karim, who educates me." She sipped the mint tea.

What was wrong? The thought filtered through Alimah's consciousness before she could even catch it. How foolish, she thought. Nothing was wrong. The girl was beautiful. Indeed, she appeared perfect in every way. She would be Karim's crowning achievement. *Independent!* That was it! Zaynab was independent. Mustafa was not used to such a woman, which was why he could not fathom her. I was once like that, Alimah recalled, but the love of my husband changed everything for me. If Zaynab could be loved, she would lose that air of self-containment, the older woman felt.

"Would you like a visitor closer to your own age?" Alimah inquired. "Karim's sister, Iniga, desires to meet you. She is a year older than you, but I believe you would like each other. She is to be wed in the spring to an old friend of the family. Have you learned to play chess yet? It is a very clever game played upon a board. Have Iniga teach you, and then challenge my son. He is a fine player. If you play well, he will be pleased."

"I thank you, lady, for your good advice," Zaynab said.

Alimah arose. She had seen what she had come to see. She had learned what she had come to learn. She bid the Love Slave farewell and departed her son's villa.

"I can see where our lord Karim gets his fine looks," Oma noted when the good lady had gone. "I am astounded that she has borne three children, and one as old as the captain. She does not look worn by it at all."

"I think this life an easier one than that we lived in Alba. The women of the rich are pampered. They do no hard work as do our women, rich or poor, but rather they spend their time preparing to please their lords. Now that I see it, I am sorry for my sister, Gruoch. She will be old before her time."

Karim returned from the mountains, where he had purchased ten fine Arabians—nine mares and a single stallion—to take to Cordoba. The horses would spend the winter months in his pastures and stables being fattened and groomed to perfection. The breeders had a tendency to keep their animals too lean. The elephants had already been bought for him by an agent of his brother Ayyub. They were being kept by their previous owner until the spring, when they would be brought north to Alcazaba Malina for transport to Cordoba.

While Karim had been in the mountains, Alaeddin ben Omar had been overseeing the building of the new ship. It would be a duplicate of *I'timad* and was to be called *Iniga*, after Karim's sister. The young girl was thrilled by the honor.

"He has always been the best brother in the whole world," she enthusiastically told Zaynab. "Not at all like Ja'far or Ayyub. They couldn't be bothered with a little sister, but Karim never felt that way." Iniga had arrived for her first visit with Zaynab just two days after Alimah's initial visit. The three young women, for Oma was included, had immediately become friends.

Iniga taught both girls how to play chess. "My brothers," she told them, "think they play better than anyone else. They are always having games, but I can beat them. Mother says I must not, for men's pride is so easily hurt by such trivial things, so I pretend to be beaten by them, and they are happy."

Zaynab laughed. Though she was younger in years than Iniga, her experiences had made her more mature. "Your mother is correct, Iniga," she told her friend. "Women are indeed stronger. I believe that is why Allah designated them the life-givers. Can you imagine a man having a baby?" She chuckled.

"Have you seen a baby born?" Iniga's eyes were wide.

She must be careful here, Zaynab thought. Iniga was the virgin daughter of a rich family. It was likely she knew little of what transpired between a man and a woman. "My twin sister and I were the eldest of our mother's children," she told the girl. "Mother had many children after us. By the time we were five, there was little Gruoch and I did not know about birthing babies. The houses of the rich in Alba are not at all like the houses of the rich here. We lived in a stone tower with a single large room upon each floor. There was little privacy for any of us. It was always cold, and frequently rainy and damp. I was used to it, but now I could never go back. I love the sunlight and the warmth of this land. Is Cordoba like this?"

Iniga nodded, her curiosity satisfied for the moment. "Aye, and the caliph's palace is, I am told, the wonder of the world. They say when he travels between Madinat al-Zahra and Cordoba, carpets are laid upon the road between the two places. And the road is lit at night by lamps upon posts! It takes six lamplighters, they say, to keep all the lamps lit upon that road! Imagine, a lighted road! I wish I could see it, but I shall probably spend all my days here in Alcazaba Malina. Once I am wed, it is my duty to produce children for my husband; but then," she said with a smile and a shrug, "what else is there for a woman to do? I think I envy you just a little going to the caliph's court, Zaynab." Iniga sighed. "You really are an extravagantly beautiful girl. I think the caliph will be ravished by you, and the other women of his harem will be jealous. You must be careful of those women, you know. Trust no one but Oma, and make certain that the eunuch they give you is loyal to you alone. You can always buy a eunuch's loyalty. You must be certain those more powerful than you don't control your servants. You are wise, and you should be able to fathom whom you can trust."

"Who are you to marry?" Zaynab asked Iniga.

"His name is Ahmed ibn Omar. He is a nephew of the lady Muzna, her sister's eldest son. I have known him my entire life. It was always assumed that we would marry. He has black hair that is like a raven's wing, and lovely brown eyes."

"Do you love him?" Zaynab wondered.

Iniga thought a long moment, and then she said, "I suppose I do. I have never thought of being with anyone else. Ahmed is kind and funny. They say he never gets angry. I am content with the arrangement that my parents have made."

In a sense, Zaynab envied the girl. Love was a painful emotion, she was discovering. It was probably better, she considered, to be *content* like Iniga. There was no hurt in being content. Her mother had never been content, certainly. For all Sorcha MacDuff's vehement anger against the MacFhearghuis, she had loved him in her strange way, and he had loved her. It had been a bitter thing for them both. Love was definitely not a desirable emotion to feel, Zaynab decided, but how did one stop loving a man?

Pleased with the progress she was making in all the areas of her studies, Karim al Malina took his pupil a step further in the erotic arts. Joining her one evening, he brought with him a delicately woven gold basket. "This is for you," he said, handing it to her.

She lifted the peach silk covering from the basket and gazed, puzzled, at its contents.

"They are a collection of love toys," he said, answering her unspoken question. "They can be used by your master or by you."

Slowly Zaynab removed each item and set it carefully on the little ebony table by the bed. There was a crystal flask with a silver stopper that was filled with a clear liquid, and an alabaster flask containing a blush-colored creamy liquid that smelled of gardenias. There were two golden bracelets, separated by a short golden chain. The bracelets were lined in lamb's wool. There were two items encased in purple velvet bags. She opened the smaller of the two and a pair of silver balls rolled into her palm.

"Why do they feel so odd?" she questioned him.

"There is a tiny drop of mercury in one of them, and a wee silver tongue in the other of them," he explained.

"What are they for?" she asked.

"Pleasure," he responded. "I will show you shortly, but first open the other bag, Zaynab."

She obeyed, and drew forth an object that brought a blush to her cheek. "What is it, my lord? It looks like a manhood, and yet . . ."

He laughed softly. "It is called a dildo. This one is an exact replica of Abd-al Rahman's manhood. It is carved from ivory, and perfect in its detail. You will note that its handle is gold and bejeweled as befits your lord. If you long for your master, and he is not there to pleasure you, you can use the dildo. It may please him to see you use it before him.

"For now I will use it to initiate you into another form of love play. You have a second maidenhead, but I will not take it myself. I will use the dildo to prepare you for your master's taking of that maidenhead. By right his must be the first manhood you take into that other orifice, but you will need to be readied for it. We will use the dildo for that purpose."

She nodded, not quite certain what he meant, but she knew he would elucidate further when the time came. She uncorked the crystal stopper and sniffed. It had a rose fragrance to it. "What is it?"

"It is a special liquor. Oma will be given its recipe. It is used to stimulate passions that are perhaps a bit slow. The caliph is not a youth, Zaynab. There is a small cup in the basket. Take it out and pour yourself a draught. You will not need it as a rule, but I want you to understand how it will affect your lover." When she had obeyed him, he said, "Now take the last item from the basket."

Zaynab removed the black onyx jar. Inside was a thick odorless cream. She set it aside, asking him instead, "What is the pale pink liquid, my lord? It smells like my gardenias."

"It will make the skin very sensitive to touch," he said. "Let me rub some on you, my flower. The caliph will enjoy exciting you in such a way, and it gives him time to become aroused as well. It is subtle, but very effective. There are special herbs in it which Oma will be told of so she can keep you well-supplied." He began to smooth the pale cream over her skin, and she purred contentedly at him.

"And the other cream? The one in the jar?" she asked.

"It is but a lubricant for the dildo," he answered.

She was silent for a short time, and then she said, "What are those dainty little chains for, my lord?"

"Playing," he told her. "The caliph may enjoy the little games that men and women often play to amuse themselves. I shall begin to teach you such games soon. Perhaps the caliph would like to pretend that he has captured you in battle. You would resist his attentions if free to do so, but he chains you, and you are forced to give him pleasure. Or perhaps he would enjoy being your captive. Older men like to play games. It keeps their bed sport interesting, Zaynab." He rolled her over, and pouring some of the liquid cream into his palm, began to massage her breasts and her belly. "Do you like it?" he queried.

"Ummmm, it feels tingly, my lord," she replied.

"All over?" he murmured, his hands kneading her legs and thighs.

"Yesss, all over!" she admitted, squirming slightly beneath his touch. In fact the touch of his hands was becoming almost unbearable.

"Roll onto your belly," he said, and when she had done so, he continued. "Now draw your legs up beneath you. Good. Arch your back deeply, Zaynab. Keep your shoulders as flat as you can. Rest your head in the cradle of your folded arms. Excellent! That is the position you must take when the caliph decides he wishes to enter into your body through your Temple of Sodom. Stay that way while I prepare the dildo." He dipped the instrument into the lubricant, and kneeling behind her, he prepared to insert it. "Do not be frightened. It is a different sensation. If you feel the need, arch your back in a deeper curve to accommodate the dildo." Firmly he spread the twin moons of her buttocks with his thumb and forefinger, revealing the small rosette between them. He positioned the dildo and applied gentle pressure until the tight flesh began to give and the head of the ivory penis entered her tense body a small way.

Zaynab gasped. It wasn't that it hurt. It was simply a wretchedly uncomfortable sensation. She didn't like it, and she told him so. "Why are you doing this to me, my lord? It is unnatural!"

"To some, my jewel, but not all," he told her. "As a Love Slave you must be prepared to accept your master in a variety of ways. You have already accepted a manhood in two of your three orifices. There can be no surprises for you once you become a member of the caliph's harem. You must be perfection in all ways." He pushed the dildo in a bit farther, and she attempted to squirm away from him, but Karim placed a firm hand upon her neck. "Obedience at all times," he reminded her.

"I hate this!" she cried to him. *"I hate this!"*

His grip on her neck was hard as he pressed the dildo its full length into her, withdrawing it halfway and thrusting it forward once more, and yet again and again, in a fierce rhythm.

She could not struggle against him, with his harsh grasp upon her. She hated what he was doing, what was happening, and then to her growing horror she felt a thrill of pleasure ripple through her uneasy body. She was pushing her buttocks back and forth in counterpoint to the thrusts of the dildo. "I hate you for this!" she spat at him, but her body was already shuddering with release even as he drew the dildo from her body, allowing her to collapse into a heap.

"It is not an activity that I enjoy," he said in a flat voice, "but you will remember that I am training you for the caliph's bed and not my own. Abd-al Rahman, I am told, occasionally enjoys this kind of sport. You must be ready to accede to his wishes should he desire you in this fashion. Twice weekly from now on you will take the dildo into your body in this fashion to prepare you."

Zaynab did not answer him. Forcing her onto her back, he saw that her cheeks were wet with her tears, although she had made no sound at all. Tenderly he kissed each tear, and then he gathered her into his arms. It was her undoing. "I hated it!" she sobbed, and then her anger sweeping her up, she cried out, "and I hate you!" Furiously, she began to pummel him with her fists. "You hurt me!"

"It will hurt less each time," he said, grabbing her wrists and imprisoning them in his grip. "In time your body will easily give, and it will not hurt you." He pressed her down upon the

mattress, his big body covering hers, seeking her mouth with
his, leaving her utterly breathless, and even angrier at him.

"It matters not even if it doesn't hurt. I hated it!" she shrieked
at him, pulling her head from his, baring her teeth in fury.

At that he lost his own control. His mouth crushed bruis-
ingly down on hers again, kissing her fiercely. Damn her!
Damn her! She was the most exciting woman he had ever
known, and he loved her. Yet he must not. He dared not. *He
could not!*

She felt the hardness of his manhood against her thigh. She
felt his kiss deepening, softening, and her anger tempered.
Ohh, why did she love Karim so very much? He was a cold and
cruel man whose only interest in her was in training her like an
animal to please the sensual appetites of some potentate. She
sighed deeply, returning his kisses. She didn't care! If this was
all she was to have of happiness, then she would grab at it for
the brief time she would have with him. It was more than
Sorcha had ever had. More than Gruoch would ever have.

Zaynab wrapped her arms about her lover, drawing him as
close as she could. Her lips welcomed him, parting to invite his
tongue into her mouth to play with her tongue. Her hands
caressed him, tangling in his soft hair, running down his long
muscled back, encouraging him in his deepening passion. Her
throat strained in a silent scream as he pressed hot kisses upon
it, inhaling the perfumed flesh. Straddling her, he leaned back,
his hands playing with her breasts until they were taut with
desire, her nipples puckering into tight points that begged to be
suckled upon. He heard their quiet message and obliged, his
mouth closing first around one nipple, and then the other. He
sucked hard upon her, sending a ripple of desire down to that
little jewel between her legs. She moaned, satisfied, as he slid
between those milky thighs and pushed his raging lance into
her eager body.

"Impatient as ever," he teased her through gritted teeth.

"You have but taken the edge off my appetite," she told him
boldly, and her nails ran lightly down his back, causing him to
shiver. "Now you are well mounted, my lord, let us see if you

can run the course like that fine Arab stallion you have brought back from the mountains!"

His knees gripped her hard. Slowly at first, and then with increasing vigor, he began to ride her. He showed no mercy, driving her up one peak and another, and yet another. Now her nails raked him cruelly, her little whimpers urging him onward until finally they both collapsed, exhausted with their passionate labors. Rolling off her, he cradled her in his arms. "If you belonged to me, Zaynab, I should never make you unhappy," he said softly. It was the closest he had dared come to admitting his love for her.

"If I belonged to you, my lord Karim, I should never be unhappy," she responded. It was the closest she dared to come to admitting her love.

But he knew, and she knew, and the pain was almost too much to bear. "I am a man of honor, my jewel. In the spring I will deliver you to the caliph in Cordoba," he said to her.

"And I am a woman of honor, my lord Karim. I will go without question, and do honor to both your name and Donal Righ's," Zaynab told him.

There was nothing more to say. There was so little time left for them. Silently, each vowed they would not waste that time.

Chapter 8

"*I* believe I have found a bride for you, my son," Habib ibn Malik told Karim. "Her name is Hatiba."

"If you think she is suitable, my father, then so be it," Karim answered. What difference did it make? he thought to himself. I will never love her as I love Zaynab.

"She is a lovely girl," Alimah added, but she could see that her youngest son was otherwise preoccupied. "Are you certain, Karim, that you wish to marry at this time? Perhaps you would enjoy one more voyage on *I'timad*."

"I will take that voyage when I sail to Cordoba with Zaynab and her train," he answered, "and then I will go on to Eire to inform Donal Righ of the caliph's delight in his gifts. It is time that I married. Arrange the wedding for next autumn."

"Let me tell you about Hatiba," said his father, who was not quite as intuitive as Alimah. "She is the daughter of Hussein ibn Hussein."

"A Berber?" Allah help him. Berber girls were noted for their docile temperaments. She would be obedient, and boring beyond belief, but perhaps that was what he needed. There could be no comparisons to Zaynab. *Zaynab*. His golden-haired passionate love.

"I have done very well by you, Karim," his father continued. "Hussein ibn Hussein is an enormously wealthy breeder of fine Arabians. The horses you bought undoubtedly came from one of his farms. He is giving Hatiba a breeding facility, one hundred mares, and two young stallions in their prime as part of her dowry. What think you of that, my son? Is it not impressive?" Habib ibn Malik was enormously pleased with this

170

match, which would add to his family's wealth and prestige.

"Most impressive. Is she ugly, then, that her father feels the need to show such generosity?" Karim wondered aloud.

"I have seen Hatiba, and she is very fair," his mother responded. "She has pale gold skin that absolutely glows with her good health. Her hair is lustrous and silky, as black as ebony. She has gray eyes and a sweet, pretty face. Her demeanor is modest and soft-spoken. If her father is generous, it is because she is his last child, the daughter of his favorite wife. I have spoken with that lady myself. She tells me that Hussein ibn Hussein dotes on Hatiba. That is why he has been so loath to make a match for her, but she will soon be too old, so he has at last relented."

"How old is she?" Karim asked.

"Fifteen, my son," his father answered.

"The same age as Zaynab," he said low, but Alimah heard him.

Later, when her husband had gone, she sat with her son and questioned him. "You have not fallen in love with this girl, Karim, have you?" Her lovely face was genuinely concerned.

"I love her," he said bluntly, "and she loves me."

Alimah's hand went to her heart. "She has told you so?" she asked him. This was all her husband's fault. When Karim, in his youth, had shown himself to be an extremely sensual man, Habib had, at the wicked suggestion of Ja'far and Ayyub, sent her younger son to the School of the Passion Masters in Samarkand. The brothers had meant it as a jest, but Habib had taken them seriously. Karim had obviously been diligent in his studies, because for a time he was successful in this field.

But Karim was a sensitive man, although men, Alimah knew, rarely admitted to such feelings. He had felt great guilt when the Love Slave Leila had killed herself over him. It had only been a matter of time before something like this was bound to happen. She had been so relieved when he decided to cease his activities, and worried once more when her son had taken Zaynab on for friendship's sake. *Now this!*

"Neither Zaynab nor I have openly admitted—voiced, if

you will, my mother—the love we have for one another. Would it change anything? The pain is already almost unbearable," he answered her.

"Send her to Cordoba now with Alaeddin," Alimah begged.

He shook his head. "She goes in the spring, and not before. She is not quite ready yet, my mother. Besides, Alaeddin will captain my new vessel, *Iniga*. It will take two vessels to carry all the gifts that Donal Righ has sent to Abd-al Rahman."

"I am sorry for you both," Alimah said quietly. "Sadly, the heart is not often wise. It cannot be controlled by reason. You may never love another woman as you do Zaynab, my son, but in time the pain will lessen and you will love again. So will she. Not as she loves you perhaps, but then you do not want her to be unhappy, I hope."

"No," he replied sadly. "I do not want her to be unhappy."

His mother put a comforting hand upon his. "Hatiba will please you, I promise you that. Be good to her, for she is the innocent in this."

"When have I not been kind to a woman?" he asked her bitterly. "I have been taught to appreciate women as no other man. Hatiba bat Hussein will be my first wife. She will be respected and honored as such."

"Then I shall tell your father to formalize the arrangements and sign the contracts?"

"How much dowry will I give my bride?" Karim asked her. It was the custom for a bride to be given a price as well as to give her husband a dowry. Islam protected its womenfolk. If in the future Karim divorced Hatiba, both her dowry and her bride price would be given to her in settlement. Her children would remain the father's responsibility.

"The bride price will be three thousand gold dinars. Such a sum honors both father and daughter," Alimah told her son.

Karim nodded. "It is generous, but fair," he said. "Tell Father I will be responsible for the bride price myself. I can more than afford it. When will the qadi come to record the contract?"

"The marriage contract will be signed the day of Iniga's wedding. Hussein ibn Hussein has been invited. He has insisted, however, that you not see Hatiba until the day of the wedding," she explained. "I know it is old-fashioned, but it is his wish as her father."

"She is obviously an obedient daughter," he replied dryly. "I suppose it augurs well for my married life. Can you imagine Iniga's reaction if you told her she was marrying a total stranger and could not lay eyes upon him until the marriage was celebrated, the deed done?"

Alimah burst out laughing, and then said, "Fortunately, we do not have that problem with Iniga, as she and Ahmed have known each other their whole lives. They are a good match."

"Zaynab and Iniga have become friends," he said.

"I know," Alimah said, frowning again. "I want to disapprove, but I cannot. Zaynab is charming and mannerly. She and Iniga are genuinely fond of one another. Who knows what Zaynab's fate is to be? Should she become the caliph's favorite, Iniga would have a very powerful friend in Cordoba."

"You like her too," Karim noted softly.

"Yes," his mother admitted, "I do. I find her a sensible girl."

"Iniga has invited her to her wedding. I will bring her and Oma. Neither of them has really known a family. They seem to bloom in the warmth of ours. I will send her back to the villa when Ahmed's procession comes to take Iniga to his father's house."

"Very well, I will allow it," Alimah said. "Iniga did not want a large wedding, and so it will be a simple affair in our gardens."

"I will leave the month after the wedding for Cordoba," Karim said. "Then I will go on to Eire, but I shall not stay there. I go but to inform Donal Righ that I have completed my commission for him. I shall stay in Eire just long enough to take on water, stores, and whatever cargo I can find before returning home."

"And you will come back to your own wedding," Alimah said.

"Yes," he agreed. He would marry a girl named Hatiba. A girl he had never met, who would never please him no matter how hard she tried; but she would never realize it. He would be kind and gentle to Hatiba, his Berber bride, and she would not ever know that he loved another woman with every fiber of his being. That he would always love her. That he would love no other but Zaynab, of the golden tresses.

Karim brought Zaynab and Oma to see the city they had but briefly passed through on their arrival. The two young women, properly garbed in their black yashmaks, nothing but their eyes showing, alighted from their litter and strolled about the market with Karim. It seemed to Zaynab and Oma that there was everything imaginable for sale, and many things they had never imagined. The awninged stalls overflowed with a plethora of goods. Colorful fabrics—silks and cottons, linens and brocades—were hung out for sale. They blew like banners in the gentle breeze. There was beautiful leatherwork, pottery, and brasswork; exquisite carved boxes of ivory, soapstone, and bone displayed with equally beautiful boxes that were delicately painted in bright colors on black lacquer.

One stall sold colorful live birds, which hung confined in their willow cages. Some of the creatures sang sweetly, while others simply shrieked raucously, hanging upside down on the bars, glaring with beady black eyes at the passersby. A poulterer and a butcher were next to one another, their wares displayed for all to see. Beef and lamb hung side by side, boys with palm fans shooing the flies from the meat. Chickens squawked, ducks quacked, and pigeons cooed, confined in their pens, awaiting a buyer. There were jewelers selling everything from cheap brass earrings to expensive baubles that glittered in the sunshine.

Rounding a corner, they came upon a slave merchant. They stopped, fascinated. Strong young black men were paraded naked, and were quickly sold to new masters. A pretty dark-haired young girl was brought from behind a curtain. She tried to cover her nudity with her hands, but the slave master spoke sharply to her, and with reluctance she revealed all to an audience of eager bidders. The bidding was spirited. The girl, advertised as a virgin with a physician's proof of her condition, sold quickly for three hundred thirty dinars.

"Would that have happened to Oma and me if Donal Righ had not bought us?" Zaynab asked Karim.

He nodded. "Yes, my jewel. A slave market is not a happy place."

Once again, Zaynab realized, but this time far more strongly, how fortunate she and Oma had been to be sold to Donal Righ. Oh, they had been told it often enough, but seeing that poor frightened girl just now had really made her understand. If men did not think me beautiful, she considered thoughtfully, I would have ended up terrified in some public marketplace, and Oma as well. She shuddered in her distaste, but her companions did not notice.

Putting a hand beneath Zaynab's elbow, Karim directed her into another part of the market, where they came upon stalls filled with fruits, flowers, and vegetables. One merchant hawked carnations, jasmine, myrtle, and roses. Another offered baskets filled with cucumbers, peas, beans, asparagus, aubergines, and onions. There was a stall filled with herbs, mint, marjoram, sweet lavender, and jars of yellow saffron. The fruit seller offered oranges, pomegranates, bananas, grapes, and almonds.

Karim bought them little cups of water flavored with lemon to assuage their thirsts, for the day had grown unseasonably warm for late winter. "Sip it through your veils," he cautioned them. "You must never show your faces in public, lest you disgrace yourselves."

They walked on, and Zaynab's eye was caught by a small stall where a silversmith worked. "May we stop, my lord?"

"Indeed," he said, "and you may each choose a gift if something catches your fancy."

The serving girl's eyes lit upon a delicate silver chain studded with blue Persian lapis, and Karim generously bought it for her. Zaynab, however, fell in love with a silver cup. It was not footed, but rather round in shape to fit comfortably in the palm of the hand. The cup was decorated with a raised design: a lily, about which a small hummingbird hovered. The flower was overlaid with gilt, while the bird was enameled in bright green and violet with a tiny ruby eye.

"This is what I desire, my lord," she told him quietly, and he purchased it for her.

"You will remember me each time you sip from this cup," he said as he escorted her to her litter.

"I could never forget you," she told him softly.

"The silver comes from mines in the nearby mountains that belong to Alcazaba Malina," he told her in an effort to change the subject. "Those mines are responsible in part for the city's prosperity."

She could not look at him. Turning her head, she lay back in the litter and pretended to doze. In a few weeks Iniga would marry, and the month after, Karim would take her to Cordoba. She would never see him again. The knowledge was like a knife to her heart. Yet did any woman have a different lot in life? Her sister had been married for expediency's sake. Zaynab wondered if the child Gruoch had borne was the hoped-for son. If it had been, then Sorcha MacDuff's revenge would have been total and complete. A true MacDuff would continue to possess Ben MacDui, as well as the MacFhearghuis's lands. I will never know, Zaynab thought.

Iniga's wedding day arrived. Zaynab had consulted Karim as to what she should wear. "I would do your sister honor, but I do not want to outshine her on her day of days," she told him.

"If you wore a sackcloth you would outshine every woman in the world," he said gallantly. "I can only tell you not to wear pink, for that is the color of my sister's garment."

"What help is that?" she grumbled at him.

"Something elegant, but simple," Oma said, drawing forth from the chest a caftan of aquamarine silk. The round neckline was embroidered in gold and silk thread flowers, as were the bottom of the sleeves. "There are matching silk trousers for beneath, my lady. We'll use the little gold slippers. The plain ones, not the jeweled."

Karim, listening, nodded his agreement. "And only earbobs for jewelry," he said. "The little gold crescent moons. Perhaps a single bracelet, but nothing more."

Oma dressed her mistress and then did her hair. She braided

the long thick gilt mass into a single plait, weaving matching silk ribbons studded with pearls among the silky tresses. When she had finished, she topped the braid with a diaphanous silk veil of blue-green shot through with gold and silver. It had a matching face veil. The servant's own garb was similar in style to her mistress's, but it lacked embroidery and was of a pretty soft green. About her slender neck Oma proudly wore the silver necklace Karim had bought her. Sadly, all their splendor was topped by the black yashmaks they were forced to wear when traveling.

The litter arrived to take the two women into the city. As was his custom, Karim rode by their side. When they reached the street where Habib ibn Malik's home was located, the litter stopped before the garden gate. Dismounting his horse, Karim opened the gate with his key.

"I must enter through another way," he said. "You will find the other women in the garden at their celebration."

"Where are the men?" Zaynab asked.

"The celebrations are separate," he explained. "It is our custom. Go now, and enjoy yourselves. My mother will tell you when it is time for you to leave. You will depart through this same gate, and I will be waiting for you. Enjoy yourselves!"

They walked through the gate and found themselves in the most exquisite gardens. There were tall graceful trees everywhere, and pools with water lilies, and fountains that sprayed showers of tiny droplets into the sweet afternoon air. Following the sound of music, they moved along a gravel path until they reached the bridal party. The two young women went immediately to the lady Alimah and paid their respects.

Karim's mother was looking particularly beautiful and happy this day. "Do you see the bride?" she asked them, and turning them about, pointed.

There in the center of the garden, Iniga sat upon a golden throne, garbed in soft pink silk sewn all over with tiny crystals and diamonds. Her hair was unbound and dusted with gold, but a delicate pink veil was placed modestly over it. Slave women came and removed Zaynab's and Oma's travel garments. Instinctively, the two shook the wrinkles from their gowns.

Alimah looked approvingly upon them. "How pretty you both are," she said in a kindly tone. "Now go, and greet my daughter."

They hurried to the center of the garden, where Iniga sat alone, surrounded by her dowry and wedding gifts. She grinned mischievously at them. "What do you think?" She laughed. "Am I not like some painted idol?"

"You are quite magnificent," Zaynab agreed. "Do you sit there all day, Iniga, or are you allowed to move about?"

"I must sit here in my solitary splendor," Iniga chuckled, "until late afternoon when Ahmed and his male relations will come to take me to his father's house, where we will live. The party will continue there, again men and women in separate areas, until at last my husband and I may escape to the privacy of our bedchamber. After that my glory is dimmed until the day I announce I am with child. Then it will brighten with each passing month until I deliver my offspring, who will hopefully be a son."

"What if you birth a daughter?" Zaynab asked her.

"A son is hoped for first, but a daughter is welcomed too. Before the prophet came and brought enlightenment to our people, many killed their female infants. The Quran, however, says: 'Do not kill your children because you fear poverty. We will grant you subsistence to feed them. Killing them would be a terrible mistake.' " Iniga smiled. "Besides, we women are lifegivers. We should not be lifetakers."

It was a pleasant afternoon. An all-female orchestra played, and often the women danced with each other beneath the eye of the bride. Slave girls passed trays of drinks, little cakes, sugared dates, and other sweets. Finally, Alimah signaled to Zaynab and Oma that it was time for them to leave. Returning to where Iniga sat enthroned, they wished her well and then bid her farewell.

"Come and see me," Zaynab said, "before we leave for Cordoba."

"When will you go?" Iniga asked.

"After Ramadan, Karim has said," Zaynab answered.

"I will come," Iniga promised her friend. "He will not leave until after Id al-Fitr, the three-day celebration ending Ramadan. The holy month begins in two days, and I will not be able to come during it, but I will come at Id al-Fitr, Zaynab, I promise."

The two girls embraced. Then Zaynab, in the company of Oma, hurried back across the garden to the little gate in the wall. Karim was awaiting them with the litter. After settling them in it, he told them, "I must remain for the rest of the celebration. I will be with you late tonight, my jewel. Wait up for me." Then he closed the curtains, and they felt the litter being lifted up and carried off.

" 'Tis funny," Oma said as they traveled along, "how the men and the women celebrated separately at the wedding feast. I had hoped to see Alaeddin ben Omar there, but if he was there, I will never know unless he tells me. He has been so busy these past months, I have hardly seen him at all. I suppose I am not important to him, though he did his best to seduce me on our voyage from Eire."

"Did he succeed?" Zaynab questioned her servant mischievously.

"No," Oma said, "but not for want of trying." She sighed. "There is no future for me there, lady, and I find for all my chatter I am not a girl for a quick kiss and a cuddle. The caliph will see you and love you, lady. You may have a child, and that child will be born free, a king's son. Any child I bear will be a slave, as I am now. Perhaps if I had not been born free myself it would not matter, but I was freeborn, and it does."

"If I please the caliph," Zaynab said, "it will be in my power to free you, Oma. I could return you to Alba. Would that make you happy?"

"Lady, I should far prefer to stay with you," Oma said. "There is nothing for me in Alba. I have no family, and the only home I have ever known was the convent. I cannot return there," she said with a little smile. "Can you see the look on Mother Eubh's face if I came tripping up the road to her gates?"

"I could send you to my sister at Ben MacDui," Zaynab said.

"*What!*" Oma cried. "Are you trying to rid yourself of me, lady? You cannot be certain your sister survived her childbirth, and how would I ever explain all of what has happened to us? Do you think your sister and the Fergusons would believe me? They'd set the dogs on me, lady! Do not send me away from you!" Tears sprang into Oma's eyes.

"I do not want to send you away," Zaynab said, patting her serving girl's hand, "but you seemed so unhappy just a moment ago."

"Ohh, it is just that Alaeddin ben Omar," Oma said.

"Perhaps then you should let him succeed at his seduction of you," Zaynab suggested. "Because you are my servant does not mean you should not have a bit of love for yourself."

"I do not want a child," Oma replied.

"You do not have to have one, then," Zaynab said. "Do you not wonder why I have not become with child all these months? Did not Karim give you a bottle of elixir back in Dublin with instructions that I was to be given some in water each morning? Have you not been given the recipe for that same elixir, and brewed it yourself for me?"

"Yes," Oma said slowly. "I never knew what it was, but I knew the master would not harm you."

"That elixir is to prevent me from having a child," Zaynab told her companion. "And there is also another method, but I am not as certain it would be successful. Iniga told me the women of the harem stuff little sponges into their sheaths up to the mouth of the womb. This is said to block their lover's seed. Take some of my elixir, Oma, and then if you wish, take Alaeddin ben Omar for your lover. You will be happier, I think, than if you don't."

"Thank you, lady," Oma said gratefully. "I will admit to desiring that black-bearded ruffian, but no child of mine will be born a slave!" Then she thought a moment. "How long must I take the elixir before yielding to Alaeddin's charms?"

"Take a dose of it tonight," Zaynab suggested. "You will be safe immediately as long as you imbibe it daily. I will not take it once we arrive in Cordoba, however, for having a child by the caliph can only increase my value to him, and my status in the harem."

"I think I will be sorry to leave this place," Oma said. "It is a fair land, and the lord Karim is a good master. When will we go, lady? Do you know?"

"In two days the month of Ramadan begins," Zaynab told her. "We will refrain from eating and drinking from sunrise to sunset. At the end of the month there will be a three-day celebration. We depart for Cordoba immediately after it."

The following morning brought a period of intensive study for Zaynab. Knowing that the time was short, her teachers pressed her, to assure themselves that she had attained perfection in their eyes. Her success in Cordoba would reflect glory on them all.

In the late afternoon Oma came to her, bringing a long, hooded white cloak. "My lord Karim says you are to put this on and come with me, lady." Then she lowered her voice so the imam could not hear. "And Alaeddin has come with my lord Karim. May I be with him?"

"Of course," Zaynab said generously. "If I cannot care for myself for an evening, then I have grown too soft with this good living. I do not expect to see you before morning, Oma," she concluded with a twinkle in her eye. "I hope you will obey me in this matter."

Oma giggled happily, leading her mistress into the courtyard, where Karim awaited her, mounted upon the handsome white stallion that he was taking to Cordoba. He bid her come to him.

"My lord?" She stood by his foot, puzzled.

Reaching down, he lifted her into the saddle before him and encouraged his mount forward. "Are you comfortable?" he asked her. "We have a ride of several miles ahead of us."

"Where are we going, my lord?" She was very comfortable upon the horse, cradled in his arms. He was garbed all in white, a small white turban with a veil atop his head. She nestled against his chest, inhaling the masculine fragrance of him, and sighed with pleasure.

He smiled, thinking how free she was with her feelings. There was no guile in her. What a refreshing change she would be to the caliph, he thought, and his smile faded. In a few weeks' time she would belong to the caliph, but for now she was his. "We are going to a small house I own," he told her. "It is in the hills upon a lake."

Zaynab said nothing more. Her fair head rested against his shoulder as she curiously watched the countryside about her pass by. She had seen virtually nothing of Malina but the road between Karim's villa and the city itself. The mountains at the edge of the plain were snow-topped. The broad fields were newly green with the recently sprouted grain. They passed by vineyards, the vines leafy with early growth. The almond orchards were in bloom, and the silvery leaves of the olive groves were ruffled by the light breeze.

"Is all of this yours?" Zaynab asked him.

"Yes," he answered her, smiling.

"You must be very rich," she considered, and he laughed. "In Alba they would think they were in paradise to have such land. Our lands were rocky. The soil there did not easily give up a crop, but here the bounty seems to spring graciously from the earth for you."

"Malina is a special place," he agreed. "The land is fertile, and the climate temperate."

"In Alba," she told him, "it is always cold, and usually gray. Sometimes we would get a few warm weeks from midsummer into the early autumn, when the men hunted the grouse, but that was all. And it rains a great deal in Alba. I love the sun of this land!"

They rode on and she noticed that gradually the landscape gave way to gently rolling hills that were covered with red anemones. Finally, he turned their mount off onto a side road that led down a hillock into a small wood, and before her was a small teardrop of a blue lake that she could have never imagined would be there. On the lakeshore was a little marble building set in the center of a garden now in bloom with yellow, white, and blue flowers. Karim pulled the horse to a stop before the building and dismounted, turning about to lift his companion down.

"I call this place 'Escape.' It is where I come when I wish to be alone. I found the lake years ago as a boy when I came hunting in these hills. My father gave me this land when I returned from Samarkand. I built my first villa within sight of the sea, but Escape here, where no one else would be likely to find it." He took her hand, and together they walked across a portico into the building.

She found herself in a single large chamber on the far side of which was another pillared portico upon which were jardinieres of pink rose trees. In one corner of the room was a small fountain of black marble from which sprang a little golden spout drizzling clear, cool water. In the center of the room, upon a dais, was a bed with a feather mattress covered in black silk and heaped with matching pillows striped in cloth-of-gold. Next to the dais was a low round table upon which had been placed a tray with a roast chicken, a dish of rice pilaf, and a bowl of pomegranates and bananas. There was also a crystal decanter of wine. Upon the floor of the room were thick wool carpets in rich crimsons and blues. There was nothing else.

He poured them each a small silver goblet of wine and handed her one.

"The imam says that wine is forbidden," Zaynab said.

"Allah has created the earth, the grapes, and therefore the wine. There can be nothing wrong with what Allah has made. It is a display of drunkenness that is wrong, my flower. You will find wine at the caliph's court in Cordoba. Drink up." He lifted the goblet to his lips and drank his wine down. Then he poured himself another draught, swiftly drinking it down as well, before slamming the goblet back onto the table.

Zaynab looked at him, amazed. Such behavior was totally unlike Karim al Malina. Then she said, "Why have we come here, my lord?" She had not yet touched her wine.

"Tell me that you love me, Zaynab," he said suddenly. "I want to hear the words from your own sweet lips." His eyes bored into hers, pleading.

"My lord, you are mad!" she exclaimed. Her heart was

beating far too quickly. She attempted to turn away from him, lest he see the truth in her eyes.

He would not permit it, pulling her about, forcing her face up so he might look down into it, but she lowered her lashes to protect herself from his look. "Fate has decreed that we fall in love and then be separated forever," he said. "I love you, Zaynab, and you love me. Why will you not admit it?"

"Have you not taught me that a Love Slave does not become entangled emotionally with her master, my lord? The wine, I fear, has gone to your head. Come, and let us eat something," she begged him. Why was he doing this to her? Was it some sort of test? She must remain calm.

In answer Karim drew her tightly against him and said in a harsh voice, "*I love you, Zaynab.* I have not the right, and I should not be such a fool, but when has the heart ever been rational or prudent, my love?" His hand caressed her shining hair. "Allah has finally punished me. It is arrogant of any man to believe he might train another human creature in the arts of love."

"You have not trained me to love, my lord, you have taught me to give pleasure," she answered him quietly.

"Tell me you love me," he pleaded, his voice ragged with emotion.

"There is no future in such a love," she replied coldly. "Have you not made it clear from the beginning that I belong to the Caliph of Cordoba? I cannot be his Love Slave and be in love with you, Karim."

"And yet you are," he insisted, caressing her cheek.

"Do not do this to us," she begged him. His touch had wrecked her resolve. "If I love you, how can I bear to leave you in a month's time? If I love you, how can I live the rest of my life without you? If I love you, how can I belong to another man, Karim, my lord?" He was not drunk on the wine, and she knew it.

"Your body will belong to that man, but your heart will always belong to me," he responded. "I do not jest, nor do I test you, Zaynab, my beloved. I speak from the heart words I have no right to say. Words that I should have never uttered to you, yet I cannot help myself. My love for you has rendered me helpless to my own moves. I love you, and I shall love you through eternity itself."

She pulled angrily away from him. "And what good will this love you have for me do, Karim al Malina? I am not yours! I can never be yours! How dare you break my heart like this? Ohh, you are cruel! Cruel! I shall never forgive you!"

"Then you do love me!" he cried, triumphant.

She looked at him bleakly. Tears ran down her beautiful face. "Yes, damn you, I love you! Are you pleased? Is your vanity satisfied, my lord? I swore to myself that I should never say those words to you, but you have forced them from me. How can I now go to the caliph, knowing that I love you, and that you love me? What have you done to us, Karim? We will surely bring dishonor upon those who trusted us."

He drew her back into the circle of his embrace. "Nay, we will not," he told her. "We will do what we must. You will go to the caliph, and I will marry a little Berber girl named Hatiba; but before that happens, we will spend a month together here at Escape, just you and I. Whatever our fates after that, we will have a lifetime of love to remember and be comforted by, my beautiful Zaynab of the golden tresses. How could I let you go without knowing the truth? Without ever knowing love?"

"Perhaps it would have been easier if you had," she said low. "I do not know if I can be as noble and as brave as you, Karim. I am a simple girl from a primitive land. We Celts of Alba know but passion and vengeance in our lives. I thought there was little else, yet you have shown me beauty, and light, Karim al Malina, and a family that loves one another. If God would grant me but one thing, I should wish to belong to you for the rest of my days. To bear your sons and daughters. To become as your mother has become, content with my lot. But you would tell me that you love me, and force the same sentiments from me. Now I shall never be content, my lord. If my fate is to suffer the knowledge of your love, then yours must be to live with the knowledge that I shall never be happy once I have been parted from you. I might have been, Karim, but not now."

"You cannot be happy knowing my heart goes with you?" he said.

She shook her head. "I shall never be happy away from you."

"Ahh, Zaynab, what have I done to us!" he cried.

"For all my anger, Karim, I do not care," she replied. "I love you, and we have so little time left. Let us not spend it in recriminations. You have broken my heart, but I still adore you!" She wrapped her arms about his neck and kissed him passionately. "I will always adore you, through eternity itself!"

Lifting her up, he laid her upon the bed and gently undressed her. Then removing his own clothing, he lay by her side. Their hands touched, fingers intertwining. They stayed that way, silent, for some time, until finally raising himself up on one elbow, he bent his head to kiss her mouth. Her jewel-like eyes regarded him gravely, then they closed as she gave herself over to the sweetness of the moment. His hands touched her as they never had before, with an incredible and unbearable tenderness that left her aching for more.

He kissed each tear from her face, and cradled that face in his hand, his lips touching her lips, her cheeks, her shadowed eyelids.

Reaching up, she caressed the strong, handsome face, her fingers memorizing each curve, each line, each bit of him. What had she done that such joy and such pain should be given to her? Love was but a terrible misery. She would be glad when he brought her to Cordoba. Glad to be rid of this pain. Surely it would leave her in time, and she would concentrate on all she had been taught. She would be the most famed Love Slave ever known. It would be all she would have.

"I love you, my flower," he murmured in her ear, his breath warm and tickly. He nibbled upon the fleshy lobe.

Turning to face him, she melted, and it seemed as if the heart within her cracked. It wasn't fair! "And I love you, Karim al Malina," she told him. "Love me, my darling! Ohh, make love to me!"

He answered her cry, filling her with his passion until they both collapsed, entwined, and the new moon rose to lightly silver the lake outside their love bower, while a night bird sang its painfully sweet song.

Part III

AL-ANDALUS

A.D. 945

▦ _Chapter 9_

Abd-al Rahman, Caliph of Cordoba, lay alone in his great bed. Outside his windows the bright dawn was beginning to color the sky. The birds were already singing. Their songs always sounded better in late spring, he thought, than at any other time of the year. Perhaps it was because they were courting. Love made a difference in everything. He smiled. It had been some time since he had been in love. Several years in fact. He was ready for a new adventure, despite the fact that he had passed his fiftieth year.

He knew what they were all thinking. His favorite, Zahra, encouraged such thoughts. It suited her vanity to discourage his younger concubines. He was a father eighteen times over. He was a grandfather. Despite his amorous appetites, which, he had to admit, had eased somewhat over the last few years, he had reigned so long, people were beginning to think of him as an old man. Well, he wasn't! He had the hard body of a man thirty years his junior, and his hair was still reddish-blond, without a trace of gray. It was spring, and he was ready for a new love!

He stretched, breathing in the sweet morning air. _Today._ What was on his agenda today? Ah, yes, this was the day of the month when he was presented with gifts from grateful subjects, friends, and would-be friends. Mayhap there would be some pretty slave girls among his gifts. Mayhap one of those toothsome creatures would appeal to more than just his lust. It was dubious, but he could hope. Yes! He was ready for a new love.

The door to his bedchamber opened, and his body slave

entered. The day had officially begun. Without any urging, the caliph sprang from his bed and followed his usual morning routine. First he bathed. Then he ate sparingly: a dish of newly made yogurt, a cup of mint tea. Washing his hands and face again, he allowed his nails and his hair to be trimmed. Then he was dressed. Today he wore green and gold, the colors of the prophet—silk trousers, a plain brocade undertunic, a wide jeweled sash, and a bejeweled open coat with wide sleeves lined in cloth-of-gold. A gold dagger studded with emeralds was tucked into his sash. Dark felt boots were fitted upon his feet. A cloth-of-gold turban with a glittering diamond set in its front was placed upon his head. The caliph was now ready to receive his visitors and all the gifts that they would bring today.

His favorite, Zahra, came to wish him a good morning. She was a handsome woman in her late thirties, with beautiful chestnut-colored hair and silver-gray eyes. "Do not let the foreign missions tire you with all their boring talk, my lord. You must take care of yourself for the sake of us all. While I love our son, he will never be the ruler that you are, my dear lord." She smiled lovingly into his face.

The caliph felt a stab of annoyance. Zahra was a wonderful woman. He loved her, and respected her, but of late she could be extremely aggravating, especially when she persisted in treating him like some white-bearded old man. She had the same effect on him that a grain of sand had on an oyster. "I enjoy the foreign missions, my dear," he told her, "and who knows what unique gift shall come to me today. Perhaps a beautiful slave girl to entice and capture my heart." He smiled down into her face, and with satisfaction saw the pique in her eyes. He would not be an old doddard to please Zahra, or their son, Hakam.

Hakam. There was another difficulty. He was a wonderful young man, but he was more a scholar than a man who would one day be caliph. His interest in books and other literary pursuits was far greater than his interest in women. He had no children, but that was because he spent so little time in the company of his harem. Abd-al Rahman blamed Zahra for that. Her son's great intellect was her pride, and she had always encouraged him to study, saying he would have time for women later on, but there she had been wrong. There was never enough time for women in Hakam's life when there was a new book to be examined and read. Nevertheless, Prince Hakam had of late become more interested in ruling al-Andalus. The caliph put that interest down to his eldest son's realization that he had six eager, ambitious younger brothers. Still, father and son loved one another, and their relationship was a close one.

The caliph, in the company of his personal guard, made his way to the Hall of the Caliphate. It was a magnificent space with a high, domed ceiling held up by soaring columns of pink and blue marble. The walls and the ceiling were sheathed with sheets of beaten gold. In the center of the ceiling was a huge pearl that had been sent from Byzantium to the caliph by the emperor Leon. There were eight doors of ebony, ivory, and gold that gave entry to the hall. The doors were set between pillars of pure crystal.

In the middle of the floor was a large crystal laver of mercury from the caliph's mines at al-Madan. At the caliph's signal, slaves rocked the laver, and the chamber would be filled with shooting rays of light that gave the impression the room was floating in midair. It was a terrifying experience for the unprepared, and an incredible wonder to those who had experienced the effect before. To complete the beauty of the hall, magnificent brocades were hung between the columns, and fine carpets were laid upon the marble floors.

The morning passed pleasantly enough with diplomats and missions from various lands coming forward to present their credentials or proffer their gifts. There was nothing unusual among them, and Abd-al Rahman concealed his boredom. Prince Hakam and the caliph's favored physician, Hasdai ibn Shaprut, were by his side.

Hasdai ibn Shaprut, a Jew, was a great deal more than a medical adviser. He had come to the caliph's attention just two years ago by rediscovering a universal antidote for poison. Poison being a favorite weapon among assassins, this find was hailed gratefully by the rich and powerful. The caliph quickly discovered, however, that his new friend was also an excellent diplomat and negotiator. In al-Andalus a man's religion was no barrier to his advancement. Hasdai ibn Shaprut's elevation into the government was assured.

Abd-al Rahman sat cross-legged upon a wide bejeweled golden throne, made comfortable by the many scarlet satin cushions upon it. The throne was topped by a cloth-of-gold and silver-striped canopy. He yawned discreetly behind his hand as the new ambassador from Persia made his way out of the Hall of the Caliphate. The caliph had been sitting for close to three hours. There had not yet been any gift that attracted his interest, only the usual number of racing camels, slaves, jewels, and exotic animals for his zoo. His early morning enthusiasm had palled. Perhaps he would go hawking this afternoon on horseback.

Then the chamberlain announced, "My lord Caliph, a procession of gifts brought to you by Karim ibn Habib al Malina, from the merchant Donal Righ of Eire. These gifts are sent you in gratitude for your friendship."

The doors directly in front of the caliph opened with a flourish and a herd of elephants began to enter the room. Abd-al Rahman sat up, his blue eyes sparkling with interest. The elephants came two abreast, every animal escorted by a keeper garbed in blue and orange silks. Between each pair of pachyderms was slung a magnificent carved column of green agate. Twenty-four animals lumbered through the huge Hall of the Caliphate, their great hooves pressing into the carpets. At a signal from the head keeper, the beasts stopped, and raising their trunks, saluted the caliph with a strident bellow before moving on and out the other side of the chamber.

"Magnificent!" the caliph enthused, and his two companions agreed.

"What else can this procession offer, that can excel such a spectacle, I wonder?" Hasdai ibn Shaprut remarked. He was a tall, slender man in his early thirties, with warm amber eyes and dark hair. Like his master, he was clean-shaven.

"Indeed, my father, the exit cannot surely surpass the entrance," Prince Hakam said. He was close in age to the physician, and a serious young man with his mother's coloring.

"We shall see. We shall see," the caliph said.

The elephants were followed by slaves carrying twenty bolts of silk, each of a different color, which were unfurled before the ruler; three alabaster jars of rare ambergris; two caskets fashioned from ivory and gold, the first filled with loose pearls, the second with flowering bulbs; one hundred skins of red fox; one hundred skins of Siberian marten; ten white Arabian horses, caparisoned with gold bridles and brocaded saddles; five bricks of gold, and fifteen of silver; and two spotted hunting cats with gold collars on red leather leashes.

Lastly came a litter, escorted by Karim al Malina and Oma. It was carried to the foot of the caliph's throne, where a magnificent carpet was spread beneath it. The captain stepped forward and bowed low to Abd-al Rahman, as did the serving girl by his side.

"Great lord," Karim al Malina began, "a year ago I was entrusted with a commission from Donal Righ of Eire. I was to bring you these tokens of his deep respect and great esteem, in thanks for your kindness toward him and his family. I was also entrusted with the education and training of a girl, who is called Zaynab. I am the last of the Passion Masters here in al-Andalus who was trained in Samarkand." Karim stretched out his hand toward the litter's closed curtains. "My lord Caliph, may I present to you the Love Slave, Zaynab."

A slim white arm came forth from the litter, its delicate little hand placed in his.

The caliph and his two companions leaned forward with curiosity.

Oma gently pulled the curtains of the litter aside, and a swathed figure stepped forward. The litter was immediately moved back, so as not to obscure the caliph's view. The serving girl carefully removed the all-enveloping silk cloak from her mistress and stepped away.

Zaynab stood motionless, head bowed, as she had been taught. Her presentation garments were chosen to entice. She wore a skirt fashioned from strands of tiny seed pearls attached to a wide gold and bejeweled band that rested just below her hipbones, leaving her navel open to view. Her tight short-sleeved blouse was made of cloth-of-gold. It had a round neck with a charming keyhole opening bordered with pearls, cut to just below her breasts. She was barefoot, but a diaphanous veil of the softest blush silk covered her head, and another veil obscured her features.

Karim al Malina reached out and drew the veil from her head while Oma swiftly loosened her mistress's hair, allowing it to fall free, spreading it out fanlike that it might display to its best advantage.

Abd-al Rahman could hear his heart beating in his ears. Uncrossing his legs, he rose from his throne and moved down the two steps of the dais to where the girl stood. Unable to help himself, he took a strand of her pale gold hair between his fingers and felt the silky softness of it. Reaching out, he unfastened one side of her veil, tipped her chin up that he might see her face. Her pale lashes lay thick upon her pale cheek. "Raise your eyes to me, Zaynab," he said softly.

Obeying him, she looked into his face for the first time. He was not even a head taller than she, and was of stocky build. The deep blue eyes staring into her own were contemplative. She was almost relieved, but her beautiful face showed no emotion whatsoever.

The caliph was staggered by what he saw. She was probably the most beautiful woman he had ever seen. Her features were perfect: oval-shaped eyes; a straight nose neither too long, nor too short; high forehead and cheekbones. A lush mouth seemingly made for kisses. A square little chin that suggested a touch of stubbornness. Good! He disliked bland women. He smiled, pleased, wondering what her smile was like. Right now, he suspected, she was terrified, although she was too well mannered to show it. Gently, he refastened the veil, covering her face, and she lowered her eyes again. Slowly the caliph remounted his throne.

"Donal Righ has outdone himself, Karim al Malina," Abd-al Rahman said. "Remain the night here at Madinat al-Zahra as my guest. My chamberlain will see to your comfort. In the morning I will receive you in private and tell you whether the

Love Slave, Zaynab, pleases me. You will then convey a personal message to my friend, Donal Righ."

Karim al Malina bowed low to the caliph, and, dismissed, backed from the Hall of the Caliphate. For a single, swift moment his eyes met Zaynab's, and his heart cracked painfully. He would never see her again. Allah watch over you, my beloved, he called silently to her, but she was already being escorted from the hall.

Zaynab did not speak as she and Oma were led from the Hall of the Caliphate. There was nothing more to say. Her heart was broken, and she would never love again. It was far better that way. She might be young, but she had no illusions left any longer. Karim was gone from her life. Her very survival and that of Oma depended upon the goodwill of a blue-eyed man called Abd-al Rahman. He was not unattractive, she decided, but she had certainly never imagined that he would look quite like he did.

The caliph was not a tall man. Though she was considered tall for a woman, he was barely taller than she was. His garments, of course, had been magnificent. What lay beneath them she could not tell, except that he was a man with a solid build. His eyebrows had been reddish. Was his hair that shade too? She would eventually know, for when he had looked upon her, his frank gaze had told her that he desired her.

They were brought to the women's quarters of the palace, which was practically an entire building of itself.

"This slave woman and her servant were brought to the caliph as a gift this morning," her escort said to the eunuch at the door. Then the guardsman departed, his duty done.

"Come in, come in," the eunuch beckoned them. "I will get the Mistress of the Women. She will assign you and your serving wench bed space. Wait here," he told them, and bustled off.

Zaynab and Oma looked about them. The pillared hall with its several sparkling fountains was filled with women of all sizes, shapes, and colors. The cacophony of their voices made it seem like they had been set down into a huge cage of chattering birds.

"What? Another girl?" the Mistress of the Women grumbled as she arrived to look Zaynab over with a critical eye. "There are over four thousand females in this place now as it is. How am I to cram another one in, I ask you? Well, you're pretty enough, but the caliph is not a man in his youth any longer. I suspect you'll grow old and fat like so many of the others. Let me think where I can put you."

"I require my own apartment," Zaynab said quietly.

The Mistress of the Women, whose name was Walladah, gaped at the young woman, astounded, then she began to laugh. *"Your own apartment?* Hah! Hah! Hah! Are you some princess, then, who is to be given special attention? You'll be fortunate if I can find you bed space at all. An apartment? Hah! Hah! Hah!"

"Lady," Zaynab said quietly, but firmly, "I am not some Galacian or Basque girl whose hair has been dyed. I am not a fearful virgin hoping to gain my master's favor. I am Zaynab, the Love Slave, trained by the great Passion Master, Karim ibn Habib al Malina. I am to be housed according to my station. If you doubt my word, I suggest that you send to the caliph for his wishes in the matter. I will abide by them and offer no further complaint."

Walladah struggled to make a decision. The well-being of the women of the harem was her duty. She was a distant cousin of the caliph, a woman widowed young, for whom no one else had asked. Only her family ties had gained her so powerful a position in Abd-al Rahman's household. It had also gained her riches and respect. She was not anxious to lose all she had attained.

"You must decide, lady," Zaynab pressed her gently. "The slaves will soon be here with my possessions. I have several trunks, and jewel cases that must be given a safe haven. I cannot have common concubines and their servants riffling through my garments. It is absolutely unthinkable. Remember who we serve, lady. I have been sent here for but one purpose. To please my lord, the caliph. I cannot do that if I have no place to entertain him, or if my personal possessions are stolen away by light-fingered females of undetermined heritage."

Walladah looked at Zaynab closely. The young woman before her was incredibly beautiful, and very self-assured, yet she was polite. A trifle haughty perhaps, but polite. "Well," the Mistress of the Women allowed, "perhaps I could find a small apartment for you, but if you do not find favor with the caliph quickly, you shall find yourself sharing a sleeping mat with your servant."

Zaynab laughed as if such a thing were impossible, and then she replied to the Mistress of the Women, "My apartment must have a little garden of its own. I need my privacy when I take the air."

Walladah swallowed her outrage. The cheek of the wench! But then, she had to admit that this was no ordinary slave. Still, her position necessitated that she maintain a certain control. "I have just the apartment for you, my lady Zaynab," she told her. "If you and your servant will follow me, please." She hurried off with the two young women behind her. The apartment she would put this girl in was at the absolute far end of the harem. It had a tiny scrap of a garden, but the garden wall was shared with the caliph's zoo. The girl would have what she had requested, but it would hardly be choice. Later, if she gained real favor with the caliph, there would be time to find a better accommodation. *If.*

Oma gasped with outrage as Walladah opened the double doors to the apartment. How dare this woman insult her mistress so? She was about to voice her opinion of this affront to Zaynab when her mistress placed a warning hand on her arm and spoke for herself.

"It is small, Lady Walladah, but I believe it can be made quite comfortable. I shall remember your *kindness.*"

The Mistress of the Women felt a momentary sense of discomfort at Zaynab's words. "I will send a cleaning woman at once, lady."

"Excellent," Zaynab purred. "I shall want to see the eunuchs available for my service as soon as possible. I shall also need to bathe soon. The caliph will desire my presence tonight."

Walladah hurried off, amazed that so young a girl could

have such presence and could have nonplused her so. She would do what she had to do to make this Zaynab comfortable. Then she would report to the lady Zahra, the caliph's favorite wife. That lady would certainly want to know all she could regarding this new creature.

"If she had sent us back to Alcazaba Malina," Oma huffed, "we could be no farther away from the center of things here. Two rooms, and neither of them big enough to swing a cat in, I might add."

Zaynab laughed, closing the doors behind them. "It is better than being assigned a bed space in the harem sleeping quarters amid a group of other women who would undoubtedly steal everything we have," she said. "These quarters may be small, but they give us status and privacy. We will turn them into an exquisite jewel box to house a perfect jewel," she finished with a chuckle.

Oma looked about her. "Well," she said, "I suppose once the dust is removed and we put our things about, it will be habitable. Let's see what we have for a garden."

They went outside to find a small square garden with a round marble pond in its center. A bronze lily rose from the middle, to spray a fine mist of water into the air. There were no plantings of any kind, although the beds had been dug for them.

"Roses, lilies, and nicotiana," Zaynab said. "And sweet herbs as well. I think the pond should have real water lilies too, don't you, Oma? And we'll perfume the water to make the effect even lusher."

The cleaning woman came, and shortly the two rooms were spotless.

Walladah returned, approved their efforts, and then said to Zaynab, "What furniture will you require, my lady?"

"Oma knows, and will go with you to select it," Zaynab said sweetly. "Where are the eunuchs for me to choose among?"

"They await outside, lady. Shall I have them come in?" Walladah responded, a little smile touching the corners of her mouth. She had already spoken to Lady Zahra. They had picked the eunuchs themselves. Only one was really suitable. The rest were insignificant. This Zaynab, with her youthful pride, would be certain to choose the one they wanted her to pick. Walladah opened the doors and commanded the six eunuchs to come in. "Here are the candidates I have chosen for you, lady," she said. "Which of them will you have?"

Zaynab looked at the six before her. Two were elderly. One was of middle years and looked half-witted. One was very young. Another was enormous in girth and looked half asleep. The sixth was a dignified dark-skinned man. Five were so eminently unsuitable that Zaynab knew it was this eunuch she was expected to take into her service. He would undoubtedly be a spy for Walladah. She contemplated the six. Among them was a fair-skinned boy with dark hair who looked nervous and wretchedly unhappy all at the same time. She pointed an imperious finger at him.

"I want him," she said in a tone that brooked no interference.

"Lady," Walladah protested, "he is too young for such responsibility! Choose someone else."

"Are you saying that you brought me someone unsuitable?" Zaynab demanded. "I choose this young eunuch because he will bend to my ways easier than any of the others." She turned to the boy. "What is your name?"

"Naja, my lady," the boy told her.

"He has no influence among the other eunuchs," Walladah protested. "He will be of absolutely no use to you, Lady Zaynab."

"It is not necessary that he have influence," Zaynab said blandly. "When I gain favor with our lord the caliph, then Naja will gain influence through me, Lady Walladah. Now, if you would go with Oma and allow her to choose my furnishings . . ."

Defeated, the Mistress of the Women retired, taking the five rejected eunuchs with her. With a grin and a wink at her mistress, Oma followed along.

When they were alone, Zaynab told Naja, "You may trust me when I tell you that I shall become the caliph's favorite. I am no mere concubine, but a Love Slave. Do you know the difference?"

"Yes, my lady," the boy said.

"Walladah wanted me to choose the tall dark man, who is undoubtedly her spy. I chose you instead because I expect total loyalty from you, Naja. If I should ever discover that you have betrayed me, I will see you die a most horrible death, and no one will be able to protect you from my wrath. Do you believe me?"

"Yes, lady," the boy replied. Then he said, "Nasr, the one they wanted you to choose, spies for the lady Zahra, not Walladah, although that one is also in her debt."

Zaynab nodded. So the caliph's favorite wife was already aware of her arrival. She would be a formidable opponent, but perhaps she need not be. They might never be friends, but they did not have to be enemies. "The lady Zahra wastes her time spying on me," Zaynab told Naja. "I do not wish to replace her in the caliph's affections. Indeed, I could not possibly do so. Replace a woman for whom a city has been built and named?" Zaynab laughed. "I only wish to please the caliph. That is what I have been trained to do: to give pleasure." Although she hoped to build a certain loyalty in Naja, she knew that he, like all the others, could be bribed by a more powerful personage. Whatever he would repeat must soothe rather than worry the lady Zahra.

Oma returned, followed by several slaves carrying the furniture she had chosen for her mistress. "That old Walladah," she told Zaynab, "would have had me take the most dreadful furnishings. Fortunately, I prevailed, my lady." Hearing a noise behind her, she whirled about, saying, "Be careful with that divan! Put it there, now." She turned back to her mistress. "I thought the caliph should have something comfortable to sit on when we entertain him."

Oma had found some lovely pieces in the harem storehouse. The divan was covered in peacock-blue silk. Its wooden legs were painted with gold. She had obtained several small tables, both round and square. One was of polished ebony inlaid with mother-of-pearl, another an engraved brass circle set upon ivory legs, a third made of blue and white tiles. Several slaves were laden down with silk pillows in shades of emerald, sapphire, and ruby. There was a wonderful standing greenish bronze lamp, several hanging lamps with amber glass inserts, and a number of polished brass lamps for the tables. There was a single chair of carved wood with a leather seat, and several charcoal braziers to provide heat on damp or chilly days. The bedchamber needed no furnishings. A dais for Zaynab's bedding was already in place, and her clothes chests would take up the rest of the room. There was a small alcove off the bedchamber, where Oma would spread her bed mat. Naja would sleep outside of his lady's door.

Finally they were alone, and Oma began to unpack her lady's chests. "What will you wear?" she asked her.

"Something simple," Zaynab answered. "But first I must bathe. Naja, are the baths available at any time?"

"Yes, lady, but the ladies of the harem usually bathe in the morning. It is their gossiping time."

"I bathe twice daily," Zaynab informed him. "In the morning and in the late afternoon. I require the services of the masseuse in the afternoon each day. My scent is gardenia. I use no other. See the bath attendants are so informed." She loosened the hip band of her skirt, and it fell to the floor with a rattle. Stepping away from the pearl-encrusted garment, she undid her blouse and pulled it off. "Oma, a robe, please." She handed the blouse to Naja as Oma helped her mistress into a white silk garment. "Take me to the baths, Naja," Zaynab commanded him.

The young eunuch passed the blouse to Oma and then led his new mistress from her apartments. As they hurried through the harem, Zaynab was the curious object of all eyes. She said nothing, but stared straight ahead, head held high. Walladah, she suspected, was already spreading tales. When they reached their destination, Naja introduced Zaynab to the Mistress of the Baths, who was called Obana.

"Well," Obana said bluntly, "remove your garment, and let's see what we have to work with." Obana was a person of great importance in the harem hierarchy, and her only loyalties were to the caliph. She could not be bribed, nor did she fear any of the women, including Zahra. A maiden's good grooming and radiant beauty reflected well upon Obana, particularly if the caliph was pleased, *and if he was*, Obana was usually rewarded by her generous master. Gaining her favor was paramount to success with Abd-al Rahman.

Naja whisked the silk robe from Zaynab, and she stood quietly under Obana's critical eye.

"Let me see your hands, lady." Carefully Obana examined the girl's hands, turning them over, running her strong fingers along Zaynab's delicate digits. "Your feet, one at a time." Zaynab patiently obeyed. "Open your mouth." She peered in at the girl's strong white teeth and sniffed hard. "Good teeth, no rot, sweet breath," was her comment. Swiftly she ran her hands over Zaynab's body. There was nothing lewd or licentious in the gesture. Zaynab might have been a fine mare being examined by a prospective owner. "Your skin is wonderfully soft and firm. You are not one of the typical harem beauties who will grow fat with age." She felt a lock of her subject's hair. "It's like thistledown, but then you know that. Do you use lemon on your hair to encourage its lights?"

"Yes, my lady Obana. I was so taught," Zaynab said in a soft voice. Her look was direct, her expression pleasant without being familiar.

"Excellent!" Obana approved. "Well, lady, I have never seen a more beautiful girl come into this harem. You are a Love Slave, the gossip says. Is it so?"

"Yes, my lady Obana. The gossip in this instance is correct," Zaynab answered, unable to keep the laughter from her voice.

Obana chuckled herself. "They are already saying much about you. Considering you entered Madinat al-Zahra but a short time ago, I find it amazing all that is said about you."

"I am but today's diversion, my lady Obana. Tomorrow the women of the harem will have something else to amuse them," Zaynab said with a small smile.

"Well, to business," Obana said briskly, nodding. "When did you last bathe, my lady?"

"This morning," Zaynab replied. "It is my custom to bathe twice daily. Naja knows my preferences and will tell your assistants."

"Excellent!" Obana replied, but then she personally oversaw

the Love Slave's ablutions. This one would definitely find favor with the caliph. For how long, she could not predict, but for now it was a certainty. She did not envy the lady Zahra and the lady Tarub, the master's two favorite wives. They truly loved their husband, and to be supplanted, even for a brief time, by so very young and fair a creature as this Zaynab, must be galling. Yet neither of those ladies ever showed their displeasure when their lord and master strayed into greener pastures. They were too well mannered. They did not have to fear being replaced in their husband's esteem, for their positions were secure by virtue of their sons and their long association with Abd-al Rahman.

Bathed, and massaged, her fingernails and toenails neatly pared, Zaynab was reclothed in her silk robe. Thanking the lady Obana, she turned to go, but suddenly Naja gasped softly, and bowing low, stepped aside, allowing the lady Zahra to enter the chamber. Zaynab fell to her knees, her head bowed.

A tiny smile of amusement touched Lady Zahra's lips. "It is not necessary for you to kneel to me, Lady Zaynab. Kneel only to our lord and master, Abd-al Rahman al Nasir l'il Din Allah, the great and victorious Caliph of al-Andalus."

Zaynab rose immediately. "I but do honor the lady Zahra, she who holds the caliph's heart, mother of his heir, for whom this city was named. I am neither meek nor humble, madame, but your status demands that I behave in a mannerly fashion, lest I shame he who trained me and he who sent me to the caliph in gratitude for his many kindnesses."

Zahra laughed a tinkling laugh. "You are clever," she said. "That is good. You will amuse my husband. He needs a new diversion, for he grows easily bored of late. Please him as long as you can, Zaynab." Then the lady Zahra turned about and departed the same way she came.

Well, well, the Mistress of the Baths thought to herself. The lady Zahra is afraid of this one. She is concerned enough to beard the girl on her first day in the harem. She has never been afraid of any of the others. Why this one? It is interesting. Yes, I shall watch this drama unfold about me with pleasure.

Zaynab walked the width and the length of the harem back

to her quarters. The other women watched her openly now; some with simple interest, some with envy, some bitterly, for her beauty was not to be denied and would draw the caliph's attention away from them.

When she was safely within her little apartment, Zaynab collapsed upon the divan. "I have met the lady Zahra," she announced to Oma. "She is already jealous of me, and so are the others. I could feel their hatred reaching out to score me as I returned from the baths."

Oma had brewed mint tea on one of the little braziers. She pressed a small porcelain cup into her mistress's hands. "Drink. You need your strength, my dear lady. It has been a hard day, and it is not over yet. Naja, we have not eaten since dawn. My lady needs food."

"I will fetch it for you," he said eagerly.

"Naja." Zaynab spoke.

"Yes, lady?"

"I have told you that I will destroy you if you ever betray me, but if you are loyal to me, your rewards will be great and many," she told him. "You were not, I suspect, born a slave, any more than I was. You are fortunate to have survived your surgery."

He nodded. "I am a Rumi from the Adriatic coast," he told her. "I was taken five years ago when I was twelve. My two brothers died of the operation. The slaves said I was the fortunate one to have escaped the jaws of death. My name means deliverance. I came into this household two years ago. I know why you chose me from among the others, but in doing so, lady, you have raised me in rank. One has but to look at you to know that the caliph will love you. Your success is mine as well. I will serve you with loyalty."

"Any fool can attract a man's attention," Zaynab said. "It is the clever woman who keeps it, Naja. Do you understand me?"

He smiled for the first time in her presence. "I will not fail you, lady," he promised her and hurried off to find them food.

"Can we trust him, I wonder?" Oma said, her amber eyes contemplative. "He's no Mustafa, is he?"

"He will serve me loyally as long as my interests dinna conflict with those of Lady Zahra," Zaynab said, switching to their native tongue. "That great lady is the real power here in the harem, nae the caliph, Oma. We must nae allow ourselves to forget it. Lady Zahra hae been wi' the caliph for many years, and she hae his love, and his trust. If I am fortunate, I will bind him to me for a wee time, and perhaps even bear him a bairn, but the lady Zahra will always be queen in this place. Naja will serve me well, but if called to choose between us, he will side wi' the lady Zahra. Guard yer tongue around him if ye can."

"Do ye think the caliph will visit ye tonight, my lady?" Oma wondered aloud. "He be a braw gentleman, I'm thinking."

"He will come," Zaynab said with certainty. "I could see the interest in his eyes when he unveiled me earlier. Then, in the baths when I met the lady Zahra, she told me that the caliph is bored and needs a new diversion. She said it to hurt me, of course. To reassure herself that she will always be first in his heart, and I but a passing fancy."

" 'Twas cruel, lady," Oma sympathized.

" 'Tis nae but the truth, my wee Oma. 'Tis unlikely this mighty man will fall in love wi' me forever, but if I can gain his favor long enough to hae a bairn of my own, then we shall always be safe here, and nae lonely ever again. To gain those ends I will do what I must."

Naja returned, bearing a tray. Upon it was a bowl of rice with pieces of capon breast in it. A second bowl held creamy yogurt with freshly peeled green grapes. There was a piece of warm flat bread and a dish of fresh fruit. Carefully he placed his burden upon the brass table where Zaynab and Oma had seated themselves. Taking a silver spoon from his robes, he dipped it first into the rice and chicken dish, tasting it, and then into the yogurt, which he also tasted. Then, nodding with satisfaction, he gave them each a spoon with which to eat from the communal bowls.

"I will taste everything for you, my lady Zaynab," Naja said. "Poison is a favorite weapon here in the harem. The bread I took myself as it came from the ovens, and the fruit I personally chose, but the kitchen slaves dished up the bowls. We cannot be too trusting, nor can we be too careful. Nonetheless, should someone or something slip beneath our guard, Hasdai ibn Shaprut, the caliph's favorite physician, has rediscovered a universal cure for all poisons. It is unlikely you would die, but you could be wretchedly uncomfortable and your innards scarred."

Zaynab swallowed hard. This was not something Karim had dwelled upon during her education. *Karim.* She had vowed never to say his name again, or even think of him, yet the sun had not even set and her thoughts were turning to him. How wonderful that last month at Escape had been. It was just the two of them. Each day food had appeared as if by magic. The wine decanter had been kept filled. They had talked, and made love, and walked in the hills together. She had wanted it to go on forever. Knowing it could not, she wished for death instead, but that did not come either. The choice, of course, had been hers; but Zaynab knew she was not a silly, weak fool like the Love Slave Leila had been. There was life, and there was death. Living was the harder, stronger choice, and she wanted to live even if she could not have Karim. A strong streak of common sense ran in her veins. No man, not even Karim, was worth her life. She would always love him, but her loyalty would be to this caliph who was to be her master.

Still, Zaynab sighed deeply, remembering. In the end she and Karim had returned to the villa, and the same litter that had brought her along the coast road from Alcazaba Malina returned her to *I'timad*. They had sailed across the Gulf of Cadiz into the mouth of the Guadalquivir, and up the river to Cordoba. He had not touched her since they had left Escape. Nor would he ever again, Zaynab thought sadly. Then she shook herself impatiently. It was over. She had another new life, and with luck, one day she might find happiness again.

Reaching out, she took a fruit from the bowl and bit into it. The sweet juice trickled down her chin. "What is it?" she asked Naja. "I like it."

"It is a plum, lady. Do you not have plums in your land?"

"Nay, there are no plums in Alba. We have apples, and some pears, but no other fruits," she explained.

The meal finished and cleared away, Naja brought them a bowl of scented water with which to wash their hands.

Zaynab stood up. "I must rest now," she told them, and disappeared into her bedchamber.

"Have you chosen her garments for tonight, in case the caliph should come to her?" Naja asked Oma.

The girl nodded. "She is so beautiful, she needs little adornment, I think. Just a silk caftan, her hair scented and loose about her. I have chosen a caftan the color of her eyes."

"Perfect," Naja agreed.

There was a knock upon the door, and the young eunuch hurried to open it. Another eunuch stood outside. Wordlessly, he handed Naja a silken packet, and turning, departed. Naja could scarcely contain himself as he handed it to Oma.

"What is it?" she asked him.

"A gift from the caliph, Oma! It means that our master will certainly come to her tonight. She has already found first favor with him. Such a thing is unheard of! No woman has ever found favor so quickly! She will be the great love of his old age. I sense it!" the eunuch said excitedly.

Open, the packet revealed a large and absolutely flawless round pink pearl.

Naja's dark eyes met Oma's meaningfully.

※ *Chapter 10*

*T*here was no knock upon the door. It simply opened, and the caliph entered the room. Jumping up, Oma and Naja bowed low.

"Where is the lady Zaynab?" the caliph asked politely.

"She is in her private chamber, my lord," Oma said softly, her eyes lowered.

The caliph nodded in answer. Opening the door of the bedchamber, he passed through.

She had heard him in the outer room. Now she bowed silently, patiently awaiting his command. He closed the door behind him and stared at her for a long moment. Zaynab did not move. Indeed she was barely breathing, for she suddenly realized that she was a little frightened, although her face showed no emotion whatsoever. She was frozen like a statue.

"I thought that I had imagined your astounding beauty," he finally said, breaking the silence between them, "but you are indeed real, Zaynab. Disrobe for me now. Those tantalizing little glimpses of your body this morning in that fetching costume you wore have made me eager to see all of you."

His tone was demanding, as if he were struggling to contain his impatience for her. The look on his face was imperious. He was obviously a man used to immediate obedience. Then, as if to put her at her ease, he smiled a quick smile at her. His teeth were square, even, and white. His hair, without the turban, was indeed a reddish-blond; the eyes beneath the sandy lashes a deep blue.

How strange, she thought. She had assumed before coming here that Moors were all dark-haired, dark-eyed men, yet it seemed they were not. Her fingers reached up to undo the tiny pearl buttons on her caftan. One by one she unfastened them, her eyes never leaving his. The last button slipped its silken loop. The caftan was open to the navel. The caliph's gaze was mesmerizing, and she still could not breathe.

Before she might shrug the garment from her, he reached out, easily parting the twin halves of the caftan and sliding it over her shoulders. It fell to the floor with a small hiss of silk. Abd-al Rahman stepped back a pace and let his deep blue eyes wander the lush curves of her body. "Where," he said softly, "in the name of all the seven djinns did Donal Righ ever find a creature as magnificent as you?"

"I was brought to him by a Norseman," Zaynab replied, amazed that she could actually speak again. "He raided the convent in which I had been placed."

"You were a Christian nun?" His eyes feasted upon her breasts, and it was all he could do not to bury his face between them.

"Nay, my lord. I was to be, but I had only arrived that same day," Zaynab explained.

"What cruel, unseeing, unfeeling man could place so beautiful a maiden within a convent's high walls?" the caliph demanded half-angrily. "You were not meant to be incarcerated, a dry virgin, for the rest of your days. Praise be to Allah that my old friend, Donal Righ, found you!"

Zaynab laughed at his ardent opinion. She could not help herself. He was certainly a passionate man. "I have a twin sister, my lord," she explained. "We are identical, but she is the elder. Our father died before our birth. We were his only legal offspring. It was decided that Gruoch would wed a neighboring lord's heir, and that I would be sent to the convent. The decision was made on the day we were born. Neither of us had any say in our fates."

"Could not a husband be found for you as well?" the caliph wondered. Allah, her hair was incredible. He wanted to feel its softness on his naked body.

"A husband for me would have caused difficulty. He would have wanted half of our father's land, my lord. The neighboring lord wanted it all for his heir and his kindred. I cannot fault him. Our two families had feuded for years. My sister's marriage put an end to the warring. There was no other place for me but in a convent," Zaynab finished.

"Your place is here in my arms," the caliph said firmly. "You belong to me, and me alone, my beauty!" Reaching out, he drew her to him. Then, taking her chin between his thumb and his forefinger, he kissed her mouth, exploring its texture, its firmness, the special taste of her. His eyes swam with a look of melting lust as he ran the very tip of his tongue across her lips. "Ummmmm, you are delicious," he declared, "and you are meant for nothing but pure pleasure. 'Tis why Allah created you, Zaynab. Your fate is to pleasure me, and be pleasured in return. I am an excellent lover, as you will shortly learn." With one hand he began to knead her left breast gently. "I am half in love with you already," he told her. "You excite my body as it has not been excited in many a year. My heart calls out to yours, Zaynab." His hand now moved to caress her face, even as his low voice caressed her rebellious spirit. "Are you afraid of me, my exquisite one? You need not be, for your sweet surrender to my will guarantees you my favor."

"I am afraid of your power, my lord," she admitted, "but I do not think I am afraid of you."

"You are wise to know the difference," he replied, smiling. He fastened his hands firmly about her waist and lifted her up onto the bed. Then stepping back, he observed her once more. "Turn for me, Zaynab," he said.

Slowly she revolved, giving him ample time to view her naked form. She was amazed at how very controlled he was with her.

He ran a hand over her pretty posterior. "You have a bottom like a perfect little peach," he complimented her. "Has the maidenhead between its halves been plundered yet?" His hand lingered, caressing the silken skin, fondling her.

"The Passion Master felt that was your privilege, my lord," she told him, "but I have been prepared to receive you." Zaynab strove with all her might to keep from shuddering. There was something sinister in the fingers now trailing over her flesh.

"Good!" he responded. "Now turn back to me, my lovely," and when she had, he said, "I know you are trained to give me pleasure far greater than that of a mere concubine, but tonight I would simply have you be a woman. Tonight I will make love to you. You will obey my every command, and together we will find pleasure." He lifted her down from the bed.

"You will find no woman more obedient or eager to please you than I am, my lord," Zaynab promised him. She felt foolish at her earlier nervousness. The caliph was no monster. He was really quite nice, and the fact that he was a stranger to her could make no difference. She was not just his personal possession. *She was a Love Slave, and she knew her duty.*

He quickly disrobed, pulling his caftan off and letting it drop to the floor next to her garment. Then he stepped back, giving her the same vantage point that he had previously had. "You may look at me," he told her. "A woman should know her master's body even as he knows hers."

Her face was grave as she examined him. Her earlier impression had been correct. He was not slender like Karim, but rather stocky. Still, he was not fat, and he was very well muscled. She knew his age to be over fifty. Yet the body before her was not what she would have imagined that of an older man to be. It was attractive and firm. He was fair of skin, but devoid of body hair. His torso was short, his length in his shapely legs. His male parts seemed well formed and of a good size. Zaynab raised her eyes back to his again. "You are most pleasing, my lord," she complimented him.

"Men's bodies," he told her, amused, "have not the exquisite beauty of women's, my lovely. Still, when put together, they usually fit well." Reaching out, he drew her back into his arms, moving to fondle her breasts with the eagerness of a young boy with his first maid.

Zaynab closed her eyes a moment. His touch was distinctly different from Karim's, but the thought, rather than distressing her, sobered her. The fact that she and her Passion Master had fallen in love was unfortunate, but they had both known all along such a love could not end happily. She would not disgrace him by behaving badly with the caliph. She must be a credit to Karim, *and* it was he who had taught her to give herself over to the pleasure of man's passion. For all their sakes, she had to do it. She was not some silly virgin with foolish dreams of true love.

She concentrated upon the hands now palpating her flesh. They were firm, a trifle insistent perhaps, yet gentle. His mouth met hers, his deep kiss warm and sensual, sending a thrill down her spine. She could not help but respond, kissing him back. He was a stranger, yet he was able to arouse her, which she had not thought really possible. There were obviously things Karim had not taught her; things she would discover for herself.

She threw her head back, and his lips followed the graceful line of her throat. She felt the warm wetness of his tongue succeeding the feathery touches of his kisses. She murmured, satisfied, as his mouth found the swell of her young breasts. He kissed and licked the perfumed skin, the scent of gardenias permeating his senses, heightening his desire for her. His mouth closed over a coral-tipped nipple, sucking hard on it, and her body arced in his possessive embrace. He bit down lightly on the nipple. Zaynab cried out softly, her senses now whirling, caught up in the strengthening erotic loveplay between them.

"Open your eyes," he commanded, standing straight again. His look was passionate as he stared directly into her gaze. He traced his fingers over her half-open lips, suggestively pushing his forefinger deep into her mouth. She sucked slowly upon it, her tongue revolving sinuously about the finger, her breasts pressed lightly against his smooth chest.

"You have eyes like aquamarines," he said softly. "A man would die for such eyes." Drawing his finger from her mouth, he ran it down the valley between her breasts. Then, hands upon her slim shoulders, he pushed her down upon her knees before him.

She knew what was expected. Taking him within the warm cavity of her mouth, she began to suckle upon him. His sharp intake of breath told her she was pleasing him. His fingers dug into her head, kneading the scalp with growing urgency as he began to burgeon. She fondled his pouch in her hand, cupping it, squeezing it gently. With a single finger of that hand she reached beneath him, seeking for a certain spot, finding it, pressing up upon it. He groaned, then shuddered as a sharp stab of desire slammed into him. Her clever little tongue encircled the ruby head of his manhood, coaxing his desire into full flower.

"Cease!" he groaned, pulling her to her feet again. "You are going to kill me with delight, Zaynab. What a naughty little witch you are, my lovely!" He was swollen with burning lust, but he yet managed to control his need to possess his new toy. He would not take her too quickly the first time. He wanted to test her mettle. If he died, it would be from pleasure.

"Sit," he said. When she had settled herself upon the edge of the bed, he knelt down. Taking her foot in his hand, he studied it intently. It was small and narrow, each toe beautifully shaped, the nails dainty and round.

Enfolding the little foot in his hand, he raised it to his lips and kissed it. He ran his tongue along the high arch, then sucked upon each tiny toe. Next he pressed slow, hot kisses from her ankle up her leg to her inner thigh. Her other foot and leg received equal treatment. She shivered with delight beneath his skillful mouth.

"You have love balls?" he asked her, and when she nodded, he said, "Fetch them, my lovely."

Reaching out to the gold basket by the bedside, Zaynab drew the velvet pouch forth and handed it to the caliph. Opening it, he spilled the little silver orbs into his hand, rolling them about his palm, smiling with satisfaction.

"They are nicely weighted," he noted. "Open yourself to me now." She spread herself before his avid gaze, and he slowly inserted the balls, one by one, pushing them deep into her love canal with a long, expert finger. Bending forward, he then spread her nether lips, staring with delight at the moist coral flesh beneath his gaze. His tongue snaked out to touch her little jewel.

"Ummmmm," she murmured, squirming edgily at the contact. Within her the silver balls hit together at the slight movement. Zaynab gasped. The sensation was incredibly intense, almost painful. Karim had demonstrated the balls once. She had forgotten the sweet torture that they could inflict upon a woman.

The caliph's tongue began to probe her in earnest. It lapped over the interior of her soft, silky nether lips; it worried at the sentient little badge of her sex until she thought she would die of the pure pleasure he was provoking. She was half sobbing as again and again the silver balls butted against one another, sending the painfully sweet sensation thrilling through her writhing body.

Finally she could take no more. *"Please!"* she pleaded to him.

Without a word he withdrew the wicked little instruments of torture from her body. Then holding her legs apart, he leaned forward once more, his tongue pushing into her passage, withdrawing, pushing forward again. She cried out with pleasure. Her love juices were flowing generously when he pulled himself up and over her and kissed her deeply, his tongue transferring the taste of her own musk into her mouth. His lips were everywhere on her body: the hollow of her throat, her belly, her lips again. She was wet with the waves of heat he was creating in her.

Zaynab was suffocating with her desire. She clung to Abd-al Rahman, feeling the hardness of his masculine body against the yielding softness of her female body. They had somehow in their love battle managed to gain the full area of the bed. Now the caliph positioned himself between his eager lover's outstretched thighs. He smiled as the girl beneath him whimpered her hunger, rubbing the tip of his manhood against her little jewel.

"Look at me," he growled low. "I would capture your soul when I mate with you. *Look at me, Zaynab!"*

She was half mad with passion, but if she let him overwhelm her now, she would fail with him. She would be just another concubine. Opening her eyes, she gazed meltingly at him. "What a lover you are, my lord!" she murmured huskily at him. "Do not keep me waiting any longer. Sheathe yourself within me! Make me ache with the pleasure that I know only you can give me!'"

Her words sent a thrill of excitement down his spine, and he thrust deep into her. She was hot, and tight. He groaned. "Ahh, Zaynab, you will surely kill me with delight!" He began to move upon her. She was wonderful, wrapping her legs about him, taking his face between her two little hands, clinging to him desperately as if she would perish if she let go.

"You are a stallion, my lord," she half sobbed. "Take me! Punish me with pleasure! *I am yours!*"

His lust was inexhaustible. It had not happened to him in years. Again and again and again he pushed into her eager body, but he could not find his release, though she certainly found hers, not once but twice. Finally he withdrew from her, saying, "Turn your body and assume the opposite stance, my lovely. I need your other maidenhead."

Her compliance was immediate. He saw no reluctance in her at all, but she dreaded what was to come. She hated this form of lovemaking. She had hated it when Karim had slowly pushed the ivory dildo into her. She hated it now. She had hoped never to be used in this fashion. In the future, she would try to find a way to avoid it if at all possible. Pulling her knees up beneath her, she arched her back, elevating her bottom for him.

He was at her in a moment, his hands pulling the cheeks of her posterior apart, his manhood pushing against the tight little rosebud of her fundament. *Pushing. Pushing.* And then it gave way. The head of his weapon gained a slight entry. His hands tightened about her hips, holding her steady as he thrust hard, ignoring her cry of pain, groaning with his own pleasure. She was incredibly tight. Tighter than any he had ever known. He pressed on, withdrawing slightly, pressing steadily forward again and yet again until finally he was fully engaged within her. She felt him throbbing, and at that very moment his crisis came.

Though his seed fell on barren ground, he sighed with relief at his release. "Ahhhh," he groaned, and slowly withdrew from her.

After taking a few minutes to recover herself, Zaynab arose from the bed. Going to the door, she opened it and gave swift orders to her two servants outside. She returned to the caliph's side with a silver ewer of scented water and several love cloths. He lay sprawled, utterly exhausted, before her. Tenderly, she bathed him, and then herself, clean of any evidence of their passion. Removing the basin, she crept back into the bed next to him.

His arms tightened about her, drawing her back into his embrace. His hand caressed her golden hair. "I will try never to use you in that fashion again. I could sense you did not like it, but tonight there was no other way for me, my lovely Zaynab. I cannot remember having ever been so aroused in my entire life by any woman as I was aroused by you a few moments ago. You are magic. You have brought me back my youth, and I quite enjoy it."

"I am your slave, my lord Abd-al Rahman. *Your Love Slave.* I will never refuse your passion no matter the form it takes," she told him proudly. "I am not some weak little concubine. I have been trained to both give and to receive the ultimate in pleasure." She would never admit to him that she had hated his perverse way of passion. It would only shame Karim. A Love Slave feared none of passion's roads. She willingly traveled them all.

"Fetch me some wine, my lovely," he ordered her.

She left the cradle of his arms, and went to the single small table she had allowed to be placed in the room. On it were several decanters. Two were of wine, but the third was filled with the restorative that Karim had given her. Pouring a few drops of it into a silver cup, she filled the rest of the vessel with sweet red wine and brought it to the caliph. "There, my lord, drink, and be revived." He quaffed the cup quickly down, shaking his head at her offer of more.

"I know I am to obey you in everything, but will you let me relax you now in my own special way?" she asked him with a small smile.

The edge had been taken off his lust. The wine was helping

to mellow him. He nodded his permission, lying back amid the pillows of the bed.

Zaynab reached into her gold basket and drew out an alabaster jar. Setting it among the bedclothes where she could reach it, she straddled him, and opening the jar, scooped a handful of pink cream from within. Rubbing her two hands together, she then smoothed them over the caliph's torso with a delicate, sensuous touch.

"It has your scent," he noted, amused.

"Do you mind?" she replied, making teasing little circles upon his chest. "You were very masterful before, my lord. I but wish to soothe you." Her slender fingers ran seductively over his skin yet again.

"I think you seek to arouse me again, little houri," he teased her with twinkling eyes. Taking the jar, he scooped out some cream, which he then began to rub over her pretty bosom. "You have adorable breasts, Zaynab. It is impossible to see them and not seek to touch them." He fondled her with his fingers, pulling her nipples out and pinching them.

"Why do you not wear a beard?" she asked him innocently. "So many Moors are bearded, but you are not, my lord. Why is that?" She could feel his arousal beneath her. The restorative was obviously most potent.

"I am fair-haired," he explained. "When my ancestors came to al-Andalus two centuries ago, we were Arabs from Baghdad and Damascus. All of us were dark-haired and dark-eyed, but we have a weakness for fair-haired women. Over the centuries my family has intermarried with light-haired, light-eyed slave girls. Both my mother and my grandmother were Galacians from the northwest. My coloring is more theirs. When I grow a beard it is red-blond, and I look like a foreigner. It is better that I remain clean-shaven, for my features are those of an Arab."

Reaching out, she caressed his face provocatively. "I like your face, my lord," she purred at him truthfully. He had an elegant head with high cheekbones, a strong nose, and a narrow sensuous mouth.

"You are a little witch, Zaynab," he told her, playfully tweaking her nipples. Then, with a swift motion, he reached up, rolled her beneath him, and laid his body atop hers. "And you are a very naughty tease, my lovely one. You must learn who is master here. I fear I must chastise you," he told her, his mouth coming down hard on hers. He kissed her slowly, completely, his lips moving from her lips to her face to her neck. His mouth scorched her skin as it followed the line of her throat. Gently, he nipped at her ear, murmuring in it, "I do not think I shall ever tire of you, Zaynab." Then he entered her slowly, tenderly. "You are meant only for love, and I mean to love you. You will pleasure me as no other woman ever has, and I will pleasure you as no youth possibly can."

She had not expected such strength from him. To her surprise, she found him a wonderful lover. Perhaps it would not be so terrible to belong to him after all. He was not unkind. He had promised to try not to use her again in that way she disliked. She tightened the muscles of her sheath about his manhood, and he groaned with delight. "Does that please you, my lord?" she asked him, knowing his answer already.

He responded by increasing his rhythm, and she gasped. "Does this please you?" he countered.

Together they taunted and challenged each other with one erotic game after another until both collapsed, satisfied for the moment. Abd-al Rahman held Zaynab in his embrace, chuckling. She was wonderful! This morning he had welcomed spring, and longed for a new adventure, a new love. Well, he had certainly found it with Zaynab.

"Why do you laugh, my lord?" she asked him.

"Because, my lovely, I am happy," he answered her. "Happy for the first time in a long while. Do not let anyone tell you you have not found favor with me, Zaynab, because you have. Tomorrow I shall have you moved to a larger apartment that suits your status."

"No, my lord, let me stay here," she begged him. "These little rooms suit me. If you will but let me have the services of a gardener, I shall soon have my little garden blooming."

"You like these rooms?" He was surprised.

"The lady Walladah gave them to me because I demanded my own apartment, my lord, but she chose a place at the farthest end of the harem to punish what she considered my arrogance. However, I like it here. It is private, and few can spy on me," she told him. "If you move me to a suite of rooms amid the rest of the harem, I shall never have any privacy, *nor will you.* Each time we cry with pleasure, it will be heard, and it will be noted by the gossips. If you cry out fewer times one night than the evening before, it will be said that I am losing your favor. No, my lord. I prefer these rooms to any others you would offer me."

He was amazed by her reasoning. She had been in his possession but a few hours, but had already analyzed her entire situation. "You are very clever," he told her. "Very well, you may have these rooms, and I shall give you a gardener of your very own."

Leaning over, she kissed his mouth lingeringly. "I have no time for the politics of the harem, my lord. My duty is to please you. If I am to do that properly, I cannot be distracted by the foolishness of jealous, silly women."

Abd-al Rahman laughed aloud, and his laughter was heard beyond the walls of Zaynab's rooms. The women still awake and gossiping looked meaningfully at one another, nodding sagely. They would have been mortally insulted had they but known the reason for his amusement.

By morning the whole harem was aware that the caliph had stayed the entire night with the new woman. The early risers saw him leave her apartments, and eagerly reported it to any and all who would listen. The caliph looked as many had not seen him look in years. He looked as many had never seen him look. *He looked happy.* There had been a spring to his step, a smile on his lips. *He had whistled!*

When Zaynab and Oma appeared in the baths later that morning, escorted by a preening Naja, the voices ceased in midchatter. All eyes were upon her. She walked proudly among them, smiling, as Obana hurried up to her, greeting the new favorite effusively. Everyone already knew that the caliph's first gifts to his beloved had consisted of the furs and jewels that Donal Righ had sent. It was an astounding first-night gift for

Abd-al Rahman to have made. The women were more than impressed.

"Good morning, my lady Zahra," Zaynab boldly saluted the older woman.

"Good morning to you, my lady Zaynab," the caliph's wife responded. "I understand that you have found favor with our lord."

"I am fortunate beyond belief," Zaynab answered her modestly. "Allah has smiled upon me. I am grateful, lady, but I am also greedy."

"*Greedy?*" Zahra cocked an eyebrow. "How are you greedy?"

"I shall not be content until I have found your favor also, lady," Zaynab said cleverly, looking directly at the other woman.

"In time perhaps," Zahra replied, half laughing. What a little devil this girl was: beautiful and seductive enough to have caught the jaded Abd-al Rahman's favor and kept it for an entire night—yet possibly she was dangerous as well. Zahra could not decide, and until she did, Zaynab would not have her acknowledged favor. "*If* you continue to please our lord and master, my lady Zaynab, *if* you do not sow seeds of discontent in the caliph's garden; then and only then will you have my favor too. Time will tell, my dear." Zahra suddenly realized that this girl could be her daughter. It was an uncomfortable thought.

If only Abd-al Rahman had not been so taken with her, Zahra considered. Perhaps she could have convinced him to give the girl to Hakam. She would be a good mate for their son. She looked like a girl who could breed strong sons. It really was time Hakam paid more attention to women. The damage was done, however. Abd-al Rahman had slept with the Love Slave and obviously been pleased. It was unlikely he would ever part with her. What a shame.

"She says she will not give you her favor yet," Obana gloated to Zaynab privately, "*but*, she has spoken at length with you before all the others. Many will consider that you already have her favor. You are an amazing girl, my lady Zaynab. In one day you have accomplished what it takes most years to accomplish. The majority of the women here have never attained the heights you have already scaled. You have made many enemies here today, I fear."

Zaynab laughed. "Not intentionally, my lady Obana, I assure you," she said. "I am the caliph's Love Slave. I seek but one thing: his pleasure. Nothing else matters to me. I will not become embroiled in female foolishness. It can only distract me from my duty."

"You are right, of course," Obana agreed, "but nonetheless you must be vigilant, my child. There are women here who have tried for years to attract our master's attention and never have suceeded."

"And never will, even if I am gone from this place," Zaynab said in practical tones.

"True," Obana nodded, "but still you must have a care for your safety."

"I will," Zaynab promised, patting the older woman's hand. She knew Obana was being kind, but she also knew that that kindness stemmed from her own success with the caliph. I have no illusions left to me, she thought, sad for a moment. Will the rest of my life be like this? Will I always have to be on my guard, to question everyone's motives? She sighed. If the truth be known, she wanted only to be a simple woman with a man and a houseful of children. That, however, would never be.

"Let us get you bathed properly," Obana said, breaking into her reverie. "I will tend to you myself."

When he left Zaynab, Abd-al Rahman had gone directly to his own private bath to sit amid the steam and revive himself. It had not been a night in which he obtained much rest. He had not had a night like that in twenty years. Yet he had enjoyed himself greatly. Zaynab was not simply the most sexually advanced woman he had ever made love to, she was also intelligent. Learning about her was going to be an absolutely fascinating experience. He exited his bath to dress.

"Do not forget, my lord, that you promised to speak with

Karim al Malina this morning," his personal body slave, Ali, reminded him.

"Send someone for him," the caliph said. "I have but to give him a personal message for Donal Righ."

"The lady Zaynab pleasured you?" Ali ventured.

Abd-al Rahman laughed heartily. "Never, Ali, in all my born days have I enjoyed a woman as I enjoy my new Love Slave. If Donal Righ thought he owed me a debt, he has repaid it a thousand times over."

Karim al Malina was sent for, and came immediately. He had not slept well. Even the lovely girl given to him for his pleasure had been unable to distract him, although she had left him declaring never to have known such a lover as he. Zaynab was lost to him, and all he wanted to do was leave Madinat al-Zahra as quickly as possible.

The caliph looked up from his simple breakfast when his visitor entered. Karim bowed low, saying as he did, "Good morning, my lord."

Abd-al Rahman looked up with a friendly smile at the serious young man. "And a very good morning it is, Karim al Malina. I have spent a night such as I never thought to spend again at my age. What an excellent job you have done with Zaynab. She is perfection! You may tell Donal Righ it is I who am now in his debt."

"I will tell him, my lord," Karim said in a lifeless voice, but the caliph did not notice.

"Besides her schooling in the erotic arts," Abd-al Rahman said, "has she had other education? She seems a clever and intelligent woman."

"She is," Karim said. "Her tutors were most satisfied with her. Among other things, you will find she has a beautiful voice and sings like a bird. My mother said it was quite the finest voice she had heard in some time. Zaynab also plays three instruments. You will not find her lacking, I assure you, my lord."

"She is a credit to your own training, Karim al Malina. Will you educate another girl soon?" the Caliph asked, curious.

"No, my lord, I will never train another girl again. That time in my life is over. I shall now sail to Eire to inform Donal Righ of your great pleasure, then I shall return home to Alcazaba Malina to marry as my family would have me do. I am the last of my father's children to take a mate. My little sister wed just a few months ago."

"It is important for a man to marry and sire children," the caliph agreed. "A man can never have too big a family about him. Tell me, how old is Zaynab?"

"She is fifteen, my lord," Karim responded, thinking, And much too young a flower for a man of your years. He swallowed hard. He must not allow his jealousy to show. Zaynab was not his. She never really had been. "Her birthdate is, I believe, in the early winter."

"I will take good care of her, Karim al Malina," the caliph said. Then he arose from his meal and held out his hand to the captain.

Taking it, Karim knelt and kissed the caliph's great diamond ring. "Allah guard and guide you, my lord," he said, then rising, left the potentate's presence. He struggled to keep his steps measured even though he really wanted to run, to shake the dust of this place from his robes. In the courtyard he mounted the horse that had been brought for him, turning its head to the Cordoba road. They would sail with the afternoon tide. *Farewell, my heart. Farewell, my love,* he silently whispered to her. Allah watch over you.

※ *Chapter 11*

Carrying a full load of freight in their holds, *I'timad* and *Iniga* sailed from Cordoba. They stopped at several ports along the Breton and Norman coast, selling part of their cargo, then traveled across the sea that separated the coast of Europe from that of England, where their luxury goods were welcomed by the inhabitants of that island on the edge of the known world. Finally, they charted a course around Land's End for Eire, sailing up the Liffey one rainy midsummer's morning.

Donal Righ greeted them eagerly, coming aboard *I'timad* himself. "A thousand welcomes, Karim al Malina!" he said jovially. "Do not keep me in suspense, I beg you, my young friend. My old heart will not stand it, I assure you. The caliph? He was pleased?"

"You have no heart, Donal Righ," Karim said, "else you would not have sent that exquisite flower of youth into the frosty embrace of the caliph. To answer your question, Abd-al Rahman was very pleased by your gifts, but of course, most delighted by Zaynab. Within a single night she had gained his favor, he most volubly assured me. I have been told to tell you that he is now in your debt. Are you pleased? You should be, Donal Righ. I trained Zaynab to be a perfect device of desire. She will probably kill Abd-al Rahman with her unleashed passions."

"If this is so, Karim al Malina, then I owe you an even greater debt than I anticipated," Donal Righ said, delighted.

Although he would not admit to it, he understood the young man's bitterness, however. Karim al Malina had obviously fallen in love with Zaynab. How could he not have? If I were a younger man, Donal Righ thought wistfully, I should have fallen in love with her. Perhaps I did a little. She was a lovely girl. "What will you do now, my friend?" he asked the younger man.

"Alaeddin and I will take what cargo you can give us and return home to Alcazaba Malina. I am to be married shortly. I will not go to sea again except occasionally." Karim then went on to explain that he had purchased elephants for Donal Righ rather than the racing camels the merchant had wanted, and told how the enormous beasts had brought the great columns of green agate into the Hall of the Caliphate. "It was a very impressive procession, Donal Righ. It was my eldest brother, Ayyub, who thought to use the pachyderms."

"Excellent! Excellent!" the Irishman enthused. "You have done me proud, Karim. I shall never be able to properly repay you." Then he said, "*You are to marry?* Who is the bride?"

"Her name is Hatiba. Other than that, I know nothing of her. You know our ways, Donal Righ. I'll never see the girl's face until after the wedding, when she enters my house and my bedchamber. My mother says she is fair enough. I can only hope my mother is right. My father is ecstatic that I have agreed to wed and provide him with more grandchildren. The girl is suitable. I care not. I will do my duty by my family. Hatiba will be treated with respect as the mother of my sons." He shrugged, his face a mask of indifference.

They remained in Eire but a short time. Karim refused to visit Donal Righ's house. He needed no reminders of Zaynab. She would be in his heart forever. In that, Alaeddin ben Omar was in agreement. He had very much wanted to marry Oma. Zaynab had given her permission, for technically Oma was hers to dispose of as she wished. Oma herself had refused him.

"It is not that I do not love you," she had told Alaeddin, "but I cannot leave my mistress alone and friendless in a strange land. It is she who saved me from a life of hardship and an early death. I owe her my allegiance."

Zaynab had assured her young servant that it was perfectly all right if she chose to marry, but Oma could not be moved. She would not be parted from Zaynab. Alaeddin ben Omar had been forced to accept her decision. In Islam there was no marriage without the consent of *both* the bride and the groom. Oma's firm refusal had put an end to the matter.

I'timad and *Iniga* departed Eire for Alcazaba Malina, encountering bad weather almost the entire way. Karim thought bitterly how different this trip was from last year's voyage, with its smooth, perfect seas and blue skies. When they gained port at last, he saw to his cargoes before going to his father's house. There both of his parents welcomed him warmly, delighted that he was safe.

"Your marriage is set for the new moon of the second month of Rabia," his father told him. "Because Hussein ibn Hussein lives in the mountains, the ceremonies will be held here in Alcazaba Malina within our house. You will take your wife from here to your own home."

"And we are going to be very traditional, are we not, my father? I shall not see my bride until she enters our nuptial chamber to reveal herself to me. Poor little girl, being married to a stranger so far from her own home and family. Must it be this way? Could not the girl and I at least meet beneath our mothers' eyes before the wedding?" Karim said.

"Hussein ibn Hussein and his family will not enter the city until the day before your marriage is to be celebrated," Habib told his son. "You may scoff at our traditions, Karim, but we follow them because they give an order and a meaning to our lives. You must begin to reconsider your attitudes, my son, as you are to become a married man. How can you guide your own children without traditions? Your carefree and irresponsible days of reckless abandon must cease now as you assume the new responsibilities as a husband and a father," Habib concluded seriously.

Alone with his mother afterward, Karim said, "I remember why I stayed away all these years. I am not my father, I fear. It is obvious that the blood of your adventurous Norse ancestors flows hotly in my veins, Mother." He kissed her cheek lovingly.

"Your grandfather was a farmer," she sternly reminded him.

"But his brother, your uncle Olaf, went a-Viking. I remember you telling us that once when Ja'far and I were small," Karim reminded her. "You said he hated farming, and there was not enough land for both your father and him, so he went to sea."

"It has been many years," Alimah said evasively, "since you were small, Karim. My memory is not what it used to be."

"Your memory is better than ever, my mother. Perhaps I am making a mistake in taking a wife. Perhaps I am not meant for marriage."

"Perhaps," his mother said, "you have not forgotten Zaynab. The best way to rid oneself of an old love is to take a new love, my son. You were foolish to fall in love with the caliph's property, and even if you shamed your family by going back on your word to wed Hatiba bat Hussein, you could still not have Zaynab for your own." She took his hands in hers, looking into the azure eyes so like her own. "Karim, you must face the reality of your situation. You have to accept your fate."

"I hate my fate!" he said heatedly.

Alimah had not heard that tone in her youngest son's voice in many years. It was the sound of pure unhappiness, of frustration, of anger against everything around him. She sighed with worry. He really was like her uncle Olaf, whom, despite her protestations to the contrary, she remembered quite well. He had loved a girl who chose another suitor. He had never really been happy after that. Some men were capable of loving only one woman. Uncle Olaf had been away at sea the day her parents were slain; the day she and her siblings had been carried off. She wondered if he had ever found happiness, or if her son Karim would find it.

"We cannot always have what we think we want from life," she told him plainly. "You agreed to this marriage, Karim, and your father gave his word. Hatiba will not be Zaynab, but she will be your wife. You made the choice months ago. Neither your father nor I forced you to it. *You made the choice*. It is past time you were married. Perhaps when you have the responsibility of a wife and children, you will stop behaving like a spoiled child yourself. Now leave me! You have made me very angry. I must compose myself before I go to your father, lest Habib learn that you are not yet the man he believes you to be."

Rising, he kissed both her hands, withdrawing his as he did

so, and then departed from her presence. He smiled wryly to himself. She had given him quite a tongue-lashing. He could not remember the last time she had been so angry with him. She had always been his strongest defender as well as his harshest critic when he was growing up. He believed that of all her children, she loved him the best, although she would certainly never say such a thing. And as usual she was right. He was feeling sorry for himself, without any thought for the girl who was to be his wife. She was coming to the marriage filled with the kind of hope a young girl has, filled with excitement, and probably even a little fear. It was up to him as a man to reassure her, to make her welcome . . . *to love her.* Could he love her? Was his mother right? Was he being childish?

He went to see his sister, Iniga. She was already swollen with her first child. There was a glow about her, a happiness he had never before seen in her face. What had happened to the dear little girl he always seemed to remember when he thought of Iniga? He almost didn't recognize this serene young woman.

"You are troubled, Karim," she said, sounding much like their mother. "Your heart weeps for Zaynab, doesn't it?" She touched his cheek. To his shock, he almost wept.

He nodded in answer to her query and then said, "I have an obligation to Hatiba bat Hussein. I must keep that obligation lest I besmirch our family's honor, but what if I cannot love her, sister?"

"Perhaps you will not," Iniga said honestly, "but the brother I know and adore will be a good husband, Karim. If you cannot love Hatiba, then I know you will at least be good to her. She will never feel neglected or ill-used by you. You will give her respect. Surely you do not imagine that Ayyub and Ja'far love all of their wives? Marriage is meant to further one's own family, to build alliances with other families. You are such a romantic, Karim!"

"Does Ahmed love you?" he demanded of her.

"Yes, I believe he does, but in that we are fortunate. It will not, however, prevent him from falling in love with another woman one day and taking another wife," Iniga said practically.

"Father loves Mother," he countered.

"But he is only fond of Lady Muzna. That marriage was arranged by our grandfather, Malik ibn Ayyub," Iniga said, checkmating him.

"In other words," he said, "marriage is a game of chance, my sister? Sometimes one wins, and other times one loses."

Iniga giggled. "Yes, Karim, that is exactly it," she agreed, "but marriage will also be like a sea voyage. You do not know what is going to happen. If Hatiba is pretty, and amenable, your voyage will be pleasant and your sailing smooth."

"And if she has a face like one of her father's horses, and a disposition like a camel, it will be rough seas all around." He chuckled. "I am not certain I find speaking with you at all reassuring, Iniga."

"Mother says Hatiba is very pretty. She saw her when she and Father went to conclude the negotiations at Hussein ibn Hussein's home in the mountains," Iniga said. "She is dark-haired and light-eyed."

"So Mother said, but then mothers are not often the best judge of one's mate, little sister," he replied.

"Shall I report to you after the bridal bath?" Iniga said mischievously. "Not that it will do you any good if she does have the face of a horse and the disposition of a camel. You'll still be stuck."

"You comfort me, Iniga," he told her, and they both laughed. Then Karim said, "Will you tell me?"

"Of course," she promised him with a chuckle.

Did it really matter if Hatiba were a pretty girl? he wondered. Well, mayhap it would make his life a little easier, he thought, but it didn't necessarily mean that he would love her. Poor little girl. She was an innocent in all of this. It wasn't her fault that he was in love with Zaynab. Perhaps what he really needed was an inexperienced virgin who would think he was wonderful because she did not know any better. That could be a blessing in disguise. If Hatiba had never known love, it was unlikely she would suffer from the fact that he would not love her.

His thoughts made him uncomfortable, for this attitude was

dishonest, and Karim al Malina was not a dishonest man. Yet how could he erase from his heart and mind the memory of golden hair, aquamarine eyes, and a body that would render a strong man weak as a baby? He couldn't. But Hatiba must not be made to suffer for his weakness of character.

The bridal bath took place the day before the wedding. The women of both families, and the bride's few friends who had come to the city with her, gathered together for an afternoon of bathing, perfuming, and gossip. It was supposed to relax the nervous bride, to reassure her that she was among those who loved her, and always would be. Afterward Iniga made her way from the baths to her brother's apartment in their father's house.

"You have seen her?" Karim had been waiting impatiently all afternoon for the ritual to be completed.

Iniga nodded solemnly.

"And?" He was almost eager.

"She is very pretty, as Mother said," Iniga began slowly, "but . . . " She paused, searching for the right words.

"But what?" Allah, what was the matter? Karim wondered.

"I found her sullen," Iniga finally said bluntly. "She does not seem to be happy about this marriage, Karim. It is not nervousness, I'm certain. She hardly smiled the whole afternoon, but when she did, I saw that her teeth were good. At least that's something."

She was sullen, and her teeth were good. It was not particularly consoling. "She has agreed to the marriage," he replied, "else it could not take place. Perhaps she is just afraid, Iniga. After all, tomorrow at this time she'll be married to a complete stranger."

"Yes," Iniga answered him. "I never considered that. After all, I married someone I knew, and did not really leave my family. You are probably right, Karim. She is afraid, but you will reassure her once you are her husband. Then she will see she need not be fearful." But Iniga did not believe her words for a moment. Hatiba had been sullen, like someone forced to do something she did not desire. She hoped Karim could help

Hatiba overcome whatever it was that was troubling her. In doing so they might find a happiness of sorts together.

The wedding day was a clear, bright day. In that they were fortunate, for the rainy season was almost upon them. The male family members and friends went first to the baths and next to the mosque, where the imam examined the contract drawn up by the qadi weeks before. He asked if the dower had been paid, and satisfied that all parties were in agreement, performed the ceremony uniting Karim ibn Habib and Hatiba bat Hussein in marriage, although the bride herself was not present. Then the men returned to Habib ibn Malik's gardens, where Hatiba, garbed in her red and gold wedding garment, sat ensconced amid her gifts, awaiting her bridegroom.

Karim went to her, and raising the red veil drawn over the girl's face and head, stared into a pair of cold gray eyes. There was no smile of welcome. Her age had been given as fifteen, but Karim had the feeling he was looking at an older girl, though perhaps it was the gravity of the occasion that made her look more mature. "I salute you, Hatiba, my wife," he said courteously.

"I greet you, Karim ibn Habib," she replied. Her voice was soft and well modulated, but it lacked emotion of any kind.

The men and the women separated, and the feasting began. Wine, cakes, fruits, and other sweets were being served. The traditional all-female orchestra played. The women danced together in celebration. The men in their part of the garden were entertained by sinuous dancers.

"She's pretty," his brother Ja'far said as they stood watching the dancers. "Berber girls are nicely docile. After you get a son on her, you can find yourself some exotic little creature who has more spirit and begin your harem. Considering your field of expertise, your women should be the happiest women in Malina." He chuckled, giving his younger brother a jovial poke.

"Her eyes are as cold as silver," Karim replied. "I greeted her as my wife, but she did not address me as her husband. She is not willing, no matter what her father told the imam. My father-in-law was evidently greedy for the bride price I paid for the girl, but he shall not have it, for no matter, I will remain married to Hatiba."

"Do not sound so grim," his brother counseled. "She is just frightened like all virgins. You'll have her warm and at ease by the sunrise, Karim. I do not have to instruct you on the seduction of pretty virgins, little brother." He laughed. Then tipping his cup up, Ja'far drank down his wine, his gaze straying to the big-breasted dancer entertaining them.

The bride was put into her litter in the late afternoon and taken in procession to her husband's home outside the city. Karim led the guests, riding upon a white stallion his new father-in-law had given him as a wedding gift, down a street strewn with rose petals. Musicians accompanied the wedding party. The bridegroom tossed gold dinars to the well-wishers along their route. When they reached Karim's villa, the household slaves under Mustafa's guidance served the guests refreshments. Not long after, they departed, leaving the newlyweds alone to get acquainted with each other.

Karim gave his bride an hour's time before he entered her chambers. Beyond the windows of her rooms the sun was setting into the western sea. "You may go," Karim told the slave girls clustered about his bride.

"You will all remain," Hatiba said harshly. The slave girls looked uncomfortable and confused.

Karim snapped his fingers sharply, saying as he did so, "I am master in this house, Hatiba." The slave girls hurried swiftly out of their mistress's apartment.

"How dare you order my servants about!" she cried to him.

"I repeat, Hatiba, *I am master in this house.* I cannot believe that your father allowed you to behave in such an unchecked manner under his domain. I will assume that you are frightened. You need not be." He took a step toward her, and to his surprise a small dagger appeared as if by magic in her hand.

"Do not come any closer, or I shall kill you," she said low.

With a swift movement, Karim grasped his wife's wrist and yanked the weapon from it. Looking at it, he laughed scornfully. "You couldn't kill an orange with that, Hatiba," he said.

"The tip is poisoned," she replied softly.

Looking closely at the blade, he saw that its pointed end was indeed darkened. Karim sighed deeply. "If you did not want this marriage," he said, "why then in the name of Allah did you agree to it? Or was it your father's decision, Hatiba?"

"He could not resist the bride price, for one thing, my lord," she told him honestly. "He never received as much for any of my sisters."

"Was there another reason as well?" he pressed her.

"Do you need to ask?" she replied. "You are the son of the Prince of Malina, my lord. What a coup for my father to have his youngest daughter married to a son of Malina's ruler. My father is no longer content with just his wealth. Now he seeks power."

"My father is hardly a mighty lord," Karim said. "He is the hereditary prince of this land because our ancestor founded the city. He governs with the aid of a council, not by his whim alone. We keep no court; the court is in Cordoba. We live like ordinary citizens. My father is respected because he rules through his council with wisdom and kindness. We give our allegiance to Allah, and to the caliph. It has always been the way of our family.

"Besides, I am my father's youngest son, Hatiba. I shall never be Prince of Malina. I do not want to be. What did your foolish father think he could gain by forcing you into a marriage you did not want?"

"It was the prestige of being able to say that his daughter Hatiba is the first wife of the Prince of Malina's son; the status and distinction of being able to claim that he and the Prince of Malina have grandsons in common. Being related by marriage to your family gives him new power among the mountain clans. That is what he wants."

"Do you love someone else?" he asked her bluntly.

Hatiba flushed, her pale golden complexion growing rosy with his words, but she answered him honestly. "Yes, and he was to have been my husband, but that your family offered for me. The contracts were already signed, the bride price and dowry agreed upon, although not paid. But then came your father's offer. My father tore up the contracts. The old qadi who had overseen them died suddenly. There was no proof that any agreement had been made. Since neither the bride price nor the dowry had been exchanged, my beloved was forced to watch as I was contracted to you. Ohh, why of all the girls you could have had did you want me?" Her gray eyes filled with tears, and she angrily wiped them away.

"I did not want you," he said quietly, deciding that her honesty deserved his in return. "I did not even know of your existence until the match was made. Last year I asked my father to find me a wife. I have spent most of my life a sea captain and trader. I knew how much it would please my father if I finally settled down.

"This spring I delivered to the caliph in Cordoba a slave woman whom I loved, and she loved me. You have been told, I know, that I was a Passion Master. The girl was put into my care by an old friend of my father's. I trained her in the erotic arts, but I broke the cardinal rule of my own order by loving her, and by accepting her love in return. Neither of us had that right. In the end, for honor's sake, we did what we had to do. Zaynab went to the caliph's bed and quickly became his favorite. I came home to Alcazaba Malina to wed with you.

"It is unfortunate that we each love another, but we cannot change our fates, Hatiba. If I sent you back to your father this very day, it would change nothing. I should not have Zaynab, nor would your father's honor permit him to let you have your lover. You know that I am right. Neither of us knows if we can love the other, but I will give you the honor and respect that you deserve as my wife. More I cannot promise. Will you honor and respect me in return, Hatiba?"

She was astounded by his speech. Suddenly her cold and distant demeanor collapsed, and her face was that of a frightened young girl. *"You must send me back,"* she half whispered. *"I am not a virgin."* Then she began to weep, childish little sobs of fear and sorrow.

"The rejected bridegroom?" he asked her gently.

She nodded, her gray eyes upon him, desperate with fear.

"When was the last time you lay with him?" Karim asked her.

"Three days ago," she said low.

"Your maidenhead is not important to me, Hatiba," he told her. "However, if you are with child by this man, I have no choice but to send you back to your father in disgrace."

"If I am with child, I could say it was yours," she replied defiantly. "No one could prove otherwise, my lord!"

"I will not sleep with you, Hatiba, for two months," he told her, "and now I will recall your handmaidens to keep you company this night. What a pity you were so foolish. I would have initiated you sweetly."

He left her weeping softly, and returned to his own apartments. "Tell Mustafa I wish to see him immediately," he told an attending slave.

Mustafa came, and Karim told him, "I must return to Alcazaba Malina to speak with my father. See that my wife and her handmaidens remain in her apartments. No one is to leave those rooms, Mustafa."

"Yes, my lord," Mustafa said with an impassive face. "Shall I have your stallion saddled for you?"

Karim nodded, and several minutes later he was on the road back to the city. Arriving at his father's house, he was relieved to find it quiet.

"Karim!" His father looked up, surprised, at his entry.

"What is the matter?" his mother said, a concerned look upon her beautiful face. "Why are you here instead of with Hatiba?"

Karim explained to both of his parents the scene that had taken place between him and his bride.

Habib ibn Malik was outraged. "You will divorce her immediately!" he said angrily. "I will find a decent girl for you, my son."

"No," Karim said. "The girl's father is to blame, but what is done is done. I will renounce her only if she has been foolish enough to get herself with child. I cannot accept another man's son as my heir. Tonight I want your physician to examine her to ascertain if she speaks the truth. Then I want her father informed. If the girl must be returned to her family, I want no doubt about the reasons why, and the bride price *must* be returned to me. That old Berber bandit will not profit at my expense and embarrassment."

Habib ibn Malik sent for his physician, and the matter was explained to him. He was then sent to Karim's home to examine the bride. He returned almost two hours later and announced, "The girl is not a virgin, my lord Habib. She did not lie."

"You will not speak of this to anyone," Habib ibn Malik said. "Later I may need your testimony before the qadi, but for now you will remain silent, Dr. Sulayman. Thank you."

The physician bowed and departed.

Habib ibn Malik then called to one of his slaves. "Go to the apartments of Hussein ibn Hussein and his wife. Tell them I must see them both at once. Then wait, and escort them here to me."

Hussein ibn Hussein and his wife, Qabiha, arrived shortly thereafter, puzzled, and not just a little frightened.

Habib ibn Malik wasted no time. "Your daughter is not a virgin," he said coldly. "She admitted such to my son, and Dr. Sulayman has confirmed her shame. I am also told that you had agreed previously to another match for Hatiba prior to my asking for Karim."

"There is no proof of such a contract!" Hussein sputtered.

"Aye, I understand the qadi responsible conveniently died," Habib returned dryly. "Nevertheless, the girl is not pure."

Hussein turned angrily to his favorite wife, Qabiha. "She is your daughter! Why could you not oversee her behavior?"

"She has been in love with Ali Hassan since she was ten," Qabiha replied spiritedly. "They would have wed three years ago but that you would not let her go, and held her suitor off demanding a huge bride price! They are young and hot-blooded. They believed they would one day wed, my lord. I could not keep her locked up all the time. Do not blame me! She is your daughter too, and more like you than she is like me," Qabiha finished.

"He will divorce her! I shall have to return the three thousand dinars, and they are already spent," Hussein hissed at his wife as if no one else were in the room.

"If Hatiba is not with child, Hussein ibn Hussein," Karim said quietly, "I will keep her. If her lover's seed has taken root, then she must be returned to you. I do not hold the girl responsible for this disaster. I hold you responsible. Do you understand me?" Karim's face was fierce with anger.

"My lord," Qabiha pleaded her daughter's cause, "Hatiba is really a good girl, but she is strong-willed and has always had her own way. When her father would not let her wed Ali Hassan, she became as I have never known her." The mother, Karim thought, very much resembled the daughter, but where Qabiha's gray eyes were soft, Hatiba's were hard and cold; except when she was frightened.

"You will stay with your daughter for the next two months," Karim told his mother-in-law. "I will expect that you monitor her behavior closely during that time and remind her daily of her duties as my wife. If at the end of that time I am absolutely certain she has proved infertile from her lover's seed, then I will return home to begin our life together. You will then be sent back to your husband."

Hussein ibn Hussein opened his mouth to protest, but an angry look from his wife silenced him. His jaws snapped shut with an audible click. "You are more than generous, my lord," he said, none too graciously.

Karim glanced at the man cynically. "You had best use the grace period I give your daughter to find the three thousand dinars of her bride price that you have so wantonly squandered. That gold is Hatiba's, not yours, Hussein ibn Hussein. It is for her safety and protection should she ever find herself without a husband. I would see it returned in two months to either me or to my wife."

His father-in-law looked away guiltily. "Yes, my lord," was all that he could now say, but his facile brain was contemplating how in the name of the prophet he would recover the money. Perhaps his new son-in-law might meet with some unfortunate accident. Then the young widow would be returned to her family, bride price and dowry intact, and available for another match.

Karim watched as Hatiba's father narrowed his black eyes

and considered his next move. It was undoubtedly under-
handed. He hoped his new wife would avoid being returned to
her father. It was not that he had any particular feeling for the
girl, but having become more closely acquainted with his
father-in-law, he was beginning to feel very sorry for her. He
turned to his own father and asked, "Will you see that the lady
Qabiha is transported to my home this night?"

Habib ibn Malik nodded. "At once."

Qabiha took up residence in her son-in-law's villa. Her
daughter looked angry and sullen upon her arrival. Qabiha
slapped her and said harshly, "You will no longer have your
father to condone your bad behavior, girl. He may protest to
the contrary and declare his innocence of the matter, but he
knew what you were doing when you would ride off into the
hills. *He knew!* Yet he placed you in this position for the sake
of three thousand gold dinars and the chance to ally himself
with the princely family of this city. You had best pray to
Allah, my daughter, that you are not with child by Ali Hassan.
If you are, your father will kill you. I cannot protect you from
him in this matter. What else can he possibly do with a
daughter who has brought such shame upon her family, and
still retain his own honor? You are fortunate in your husband,
Hatiba, if indeed he remains your husband. If you are not with
child, he says he will keep you. I cannot imagine any other man
being so generous."

"Generous?" Hatiba sneered. "He loves another he cannot
have, Mother. My lost virtue means nothing to him. If he keeps
me, it is for his benefit, not mine. He will never love me."

The days passed quickly by. Karim rode with his two brothers
and a group of friends most mornings, hunting in the fields and
hills about the city. In the afternoons he visited Hatiba, always
in her mother's presence. He discovered she was an appallingly
ignorant girl. She could not read or write. She had no ear for
music. When he brought tutors in to help educate her, she grew
quickly bored and wept.

"She has absolutely no attention span, my lord," the tutor he respected most told him, speaking for them all. "She cannot be taught, but worse, she does not want to learn."

Afterward Karim groaned to himself, wondering what they would possibly have in common if she remained his wife. He found she was an enthusiastic game player, however. She played both chess and backgammon with a childish zeal, wagering wildly, clapping her hands gleefully if she won, pouting if she lost. It was something. He remembered his brother Ja'far's advice to get her with child and then find some exotic creature to start his harem. He sighed sadly. He didn't want a harem of exotic females, or a wife named Hatiba who was already proving more trouble than she was worth. He wanted Zaynab, and he would never have her. She was beyond his reach forever.

Finally the waiting period was at an end. Hatiba had bled twice since their wedding day, Dr. Sulayman coming to examine her during each cycle to be certain there was no fraud. Now the physician declared his wife not with child.

"You may enter her without fear, my lord. Any issue she produces in the next year will be your child without a doubt. She is healthy, and free of disease. She should prove a good breeder."

Karim sent his mother-in-law back to the mountains. He dismissed his wife's serving women for the next few days. He entered his wife's apartments, where Hatiba awaited him. There was no turning back. No excuse for putting her aside. It was time to begin his life anew.

Chapter 12

"*D*rink this, my lady Zaynab," the physician Hasdai ibn Shaprut said, his arm bracing her, his other hand holding a cup to her lips.

"What is it?" she asked him weakly. Her head ached so.

"More of the antidote I have been giving you. It is called theriaca. Allow me to reassure you that you are going to be all right," the doctor told her. "We are fortunate you reacted so quickly to the poison you were given. It allowed us to diagnose you and save you."

"*Poison?*" A look of shock crossed her beautiful face. "I was poisoned? I do not remember. Who would poison me?" Zaynab asked, confused. How could she have made so strong an enemy so quickly?

"We do not know the culprit yet," the caliph answered her, "but if I find out who it is, she will die the very death she planned for you, my love." His face was grim with anger and frustration. His harem had over four thousand women in it: his wives, his concubines, those who hoped to gain his favor, his female relations, and their servants. It was impossible to keep track of them all. The assassin had been very clever. It was most unlikely they would ever find out who it was.

"How was I poisoned?" Zaynab queried Hasdai ibn Shaprut. "Is my poor Naja all right? He tastes everything I eat or drink."

"Other than the fact your eunuch is beside himself with worry and remorse, he is fine," the physician assured her. "The poison was ingrained into a shawl you wore. It seeped into your skin. It should have worked gradually, over a period of time, but instead the first time you wore it you reacted violently. You are obviously very sensitive to foreign substances, my lady, and a good thing too." He turned to his assistant. "Rebekah, show the lady Zaynab the shawl."

The older woman opened a metal container and displayed the contents.

"Who gave you this shawl, lady?" Hasdai ibn Shaprut asked her. "If you can remember, perhaps we will have our culprit. Do not touch it, I beg you. It is quite lethal, and must be destroyed. Just look."

Zaynab looked at the shawl. It was a particularly lovely fabric: a light, soft wool, dyed a rich rose color, with a fringe of even deeper pink. She had absolutely no idea where it had come from, and looked to Oma, who shook her head in bewilderment.

"It was not among the garments you brought from Malina," Oma said. "Remember this morning we were looking in the trunk for a shawl because the day was proving to be chilly? It was simply there on top of all the others. I did not stop to think where it had come from. I thought perhaps our lord, the caliph, had given it to you."

"Lady, I must ask this question," the physician said. "Can you trust your maidservant?"

Zaynab was outraged. "How dare you?" she said icily. "I would trust Oma with my life, sir. She is with me by choice. I offered to free her and send her back to Alba. She refused. She even refused to marry Alaeddin ben Omar because she would not leave me." Zaynab reached out for her friend, and Oma, tears in her eyes, took her hand. "Oma is faithful. She would not harm me."

"Lady, I beg your pardon, but I had to ask," the physician said.

"Can she travel?" the caliph interjected, surprising them all.

"Where would you take her, my lord?" Hasdai asked.

"Al-Rusafa. She will be safe there while she recuperates," the caliph replied. "We will travel in stages, first to the Alcazar in Córdoba, and then the next day to al-Rusafa."

"Yes," the physician said thoughtfully, "yes, that would be a good idea, my lord. At al-Rusafa you can control her situation much better. Is the palace still habitable? You have not been there since the court removed to Madinat al-Zahra."

"I shall keep her in a little summerhouse in the gardens that is quite habitable. It will not be the first time I have taken a pretty girl there," Abd-al Rahman said with twinkling eyes. "It is peaceful there," he amended, a bit more soberly.

"All her clothing will have to be burned," the physician decreed, "and her jewelry boiled in vinegar. We cannot be certain that the poison has not been infused into other of her possessions."

The caliph saw the storm building in Zaynab's eyes, and quickly said, "I will have a brand-new wardrobe made for you, my love. Besides, I like you best as nature has fashioned you. There is none fairer than you, my darling Zaynab. I thank Allah that you were not taken from me."

"Oh, my lord, you are so good to me," she answered him sweetly, but she was both angry and frightened at the same time. Iniga had warned her of such things as poison, but she hadn't taken her friend seriously.

Hasdai ibn Shaprut thought to himself that the caliph was falling in love with her, or at least believed he was. In the few years he had known Abd-al Rahman, he had never seen him act this way with a woman. What had begun as blind lust was softening as his master learned more of the Love Slave than just her nubile body. As for Zaynab herself, the physician did not believe she was in love with the caliph. She respected him, was perhaps a trifle afraid of him, and might harbor a small affection for him, but love? No. Whether she was even capable of love he could not ascertain, not knowing her well enough. Did a female trained to lead such an unnatural existence really know how to love? It was a challenging conundrum.

She was frankly the most beautiful female the physician had ever seen. He understood the caliph's fascination with her youth and beauty. Zaynab was the love of Abd-al Rahman's old age as Abishag had been the last love of King David. He would probably get a final child on her. Even though he was over fifty, the caliph was yet potent, as the existence of his two youngest sons proved.

*   *   *

"How is she?" the lady Zahra asked Hasdai ibn Shaprut. She had requested that he come to her apartments before he departed the harem. "What was the matter with her? Is she with child?"

"Someone tried to poison her," the physician said quietly. "The caliph is very angry. Fortunately, I was able to save her." And why is the caliph's first wife concerned? he wondered. Zahra did not usually bother with those she felt beneath her.

"Then she will live," Zahra said calmly. "He is too old for such a plaything, you must agree, but will he listen to me? No! It would have been better if he had given her to Hakam, do you not think, my lord?"

"I think my master, the caliph, is happy with the lady Zaynab. I think him fit enough to indulge his passions with a beautiful girl," Hasdai ibn Shaprut answered her. He had never before seen the lady Zahra exhibit such rancor. Why was she jealous? Her own position was secure, as was that of her eldest son.

"Men!" Zahra said disgustedly to the caliph's second wife, Tarub, after the physician had left. "They are all alike! Our lord endangers his health with that girl. He does not think of his value to al-Andalus."

"If he is happy," Tarub said wisely, "is he not of greater value to al-Andalus? What do you have against Zaynab that your jealousy burns so hot? None of the others have ever caused you to turn a hair, Zahra. From the beginning this girl has been mannerly, and has politely deferred to you. She causes no dissensions among the other harem women. Indeed, she keeps more to herself than any I have ever known. I have heard no complaint against her, nor would she appear to have any fault that should distress you. Why do you dislike her so?" asked Tarub, a Galician whose once red hair was now faded.

"I do not dislike her," Zahra protested. "I am simply concerned over our dear lord's health." The first wife was a Catalan, from a country known for the intellects of its people. It had been that which had first attracted Abd-al Rahman to Zahra.

"It is not *his* health that is in question," Tarub said with some small humor. "It is poor Zaynab who was poisoned."

"He loves her," Zahra almost whispered.

"Ahh, so that is it," her companion replied. "Oh, Zahra, what matter if he loves her? He loves me, and you are not the least jealous. He loves all the charming and not so charming concubines who have given him children, particularly Bacea and Qumar. You are not jealous of them in the least. If he loves Zaynab, he loves you better. Indeed he loves you best of all. He always has. Did he not name a city for you? *Madinat al-Zahra.* How marvelous that a man of Abd-al Rahman's age can still find new love!" She laughed.

"Praise Allah for it! We came to Abd-al Rahman at the same time, you and I. How many years ago was it? We were young girls. Your son was born but two months ahead of mine. I do not curse Allah that it happened that way. I rejoice in my children and my grandchildren. I accept that time has passed. You seem unable to do that, Zahra. It is growing worse for you with each year. You are no longer a girl. You never will be again. I think your jealousy lies not so much in that Abd-al loves Zaynab, but that she is young and extravagantly beautiful. You cannot change that any more than you can change the fact that you are past forty."

"You are cruel!" Zahra cried, tears springing to her eyes.

"I am honest with you as I have always been, dearest friend," Tarub replied. "I tell you that our husband will always love you best, Zahra, no matter who else he may love as well. Accept that truth and let your anger and your jealousy die, lest in the end they kill you, or the abiding love that Abd-al Rahman has for you. Will you throw away all those happy years?"

Zahra did not reply, but rather she turned her head away from her friend. Was Tarub right? she wondered. Or was her fellow wife simply saying those things to soothe her feelings? Abd-al Rahman did not seem to rely upon her as he once did. She remembered when his oldest concubine had died. The lady Aisha had been the first woman he had ever known. She had been older than he was.

Aisha was a gift from the old emir Abdallah, the caliph's grandfather, who had raised him. Abd-al Rahman had genuinely liked her. She had initiated him into the erotic arts, but she had also become his trusted friend as well. Long after they ceased their amatory adventures, he regularly visited her apartments, and he held her in the highest esteem. When Aisha had died, she directed that her vast fortune be used to ransom men and women of Islam held captive in Christian lands. So few were found that Abd-al Rahman was at a loss as to what to do with Aisha's monies. Whatever he did, he wanted it to be something Aisha would have approved. It was Zahra who had suggested that he build a new city.

It was more a walled town than a city. The site chosen was on a slope of the Sierra Morena overlooking the Guadalquivir River, to the northwest of Cordoba. It had been begun almost ten years ago, and was still not finished. There were three levels, the first of which was completed and held the royal palace. Ten thousand laborers were used in the city's construction as well as fifteen hundred beasts of burden—mules, donkeys, and camels. Six thousand stones were hewn to fit the buildings and walls each day. The roof tiles were covered in gold and silver leaf. The city was a full mile wide east to west, and half a mile north to south.

Each of the three levels planned for the city was set high enough to allow the level below it a clear view. Beneath the royal residence was a level consisting entirely of gardens, orchards, a zoo for the caliph's exotic creatures, and an aviary filled with wonderful birds. The bottom level of the town held the government offices, residences of those important people attached to the court, public baths, workshops, armories, the mint, barracks for the vast royal guard, and a mosque.

Although Zahra had joined the caliph on his expeditions to the construction site in the early years of its building, he gave her a marvelous surprise the day he moved the inhabitants of the royal palace there from Cordoba. As they approached the entry gate, he had advised her to look up. When she did, she saw a marble bust of her own head over the entrance to the city. Wordlessly she looked at him, and he told her that the city's new name would be Madinat al-Zahra, the city of Zahra.

"But should it not be Madinat al-Aisha in honor of your old

friend, whose vast funds provided the wherewithal for the city?" she asked him, heart beating excitedly. She knew he would refuse, for he did love her above all women. In deference to Aisha, however, she felt she should at least ask him. Allah! Had any woman ever been so honored?

Now, however, Abd-al Rahman had a new interest in life. The Love Slave, Zaynab, consumed him entirely, it seemed. Zahra sighed. She was working herself into a jealous fit again. Was Tarub right? Tarub was not a woman to lie, even to herself. She was kind and practical and honest to a fault.

Still, each time Zahra looked at Zaynab, she felt uncontrollable anger. She could not seem to help it. What right had this girl to take the caliph from her? And what if Zaynab had a child? Not that she really expected any child of any of her husband's women to supplant her own son, Hakam. Abd-al Rahman had always made it quite clear that Hakam was to follow him as caliph. But what if he changed his mind? What if he came to love Zaynab more? She laughed shakily. Why was she so upset? There was no danger to her high position or to her son. Yet she did not know that for certain. An older man in love with a young girl might act foolishly.

Her choler was not improved by the knowledge that Zaynab and her servants were to be moved to al-Rusafa. "From whom is she in such danger here that he must move her?" she said bitterly to Tarub. "It is ridiculous! Simply ridiculous!" Zahra's color was high.

Tarub attempted to soothe her friend, her warm brown eyes brimming with sympathy. "Do not fret yourself, Zahra. The caliph plays at being the concerned lover with Zaynab. He merely wishes to be alone with her for a time. It is natural. Do you not remember how we used to sneak off to the summer palace with him? When she is recovered, he will bring her back. With al-Rusafa to the northeast of Cordoba, and Madinat al-Zahra to the northwest, he will spend more time on his horse than in Zaynab's arms." Tarub chuckled. "She is young, and probably frightened by what happened. Whatever the caliph may have told her, Zaynab is not stupid. She knows the chances of finding who poisoned her are small at best. By taking her to al-Rusafa he merely reassures her, and eases her fears."

But Zaynab was not frightened. She was angry that someone would have tried to kill her. To her knowledge, she had no enemies. It was therefore some silly girl who actually believed that by killing the caliph's Love Slave she could win his attention herself. It was unlikely she would ever know who had done it, but she certainly intended to be on her guard from now on. She watched, furious, as her clothing was carefully removed for burning as per Hasdai ibn Shaprut's instructions.

"It is ludicrous that all of my clothing must be destroyed," she fumed. "It could not all be poisoned! And my jewelry will be ruined, being boiled in a vinegar solution! Damn that meddling physician!"

"He saved your life, lady," Oma said sharply. "Surely that is worth a few garments and trinkets. Besides, the caliph has promised to outfit you like a young queen. The twenty bolts of silk that Donal Righ gave him have all been allocated for your use."

"How do you know that?" Zaynab demanded of her.

"Naja told me," Oma said, "and you know he knows everything that goes on in this palace. He even knows that the lady Zahra is jealous of you. He's friends with one of the girls in the favorite wife's apartments."

"Do you think she is the one who poisoned me?" Zaynab wondered.

"Anything is possible," Oma said, shaking her head, "but I would not think so. Even though the chances of being caught are slim, if the culprit is caught, it would mean her life. I do not think the lady Zahra would endanger her position simply because she is jealous and feeling her years. Nay, it was probably someone insignificant."

They left for al-Rusafa, traveling with the caliph down the carpeted highway between Madinat al-Zahra and Cordoba. Zaynab was astounded by the size of the capital city, and begged to be allowed to see it.

"You may go with Naja and a suitable guard," Abd-al

Rahman told her. "If I appear on the streets, we will be mobbed. By keeping a respectable distance from the people, I ensure their respect."

"Tell me the city's history," she begged him, and he laughed.

"Any other woman I know would want directions to the nearest marketplace so she might buy herself something. You, however, want to know Cordoba's history. Very well, my funny love, I shall tell you. It was founded by a race of people called Carthaginians, and captured by the Rumi in the days of their great empire. The next to hold sway here were the Visigoths, and we captured it from them over two hundred years ago. Over a million people live here. We have six hundred mosques, eighty schools of higher learning, and a public library with over six hundred thousand volumes. Hasdai would like a medical school built here, and eventually he will have one, for I agree with him. Now, all of our physicians have to travel to Baghdad to be trained."

"There is no such number as six hundred thousand, let alone a million," she said disbelievingly, and he laughed again.

Zaynab went out into the city with Oma and Naja, ensconced within a litter, surrounded by a suitable guard, and muffled to her eyes. She didn't know where to look next. Everything was so exciting, so interesting, so busy! When they had arrived in Cordoba aboard Karim's ship, she had been transferred to a barge that transported her up the river to Madinat al-Zahra. She had had no chance to really see the larger city.

Everywhere they went, commerce flourished. The city was famous for its leatherwork, its silversmiths, and the women who did silk embroidery. There were people from all the known world walking through Cordoba's streets. The different faces and clothing fascinated Zaynab. The caliph assigned fully one-third of the state budget, more than six million dinars yearly, to building and maintaining the canals of the city, its irrigation systems, and its public structures, Naja informed them proudly. "Cordoba," he assured them, "is the finest city in all of the world, and it is the most prosperous."

"What do you think of the city?" the caliph asked Zaynab when they returned to the Alcazar palace that afternoon.

"It's wonderful," she told him, "but much too big a place for me to live in, my lord. It makes Madinat al-Zahra seem small by comparison. I have never seen so many different people!"

They traveled on to al-Rusafa the next day. Once the summer palace for the rulers of al-Andalus, it had fallen out of favor after the construction of Madinat al-Zahra. It was a very romantic place, set among wonderful gardens by the riverside. It had been built by the first Abd-al Rahman, re-created from the original al-Rusafa, which had been erected by Caliph Hisham along the banks of the Euphrates River outside of Baghdad. These gardens were irrigated by the river just as the original gardens had been. Zaynab was enchanted by it all.

She settled into a small marble house in the middle of the gardens, by a little lake that had been artificially created by the waters of the river. In the center of the lake was a wonderful summerhouse that the caliph promised Zaynab they would visit. She loved her new house. It had a spacious bright day room where they might while away the hours playing chess or singing together as she played her rebec. There was a bed-chamber for her, with a bath that opened off it, two smaller chambers for Oma and Naja, and a room where Naja would prepare their meals. Zaynab clapped her hands gleefully when she saw it.

"I do not have to share any of it with anyone!" she chortled.

"Do you dislike the harem so?" he asked her, his hand smoothing her fair hair. "Do you not enjoy the company of other women?"

"My lord, if you knew how I was raised, you would understand," Zaynab explained. "Other than two female servants, my mother, my sister, and I were the only women at Ben MacDui. My mother favored my sister, and I spent more time alone than with them. Oma is the first real friend I've ever had of my own sex. I am not certain that I like other women. They gossip too much and can be cruel. I am more interested in the world about me than in spending hours beautifying myself. The women in the harem are mostly an idle lot.

"My world before al-Andalus was so narrow, my lord. Here there is so much to see and to learn! I was trained to be a Love Slave, to know nothing but the giving and receiving of pleasure, but it is an unnatural life for me now that my eyes have been opened to the wonders of your world! I hope I do not disappoint you, my dear lord, for I should not like to do so." She nestled into his arms. "You are so good to me."

She is a miracle, he thought to himself, lying by her side in their bed. She had begun by being the most erotic woman he had ever known. There was still nothing he desired of her physically that she would not give him; but there was so much more to this girl-woman who was his possession. Not a day went by that he did not find himself amazed and delighted by her. That she should have come to him now in the late afternoon of his life was the pity. Had they only come together in his youth, they would have bred a race of giants!

"You will never disappoint me, Zaynab," he told her sincerely. Then he said, "I have heard of a game that Love Slaves are taught. It is called the Rose in Bondage. Did Karim al Malina school you in this entertainment, my beauty?" His deep blue eyes looked directly at her.

Zaynab nodded slowly. It was a game of unbearably sweet sexual torture. She was not certain the caliph was up to such a game, despite his vigorous health. "I will play it with you only, my lord, if you allow me to direct our game. It can be dangerous, you understand. Have you played it before?"

"In my youth," he said, "and I agree to your terms."

"I shall gather what we need, then," she said, rising from the bed. "Very shortly, my lord, I shall be at your complete mercy."

He watched her through half-closed eyes as she returned to him carrying a basket containing the silver love balls, four silken cords, a narrow band of white silk, a large fluffy plume, and a long, sharply pointed egret's feather. Setting the basket next to him, she lay upon the bed, spread-eagled, and smiling, said, "I am at your mercy, my lord. Once you have rendered me helpless, you may have your way with me, and I shall not be free to protest."

His eyes widened just the tiniest bit. She had never refused him *anything*, yet he had never felt he was in complete possession of her, body and soul. That invisible independence fretted him the way a grain of sand might fret an oyster. She was his slave, and he wanted some acknowledgment from her that he held the power of life and death over her. To his amazement, he had actually fallen in love with her, and if she did not love him, she would at least admit to his mastery of her by the time they were through. Kneeling, he drew the twisted silken cords from the basket, then firmly but gently bound her to the four corners of their bed. Making four loops, he slipped them over the short carved bedposts that decorated the dais. The four matching loops he slipped about her slender wrists and ankles.

"Struggle," he commanded her. "I want to ascertain that you are bound fast, yet comfortably, my beauty."

"Who taught you this game?" Zaynab asked him. She tested her bonds. She was quite helpless. "They are fastened well, my lord," she assured him with a small smile.

"Years ago when I was but a young prince," he told her, "a friend's father possessed a Love Slave. One day my friend and I went hunting. When we returned, I spent the night. His father loaned me the girl in a gesture of great hospitality." He looked at Zaynab's breasts thrusting upward, her torso tightening as she strained at the silken bonds, and grew very excited.

She watched the play of emotions across his face. How like little boys men were, but then had not Karim told her that some men enjoyed playing these sensual games? She was fortunate the caliph was not a man who enjoyed inflicting pain as some men did.

"I am going to gag you, but only for a short time," he told her. "I will soon have a better use for your mouth." Gently, he tied the silk band around her mouth. "Can you breathe properly?" he inquired solicitously, peering down at her.

Zaynab nodded. The trick to this was to remain calm, to allow yourself to trust your partner totally and completely.

The caliph reached for the pouch that held the silver love balls, spilled them into his palm, and then slowly, slowly, pushed each of the perfect little orbs into her love channel. Sitting back

on his heels, for some long moments he contemplated his beautiful captive. She was totally and utterly at his mercy. The realization excited him. Soon her exquisite body would ache with
his delicious torture.

Zaynab was fascinated as to what he would do next. She lay
very still, for movement would set the love balls into motion,
and she would be afire. It was really quite cruel of him to have
inserted them, considering what was to come.

Reaching out, the caliph began to caress her with a single
hand. His touch was very gentle as it moved in leisurely
fashion over her body, down her silken torso. He brushed his
fingers around her nipples, smiling slightly as they puckered
for him like rosebuds touched by the frost. His fingers trailed
slowly across her belly, causing goose bumps; over her plump
mont, then back up again in the crease between it and her left
thigh; sliding around her hip to fondle a buttock before moving
down her leg.

She moaned through the silk gag as the love balls met within
her, sending a jolt of painful pleasure through her.

His eyes met hers in triumph, seeming to say, You see, you
really are mine to do with as I please. Then taking one of her
feet in his hands, he stroked it. "You have the loveliest feet," he
commented. He kissed it, then began licking her flesh at the
ankle, moving up again over her rounded knee, her shapely
thigh. His tongue was now teasing at her navel, then pushing
his face farther up her torso, he moved into the valley between
her breasts, licking and blowing alternately.

Her body strained against the cords as he worked over her
flesh, and the little silver orbs clanged silently within her, setting her afire. She moaned a second time, the sound coming in
small pants.

The caliph picked up the white plume and began to stroke
her with it. "Do you enjoy this, my beauty?" he murmured. The
fluffy plume slid with a soft, teasing motion around her breasts,
over her chest and shoulders, and down each arm, before sliding across her belly and down both legs in turn. Drawing the
wide plume back and forth over her mont, the caliph suddenly
laid it aside and pressed the heel of his palm down upon the

plump flesh, smiling wickedly as Zaynab's eyes widened; she made a muffled little noise of surprise as the pressure from his hand sent another bolt of desire racing through her.

Leaning forward, Abd-al Rahman began to suckle her nipples, each in its turn, drawing strongly upon her until she was squirming beneath him, making mewling noises from behind the gag as her arousal increased. He bit down upon the flesh, then fiercely licked the hurt away, pleased by the sound of her breathing, which had become sharper. Delving into her love channel, he withdrew the love balls, but before she might recover, he settled himself comfortably between her spread legs. Taking up the pointed-tipped egret feather, he leaned forward, parting her nether lips to reveal the tiny badge of her sex to his gaze. Then holding the flesh apart on either side of it, he applied the narrow tip of the feather to her little jewel, experimenting with just the right touch and frequency of movement, which he ascertained by her increasing struggles and the rasping sounds of her breathing.

Fascinated, he watched as the deep rosy inner flesh began to grow moist with a pearly dew and the tiny nub of her little jewel burgeoned with rising excitement. He moved the pointed feather relentlessly back and forth over it until Zaynab arched her body, then shuddered almost violently, collapsing weakly with her utter pleasure.

Immediately the caliph laid aside the feather and, reaching out, untied the gag about her mouth, kissing her tenderly as he did so, beginning a sweet new erotic torture. His tongue slipped between her lips, and she sucked on it hungrily while he gave her a brief moment to recover herself. Then, as his member was in great need of calming, for his labors had not simply aroused Zaynab, but his manhood as well, he moved his muscular body up to sit lightly upon her chest, presenting himself to her mouth for soothing while he reached back with one hand and began to play with her.

"Loose my hands," she said.

"Nay," he told her.

"One hand," she begged.

"You will use only your mouth and tongue, my beauty," he said sternly. "Remember that I am the master here."

She began to lick at him with slow strokes of her tongue, encircling the ruby head of his manhood even as his fingers brought her to another sweet crisis. He was driving her wild with his teasing, and Zaynab was most impressed by his skilled naughtiness, for he was obviously as facile at this game as she was. She quivered as the pleasure raced through her once again. He really had the most talented fingers, she thought muzzily.

Pulling away from her, he gazed on his captive possessively. Then he pushed his fingers into her mouth to suck upon. "Your love juices are flowing most copiously, my beauty," he murmured low, "even as I promised you that they would. I will enjoy drinking from your fountain, Zaynab. There has never been a woman like you before, and *you are mine!*" Then carefully he reversed his position on her body, his head between her thighs, giving her full access again to his own sex.

His tongue lapped at her, teasing and torturing her almost beyond bearing. In return, however, she suckled upon his raging member, drawing her tongue slowly over his sensitive skin. Together they allowed themselves to be swept up in the raw passion of their lovemaking. She skillfully managed his wild lust, even while giving in to her own. Finally, when the caliph could bear no more, he reversed himself yet again, plunging deep into Zaynab, pumping her hard, reveling in the rising crescendo of her cries of pleasure.

He was bigger and harder in her than he had ever been. Zaynab could feel him throbbing insistently, hot with his insatiable hunger for her. For a moment her eyes fluttered shut as she let the incredible excitement sweep over her, enveloping her in the mindless, blind desire of the moment. *A Love Slave never loses control.* But for a moment she flew with the birds, soaring in a rainbow of wildly spiraling emotions.

Abd-al Rahman's crisis approached and he could no longer hold himself back. All control lost, he cried out with his pleasure as his manhood pumped a torrent of his love juices into her. He collapsed atop Zaynab with a gusty sigh of relief and utter gratification.

"My lord, release me!" Zaynab managed to gasp, and to her relief he did so before succumbing to exhaustion upon her breasts.

"Wonderful!" he said. "That was absolutely wonderful. You are surely the finest Love Slave ever trained, my beauty. I prize you above all my other possessions. Allah bless the day Donal Righ found you and gave you to Karim al Malina for training. His reputation is more than justified. What a shame he will train no more women."

"I am happy that I please you, my lord," Zaynab said softly. *Karim!* Why was it the mere mention of his name brought back the memories of those wonderful days in Malina? Those times were gone. She knew it. He was married to another woman now. Fate had taken them in two different directions. There was no going back. She did not love Abd-al Rahman, but the caliph was a kind man, and he encouraged her desire to learn. *She would not think of Karim al Malina again!*

For the next few weeks Zaynab lived happily at al-Rusafa. The caliph left her during the day but returned most nights. Abd-al Rahman was a ruler who truly ruled. He did not allow the bureaucrats who peopled his government to rule for him. They did their jobs, but he did his. His grandfather had brought Slavic warriors from northern Europe to form a personal guard for the rulers of al-Andalus and their families. These men provided protection from the various court factions. The Saqalibah, as they were called, were loyal to the caliph, and to the caliph alone.

Abd-al Rahman had introduced a program of social integration into his government which allowed the newer Muslims, the Muwalladun, to participate. Those were people whose ancestors had followed other faiths but who had converted over the two centuries since the first Abd-al Rahman had conquered al-Andalus. Non-Muslims were in the minority in al-Andalus, but they were also in the mainstream of society. Each faith was protected by its own religious law. Every citizen could own property, and each religion had complete jurisdiction over its own marriages, divorces, dietary laws, families, and civil affairs. They joined craft guilds and engaged in other trades.

Non-Muslims, of course, paid a poll and a land tax. They could not bear arms or propagate their own faith to others. They could not testify in the courts against a Muslim when that Muslim was legally entangled with a non-Muslim. These were not particularly onerous restrictions for the Christians and Jews to bear. All the faiths lived in peace.

The caliph's court, however, was filled with various factions. There were Muwalladun; Mozarabs, who were Arabized Christians; Jews; Berbers; and Arabs. Each faction pursued its own agenda while Abd-al Rahman navigated his way through them all, his sole purpose the good of al-Andalus. It was a difficult game he played, but his predecessor, his grandfather, Emir Abdallah, had taught him well. The caliph was a skilled player of the game of government. He was respected by Christians, Jews, and Muslims alike, and his wise counsel was sought after by foreign governments of all faiths.

As the caliph worked hard, his leisure hours were important to him. He had always enjoyed the company of beautiful and clever women, but Zaynab brought a new peace to his life, one he had never before enjoyed. She truly existed for him, and him alone. She had not allowed herself to be drawn into harem politics. So it disturbed him that someone would have attempted to harm her. She had made him happy. He wanted her to be as happy, and completely free from fear.

He gave orders for certain work to be done in the harem while she recuperated at al-Rusafa. New apartments within yet separate from the rest of the harem were created. It was to be called the Court of the Green Columns. The court itself was square. Each of its four sides was edged in a portico held up by three of the green agate columns sent the caliph from Eire. There was no roof over the court. In its center was a fountain of green marble in a frame of gilded bronze. It was ringed by twelve different creatures: on one side of the fountain a lion, an antelope, and a crocodile faced a dragon, an eagle, and a vulture; on the other side, a pigeon, a falcon, and a kite faced a duck, a hen, and a cock. The creatures were made of pure gold, and studded with jewels. Water came forth from their mouths. The floor within the court was fashioned of large squares of both white and green marble.

On one side of the court a narrow door entered from the main section of the harem. On the opposite side of the court there was but a single entry into the new apartments—double doors made of ebony, banded and studded in gold. There was a gold lion's head knocker on each side of the doors, outside of which the Saqalibah would stand guard twenty-four hours a day. Green and white porcelain tubs of gardenias were set about the court to perfume it.

Within the new apartments were several spacious rooms, including a large day room where Zaynab might entertain the caliph, a comfortable bedchamber, a kitchen, and several rooms for her servants and for storage. The apartment was lavishly decorated with rich velvets, silks, and satin. The furnishings and other fixtures were of the finest.

Naja was sent to the main slave market in Cordoba to purchase a cook. The woman, a Negress named Aida, was brought before the caliph himself and personally given his instructions. Her loyalty was to belong to Abd-al Rahman first, and his beautiful Zaynab second. Should anyone attempt to bribe her, she was to report immediately to Naja, who would so inform the caliph. She would take orders only from her mistress, the caliph, Naja, or Oma. No one else was to have authority over her. If they said they did, Aida was to report the miscreant to Naja.

The inhabitants of the caliph's harem watched the construction of the Court of the Green Columns with varying degrees of interest. To some it was no more than an interesting diversion. Many cared not at all. But Zahra was astounded by what was happening before her very eyes in the city named for her. Outrage followed astonishment. The girl was a concubine, not a wife. True, the caliph's favored women had their own apartments, but nothing like the rooms now being prepared for Zaynab. Abd-al Rahman was treating the girl like a royal bride. Had he lost his mind entirely? Or had she influenced him to supplant Zahra and the others? And if she had, what other demands would she make on the besotted caliph?

Again Tarub tried to calm her friend, and Zahra's eldest son, Hakam, was amazed by the depth of his mother's anger.

"It is wonderful that he has found love again at his age," Hakam said generously. "What is the matter with you, Mother?"

"He gives her too much, and elevates her too high," Zahra sputtered furiously. "He is behaving like an old fool. I question his sanity in this matter. *Or has the girl bewitched him?*"

"What he gives is his to give, and if he heaps honor upon her, it is his right to do so, Mother," Hakam replied, sounding very much like his sire. "Father's mind is sounder than it has ever been. There is no bewitchment involved, as you well know." Hakam took his mother's hand in his. "You are making yourself ill with this terrible jealousy you have for the lady Zaynab. You must cease, lest you displease my father, the caliph."

She snatched her hand away from his gentle grasp. "Do not presume to tell me what to do, Hakam! As for your father, do you think I care what he thinks, the old satyr? Let him have his young Love Slave! Let him make her queen of al-Andalus! I will not stop hating her!"

"I cannot understand her ire," Prince Hakam said to Tarub privately. "Has the lady Zaynab offended her in some way?"

"Indeed she has," Tarub answered the prince, "but her offense is not deliberate, nor can she help it. She is young, and she is very beautiful, my lord. It was bound to happen one day that such a girl would come along to offend your mother. I am content with the passing years. If I have grown plump with age, and childbearing, and a fondness for sweets, I accept it as my lot. My kismet has been a kind one. Your father is fond of me. We share a son and two daughters. My grandchildren are many, and delight me.

"Your mother, Hakam, has always been your father's acknowledged favorite wife, his most favored woman. In her mind's eye she is still young and beautiful and desirable. When she gazes in her mirror, she has never seen herself grow older. *Not until the lady Zaynab came among us in all her youthful radiance.* Now Zahra must admit the truth to herself. It angers her. She must face the fact that although your father loves her, he has not visited her bed in over five years.

"You see, Hakam, the caliph is also reluctant to admit the passing years. An exquisite young Love Slave helps him to avoid that difficult issue. We women, however, do not have such broad choices. We must either accept our fates or grow bitter with the passage of time."

"Did my mother poison the lady Zaynab?" Hakam asked Tarub.

Tarub's warm brown eyes grew disturbed. "I honestly do not know the answer to that question, my lord," she said. "A year ago I would have said it would be very unlike her, and also most foolish. Now, however, I do not know. Your mother has not been her old self in the last several months. If it were so, I do not believe Abd-al Rahman would forgive her easily."

"You are her best friend, my lady Tarub," the prince said. "Watch over her as best you can. If you believe that she might do herself or any other harm, send to me immediately. I must protect her."

It was all they could do. In a few weeks the caliph would bring Zaynab back from al-Rusafa. It was late autumn now, and the days were not only shorter, but they were growing cooler. Al-Rusafa was a summer palace, and not at all suitable for a winter's stay. The builders worked night and day to finish the new favorite's apartments, and finally they were done.

"Tomorrow," Abd-al Rahman told Zaynab, "you will begin your journey back to Madinat al-Zahra. I have a fine surprise for you, my love, when you return. I know you will be very pleased."

"You spoil me," she replied with a smile, "but I confess to enjoying it, my dear lord. We cannot go, however, until we have visited the little summerhouse in the middle of the lake. You promised me we would see it together."

"We will go now," he told her.

"It is evening, my lord," she said. "The moon is already up."

"That is the best time to see this particular little summer-house," he replied, taking her hand and leading her from their chamber outside to the lake, where a small boat awaited them. Helping her in, he pushed the tiny vessel into the water, and joining her, began to pole the cockle from the shore out toward the center of the lake. It was not a long voyage, and within a very few minutes he was tying their boat to the railing of the summerhouse. Stepping out, he took her hand and drew her up behind him.

Inside the summerhouse, Zaynab looked about her. It was built of wood that was gilded, and its roof was a glass dome. As she looked up, the caliph shifted a small lever in the wood-work. Suddenly water began to rise up and over the glass dome, falling in a transparent sheath down the hemispherical roof; yet within the summerhouse they remained dry. "Ohhhh!" she cried in wonder.

"Do you like it, my love?" he asked her.

"It is wonderful!" she exclaimed. Then she saw that the house was furnished with a single double couch and a small table by its side that held wine, fruit, and a softly flickering oil lamp. "You meant to bring me here tonight!" she said, clapping her hands with delight.

At that moment the moon rose over the trees, silvering the water around and above them. The caliph removed his embroidered silk caftan even as Zaynab removed hers. He drew her into his arms and kissed her tenderly. His fingers caressed her face, and she smiled radiantly at him. "You are the most beautiful woman in the world," he told her. "I will give you anything within my power to give you, Zaynab, my love. You have but to ask it of me, and it shall be yours."

"There is but one thing I long for, my lord," she answered him softly. Her little hand reached up to stroke his strong facial features.

Catching her hand in his, he turned it over and placed a burning kiss upon her palm. "Tell me, my love, and it is yours!" His gaze burned into her eyes. Their time together in the solitude of al-Rusafa had rendered him obsessed with her. What had begun in lust for him was turning to love.

"Give me your child," she said simply.

"You would bear me a child?" His youngest sons were already five and seven. He was surprised, yet elated by her response.

"You are startled," she said with a smile. "Does my wish displease you, my dear lord?"

"Do you love me, Zaynab?" he asked her, curious.

She thought a long moment and then said, "In honesty, my lord, I do not know. Once I thought I loved a man, but my feelings for you are different from those I had for him. I do not believe, however, that I should want your child if I did not feel some tenderness toward you." She smiled almost shyly at him, laying her golden head upon his shoulder. "I must care for you, else I should be heartless."

He wrapped his arms about Zaynab in a tender embrace. His lips touched her soft hair. "I have loved you from the moment you stepped from your litter that day in the Hall of the Caliphate," he told her.

She laughed softly. "You lusted after me that day," she accused.

He laughed back. "I did," he admitted, "but I loved you then too. Not as I love you now, Zaynab, but I did love you."

His eyes told her that he spoke the truth. He did love her, or at least he believed he did. More, she comprehended that she cared for him. She sighed as his hands began to caress her. This was all that mattered now.

He turned her about, and began to fondle her breasts. "They are like young pomegranates, ripe and bursting with their sweetness," he whispered in her ear. His thumbs rubbed her sensitive nipples. "And these are like the little cherries that come to al-Andalus from Provence in early summer."

She reached up and wrapped her arms about his neck, allowing him free access to her entire body. He put an arm about her waist, drawing her as close to him as possible. She laid her head back upon his shoulder as his lips moved hotly over her neck and up to her ear. He nibbled delicately upon the lobe, then swirled his tongue about the whorled interior. A hand kneaded her breast. Rubbing herself provocatively against him, she felt his maleness pressing into her flesh. His hands crushed her hips in a fierce grip. Removing those hands, she turned about and led him to the double couch, pushing him down upon his back.

Kneeling next to the couch, she began to caress him with her hands. He sighed, deeply affected by her tender touches. Zaynab slid herself up on the couch to join him. Crouching over him, she pressed teasing little kisses over his whole body. Her long golden hair brushed his naked body with such a sensual touch that he shivered with delight. It formed a curtain shielding her from his view as she grasped his manroot in a firm grip. Slowly and with long, leisurely strokes she licked its length again and again. She took its tip between her lips and applied a firm pressure. He shuddered with pleasure. Deliberately and with great care she took him in her mouth and suckled upon him until she tasted the first sweet drop of his love juices.

And while she pleasured him, he reached out and found her plump Venus mont. His fingers insinuated themselves between her nether lips, stroking, stroking, seeking out the tiny badge of her sex, finding it. He teased at it for a time, and then when she whimpered softly, even as her tongue encircled the ruby head of his manroot, he pushed two fingers into her eager body, moving them back and forth until her own love juices sprinkled his fingertips with a generous effusion.

Zaynab drew away from him and then mounted her lover, sheathing his length in a single graceful motion. His hands reached up to touch her breasts again. She closed her eyes, leaning back slightly, and felt the hardness within her throbbing hotly with passion. She rode him for a short time, but then he rolled her over so that he became the dominant one. Holding her legs open and back, he pushed into her again.

It is so sweet, she thought lazily as he moved hungrily upon her, pistoning her with his lust. She tingled from the soles of her feet to the top of her head, her body shuddering as she reached the first plateau, and then the second, and finally a third. With a cry she dug her nails into his shoulders, raking them down his back. She gasped for breath, sensing his expansion and then feeling the explosion of his seed as it thundered into her waiting, eager body. Then she swooned, the pleasure overtaking her like a wave hitting the beach.

Afterward they lay happily together upon their backs, sated for the moment. Above them the water device cascaded down over the glass dome; a night bird called sweetly, poignantly, to its mate, and the moonlight silvered their fevered bodies with its light.

❧ *Chapter 13*

"*S*he is with child," Zahra said grimly to Tarub. Her face was pinched with her anxiety. She had not slept decently in days.

"You must stop it!" Tarub spoke sharply. "Our lord Abd-al Rahman has fathered eighteen children already. This will be but another."

"What if it is a son?" Zahra said, a desperate tone to her voice. "What if she convinces him to displace Hakam for her son?"

Tarub could not believe what she was hearing. Zahra had always been sensible, clever, and practical. Now she was behaving like a madwoman. "Zahra! Zahra! Get a hold of yourself," Tarub begged her friend. "Our lord will never replace Hakam as his heir. He loves Hakam above all his children. The caliph is not a young man any longer. He would not supplant Hakam, a grown man, with an unborn infant. It would be too dangerous. It could destroy the Caliphate! Besides, Zaynab might have a daughter."

"I had not thought of that," Zahra said tonelessly.

"She is very happy," Tarub told her companion.

"You have been to see her?" Zahra was surprised. Why had Tarub been to see *her*? Was Zaynab making a new and influential friend? Tarub, she suspected, had always been secretly ambitious for her children, and now for her grandchildren. Tarub had never really been her friend. I have no friends, Zahra thought.

"She would welcome you if you would but come," Tarub said, unaware of her companion's speculations. "You have never taken the time to know her, Zahra. You have built her up in your mind as some dreadful villainess, and she really is not. She is a simple girl who wants nothing more than a man to love her, and to bear that man's child. I like her."

"You like her?" Zahra's look was incredulous, and then it turned angry. *"You like her?"* she spat. "It is not Zaynab who is simple, Tarub, it is you! She has bewitched your already addled wits. You are a fool! A fat, stupid fool!"

Tarub's eyes filled with tears. "You have no cause to be cruel to me, Zahra. I have always been your friend. I have been loyal and stayed by your side all these years; swallowing your insults, putting up with your arrogance, and excusing it to others whom you have offended. You have no cause to dislike Zaynab. You do not even really know her, and your irrational suspicions of her are unfounded! Yes, I like her. *I like her!*

"If you loved Abd-al Rahman as you have always claimed, you would be glad that he is happy with this new love; but all you care about is your high position; the fact that a city was named for you; and that your son will follow his father one day. You do not truly love our lord! I suspect that you never have. You are only afraid that you will lose your vaunted place to Zaynab. *I hope you do."*

And so saying, Tarub heaved her plump form up from the cushions where she had been sitting. Her orange silk skirts swaying indignantly, she stamped from the lady Zahra's apartments.

This display of anger, so uncustomary for fat, amenable Tarub, caused Zahra's sense of proportion to be somewhat restored. She was allowing her unreasonable hatred of Zaynab to blossom out of control. She would draw attention to herself, and make herself a laughingstock within the harem. She knew there were many who had always been envious of her, and of the caliph's affections for her. They would be delighted to see her fall. It was ridiculous that she be jealous of Zaynab simply because she was young and beautiful. With every passing day she grew older. Her beauty would eventually fade. *She had no real power over anything.*

And power, Zahra knew, was the real key to happiness.

Without power you became a victim. If Zaynab was honestly content to simply make Abd-al Rahman happy, happy to bear his children, then Zaynab was really a victim; a victim of her own success and lack of personal ambition, for the caliph would certainly lose interest in her as she grew swollen with the child. And after her brat was born, would Zaynab still hold his interest? Would she be able to regain it? Or would she be like so many of the other women Abd-al Rahman had loved— *forgotten*?

Let Tarub run daily to the Court of the Green Columns to pay homage to Zaynab, the soon-to-be-forgotten concubine. They were two of a kind. Silly and weak. Their children would amount to nothing. Let Zaynab think by Tarub's befriending her, that she herself would shortly extend her favor. She remembered the boldness of the girl in the baths in her early days at Madinat al-Zahra, asking for her favor, trying to wheedle her with a smile. I will never give her my favor, Zahra thought darkly. In fact I will ignore her entirely. She is nothing to me, and soon she will be nothing to the caliph.

But the caliph was delighted that his favorite was expecting his child. He knew it had been conceived in that last passionate night they had spent in the summerhouse at al-Rusafa. The child would be born next summer. When Zaynab's symptoms became unmistakable, he had called upon Hasdai ibn Shaprut to be certain that Zaynab was healthy and that the child would come to term. It would have been a scandal, had the doctor not been brought into the harem in secret. He came accompanied by his female assistant, Rebekah, and the caliph himself.

"You are with child," he said to Zaynab. It was not a question.

"So I believe, my lord doctor," she answered.

"Tell me the signs that indicate this to you," he said.

"My link with the moon has been broken," she began. "I am nauseous much of the time. Strong smells, particularly that of food cooking, give me a headache. My breasts are beginning to ache all the time, and the nipples are very, very tender; so much so that my lord cannot touch them any longer without giving me pain."

Hasdai nodded to himself, and Rebekah handed Zaynab a small glass bowl. "You must pee into it," she instructed the patient. "My lord Hasdai needs to examine your urine."

Zaynab went behind a screen, with Oma holding the bowl. A few moments later Oma emerged and handed the bowl to the doctor. Zaynab came back and settled herself into a comfortable chair with a wide leather seat, watching.

Hasdai ibn Shaprut held up the deep crystal bowl and peered closely at it. "Her urine is almost perfectly clear, my lord," he said, "but you will note the faint, almost imperceptible cloudiness beginning." Lowering his head, he sniffed strongly. "Healthy," he commented. Then dipping his finger into the glass bowl, he tasted it. "Healthy," he said. "A faint sweetness, but healthy." Turning to the caliph, he said, "I would like your permission to examine her briefly, my lord."

The caliph nodded. "You may touch her, Hasdai. I know that you are not lustful."

The physician acknowledged his master's words, saying to Zaynab, "Hold out your hands for me, lady," and when she did, he looked carefully at them. "Her hands are not swollen, a good sign," he told them. "Her nails are healthy, not blue, the little moons white, as they should be." Then he said, "I must ask you to come out and lie down, lady." When she did so, he gently palpated her belly. Satisfied, he thanked her and then said to the caliph, "She is positively with child, my lord, and healthy, in my opinion. She is broad in the hips and should give birth easily."

"I am not broad in the hips!" Zaynab said indignantly, sitting up again. "I am a slender girl, as my lord can attest."

"I chose the words badly, my lady," Hasdai said. "The space between your hipbones is not narrow, which is a good sign."

"Indeed," Zaynab replied irritably.

"You are slim as a young nymph," the caliph told her indulgently, an amused smile upon his face.

"You mock me!" Zaynab cried, and burst into tears.

"Irrational behavior, another sign that a woman is breeding," Hasdai ibn Shaprut said dryly. "Emotions run high at a time like this."

"See my learned physician friend and his assistant out, Naja," the caliph said solemnly, struggling to keep his laughter in check. He enfolded his beloved in his arms. "There, my love, do not weep. I adore you, Zaynab, and we shall have the most beautiful child. I pray Allah will bless us with a daughter who is as beautiful as her beautiful mother. We shall call her Moraima."

"We will?" She sniffled against his shoulder. His strong arms were comforting, and she nestled against him.

"Yes, we will, my love," he said quietly, kissing her soft lips. The door closed behind the others.

Lifting her up, the caliph laid her upon her bed. Kneeling next to her, he undid the buttons upon her caftan and stroked her breasts. "You are so beautiful, Zaynab," he told her tenderly, kissing her faintly rounded belly. "I love you, and I love our child."

Winter came, to be followed by a bright spring and early summer. Zaynab's belly grew swollen with her child. To everyone's surprise, the caliph did not lose interest in his beautiful concubine. Indeed, his passion for her seemed to deepen with each passing day.

"I believe he will make her his third wife," Tarub said to Zahra. They were barely speaking, but with uncharacteristic meanness, Tarub wanted to hurt Zahra. She had not forgotten the other woman's cruelty. "He is more interested in this child than any of the others he has had."

"She could perish in childbirth," Zahra said coldly. "She is small-boned and undoubtedly weak. Or," she smiled cruelly, "the child could die shortly after its birth."

"The caliph would not like to hear you threatening either his beloved or their child," Tarub replied, smiling back at Zahra. "It is careless of you to do so in the presence of someone Abd-al Rahman would believe, Zahra. Your unreasonable jealousy makes you incautious."

"He will never take her as his wife," Zahra said, though she was less than certain.

Tarub laughed mockingly, and left Zahra to her black thoughts.

Midway through the month of Muharram, which in Christian Europe would have been the end of July, Zaynab went into labor. The birthing chair, gilded and bejeweled, was brought into the Court of the Green Columns. Although they were not allowed inside, many harem women gathered in the court-yard to await word. Tarub came in the company of the caliph's concubines Qumar and Bacea, who were also mothers of Abd-al Rahman's children, to attend Zaynab. Naja admitted them, bowing respectfully. Qumar was a Persian, known for her healthy progeny. Bacea was a red-haired Galacian, mother of the caliph's youngest son, Murad. Both concubines were in their mid-twenties.

"Are your pains hard yet?" Tarub's motherly face showed her concern.

"She looks strong," Qumar said cheerfully. "She will birth her child well, I can tell."

"You must not be afraid," Bacea told the younger girl. "Birth is a natural function of the female body. We will be with you to help you. I have a son and a daughter, and Qumar has a son and two daughters. Do you want more children after this one?"

"What a question to ask a woman in labor!" Qumar laughed. "Bacea is a pretty girl, but Galacians are not too intelligent."

"And Persians are?" Bacea shot back. "You didn't even know you were with child the first time." She laughed, and then said, "I will admit the timing of my question is poor, however."

"Be silent, the two of you," Tarub scolded them. "You chatter like magpies. We must help Zaynab to birth her baby successfully."

The subject of their concern gasped as a strong pain swept over her. *"Allah!"* she cried.

"That is good!" Tarub said piously. "Call upon God, and He will deliver you, and your child."

The two concubines swallowed their laughter, their eyes

meeting Zaynab's. It had been a long time since Tarub had birthed anything. She had obviously forgotten that the laboring woman's cry was more an imprecation than a prayer.

"This is the price we pay for all that sweetness," Bacea said, a twinkle in her hazel eyes, and Zaynab was forced to grin.

"I will know better next time." She giggled, and then groaned again as pain washed over her.

For the next several hours they alternately cajoled and encouraged her in her labor. Qumar, being more supple than Tarub, knelt and spread a layer of cloth beneath the birthing chair where Zaynab now sat. Outside her bedchamber the caliph waited in the company of Hasdai ibn Shaprut, whom he had called in case of any emergency. The physician was not needed, however. A cry was heard from within, and shortly thereafter Tarub, her face wreathed in smiles, came forth from the chamber, a swaddled bundle in her arms.

"My lord husband," she said, "here is your daughter, the princess Moraima. Zaynab is well, and hopes you are pleased."

Qumar and Bacea now joined Tarub, each smiling and cooing over the child.

The caliph took his new daughter in the presence of his wife, his two concubines, and Hasdai ibn Shaprut. Cradling the baby gently, he looked down upon her. To his delight, the infant gazed back solemnly at him from serious blue eyes. The down upon her head was her mother's pale gold in color. "I accept this child as my own blood, my daughter," Abd-al Rahman said in a strong voice to his witnesses. Then carrying the baby, he entered Zaynab's bedchamber. He knelt by her bedside. "You have done well, my dearest love," he told the exhausted girl. "I have formally recognized our daughter before witnesses. Now none will doubt her paternity, and none shall have her to wife but the finest prince, when she is old enough," he told Zaynab. "Sleep now."

Rising, he handed the baby to Oma and left his favorite's apartments.

Zaynab lay exhausted, yet awake. She had a daughter, and the child was a princess. She wondered whether Gruoch had borne a son or a daughter, and if there had been other children since. Wouldn't her twin be amazed to know that the sister she had known as Regan was not moldering away in a convent, but the pampered concubine of a great ruler, and the mother of a princess. *And Karim . . .* Why on earth had she thought of *him*? She had kept him successfully from her mind these past months, but now suddenly he was there. Would he learn she had borne the caliph a daughter? Was he a father himself, by the wife he had returned to Malina to wed? Of course he was. What would her life have been like had she been that bride instead of Abd-al Rahman's Love Slave? It was useless to think such thoughts. She would sleep, and when she awoke, it would be all the same. She would be the caliph's adored favorite, the mother of his daughter, and Karim al Malina would be but a memory. A single tear slipped down her cheek. She would never love Abd-al Rahman, but she would honor and respect the caliph, and he would never know her true feelings. Turning her face to the wall, she willed herself into a slumber.

"She could only give him a puny daughter," Zahra sneered when she later met Tarub in the baths.

"They wanted a daughter," Tarub said sweetly. "They had her named months ago. They never even considered a son. It should please you, Zahra. Now you do not have to worry that Zaynab's child will supplant Hakam." Laughing, she went on her way.

Despite Zahra's dislike of Zaynab, the caliph's goodwill meant more to the women of the harem than the first wife's ire. They sensed Zahra's star was finally waning. They flocked to the Court of the Green Columns, bringing their gifts to the new princess, who was admired by all and praised mightily. Even Prince Hakam came to visit his new sister, bringing a small silver ball that was filled with bells to amuse the baby.

"I have no children of my own," he explained to Zaynab, "but I do remember having a toy like this one when I was small. I loved it." He smiled warmly at her, and when she smiled back at him, giving him her thanks, Hakam understood why his father loved her. He pitied his poor mother. Zahra might have been the love of Abd-al Rahman's youth, but there

was no doubt in the prince's mind that Zaynab was the love of
his sire's later years. She was a delightful girl. "My sister
Moraima will always have my affection, and the security of
my protection, lady," he told her.

Tarub, of course, rubbed salt into Zahra's wounds by telling
her former friend of the prince's visit. "I believe Hakam is as
charmed by Zaynab as is the caliph," she said with a false
smile. "The whole harem is, you know."

Zahra said nothing, but she was amazed at the depth of
Tarub's venom. She had always thought the second wife a
simple plump fool, but it was obvious that she was not. She
was a very dangerous bitch. If the caliph made Zaynab his third
wife, as was rumored throughout the harem, then together
the two of them would become a force to be reckoned with.
Tarub's son, Abdallah, was Abd-al Rahman's second son. What
if these two women worked in concert to supplant Hakam? She
had no proof of such a scheme, but she did not need it. It would
have been what she would have done had her position and
Tarub's been reversed.

The new favorite suddenly sickened, as did her child and her
waiting woman. Normally the baby would have been sent to
a baby farm to be nursed, so that the Love Slave could again
serve her master; but such a thing was anathema to Zaynab. The
women of Alba, even the highborn women, did not farm their
infants out as a general rule. She had begged the caliph to be
allowed to keep Moraima with her for a few months before a wet
nurse would be brought into the Court of the Green Columns. It
had pleased Abd-al Rahman to grant her request. He liked sitting
by her side as she nursed their child. It made him feel like an
ordinary man, if only for a short time. But now Zaynab, Moraima, and Oma were sickening.

Hasdai ibn Shaprut was called in, for poison was immediately suspected. The only two members of the favorite's household not to grow ill were Naja and Aida, the cook, which
naturally set the suspicion upon them. The physician, however,
gained some measure of Zaynab's favor by immediately ruling

out the poor eunuch, who was terrified by the turn of events, and Aida, whose loyalty was simply too strong.

"Too obvious," the physician said. "It is something that the lady Zaynab and Oma alone share. The little princess is being poisoned through her mother's milk. She must be sent away if she is to be saved."

Weeping, Zaynab gave her daughter over to the physician's assistant, Rebekah. "Do not fear, great lady," Rebekah said. She was a mother herself, and Zaynab's devotion to her child had already gained her approval. "I have an excellent wet nurse in the Jewish quarter. She is a big, healthy girl with more milk than her own child can consume. She will care for our little princess as if she were her own child, and you may see her any time you so desire."

"Why can this woman not come here?" Zaynab sobbed.

"Because," Hasdai ibn Shaprut explained patiently to her, "whatever is causing you and Oma to sicken could cause the wet nurse to sicken also. Until I find the cause, we must protect your child."

"Yes, yes!" Zaynab agreed, and turned to the caliph. "Oh, my dear lord, do not let anything happen to our child! She is all I have, and I will die if anything should take her from me forever!"

"Hasdai will find the answer," the caliph promised his beloved, enfolding her in his loving embrace, which caused Zaynab to weep all the harder.

It was poison without a doubt. Within just a few days the baby was healthy again, but her mother and Oma sickened further. *How was it being administered to the favorite and Oma,* the physician wondered, *yet not to Naja and Aida?* Their clothing was removed and replaced, but there was still no change. Hasdai examined all the foods being prepared by Aida, but the food was fresh, and they all ate from the same pots. What was it? *What?* What did Zaynab and Oma do that the others did not? Then Hasdai knew.

It came to him like a bolt from the blue. *They bathed together!* They bathed twice daily in Zaynab's private bath. Immediately the physician ordered a sample of the water to be brought. He forbade Zaynab and Oma to enter the bath again until he was certain. Testing it, his suspicions were confirmed. The water flowing into Zaynab's private bath had been poisoned! The poison was being absorbed through their skin, and slowly killing the two girls. He prayed his discovery was in time, and began administering theriaca.

The caliph was told, and he knew without a doubt who was behind this attempt on Zaynab's life, and probably the first attempt as well. There was only one person in his harem who had the kind of power to arrange such harm. He set a trap, and sprang it.

"I found the slave who poured the daily dose of poison into the cistern serving Zaynab's bath," he told Hasdai ibn Shaprut. "I had two of my most loyal guards wait in the shadows until she came. She needed little persuasion to tell me that the lady Zahra was behind it. They strangled the slave afterward."

"What will you do, my lord?" Hasdai asked.

The caliph sighed as deeply as a man in pain. "I cannot protect Zaynab from Zahra, Hasdai. In order to do so I must cast Zahra off publicly. She is the mother of my heir, and should I divorce her, I will cause a wedge between either Hakam and his mother or my son and me. I cannot do it. I decided years ago that Hakam would follow me as caliph. Because I did not vacillate in my choice, I have built the loyalty of his brothers and uncles, and his male cousins. There is no doubt, no confusion, nor has there ever been. *Hakam is the heir.*

"If I repudiate Hakam's mother, there are those who will be convinced it is but the first step to renouncing my eldest son. There will be nothing that I can say that will induce them to believe otherwise. Factions will form about my other sons. Four of them are, as you are well aware, old enough to be encouraged to sedition. Power is the greatest tempter of all, Hasdai. Gold, victory in battle, beautiful women; they all fade before the specter of ultimate power. My father was murdered by a brother who could not accept my grandfather's decision in the matter of the succession. I cannot even remember my father, but my grandfather chose me over his other sons to replace him, and then lived long enough to raise me to an age where I might grasp the reins of al-Andalus strongly.

"I have ruled this land for over thirty years now, and we have been at peace most of the time. Peace encourages prosperity. Al-Andalus is the most powerful and prosperous country in the world today. It will remain that way, my friend, because I will not permit any dissension to form that I cannot personally control. Sadly, I cannot control a war within my harem without it going beyond the walls of my gardens. Twice Zahra has attempted to murder my beloved Zaynab. To prevent any further attempt, I must either rid myself of Zahra or send Zaynab from me in order to protect both her and our child. I have no other choice in the matter."

"Will you free her, then, my lord?" the physician asked. He didn't like the way Abd-al Rahman looked at the moment. The caliph was pale, and his skin was shiny with sweat. He was obviously very distressed by this situation.

"I cannot free her, Hasdai," the caliph said. "Even though women are permitted under Islam to own their own property, a woman without the protection of a man, or a family, is helpless and in danger. No, Hasdai, I will not free Zaynab. I am giving her to you. You have no wife to object, and I shall be very generous. She will have her own house on the river outside of Cordoba, and her servants, and an income to support her, and our child; but she belongs to you from this moment on, Hasdai ibn Shaprut."

The physician was astounded. He could not quite believe what the caliph was saying to him. "You will visit her, of course," he ventured.

Abd-al Rahman shook his head. "Once she leaves Madinat al-Zahra, I shall never see her again. She will no longer be mine."

Hasdai's head was spinning with the implications of what the caliph was saying. "What of the little princess?"

A spasm crossed the caliph's face. "I will, of course, want to see my daughter from time to time," he said. Then he staggered.

"Sit down, my lord," the doctor said, reaching for the caliph's wrist and checking his pulse. It was fast and erratic. Reaching into his robes, he drew forth a tiny gilded pill. "Put this beneath your tongue, my lord. It will ease the pain in your chest."

Abd-al Rahman did not ask Hasdai ibn Shaprut how he knew of the pain in his chest. He simply took the pill and followed his instructions. Finally, when the ache began to subside, he said, "How am I to tell her, Hasdai? How am I to tell this girl I love that I will never see her again?" His deep blue eyes were moist.

"Let us move her from the Court of the Green Columns today, my lord," the physician said quietly. "We will tell her nothing except that it is for her safety. In a few days, when she and Oma are well again, you will come to her and tell her, but not today. You need time to regain your strength."

The caliph nodded slowly. "No one must know where she is, Hasdai. It will be enough for Zahra that she is gone. I will speak to her myself. You will be good to Zaynab?"

"My lord, I will respect her greatly," was the reply.

"Respect her if you will, Hasdai, but you must love her, too," Abd-al Rahman said. "She needs to be loved, and she will give you great pleasure, my friend."

To the caliph's amazement, Hasdai ibn Shaprut blushed. "My lord," he said, "I have little experience in matters of the heart. I have spent my life in the pursuit of learning, that I might be of value to my country. The delegation from Byzantium is expected any day. They are bringing the *De Materia Medica* for translation, so we may soon have our medical school in Cordoba. My time must be spent with their Greek translators. I will have time for little else. This is why, to the despair of my father, I have never taken a wife."

The physician's words cheered the caliph, for he realized that after her disappointment lessened, Zaynab would eventually want to be loved again. Hasdai ibn Shaprut had little chance against her seductive wiles.

"You will do your best by Zaynab, I know," Abd-al Rahman said, thinking, *and she will do her best by you.* "I will give orders to have her removed with all her possessions this day. Then I will go to see the lady Zahra. Accompany Zaynab, my friend."

The physician bowed low. His patient's color was better now. "Do not allow the lady Zahra to upset you again, my lord."

The caliph nodded, and departed from the Court of the Green Columns. He would have it torn down and destroyed when she was gone. No woman should ever inhabit it again. Like Zaynab, it would be but a sweet memory. Finding the Mistress of the Women and the Chief Eunuch, he gave them his instructions concerning Zaynab.

"I warn you both," he said grimly, "that should you speak of this to *anyone*, I will know it, and your tongues will be torn from your heads. You will be of little use, Walladah, to the lady Zahra then. As for you, Nasr, remember your first loyalty is to me, *and not to the lady Zahra*. I rule in all of al-Andalus, especially in this harem, not she."

He left them amazed by his hard words, and found his way to his first wife's chambers. Entering it, he dismissed her maids, all of whom were startled to see him in these environs, which he had not entered in years.

Zahra looked up, her face bland and smooth. "How may I serve you, dear lord?" she asked him.

"I know what you have done," he said harshly. "I caught your slave. She needed little persuasion to tell me the truth before she died. You are a wicked woman, Zahra!"

"If I have done something wrong," Zahra said sweetly, "then it is up to you, my lord, to correct and chastise me." She smiled at him.

"You might have killed Moraima too," he said.

"You have other daughters," she responded coldly, all pretense gone. Her eyes were icy. He had never known her like this. He suddenly realized he was really seeing her for the first time. "Did you think I would let you replace my son? Supplant Hakam with one of *her* brats? I will die first, my lord! *I will die!*" she shrieked.

"I wish you would die," he said brutally. "Hakam, I know, has no part in your treachery, Zahra. For his sake, for the sake of our country, I will not divorce you. I know there is nothing I can say that will convince you that Zaynab and her daughter are no threat to you. To preserve peace in al-Andalus, I have sent the woman I love and our child from Madinat al-Zahra. I shall never see her again, for I know I cannot protect her from you if I do. For Hakam's sake, and for al-Andalus, I have deprived myself of happiness in my last years. It is, Zahra, the greatest sacrifice I have ever made, *and I will never forgive you for having forced me to it.*"

"Ohh, my dear lord, you have done this for me!" The pinched look was suddenly gone from her face.

"*For you?* Do you not listen, Zahra? I have done nothing for you, nor will I ever again. I held you in my high esteem. I named a city for you, but you have, in your selfishness and pride, destroyed any feeling I might have had left for you. If you truly loved me, you would have wanted my happiness. All that concerned you was your position. I never want to see your face again. To ensure that, you will be confined to these rooms and your garden for the rest of your days. You will go to the baths at night when all are sleeping, so you may not contaminate any of my other women. You will be treated with deference, and you may have guests, but your reign is over, *my wife.*"

"You cannot—" she began.

"*Cannot?*" he thundered. "Lady, I am your lord and master! You may continue to sit like a spider in your gilded web, shooting your venom, *but you will obey me!*" So saying, he turned on his heel and left her.

"I do not care," she whispered to herself. "*I do not care!* I have saved my son's place from Zaynab, and she is gone from here. I will endure whatever punishment I must. He will relent. In a few days his anger will cool and he will come back to me with some charming little present. He is too old for maidens now. He needs me."

The caliph next went to his eldest son and told him of Zahra's deceit. "I have sent Zaynab and Moraima to safety. I shall not see them again," he told his heir. "The union of al-Andalus must be maintained at all costs, Hakam. Even if it means my own personal unhappiness. Do not be angry at your mother, my son. Tarub tells me that Zahra truly believes Zaynab, and any children she might have, would be a danger to you. She is half mad now. She honestly believes that she is protecting you."

"And you want me to take wives, and form a harem of my own?" Hakam said. "I think, Father, that I prefer my books."

"It would be better, my son, if when you have concluded your life's course, you were followed by your own son, but if you do not take a favorite and father a child, then choose your heir almost at once upon your ascension. Let there be no doubt as to who will lead al-Andalus when you are gone. When my father, Prince Muhammed, was murdered by his own sibling, my grandfather, Emir Abdallah, did not hesitate. He had other sons, but he had chosen Muhammed to follow him. So he chose me next, even though I was not yet three years of age. He educated me, loved me, and taught me to rule. So you must do with your heir even as he did with me and I have done with you. The people need to know that they will be in safe, sure hands. The governmental bureaucracy needs a strong rein. Do not allow *anyone* else to rule in your name for you, Hakam. I never have."

"I am ashamed of what my mother has done," Hakam said quietly. "I know that she loves me, but I would not have believed her capable of such evil." He took his father's hands and kissed them in a gesture of submission and affection.

"A mother's love is the strongest bond of all, Hakam," Abd-al Rahman told his eldest son, and then he embraced him. "Praise Allah that you have grown into a fine man!"

❧ *Chapter 14*

"*Y*ou are sending me away from you forever?" Zaynab's aquamarine eyes welled with tears. "Ohh, do not send me from you, my lord!"

Abd-al Rahman, looking into those eyes, felt the bands tightening about his chest again. "My precious love," he said, "I have explained it all to you. I had no other choice. I could not protect you as long as you remained at Madinat al-Zahra."

"Then let me live at al-Rusafa," Zaynab pleaded.

"Zahra hates you, my love," he said sadly. "She will continue her attempts on your life and that of our daughter if you remain my concubine." He sighed. He would not tell her that he had intended to make her his third wife; the wife who would comfort him and be a joy to him in his old age. He would never forgive Zahra.

"Why do you not send Zahra away instead of me?" Zaynab demanded, suddenly angry. "The jealousy is hers, not mine! How can I believe you love me when you would put me away!"

"I cannot put the mother of my heir aside publicly," he said patiently. "Many would not understand. They would think I meant to put Hakam aside in favor of another son. I have explained it all to you, Zaynab. You are not like so many of my women. *You do understand.* You may not like what I am telling you, but you understand why I must do this. And never again say that I do not love you, for I do. So much so that I will deny myself your company for the rest of my days in order to save your life, and that of our little Moraima."

"Ahh, Abd-al, I cannot bear it!" she whispered. "Where will I go? Will Moraima ever know her father?"

"How can you believe that I would set you adrift?" he cried. "I have given you this fine house on the al-Rusafa road. It has a vineyard and an orchard, and overlooks the river. It belongs to you, Zaynab. I will not free you, however, for you surely understand that in this society a woman without the protection of her family is at risk. I have given you to Hasdai ibn Shaprut. He will be your new master. He will protect you, and Moraima."

She was astounded. *Hasdai ibn Shaprut?* The serious, long-faced physician? She suddenly giggled, and when the caliph looked at her, she said, "He is a pleasant enough man, my lord, but does this physician know what to do with a Love Slave? Or am I expected to remain celibate the rest of my days?" She cocked her head at him questioningly. "Perhaps you mean to come to me secretly? I would welcome it, my lord!"

He felt the dull pain in his chest once more, and struggled discreetly to draw a breath. "You will belong to Hasdai ibn Shaprut in every sense of the word, Zaynab. When this interview is concluded, I will not see you ever again, my beautiful love."

"And Moraima?" she questioned him. "Will you cast our daughter off too, my lord?"

"Oma will bring her to me once each month," the caliph said. "I do not intend to lose my youngest child. Zahra will not be jealous of Moraima if you are not in evidence. Besides, I have told Zahra I do not want to see her face ever again. She is confined to her apartments, not that that will prevent her continual meddling, I fear. And when I am gone from this earth, Zaynab, you need have no fears for our daughter. Hakam will look after her. You can rely upon and trust Hakam even though he is Zahra's son. Now, my love, I must go from you." He turned away from her.

"One kiss, my lord!" Zaynab cried.

He turned back, his face anguished.

"Of all the wonderful things you have given me, my lord, I have but asked you for two. Our child, and a kiss of farewell. Will you deny me this last request?"

With a cry of despair he swept her into his arms. They closed about her in a fierce embrace. His mouth found hers, and he experienced her lips for the last time; their sweetness, and softness, the taste of her, her scent. He would never again smell gardenias without thinking of her. She felt his heart hammering wildly and her own beating madly in return. *And then it was over.* Without another word he left her.

Despite his reassurances, Zaynab was frightened. The caliph had been demanding of her, but as his Love Slave, she had had a measure of security. What if Zahra was not satisfied to have her gone from Madinat al-Zahra? What if she was able to reach out from her confinement to harm Moraima? Zaynab had not loved the caliph, but she was fond of him, and he was the father of her child. She knew that she had made him happy. He had said he would never see her again because of the pain it would give him. What if he began to feel that way about Moraima? Without her powerful father to protect her, to make a princely match for her, the child would have nothing. Zaynab wept bitterly.

Oma came running and tried to comfort her mistress, but she could not. Weakened by the poison, distraught over what was happening, Zaynab collapsed in a heap upon the floor.

When Zaynab finally became aware once more, she was in a bedchamber. "Where are we?" she asked Oma, who was seated by her side.

"In our new home, lady," the young girl replied. "Have you forgotten? You fell into a swoon when the—" She hesitated, but then not knowing how else to express it, said, "—when the caliph left you. You have been unconscious for almost a day, my lady. The physician said you were in no danger and would heal in time. Ohh, mistress, what has happened to us? Why have we been taken from Madinat al-Zahra?"

"Help me to sit up," Zaynab said, "and then fetch me something cool to drink, my good Oma. I will tell you everything as it was told to me, but my throat is very dry."

Oma helped her lady into an upright position, plumping pillows behind her to make her more comfortable. Then she fetched her a goblet of fruit juice mixed with a little snow from the nearby mountains. When Zaynab had slaked her thirst, she explained in quiet tones why they were now living in this new place.

"That lady Zahra!" Oma said angrily. "I wish she would die! Perhaps if she does, the caliph will take you back, my lady."

Zaynab shook her head. "It is over, Oma. The caliph did not free me. He gave me to Hasdai ibn Shaprut. I now belong to the physician. At least we were not given to someone from a far place, or sold in the open market, Oma. Do you remember the market in Alcazaba Malina where we saw the slaves being sold? We are fortunate."

Without warning Hasdai ibn Shaprut entered the room. "You are awake," he said. "That is good. How do you feel, Zaynab?"

For a moment she was about to reprimand the physician for not addressing her properly. Then she remembered she was his property now, not the caliph's. "I am thirsty," she replied, nodding at the goblet of juice with snow.

"It sits well? You have lost the nausea the poison was causing you?" He peered closely at her, then took her hand and looked carefully at it, his fingers seeking her pulse. He cocked his head to one side, humming and nodding to himself.

"The juice tasted good," she said. "The nausea seems to have vanished, my lord. Am I getting better?" She put her hand to her head and grimaced. Her hair was all matted and tangled. She must look an absolute fright!

Hasdai laughed. "You are feeling better," he said, chuckling.

"What do you find so amusing, my lord?" Zaynab snapped at him.

"I do not mean to offend," he said, "but you are suddenly aware of your appearance. Only a woman on the mend would care."

"Your experience with women then is vast?" she sneered.

He flushed. "I am a physician, Zaynab. We are taught to observe not simply a patient's body, but their state of mind as well. Right now, for instance, you are angry because of your situation."

"And should I not be angry, my lord? I have been sent from the caliph, and given to another man, all because of the irrational fantasies of a deranged woman who tried to murder me and my baby, whom she deemed a threat to her grown son! Do you believe that I should accept this situation meekly? Do you think a woman's feelings are like a spring rain, pouring one moment and stopping the next? Yes, my lord, I am very angry!"

"I will leave you, then," he said, rising from her bedside.

"Wait!" she commanded him imperiously. "Do you live here too? My lord, the caliph, said he was giving me this house."

"I have my own home," Hasdai told her.

"Why am I not there, then? I am now your Love Slave, my lord. Surely you are aware of all that entails," she said quietly.

"I am a Jew, Zaynab." He laughed, almost to himself. "You do not know what that means, do you? I am of the tribe of Benjamin, an Israelite. I am not of Islam. I am not a Christian."

"Why should I care?" she asked him curiously. "You are a man. Are not all men basically alike, Hasdai ibn Shaprut? Two arms. Two legs. A manhood. Is a Jew any different from a man of Islam or a Christian?"

"History has made us a scorned race," he explained.

Now Zaynab laughed. "Yet the Jews call themselves God's chosen people, the imam told me. If God has chosen you, then how can your fellow man be against you? It does not make sense, my lord. And you have still not answered my question. Is it that you have a wife? I am certain the caliph would not have given me to you if he did not think it was proper."

"I have no wife," he answered her. "However, we Jews live by a set of special laws. I cannot have you in my house for you are considered unclean as both a non-Jew and a concubine."

"Then you will visit me here?" How silly this all was, she thought.

"If you desire my company, Zaynab, I shall visit you, of course," he replied. "You know that if you go into the city you must be well veiled, escorted by both Oma and Naja, and in a litter."

"I may travel to the city?" She was surprised.

"You may do whatever you wish, Zaynab," he said.

"I am your Love Slave now, Hasdai ibn Shaprut. I know that you know what that means. I asked the caliph how I was to serve you, and he told me that I belonged to you completely, and in every way. Do you not find me attractive, or is it that you are in love with another woman?" She looked up at him.

Hasdai had never had a woman look directly at him. It was startling. "I find you very attractive," he said.

"Then when I am well you will come to me, and I will give you pleasure such as you have never known, my lord." She smiled a beguiling smile at him. "No woman will ever please you as I will."

He nodded gravely at her, and left the room.

"He is shy," Oma said with a little chuckle. "I think you may have frightened him just a little."

"He should be frightened," Zaynab answered. "He must follow in the footprints of Karim al Malina and Abd-al Rahman." Then she laughed. "He is tall, and handsome. I never really looked at him before. Did you note his hands? They are big, and the nails are beautifully shaped."

"It is his mouth that I like," Oma said. "It is a big and sensuous mouth. Alaeddin had a mouth like that." She sighed.

"I have not asked you how you feel, Oma," Zaynab suddenly realized. "You are better too, aren't you?"

"Oh, yes, my lady. The physician gave me that theriaca, and I got better within a day. He is a kind man, lady. We are very fortunate, as you have already said."

Over the next few days Zaynab's strength increased, and she was able to get out of bed without feeling dizzy. Her first trip was to her new baths, where Oma was only attendant. Her cook, Aida, and Naja had also come with them to the new

house. There were several other women of intermediate age
who kept the place in order.

"When will Moraima be returned to me?" Zaynab asked
Hasdai ibn Shaprut daily. "I miss my daughter."

"I will have to find a wet nurse for her," he said.

"Why can I not nurse her again? My milk has not dried up
entirely, and if my daughter returns to my breast, it will come
again. Aida, the cook, says it will," Zaynab told him. "I do not
want a wet nurse."

"You have no other choice," he said. "I know you feel
stronger every day, Zaynab, and indeed you are growing well
again. Unfortunately, I do not know for how long the poison
will remain in your system. It could be a year, or more. I cannot
allow you to nurse your daughter under those circumstances.
Moraima is safe for now with Rebekah's niece in the Jewish
quarter."

"But I am her mother!" Zaynab said angrily. "She will not
know me if you do not return her soon! I am not some lazy
Moorish concubine who sends her child to the baby farm to be
nursed. I want my daughter!"

"I will find a good nursemaid for her," he promised. To his
surprise, she grasped an earthenware trinket and flung it at him.

"Give me back my baby!" she shrieked at him.

"You are becoming irrational," he said calmly. He ducked
as another missile flew in his direction, this one better aimed,
he thought wryly. "Did you ever show your temper to the
caliph?" he asked her. "This is not, I believe, correct behavior
for a Love Slave, Zaynab. You are not supposed to kill your
master, except with passion, I was given to understand."
His brown-gold eyes were twinkling as he attempted to turn
her fury.

"How would you know that, my lord?" she demanded scathingly. "You have never once attempted to arouse my passions." Then she ran from the room so he would not see her
angry tears.

"I have never seen her like that, my lord," Oma said.

"Mother love is very strong," Hasdai answered the girl. "I
will make an effort this day to find a suitable slave woman to

nurse and care for the little princess. Your mistress is a good mother."

"My lord," Oma said boldly, "will you permit me to speak frankly?"

He nodded, wondering what the girl had to say that would be of import.

"You must address my mistress's other needs as well, my lord. She is too young to live without passion, having been trained in it. The caliph gave her to you because he believed you would protect her and make her happy."

Hasdai ibn Shaprut was astounded by her speech, although his face remained a pleasant mask. He had thought only Jewish women were so outspoken. Obviously he had been wrong. "Your mistress is still not well enough for activities of an excitable nature. In time, of course, she will be, I realize," he said. Then, with a bow in Oma's direction, he departed.

Oma thought nothing more of it, for she had had her say. The physician would certainly, when Zaynab was well enough, become her lover. In the meantime they had to get settled into this new dwelling. It was located two miles outside the city of Cordoba, off the main road, behind whitewashed walls and down a narrow lane. There was a gatehouse kept by a gatekeeper.

The house itself was built in traditional style about a court-yard with a tiled floor. In the courtyard's center was a tiered fountain that drizzled its water into a pool of water lilies and goldfish. Fat, squat vases were set about the portico of the courtyard. They were filled with gardenias whose heavy scent would, in warm weather, perfume the air. Beyond the court-yard and the house was an orchard that spread away to the low bluff overlooking the river. Next to it on either side was a vineyard.

The house was spacious. The ground floor consisted of day rooms, servant's quarters, a library, and the kitchens. The second floor of the dwelling consisted of several sleeping chambers and a large bath that was completely tiled and had gold fixtures. Throughout, it was beautifully and quite famil-iarly furnished, with carpets on the polished wood floors

and tapestries on the walls. In fact, all of Zaynab's furnishings had been transported here from the Court of the Green
Columns. The caliph had made certain that his beloved Zaynab would always be comfortable. She did not know it yet,
but Abd-al Rahman had deposited in her name fifty thousand
gold dinars with Hasdai ibn Shaprut's third cousin, who was
a goldsmith.

Hasdai ibn Shaprut came every day to monitor Zaynab's
health, but other than that, he seemed to have no interest in her.
For the moment, Zaynab did not care. Her main focus was the
return of her daughter. Finally, when she had been separated
from the child for almost a month, the physician arrived one
afternoon with Moraima and a plain-faced girl he introduced
as Abra.

"Her husband was killed in an accident, and her child was
born dead. She has suffered, but Rebekah has assured me that
she is healthy, obedient, and of sound mind."

"Why did her child die?" Zaynab demanded, her main concern for her own baby.

"It was strangled with its own cord," he said bluntly. "It
was an otherwise healthy boy. Abra has been nursing the
princess for a week now. As you can see, she is healthy and
thriving."

Zaynab took her daughter from the nursemaid. Cradling the
baby in her arms, she smiled down into its little face and
crooned in her native tongue. "There's a fine bairn, she is, my
wee sweetheart. Yer da has sent us away, but I hae ye back
now. We'll manage, Oma, and yer mam, and ye, my wee
Moraima." Tears sprang quickly to her eyes as her daughter
reached up and grasped the finger with which she had been
stroking the little pink cheek. "Ohh, she remembers me!" the
happy mother cried.

"What language did you speak to her?" he asked. "I have
studied many languages, but I did not recognize any of your
words, Zaynab," Hasdai ibn Shaprut asked.

"It is the Celtic tongue of my homeland," she explained.
"Oma and I use it when we don't want anyone to know what

we are talking about. It served us quite well in the harem at Madinat al-Zahra. I want Moraima to learn it from birth. When she is old enough, I shall find her a slave girl her own age from Alba to be her confidante."

"You are a clever woman, Zaynab," he remarked.

"So the caliph said," she responded, and then she handed the baby to her nursemaid. "You are welcome in this house, Abra. I thank you for the nourishment with which you will provide the princess. Oma will show you to my daughter's quarters."

Abra nodded her acknowledgment. She was a big girl with dark braids, black eyes, and a pillowy bosom. She would be paid for her services because she was a freewoman. She followed Oma from her new mistress's apartments, holding Moraima quite competently in her arms.

"Moraima's return has made you bloom," Hasdai ibn Shaprut noted. "I am pleased to see you so well, Zaynab. I know you will be happy now."

"When do you mean to lie with me?" she asked him suddenly.

He swallowed hard. "You are not well enough," he told her, a flush coming to his cheeks.

"I have never felt better, my lord," she murmured. "I am well rested, and content but for one thing. Are you shocked? Do the women in your family hide their lust for their men?"

He was fascinated by her; the pale golden hair loose about her shoulders, the direct gaze of her aquamarine eyes, the creaminess of her fair skin. Her caftan was white, embroidered with seed pearls. He could see the steady beat of the tiny pulse in her throat. He could feel the heat of her body as she leaned toward him, and the scent of her gardenia fragrance was intoxicating. He could not, for the life of him, however, answer her question.

"Do you not desire me, my lord?" Zaynab asked him. Then a strange look came over her face. "Are you a man who prefers boy lovers perhaps?" she queried. "I did hear of such men in the harem."

"N-No," he managed to gasp. "I am not a lover of boys." He arose quickly. "I must leave you now," he said, and was gone before she might pursue further this line of questioning.

Zaynab was completely puzzled, and her puzzlement but grew during the next few days. Abra, her initial shyness over, was a delightful, burbling font of information regarding Hasdai ibn Shaprut, the Jews, and Jewish history. The plump girl with her currant eyes nursed her little charge while chattering merrily.

"We call him *Nasi* in the Jewish quarter, lady," she said.

"What does it mean?" Zaynab asked.

"Prince, lady. Hasdai ben Isaac ibn Shaprut, Prince of the Jews. His family is *very* distinguished, even before Nasi's success at the caliph's court. He is the despair of every mother with an eligible daughter, not to mention his own parents. He will not marry."

"I wonder why," Zaynab said, and then, "Is it forbidden for a Jew to have a concubine, Abra?"

"Once, in ancient times, the men of our race took more than one wife and kept concubines. Now, however, it is frowned upon, but that does not mean it is not done, lady. Besides, the Nasi is not a married man. Do you wish to be his concubine?"

"I was given to him for that purpose by the caliph," Zaynab answered her, amused. Abra would have some fine gossip to impart when she went home to the quarter for a visit. She wondered if it would enhance or detract from Hasdai ibn Shaprut's reputation.

"We might as well be back in old Mother Eubh's convent," Oma grumbled when, after another month had passed, there was no further visit from Hasdai ibn Shaprut. "Here you are, the most perfectly trained Love Slave, and yet you live like a nun. I thought the caliph meant for you to be happy, my lady. What kind of a man is the physician? Is he a man at all?"

"Hasdai ibn Shaprut is not meant for my sole amusement, Oma," Zaynab said calmly. "He has many important duties within the court. He will come when he can spare the time."

"The caliph rules al-Andalus himself, yet he always had time to devote to his harem, my lady," Oma pointed out. "This man has not once taken a moment to enjoy your favors. It's a disgrace!"

Zaynab did not disagree with her serving woman, but she would say nothing further on the matter. For better or for worse, Hasdai ibn Shaprut was her master. If he did not shower her with his attentions, at least they were comfortable, and safe from Zahra's murderous intent. Abd-al Rahman had thought carefully before giving her to this man. Zaynab knew that the caliph had truly loved her. He would want her happiness even if they could not be together. She was content to wait.

Finally the physician came once again. Zaynab welcomed him in a cool, correct manner. She invited him to play a game of chess, and then when the refreshments were served, she told him that she had sent Abra into the quarter to fetch a separate set of dishes that would be used only for his visits. The food offered him was not only delicious, but consisted of all his favorites. He did not bother to tell her that it should be prepared in vessels separate from those of the rest of the household. When he ate at the palace, he was not treated with as much courtesy. Besides, he thought some of the dietary rules foolish and unnecessary.

"Why have you come to see me?" she finally asked him.

"The Byzantine delegation arrived from Constantinople," he said. "I have been very busy preparing for the translation of an important book they brought to the caliph."

"What kind of a book?" She leaned toward him a bit.

"It is called *De Materia Medica*. Unfortunately, it is in Greek. Although I speak Romance, Arabic, Hebrew, and Latin, I do not either speak or read Greek. The emperor Leon sent a translator along with the book. He will translate it from the Greek into Latin, and I will translate it from the Latin into Arabic." He seemed very excited, and did not even notice when she put her little hand upon his arm.

"Why?" she demanded, looking up into his handsome face.

"*Why?* Zaynab, this is the premier book of medicine!" he said enthusiastically. "There is a volume of it in Baghdad, but the government there will not allow us to copy it. That means that every time one of our young men wants to become a physician, he must go to Baghdad to study. It is ridiculous that we should have to go so far, and many are discouraged from doing it. When I have translated *De Materia Medica*, we will found our own university for medicine right here in Cordoba! The caliph has wanted one for years."

"How wonderful!" she told him. "It will be very hard work, my lord, I can see. You will need to learn how to enjoy your leisure time better. My lord, the caliph always said he worked better, and his mind was sharper, for the time he spent at his ease with me." She looked up into the physician's face. He really was very handsome, and his mouth was most sensuous. It seemed to fit his long face, with its high cheekbones. Reaching up, she ran a teasing finger along his mouth.

His wonderful dark eyes widened with surprise.

"I will teach you how to enjoy your repose, my lord," she said, enveloping him with a melting glance. She moved closer to him, a half smile upon her lips. Then she caressed his face gently with her hand. "Why are you smooth-shaven?" she asked him, her fingers trailing along the line of his jaw. "Most men are bearded here, I have noted."

"I ... I b-but follow the example of the c-caliph," he stammered.

"Do you follow the example of the caliph in all matters, Hasdai ibn Shaprut?" she lightly teased him, moving closer to him amid the pillows about the chessboard. Her eyes were twinkling.

He scrambled to his feet. "I must leave you now, lady. I am happy to find you so well," he said. He was considered the most sophisticated man at Abd-al Rahman's court, and yet this slip of a girl with her tempting body and seductive ways made him feel like a little boy. His heart was hammering. He could not rid his nostrils of her scent.

Zaynab jumped to her feet. "If you leave me before the morning, Hasdai ibn Shaprut," she said grimly, "I shall send to the caliph! I should rather take my chances with Zahra in the harem than live without love! Abra tells me there is no reason you cannot have me for your concubine, and you yourself have sworn to me that you are not a lover of men. Why will you not use me as you should? Do I displease you so?"

"Displease me? You would not displease the gods," he groaned. "You are the most beautiful and enticing creature that I have ever beheld, Zaynab, but our lord, the caliph, erred in his judgment when he gave you to me. I am not the correct master for you." He looked very unhappy.

"Why not?" she demanded of him.

"Do not ask it of me, I beg you," he pleaded with her. Oh, God! Why was this happening? She tempted him as no woman ever had tempted him, but . . .

Just then Zaynab had an incredible revelation. When it burst upon her, she knew that it could be the only reason he had not made love to her, and sought excuses to escape her company whenever the situation began to become exciting. *"You have never had a woman, have you? That is it! You have never had a woman!"*

A deep flush crept up his neck and suffused his face. "You really are too clever," he said low. "No, Zaynab, I have never known the pleasure of a woman's body. It is not that I did not want to, I simply never had any time. As my father's eldest son—and for ten years I was his only son—it was up to me to excel. I was sent to Baghdad when I was just fourteen to become a physician. When I returned, I practiced my craft in the quarter, but I also wanted to find the universal remedy for common poisons.

"It was originally called Mithradatum, after a king of Pontus who first discovered it. Two hundred years later a physician at the court of a Rumi emperor improved upon it by adding additional ingredients, including the chopped meat of venomous snakes. That gave the formula its new name, theriaca, meaning *wild beast*. Unfortunately, the formula was lost, until, using my linguistic skills, I deciphered some old scrolls and rediscovered it. The caliph was so delighted, he made me Director of Customs for al-Andalus as well as governor of the quarter, and ombudsman for all the Jews of al-Andalus."

"And in all that time you never had a moment for a pretty girl?" she said, disbelieving.

He laughed. "I was only just discovering girls when I was sent off to Baghdad. There, I lived in the house of an elderly relative, whose greatest fear was that something should happen to the scion of the house of Shaprut while in his charge. I was escorted to the university by guards and brought back after my classes the same way. My studies were difficult and all-consuming. There was no time for leisure. Besides, the old cousin knew only old men.

"When I returned home, my family wanted to make a match for me, but I put them off until I was certain I could support a wife without my father's aid. And then I began my research, and translation, and I could not quite find the time for a wife, or any woman. When the caliph heaped me with honors," he sighed, "I seemed to have even less time for myself. I felt that the entire weight of the Jews of al-Andalus was upon my shoulders, Zaynab. I have a duty to them."

"Do you like women?" she demanded of him.

"Yes," he said.

"Then you cannot remain a virgin the rest of your life, my lord. It is, I believe, unhealthy for a man not to release his love juices regularly. Surely you will poison yourself, and no amount of theriaca will restore you. If you choose not to take the responsibility of a wife, and father children, that is one thing. But to deny yourself the sweet communion of joining your body to a woman's is a terrible thing."

"Tomorrow I meet with the translator from Byzantium," he said weakly. "I need my sleep, Zaynab."

In response she pulled her caftan off, saying, "You will sleep better after I have pleasured you, my lord. If you refuse me, I shall expose your secret to the caliph. He will be very dis-appointed to think he gave his most precious possession to a man who does not appreciate her." Zaynab reached up, and pulling the pins from her hair, let it fall loose about her. "Touch it," she commanded him.

Hasdai reached out and fingered her soft tresses. "I am not certain what—" He stopped, embarrassed.

"*I am,*" she replied softly. "Trust me, my lord, and you will soon feel foolish that you ever feared this pleasure." She moved close to him. "I think you will be a wonderful lover, Hasdai. Now, put your arms about me, and I will teach you how to kiss properly." She slipped her slender arms up about his neck and drew his head down. He was tall, and she had to stand upon her tiptoes. Zaynab brushed her mouth lightly over his with the most delicate of touches.

His eyes closed and he sighed deeply. Her mouth was so sweet. She tasted like summer fruit. Her full breasts pushed against his broad chest. *"Zaynab,"* he murmured, caught up in the magic of her.

"Very nice, my lord," she purred at him.

His eyes flew open, the spell broken at the sound of her voice.

She smiled at him warmly. "You have a delicious mouth, Hasdai, but the embroidery on your clothing is wreaking havoc with my sensitive flesh." Reaching up, she divested him of his wide-sleeved tunic. Her fingers expertly unlaced his shirt, pushing it off his shoulders. Her hands moved to the belt that held up his baggy trousers. She removed it, dropping it to the floor with his other garments, and slowly, slowly, drew his pantaloons down over his narrow hips, letting them slide the rest of the way to the carpet. Then she ran her hands up his smooth, broad chest. "There," she said, "isn't that much better?"

Without a word he kicked off his slippers and stepped from his trousers. His eyes met hers. "I have never been naked before anyone since my childhood," he told her.

Stepping back, she swept her eyes over his form. "You are not just fair of face, my lord," she said honestly, "you are also fair of form, and your manhood," she brushed it with quick fingers, "shows much promise. We will give each other great pleasure."

He couldn't take his eyes from her. She was like a young, primitive goddess, vital and exciting. He wanted to touch her, and to his surprise, she seemed to sense it.

"Come," she said, and turned about so that her back was to him. Reaching down, she drew his arms around her. His hands cupped her marvelous breasts. For a moment he was frozen, and then she murmured, "Fondle them, my lord. They are meant to be played with by a lover. Gently, though, for they can be tender. Use your thumb and your forefinger to tease at the nipples. Ahhh, yess, that's it! You are going to be an excellent pupil, Hasdai." She rotated her bottom into his groin. "Hummmmm," she purred.

Her flesh was so exciting, pliant, yet soft as silk. He felt more aware than he had ever been in his entire life. Her fragrant hair tickled his nose. The tight little nubs of her nipples speared into his palms. His whole body was tingling, and the core of the sensation seemed to be focused between his legs.

Then she was taking his hands from her breasts and running them down her torso. His fingers molded her waist, her hips. She took one hand and pressed it against her mont. Without instruction he pushed a single finger between her nether lips. She was moist as he rubbed her.

"Your instincts are good," she approved his actions. "Take your hand away now. In time I will show you that little hidden jewel of mine, and how to make it shine." She revolved so that she was facing him once more. Standing on tiptoes again, she drew his head back down to hers. The tip of her tongue ran slowly over his fleshy mouth, first the top lip, and then the bottom. "Open your mouth and give me your tongue," she commanded him. When he did, she taught him how two tongues might dance together. "Isn't that nice, my lord?" she asked him afterward, and then she nibbled on his bottom lip.

He could both hear and feel the blood pulsing through his body. The tingling sensation was growing stronger. His vision seemed a little blurred, and he wasn't certain that he was breathing properly. "As a physician," he said slowly, "I know what transpires between a man and a woman. At this moment I want to fling you to the floor and push myself into you as far as I can go, Zaynab. You are a temptress!"

"It will be better if you have patience, Hasdai, my lord," she promised him, and leading him by the hand, brought him to the bed. "At least three times this night," she said, "I shall draw your love juices from your body. You will have an over-abundance of them because of your abstinence. Now lie back, and I will minister to your body."

He positioned himself in the center of the bed, and she crouched by his body. Beginning with his forehead and mov-ing down, she began to cover his handsome body with little feathery kisses. When she licked at his nipples, his head spun with the delightful sensation. He watched, fascinated, as her golden head moved lower and lower, and suddenly she was grasping his manhood. Her lips pressed hot kisses on the hard shaft, and when she ran her tongue about the ruby knob, he cried out, unable to help himself. Her mouth closed over him, and he groaned as she drew once, twice, and finally a third time upon him before releasing him. "I am close to spending," he moaned.

"Not yet," she cautioned him, and swung herself over his body. "Concentrate upon my breasts, and not the randy fellow between your legs, Hasdai. That's it," she encouraged him as he reached out to fondle the ivory orbs once more. Then positioning herself carefully, she lowered her supple body, absorbing his love pillar slowly, slowly, until he was fully encased within her. The look on his face was one of disbelief and wonder. He was close to weeping.

He could feel the walls of her sheath closing about him, squeezing him gently but firmly. He crushed her breasts, strug-gling not to lose the small control that he had. She rose up off him, but before he might protest, she was pushing down again, and again, and again. Her thighs held him in a sensuous grip as she rode him. He wanted it to go on forever, but he could feel himself swelling, throbbing, bursting as his love juices exploded from their long captivity to flood her secret garden with his life's essence. Above him her body arched, head thrown back, and then she collapsed upon him. His arms closed about her tightly.

They lay silent for some time, and he wondered if perhaps she had fallen asleep, but then she stirred. Arising from the bed, she busied herself heating water over a charcoal brazier, pouring it into a silver ewer, mixing a little bit of her fragrance in the water. She brought the basin to the bed, setting it on the little table, which was piled high with neat squares of soft cotton. Taking one, she dipped it in the water and wrung it out. Then she tenderly bathed his now subdued member. He felt more relaxed than he had ever felt in his entire life. It was a totally new feeling, quite unfamiliar to him.

When Zaynab was content that he was properly cared for, she cleansed herself. Then she disposed of the water and the used love cloths, wiping the basin out carefully, setting an earthenware pitcher upon the charcoal brazier and filling it with fresh water to heat. Returning to the bed, she reached into her little gold basket and drew forth the cup and the bottle of restorative. She poured him a draught and encouraged him to drink it down.

"You will not normally need this," she explained, "but as it is your first time, I thought perhaps it would revive you."

"You were wonderful," he said admiringly, having downed the contents of the cup in a large swallow. "In my wildest dreams I never imagined that a woman could be . . . could feel . . . *You were wonderful, Zaynab!*"

"Every man says that to his first woman, I am told, and every woman says it of her first man." She laughed. "I have pleased you, then?"

"Is there any doubt in your mind? I shall be forever grateful to you, my beautiful friend," he told her sincerely.

"Perhaps now you will please your family and take a wife," she teased him.

"I have no time," he protested. "It will be all I can do to serve my lord, the caliph, and my exquisite Love Slave, Zaynab." He reached up and pulled her down onto the bed with him. "Teach me more, Zaynab. I know that was but the beginning of passion."

"I but live to serve you, lord," she said with mock humility.

"Is it permitted to beat one's Love Slave?" he asked seriously, but his warm eyes were twinkling.

"If the pain can bring pleasure," she replied, and leaning forward, bit his earlobe. She followed the nip with a lick and a kiss, blowing softly into the shell of his ear.

He responded by rolling her beneath him and biting softly upon her nipple. Then he licked and kissed the tender flesh, asking, "Like that, Zaynab?"

"Indeed, my lord learns swiftly," she praised him. Then she leaned over him again, bending forward to take the defeated bud of his manhood, and its sac, completely into her mouth. Slowly, gently, she worked him with her tongue and lips, carefully rousing him until he was throbbing with a desire he had not believed could be brought forth again so quickly. Finally, he gripped her hair and drew her up again.

"Enough," he said. "Now answer me this, Zaynab. Can I do the same to you? Can a man taste of a woman too?"

"Yes," she told him, and lying upon her back, she opened her legs for him. "Use your thumbs to part my nether lips, my lord, and then you will see the bud of my womanhood. The tip of your tongue, gently used, will excite it, excite me. You may even put your tongue into my sheath, using it as you would your manhood."

Carefully, he followed her instructions. With almost clinical fascination he viewed her most intimate charms. Tentatively his tongue reached out to touch the dainty organ that seemed to quiver before his gaze. Within moments it was obvious that he had a talent for what he was doing, for she was whimpering and straining with pleasure. His tongue flicked back and forth. He was almost lost in his task, and then she cried out softly and her body shuddered. He had brought her to the apex of early pleasure, and he was iron hard with his own lust.

He pulled himself level with her again, and she eagerly took him into her arms. "Put yourself inside me," she whispered to him, "and then use me as I did you earlier. Move yourself back and forth within me, my sweet lord. Ahhhhh! Ahhhhh!" she cried as he complied. She was amazed. This inexperienced man was bringing her to a perfect crescendo of passion. It was impossible, *but he was*.

And it was wrong, she thought sadly. Wrong that she should

experience pleasure with this man who neither loved her, nor whom she loved.

There was a bitterness in their coupling, a hollow feeling. She had felt it with the caliph too. It would always be that way for her without Karim.

⬛ *Chapter 15*

*H*asdai ibn Shaprut seemed to be making up for all the years he had remained a voluntary celibate. He had, in a relatively short time, become a tireless and skilled lover under Zaynab's tutelage. He wanted to know everything that she knew. He wanted to try it all, although he drew the line at sodomy. It was a form of passion that did not appeal to him, although he knew that many men enjoyed its practice, not just with their women, but with an occasional boy or two for diversion.

He enjoyed having her kneel before him, her golden head against his belly, using him with her mouth. Afterward she would kneel on all fours, and he would enter her female passage from behind her. He enjoyed it when she sat facing him, his member deep inside her, while he kissed her with lips and tongue. Once she sat with her back to him, and he sheathed himself within her, his big hands playing with her breasts. There were so many exciting variations, and if it had not been for Zaynab, he might have gone his entire life without knowing them. His former virginity had been his darkest secret, known to no one.

"You will make some girl a fine husband," she told him one day as they sat playing chess together. She thought a moment, and then carefully moved a piece upon the board.

"I do not want a wife," he said, studying his own pieces as thoughtfully.

"Why not?" she demanded.

"Because," he said, moving his warrior piece, "I do not have the time for a wife, and the family that would follow our

303

joining. You, my dear, are a delightful distraction for me. You have opened my eyes to physical pleasures, and you serve me well, Zaynab. But if I come home late, or perhaps do not come home at all, you will not complain about it when you next see me. You will not whine because my duty to the caliph, to al-Andalus, to the Jewish community, override all else, and make me forget the New Year, or Hanukkah, or Passover. You will not burden me with sons whom I must personally take the time to raise properly, or daughters whom I must make good marriages for else I be shamed before my own people. These are the reasons I will not wed. Jewry is full of men who take wives and have children. I am unique in that I can be of great value not just to the Jews, but to my country as well. I have two younger brothers who will carry on the family name for our father. Alas, my parents do not understand me, but they have at least managed, in their pride over my accomplishments, to accept my decision in this matter."

"I bore the caliph a child," Zaynab said quietly. "I could as easily bear you one, Hasdai."

"I know," he answered her, "that you have the means to prevent such a child, and I hope that you will use it, my dear. But if you had my child, it would not, under Jewish law, belong to me. In my world a child belongs to its mother. Such a child could not bear my name nor inherit my estate. When the caliph gave you to me, he naturally assumed that we would become lovers, but I do not think he ever considered that you would have another child. As long as your only child is his, he will not forget you, or Moraima. Become the mother of several other children by another man, and you will quickly lose his interest. He might even forget the daughter you share. As long as Moraima is your only child, you yet have a hold on Abd-al Rahman."

"Checkmate!" she said, moving her king in a manner he had not anticipated, and she smiled mischievously at him. "You need not fear that I will have a child, Hasdai. I do not want another one. I desired Moraima because I cared for Abd-al Rahman, and I knew his child would help me retain his affections, or so I had been told. I could not have anticipated the lady Zahra's delusions."

"Do you love me?" he wondered aloud, curious as to her feelings for him. She was usually so careful about revealing anything of herself that he could not help but wonder.

"Do you love me?" she countered.

He laughed. "You have checked me again, Zaynab," he said.

"You are my friend, Hasdai, and I am glad of it," she told him. "You are my lover, and I am glad of that also, but at this moment in time, no, I do not love you."

"I've never been in love," he said. "What is it like?"

"You will know if it ever happens to you," Zaynab told him. "I cannot really explain it. I doubt that anyone can."

Their lives settled into a pattern that seemed to please them both. She was there for him, and he seemed to spend all his leisure hours with her now. So much so that his father complained that their family never saw him anymore. He did not tell Isaac ibn Shaprut that the caliph had given him a Love Slave. His father would not have understood it. He would have said that if Hasdai would only take a wife, he would have no need for this concubine. Instead Hasdai apologized, and visited his parents with lavish gifts for them both. Then he returned to Zaynab.

The months went by. Hasdai ibn Shaprut was deeply involved in the translation of *De Materia Medica*. Sometimes he would come home so exhausted that he fell into bed and slept for ten hours. *I may not be his wife,* Zaynab thought wryly one evening as she picked up the clothes he had scattered about the room, but *would my life be any different if I were?*

Her life. She was pampered and had no worries, but had it not been for her daughter, she would have been totally bored. Watching Moraima grow was fascinating. She had her mother's coloring, but she looked like her father right down to her imperious little hawk nose. Even if no one had told her, and even if Moraima did not understand, she was a little princess in her behavior.

Although Zaynab had not been fond of the city since her

removal from the caliph's court, she would occasionally venture out into Cordoba on the days that Moraima visited her father at the old imperial palace next to the Grand Mosque. Abra would take her to Abd-al Rahman, while Oma and Zaynab, accompanied by Naja, would visit the market, or a silk embroiderer's workshop, or a silversmith's. Sometimes they simply walked through the narrow, winding streets exploring the city. They never knew what would be around the next corner.

One day they came upon a tiny square, surrounded by the white, faceless walls of the houses. The square had a stone fountain in its center. About the fountain's rims were set pots of bright flowers. There were several open gardens between the houses and the street. They were filled with Damascus roses, orange trees, and shiny green myrtle. Even on such a hot day, this little hidden square seemed cool, and very peaceful.

One day they even visited the Grand Mosque itself, leaving their slippers outside, walking about beneath the soaring arches with their dowels of red and yellow. The fragrance of aloe and amber permeated the air, and added mystery to the quiet of the holy place. Zaynab realized she had never been in a real church before.

Moraima was already toddling. Her first birthday had come and gone. She knew exactly who was who in her small world. The caliph, who according to Abra adored her, was *Baba*. Zaynab was *Maa*. Oma became *O*, and her nursemaid was *Ahh*. Abd-al Rahman had given his daughter a fluffy white kitten, and the two were rarely apart. Zaynab named the kitten Snow.

On a bright spring day Hasdai arrived at the villa in midafternoon, which was odd, for the translation kept him so busy he did not usually come until late in the evening. "I must make a journey for the caliph, my dear," he told her. "I may be gone several months."

"Where do you go, my lord?" she asked him, signaling to her servants for refreshments.

"To Alcazaba Malina," he answered. "There has been a tragedy of horrendous proportions in that little kingdom. The prince and his whole family, but for one member, were slaughtered in some sort of tribal feud. The new Prince of Malina is suffering deeply from the loss of his kin. I am being sent to see if he can be cured of his melancholy so he may continue to rule for the Umayyads, as his family has these last centuries, or if he must be replaced by a governor of the caliph's choice. It is a terrible situation. The city is in chaos over the massacre. Its council is holding the peace by sheer force of will. I will be leaving in a very few days' time." He gratefully accepted the chilled wine offered him. The day was warm, and he had ridden all the way from Madinat al-Zahra.

"Let me come with you," Zaynab suggested. "I am bored here, and without you, Hasdai, I shall be even more bored."

"I do not know," he said, contemplating her proposal. The thought of being away from her delightful charms for so many weeks was not one he relished. She had become as addictive to him as sweets to a sweet tooth. "I am not certain that the caliph would approve, Zaynab."

"I do not belong to the caliph," she said mildly. "I belong to you, my lord. Why should you not take me? This is not a secret mission. I was trained in Malina. Its city is a lovely one, and Oma's sweetheart is there. He wanted to marry her, but she insisted on coming with me to al-Andalus despite the fact that I know she loves him. Perhaps he will still want her. Seeing how safe and happy and well-cared-for I am, she may change her mind if she sees Alaeddin again. She has been so loyal to me, Hasdai. I want her to have a little happiness too."

"What of Moraima?" he asked her. "I think she is too young for such a journey. I would not expose the caliph's daughter to danger."

"You are correct, my lord. Moraima will remain here with Abra, continuing to see her father on a regular basis. I do not want to disrupt her life. She will be quite safe. We will tell the caliph I am going with you, and ask him to send a contingent of his guards to protect his daughter while we are away," Zaynab said sensibly. Then she leaned over and slipped her arms around his neck. "You do not really want to leave me behind, do you, my lord?"

He slipped one arm about her supple waist, his other hand sliding into her caftan to cup a breast. Her mouth was tempting, and he succumbed, kissing her slowly, their tongues intertwining sensuously. "No," he murmured against her mouth. "I do not want to leave you, my beautiful Zaynab." His fingers pinched her nipple, and she hummed softly.

If Hasdai ibn Shaprut had believed in witchcraft, he would have said Zaynab was a sorceress. But he did not believe in it, even if the Love Slave had the ability to intoxicate his senses to the point where nothing else mattered but her kiss, her caress. Nonetheless, he was a loyal servant of the caliph before he was Zaynab's lover. The next day he spoke with Abd-al Rahman in a private chamber at Madinat al-Zahra.

"Would you object if I took Zaynab with me to Malina?" he asked his lord. "She would like to accompany me, my lord."

"Why?" the caliph wondered aloud, more curious than forbidding.

"She says she is bored, my lord," Hasdai answered truthfully.

Abd-al Rahman chuckled. "The curse of an intelligent woman, my friend. Passion is not enough for her. My Aisha used to tell me if I wanted peace in my house, I would choose women who were interested only in themselves. The others, she warned, are never content with their lot. They know there is more to life, and this, I fear, is Zaynab's burden. Of course you may take her, Hasdai. She is yours to do with as you wish. My only concern is for my daughter."

"Zaynab feels she is too young to travel. She will leave the princess behind with her nurse, Abra. She does, however, request that you post a guard about the child's dwelling while we are not there to watch over her ourselves," Hasdai said.

"Agreed!" the caliph replied. "She is a good mother, my friend. Why do you not have a child with her? Perhaps with more offspring to worry over, she would become less restless."

"My lord, the laws of my faith would not allow me to accept any children Zaynab bore me. They would have no legal standing. You know the importance of family in this world. We have agreed, she and I, that there will be no children," Hasdai ibn Shaprut told him.

Abd-al Rahman nodded. He had not thought about such a thing when he had given Zaynab to Hasdai. His first concern had been for her safety and the safety of their child. He had wanted them near that he might see his youngest child as she grew. Was Zaynab still as beautiful as she had been? He wanted to ask Hasdai, but he did not. It would have been impolite. He knew the answer at any rate. He wondered if she loved Hasdai, or if her affection for him had waned when he had given her away. Those were questions he could also not ask. He would never know the answers. They would haunt him the rest of his days. He silently cursed Zahra for her vicious jealousy, which had brought him to this unhappy state.

He shook himself from his reverie.

"The reports I have of the Prince of Malina are confused, Hasdai," he said. "He was away when the family was murdered. When he was sought after and told of the tragedy, he fell into a stupor for several days. He was finally roused, but they found him incapable of making any decisions. He could only mourn, poor fellow.

"The family physician believes it is a temporary state of affairs. He says it is the prince's way of dealing with the loss of his family. I want to know what you think, Hasdai. Can the prince be cured? Or must I replace him with a governor, and if I do, should that governor come from al-Andalus proper, or from among the council of Malina? I want the truth of this matter, and I need it quickly. You are the one man within my government I can trust completely, Hasdai. I am singularly fortunate in having you in my service."

"What of the assassin, my lord? Do you want him caught, and is it up to me to administer your justice on this man?" Hasdai asked.

"Absolutely!" Abd-al Rahman said firmly. "I cannot allow murderous bandits like this one to run loose within even the farthest reaches of my kingdom. If you allow one to get away, then others spring up like so many weeds in a field of grain. Find this man, and punish him, my friend. He must not be allowed to roam unchecked. Make his punishment a particularly unpleasant one. Use public torture, and draw it out for as long as you can. Discipline the underlings first, and save their leader for last. Be as cruel as you wish. It will offer solace to the people of Malina, and give their prince even greater status that I sent you to administrate the caliph's own justice. You will sail in one of my own ships, and have a troop of one hundred Saqalibah to help you dispense my law, Hasdai."

The doctor nodded, and bowed to his master. "It will be as you desire, my lord Caliph," he promised. "When are we to leave?"

"Can you be ready in three days' time, Hasdai?"

"We can, my lord," was the dutiful reply.

"I will send ten Saqalibah to the villa tomorrow. They will remain until you return," the caliph said. "They will have their orders from my mouth, and no other. Moraima will be perfectly safe."

By the time Zaynab and Hasdai were ready to leave, the caliph's guard had been fully integrated into the household. Aida was delighted to have a group of men to cook for, and little Moraima had already wrapped the captain of the Saqalibah about her tiny finger. Abra was utterly devoted to the child. Zaynab was content that her daughter would be secure and well guarded during her absence. She did not bother to explain in great detail to her child that she would be gone for several months. Moraima would not have understood. She simply told her that Mama would be away, but she would come back. To her pique, Moraima was not in the least affected by the news.

"Maa come back?" she demanded.

"Yes," Zaynab reassured her, tears in her eyes.

"See Baba?" the little one wondered.

"Of course you'll see your father," Zaynab replied.

"Good!" said Moraima, and turned her attention to Snow.

"I do not think she cares one bit that I am leaving her," Zaynab said, weeping in Hasdai's arms. "She is like my mother! Heartless!"

"She is not quite two," he explained, "and she does not really understand what you have told her, my love. It is better that way. You don't want her crying when you leave, do you?"

"No," Zaynab admitted, "I really do not. I just want her to be safe and happy."

"And so she shall be in her own home," he replied.

They sailed from Cordoba on a ship larger than any Zaynab had seen before. She and Hasdai had a huge airy cabin above deck, while belowdecks the one hundred Saqalibah were housed, if not not as luxuriously, at least comfortably. Even Oma had her own tiny cabin next to her mistress.

They made good time down the many miles of the Guadalquivir. It was late spring, and everything was in bloom, the orchards pink, white, and yellow with blossoms; the fields of grain already greening up. The second day they passed between fields of red anemones and white daisies blowing in the afternoon breeze.

They sailed by Seville in early morning. It was, Hasdai told her, a typical Moorish city, with small winding streets and low white buildings, with balconies, courtyards, gardens and fountains everywhere. He promised they could stop and see it on their return from Ifriqiya.

"Why did you want us to go to Alcazaba Malina?" Oma asked Zaynab one day as they sat in a sheltered location upon the deck. "Do you hope to see the lord Karim?"

"No," Zaynab answered. "Karim is a married man now. There is no point to seeing him. But perhaps we could find your Alaeddin, Oma. Wouldn't you like to marry, and have children of your own? My life, while comfortable, is hardly exciting. I shall never have any other children. Hasdai does not want them. I must accept this fate, but you do not have to, Oma. You are mine to free, dear friend, and I want you to be happy. What would I have done these last few years without you to give me courage and comfort? Let me give you your freedom, Oma, and make this match for you with Alaeddin ben Omar. I will dower you myself very generously. It is time you lived your own life."

"I do not know," Oma replied. "Alaeddin and I have been parted for several years now, lady. He may have wed already, and I will not be a second wife. Besides, I do not know if I still love him, the black-bearded rogue. And who would look after you, I should like to know? You never filled your household with a bevy of maidens like other women. It has just been you and me, Naja and Aida. The old women who keep the house clean are practically invisible. And have we not been happy?"

"I will force you to nothing," Zaynab said, "but let us find Alaeddin ben Omar and see how you feel about him. It should not be difficult. Alcazaba Malina is not a large place. Then, if you do not marry him, when we return to al-Andalus I will give you your freedom. You may remain with me, and I will pay you for your services as I do Abra. Otherwise, what would happen to you if something happened to me, Oma? I want you to be safe. You are my friend, and your loyalty means a great deal to me."

As she lay next to Hasdai in the night, the gentle swell of the sea half lulling her, Zaynab wondered if she had meant what she had told Oma. What if she did see Karim again? Would the love she had for him be reborn? Or had it died when he presented her to the caliph? Nothing, of course, had gone as either of them had anticipated. He was married now, and probably the father of a son or two. She was the mother of the caliph's youngest child, even if she no longer belonged to him. She sighed sadly. She was not happy, and yet she did not know why. She had everything a woman could want: wealth, a child, a man to protect her. What more did she really need? But still she was melancholy.

She had been wrong to come with Hasdai. She had put her mood down to boredom, and not until they had been under way had she realized that it was not boredom, but unhappiness that was driving her. Still there was nothing for her in Alcazaba Malina but memories that were too painful to even contemplate. And passion without love, she had quickly discovered, was a very bitter thing. That, however, she hid from Hasdai. Neither of them loved the other, although they had become good friends; and he did enjoy making love to her. It would have distressed him to learn the extent of her deception.

Finally, one afternoon the twin lighthouses of the harbor of Alcazaba Malina came into view. The sky above the ship was flawless. The gulls swooped and soared on the whorls of the wind, their mewling cries both raucous and mournful at the same time. It was, Hasdai had told her, a city in chaos because of the deaths of the ruler and his family, but looking upon it, Zaynab thought it seemed quite unchanged. When their vessel had been made fast to the dock, the captain came to tell Hasdai ibn Shaprut that a litter was awaiting him on the dock to transport him to the prince's home.

"There is also a horse, should your excellency prefer to ride," the ship's captain said politely.

"Is it safe to transport the women through the streets at this time?" the Nasi asked the captain.

"I have spoken to the prince's servant who has come with the transport," the captain said. "The city is peaceful in itself, my lord. There have been no riots or civil disturbances. It is just that the people are yet in shock over the deaths of their ruler and his family."

Hasdai nodded his understanding. "Then I shall ride. My lady and her servant will be transported in the litter."

Zaynab and Oma, properly muffled in the traditional street-wear of the respectable Moorish woman, were escorted by the Nasi to the litter. After they had settled themselves, the Saqal-ibah marched in orderly fashion off the ship. They were dressed in full battle gear and looked most fearsome to those onshore. Immediately, word began to spread through the city that the caliph's representative, the famous Hasdai ibn Shaprut, had arrived. He would help the surviving prince, and all would be well again. He had come with a small army. The bandits who had murdered their late ruler and his family would be hunted down and destroyed.

Leading the way, Hasdai ibn Shaprut, with the aid of the prince's representative, made his way to the home of Malina's

ruler. The citizens of Alcazaba Malina came out onto the streets
and cheered them as they passed.

When they had reached the royal gates and passed through
into the courtyard, Zaynab leaned over, saying to Oma, "I
thought a prince would live in a palace. This is no more grand
than the house the caliph gave me."

Immediately, however, slaves in long white robes came forth
to greet the doctor and his party, bringing them inside.

A tall man with a black beard came forward and bowed to
Hasdai ibn Shaprut. "Welcome, my gracious lord," he said. "I
am Alaeddin ben Omar, the prince's vizier. We are grateful
that you have come."

Oma gasped softly, clutching Zaynab's hand hard.

"We did not realize you would travel with your wife, my
lord," the vizier continued, "but she can be made comfortable
in the harem of the house. It is unoccupied at the moment."

"The lady is my concubine," the Nasi answered. "I am not a
married man, to my father's regret." He smiled slightly.

"Then our fathers would have their grief in common," came
the reply. "Mustafa, take the women to their quarters," Alaeddin
ben Omar told the waiting eunuch. He turned back to Hasdai
ibn Shaprut. "Prince Karim is awake now, if you would like to
see him, my lord."

Now it was Zaynab who gasped, but recovering, she cried,
"Alaeddin ben Omar, is it Karim ibn Habib of whom you
speak?" The question surprised even herself, and she knew
the answer before it was spoken. Allah! Why had she come?
She did not know if she could bear to see Karim, to be in
the same house with him. She strove to maintain the dignity
expected of the Nasi's Love Slave, but her heart was pounding
and she was pale.

"Lady, who are you?" the vizier said, all protocol aside.

Oma yanked her own veil from her face and replied sharply,
"Who do you think she is, you great oaf! It is my lady
Zaynab!"

Alaeddin ben Omar stared at her and the still-muffled figure
in turn. "Is it really you, lady?" he finally asked.

Zaynab nodded. Her innards felt like jelly. She mustn't

faint. If she fainted, Hasdai would surely know something was wrong. *She mustn't faint!*

"How did the caliph know to send you, my lady?" Alaeddin was saying excitedly. "You may be the one person who can bring him back! Praise Allah, the all-compassionate, for His mercy!"

"I do not understand any of this," Hasdai ibn Shaprut said sharply. "What do you know of this matter, Zaynab?"

"We should not stand here in the public entry discussing it, my lord," she answered him. "My lord vizier, where may we speak in private?" Her voice was cool and impersonal. By some miracle, and even she didn't understand it, she had managed to regain her equilibrium.

Alaeddin led them quickly to a light-filled room overlooking a familiar garden. Zaynab's head was whirling. *Karim, the Prince of Malina?* How could this be so? She wanted the answers to her questions every bit as much as Hasdai ibn Shaprut wanted his own.

"How do you know the prince, Zaynab, if indeed you do know him?" Hasdai asked her, confusion in his eyes.

"I did not know that I knew a prince, my lord," she began. "Karim al Malina, formally known to me as Karim ibn Habib ibn Malik al Malina, is the Passion Master who trained me to be a Love Slave. How is it that he has become the prince of this city?"

"Perhaps," Alaeddin interjected, "I might help in the explanation, my lord, with your permission, of course." When Hasdai nodded, the vizier continued, "Karim al Malina was the youngest of three sons of the former prince, Habib ibn Malik. Karim al Malina was a sea captain and trader, as well as a Passion Master. It was into his hands that the merchant, Donal Righ, placed the lady Zaynab for training. She had no idea that he was a son of the ruling prince."

"How could I?" Zaynab said. "Look about you, my lord Hasdai. Does this look like a palace? It is no bigger than my own house. I never met the late prince, or my lord Karim's brothers. I knew his mother, the lady Alimah, and his sister Iniga was my friend. At no time, however, was I made aware that they were royalty. I came here once, entering through a garden gate, to partake in Iniga's wedding feast. Never did she or my lord Karim say his father was the prince of this land, my lord Hasdai. *Never!*"

Hasdai was silent, lost in her words, pondering them.

"How is it that you are here, then?" the vizier asked, unable to help himself. His curiosity was great. "Are you not the caliph's property, my lady Zaynab?"

"I am the Love Slave of my lord Hasdai," she answered him softly. "The caliph gave me to him, my lord Alaeddin."

He wanted to ask why. He had thought she'd pleased the caliph. His dark eyes strayed to Oma, who sat quietly by her mistress's side. The girl's gaze met his and she blushed, but not before giving him a little smile. Oma, he knew, would supply him with the answers he needed. Now, however, it was Karim who was important. "May I have the ladies escorted to the harem, my lord?" he asked the Nasi.

Hasdai ibn Shaprut nodded. "Yes, and I will want to see Prince Karim immediately, my lord vizier."

"Mustafa, take the women to their apartments," the vizier ordered the eunuch as Zaynab and Oma scrambled to their feet.

Zaynab wanted to question Alaeddin ben Omar more closely. What exactly was the matter with Karim? Was he injured? Where was his wife? Did he have children? Had all of Habib ibn Malik's family been destroyed? Even Iniga? Dear heaven, not Iniga! Instead, however, she dutifully followed the familiar form of Mustafa. Perhaps he would provide some answers for her in the privacy of the harem. Mustafa always knew everything.

The doors of the women's quarters, empty and desolate, had no sooner closed behind them than Oma said, "Mustafa, tell me true! Is my lord Alaeddin wed yet? Does he have a wife?"

"Did you not listen, girl, when he told Hasdai ibn Shaprut that he had no wife? Nor concubine either, I might add," Mustafa said with a little chuckle. "If you had taken him when he asked, you would have been a mother three times over by now."

"There is still time for that," Oma said pertly.

"What happened, Mustafa?" Zaynab asked him softly.

"It was my lord Karim's wife, the lady Hatiba," Mustafa began, explaining to her what had transpired on the wedding day and in the two months following. "She was difficult from the beginning, and afterward the lady Hatiba could not seem to get herself with child. Both she and my master were saddened. Prince Habib began to say that his youngest son should put his wife aside, and marry a girl who could give him children, but my lord Karim would not do it. Finally the signs were good and the lady Hatiba was to have a child. A message was sent to her family in the mountains, but there was no word in return.

"Prince Habib asked my master to go to Sebta, which is south of Jabal-Taraq. Ironically, he wanted him to select fifty northerners, like the caliph's own Saqalibah, in the slave markets there; they are the best markets in the world, lady. These men would be trained as a personal guard. Prince Habib had always thought the caliph wise to put the safety of his family in the hands of those loyal to him alone, men untainted by the politics of al-Andalus. He felt the caliph set a wise example. And the lady Hatiba was sick and irritable in her early days of pregnancy. Prince Habib thought the separation would do them both good, and so my master went."

"Did he love her?" Zaynab asked quietly.

Mustafa shook his head in the negative. "They had accepted their fate," he replied dryly, and then continued. "Ali Hassan, he who had been the lady Hatiba's lover before her marriage to my master, then slipped into Alcazaba Malina with his men. They did not come boldly, but rather like the jackal, skulking and slinking furtively into the city. They attacked in the deep of night, blocking one end of the street quietly, leaving the other open for their escape. They came on foot. They broke through the gates of the house, catching the few guards the prince kept unawares, slaughtering them in their tracks.

"They had chosen their time well. All the family but for my lord Karim were here. There had been a celebration for my lord Ayyub's birthday. He, his two wives, and their children were killed, as was my lord Ja'far, his wives and children; the old

prince, the lady Muzna, and the lady Iniga's husband Ahmed.
They killed the lady Alimah last, but not before she had thrust
me and her grandson, little Malik ibn Ahmed, into a cabinet.
I hid the boy beneath my robes, my hand over his mouth,
watching them complete their butchery. Then Ali Hassan came
to where the lady Iniga and the lady Hatiba stood, clinging to
each other in their fear and horror.

" 'Bitch!' he said to the lady Hatiba. 'You swore that you
would bear no man's child unless it was mine.'

"His eyes blazed with madness, it seemed to me," Mustafa
continued. "He tried to pull her away from the lady Iniga, but
they would not be parted. Reaching out, he fingered the lady
Iniga's golden hair, an evil smile upon his lips. I could see it all
from my hiding place.

" 'You have betrayed me, Hatiba,' he told her.

" 'You did not love me enough to fight for me when my
father gave me to my lord Karim as a wife,' she answered him
bravely. 'It is my duty to bear my husband's children, Ali
Hassan.'

"My lady Zaynab, her words seemed to drive him into a
frenzy of unbridled fury. He tore her away from the lady Iniga,
wrapped her hair about his hand, and slit her throat in a single
motion. The blood spurted out, staining the lady Iniga's robes,
and the robes of Ali Hassan as well. The poor girl was frozen
with her terror, having been forced to watch the murder of her
husband, her mother, her family. She stood helpless, unable to
even scream, as that devil tore her clothing from her, then carried her off, along with the few young female slaves who had
not been killed. I waited for what seemed an eternity in my
cabinet, the lady Iniga's little son clutched to my breast. I could
hear them going through the house, stealing what they could,
but then it was all silent. Still I remained hidden.

"Finally I crept from my place. The child had fallen asleep,
praise Allah, and did not see the carnage all about us as we
made our way from the harem. Ali Hassan and his men at last
were gone. They had made their escape upon horses from the
prince's stables. They took only the finest animals, I might add.

I ran, with little Malik still in my arms, to the house of the head of the city council, and told my tale. His women took the child from me, and I returned with the entire council to this house.

"At the sight that greeted them, their cries of lamentation could be heard throughout the entire city. A messenger was sent overland to Sebta to bring my lord Karim back. We had already buried his family by the time of his return, and cleansed their blood away. We could not, however, get it out of the stones in the courtyard where the first few poor souls were slaughtered.

"When the prince was told the scope of the tragedy, he fell into a state of torpor from which we have not been able to rouse him. He will not eat. He barely sleeps. He simply sits and stares," Mustafa concluded.

"So the council sent to the caliph," Zaynab said softly. She could barely comprehend the scale of the tragedy that had befallen Karim. "Have they found Iniga, Mustafa?" she asked him. "Surely they sent after Ali Hassan to punish him."

"The destruction of Prince Karim's family was not the first of its kind carried out by Ali Hassan. He had already murdered Hussein ibn Hussein and his family. He has become very powerful, and very feared among the mountain clans. We have no army in Malina. There has not, until recently, been any need for an army. There is peace in al-Andalus."

Even now Zaynab could see that poor Mustafa was still suffering from the tragedy he had witnessed. The dead had not been Ali Hassan's only victims. "Has no one rescued Iniga, or paid a ransom?" she asked him once again. If Iniga had been alive when Ali Hassan carried her off, she might be alive still. She had to be found, and rescued.

"They will not seek after her, my lady," the eunuch said sadly. "When Ali Hassan carried her off, he was certain to violate her. She is disgraced now, and better left wherever she is, if she yet lives."

"What are you saying?" Zaynab said angrily. "Iniga has a child who survived this catastrophe. Little Malik has lost his father. Must he lose his mother too? Karim would not let that happen!"

"Malik ibn Ahmed has gone to his father's family, where he belongs. They will raise him properly. He is so young that he will never remember his parents. How can he lose what he will never recall possessing?"

"Do ye think this place be haunted, lady?" Oma said in their own tongue. "I dinna know if I can be comfortable in a place where so much death and violence happened." She shivered. "I can almost hear the screams of the women."

"I agree," Zaynab told her servant, and then turning to the eunuch, she said, "We will not stay here, Mustafa. Both Oma and I can sense the terror in these rooms. I know that you were not expecting us, but surely there is somewhere else that we may stay."

He nodded, understanding, and replied, "I will take you to your master's apartments. I am certain he will not mind sharing his rooms with you, my lady Zaynab."

Hasdai ibn Shaprut had already been brought to see his patient, Karim ibn Habib, the Prince of Malina. The young man sat in a comfortable chair upon a portico overlooking the large garden belonging to the house. His manner was lethargic, his color pale. There were dark circles beneath his eyes, and he appeared to have lost weight since Hasdai had last seen him in Cordoba.

"My lord," the vizier said, "I have brought you the caliph's representative."

Karim looked up, disinterested, at the tall man who bowed politely to him. Then he looked away.

There had been comprehension in those blue eyes, Hasdai saw. This prince was not mad. He was simply coping with his pain as best he could. There was hope. "My lord, I am the Nasi, Hasdai ibn Shaprut. While I advise the caliph in many capacities, I am also a physician. I would help you heal yourself so you may rule effectively here in Malina for our master, Abd-al Rahman. Your family, I am told, founded this city and have governed for the Umayyads for over two hundred years."

"They are all dead," Karim said low. "All but my sister's

child, but he is not of my family. Malik belongs to his father's people."

"Your sister, I am told, was carried off," Hasdai continued.

"My wife was killed," Karim replied. "She was with child."

"But your sister may live," Hasdai said.

"If she does, it were better if she were dead," he answered.

"Why?" the Nasi probed. "She has a son. The child needs her, my lord."

"She is disgraced, shamed forever," Karim said stonily. "Do you not realize what has happened to my sweet little sister? They will have raped Iniga. Perhaps only Ali Hassan, but may-hap others. My brother-in-law's family has my nephew. They would not let Iniga have him back even if we found her and brought her back. She is lost to me even as the rest of them are lost to me."

"If that is so, my lord, it is a sadness that will remain with you always," Hasdai said honestly. "It cannot be changed, but the people of Malina need you to be strong now. There is no more time left to you for mourning. You must lead! You must seek out the bandit, Ali Hassan, and destroy him so that his power will not cause further chaos in the caliph's land."

"I am the youngest son," Karim cried plaintively, the pain in his voice cutting. "It was not meant that I rule. It was to have been Ayyub, or if he had not lived as long as our father, then Ja'far. I know naught of ruling, Hasdai ibn Shaprut. Leave me to mourn in peace, I beg you!"

"I have brought with me one hundred Saqalibah. Your vizier tells me that you found fifty healthy, strong northerners in Sebta, who have since been brought back to Alcazaba Malina. In a month's time my men can have your men trained well enough for us to go after Ali Hassan. The caliph has ordered that he be caught and punished. Will you sit here like an old woman, when you could be revenging yourself upon the man who brought about all this unhappiness to you, to your people? Will you permit this Ali Hassan to swagger his way among the mountain clans, inciting them to further violence and eventual rebellion against the caliph? This is not the loyalty that I was told to expect from you, Karim ibn Habib," the Nasi finished, the scorn in his voice plain to hear.

"And when I have *revenged* myself, and the people of Malina," Karim shot back, his voice stronger than Alaeddin had heard it in weeks, "what is left for me? *I have nothing!*"

"You must take another wife, and sire a new generation for Malina, my lord," the Nasi said. "Your ancestor was but one man when he came to this place and built a city."

"I will not marry again without love," Karim said. "I did not love my poor Hatiba, for I loved someone else I could not have. I thought my devotion and respect would be enough. Perhaps if she had not died as she did, it would have been, but I am racked with guilt now when I remember."

"Love is not always an advisable virtue, my lord," the Nasi replied. "Ali Hassan loved Hatiba, and because of it she and your family died. Think on it when you choose another wife."

"A marriage without love is like an empty sky, Hasdai ibn Shaprut. It stretches out forever in loneliness," the prince answered.

The Nasi acknowledged the wisdom of Karim's words with a tilt of his dark head. "Your point is well taken, my lord," he said with a faint smile. This prince who for days had sat overwhelmed with lassitude by his pain was beginning to come to life again. It had just taken a little conversation, a challenge, a tweak of his pride. Hasdai suspected that no one had even considered such a thing, for they were all too busy encouraging Karim's mourning. They had been digging this poor prince a deep pit from which he would have never escaped.

"I have brought someone with me whom you will know," the Nasi told Karim. "Her name is Zaynab, and I am told that it was you who trained her. If that is so, then you have my undying gratitude, my lord. She is perfection."

"*Zaynab?* She is here?" The excitement in Karim's voice was barely masked. "How did you obtain her? She was given to the caliph."

"I will let her tell you herself in a few days' time, when you are stronger physically," Hasdai said. "I can see that you have not been eating. I am going to prescribe a diet for you that will help you regain your strength. Your vizier will work with the captain of my Saqalibah to plan a training schedule for your northerners. Ali Hassan's days are numbered, my lord prince, are they not?"

Karim looked up at the Nasi. "Yes," was all he said, but there was a grim determination in his voice that neither Alaeddin ben Omar nor Hasdai ibn Shaprut could miss.

Afterward, the vizier thanked the Nasi. "You have reached him, my lord, when the rest of us could not. It is going to be all right now. I can see it!"

"It was the mention of Zaynab that touched him most, my friend," Hasdai said quietly. "Nothing else I said influenced him as much as the mere mention of her name. *Why?* Tell me."

Alaeddin ben Omar shook his head. "It is not my place to speak of them, my lord Nasi. You must ask either Zaynab or the prince, but do not ask me."

"Very well," Hasdai said. "I will ask Zaynab."

◾ *Chapter 16*

"How is the prince?" she asked him after they had made love that night. "Will he survive?"

"Yes," Hasdai replied. He had heard nothing in her voice that indicated to him how she might feel about Karim ibn Habib. He asked himself if he really cared, and knew that he did. It wasn't that he loved her. He wasn't even certain he was capable of such an emotion. But she had become his friend, and he enjoyed their shared passion. He somehow knew it would not be the same with another woman. There was more to Zaynab than just a skillful concubine, and he didn't want to lose her.

"The eunuch Mustafa told me what happened," she said. "It is horrific. We must learn if the prince's sister, Iniga, is still alive. If she is, she must be rescued, my lord Hasdai." She put her head on his shoulder. "Iniga is the sweetest girl."

"The prince says she might as well be dead, for she has been shamed and defiled," Hasdai told her. "There is a strong code of morality here in Ifriqiya. While I may not always approve it, I do understand. If this poor girl has been violated—and it is possible that she has—no respectable man will want her for his wife. Ali Hassan might as well have killed her. That he did not bespeaks to me a man of vast cruelty."

"Is my friend then to be left to her fate?" Zaynab said furiously. She sat up and, crossing her legs, looked seriously at the Nasi. "Tell me you will rescue her, Hasdai. I will take her home with me, and at least she may live her life out in peace. Do not leave her to that beast, Ali Hassan, if she yet lives. *Please!*"

"The prince bought fifty northern warriors in Sebta. They will be trained by our own Saqalibah. In a month's time we will go into the mountains after Ali Hassan. Prince Karim must lead his soldiers. He is not strong enough yet to do so," he told her.

"So Iniga must languish further? At least send a spy to ascertain if she is alive or dead, my lord. I know you must send out spies to reconnoiter the territory held by Ali Hassan and determine his support among the mountain clans."

"How would you know such a thing?" he asked her, amused, yet surprised. She was always astonishing him when he least expected it.

"I grew up in a land of clan feuds, my lord. Such a strategy is commonplace among my people. If you do not know your enemy's strength, you can easily lose your castle, or your land, or your cattle," Zaynab explained in matter-of-fact tones. "There is nothing surprising there."

"Our chief objective is to destroy Ali Hassan and his influence," her lover replied. "If the lady Iniga can be found alive, then we will determine what to do with her." He reached out for her, but Zaynab drew back, her beautiful face angry.

"Iniga has become a victim of evil, my lord. That in itself is horrendous. Why must she suffer further among her own kind for what has happened to her? Why is she suddenly disreputable? The shame should not be hers, but rather those who have harmed her. I am a concubine, my lord. Am I not as disreputable?"

"Zaynab," he said patiently to her, "you must understand. I know that you are intelligent enough to do so. Iniga was the daughter of Malina's prince. She was a wife. A mother. Once she was carried off by Ali Hassan, her mantle of respectability was stripped away from her because of her carnal knowledge of another man, or men. You, however, are a concubine. It is your place to be seductive. It is your place to know men carnally. You have a cloak of respectability of a different sort, my dear."

"And if it had been me who was carried off by Ali Hassan

and violated, would I not be as disreputable as you claim poor Iniga now has become?" she demanded.

"Of course not," he responded to her. "You are a concubine."

"That," Zaynab said scathingly, "is absurd reasoning, my lord."

"I have never known you to be this way," he said to her, and indeed he was surprised by the depth of her feelings in this matter.

"I have had two close women friends in my life, Hasdai, and one of them is Iniga. I was not born a slave, but my slavery has been a benign captivity. I have been pampered and adored. Not so my poor friend. She was forced to watch as her family was slaughtered before her eyes, kidnapped, and most certainly violated. Until now Iniga was sheltered, and loved by all who knew her. She has a child. She does not deserve this, and I will do all I can to see she is rescued! I cannot stand idly by while you men debate the issue of her lost *virtue*. It is ridiculous! What has Iniga's virtue to do with any of you? It is her life that is in danger!"

"I promise you, my dear," he said, taking her hands in his, his amber eyes sympathetic, "that those who scout Ali Hassan's territory for us will seek word of Iniga. For now it is all I can do, Zaynab. Come now, and kiss me. I am hungry again for your lips."

Stretching out, she drew his head down to hers, but her mind was far away as she automatically elicited sighs of rapture from him with her kisses. She was somewhat appalled at herself to realize how perfunctory her actions had become. She wished it could be otherwise, but it was not. She might have felt guilty had she not known he did not love her. Instead she thought of Karim, who was in this very place as she lay in the arms of another man. Did he know she was here? Did he think of her?

He did. He wondered as he lay alone in his bed how she had come to be the property of Hasdai ibn Shaprut. The Nasi was young and handsome, and looked virile. Did he please Zaynab? Karim sighed. Was she happy? Why in the name of Allah had she been brought back to him when he could not have her? Was his pain not great enough? Alaeddin had promised him that Oma would answer all their questions in the morning.

Karim couldn't sleep, nor did he want to sleep. The caliph's representative had forced him by his sharp words to face the fact that he was now responsible for Malina and its people. He could not, would not, disgrace his father and those others who had come before him. They had founded this city, and brought it to its current prosperity. He could not allow their efforts to be for naught because of the terrible tragedy that had taken place.

When the dawn came he was still awake. A servant came with a tray of food. Karim looked at it and wrinkled his nose. The servant, an old woman who had known him since he was a child, said sharply, "The physician said this is what I was to bring you, and this is what you must eat, my lord. You have not the strength of a baby right now, but you must grow strong again so you may seek out and destroy Ali Hassan!" She plunked the tray on the table before him. "Eat it all, my lord!" Then she shuffled off.

Karim gazed down at the bowl of hot millet cereal, and with a sigh began to spoon it into his mouth. When he had finished it, he peeled himself a hard-boiled egg and ate it, then nibbled upon the slice of sweet melon upon the plate. There was a small goblet of wine for him to drink, and a slice of bread with a slab of goat's cheese, but he could not finish that. Still, he did feel better for the meal, he thought, as the slaves removed the tray.

Alaeddin came, bringing Oma with him, and the girl explained to Karim why Zaynab was now in the possession of Hasdai ibn Shaprut.

"Does she love him?" he asked Oma.

"Of course not, nor he her," Oma replied. "She was fond of the caliph, I know, but she and the Nasi are but friends."

"And she has a child?" Karim's eyes were wistful.

"A daughter, Moraima," Oma said. "The caliph loves the little one and is very good to her. My lady would not bring her with us for she feared that travel could prove a danger to the little princess."

* * *

Afterward, when Oma was back with her mistress, she said,
"He asked if you loved the Nasi, my lady. I think he still cares
for you. When I spoke of your child, he was very sad."

Zaynab held up her hand. "Do not tell me any more. I do not
want to know, Oma. I have had no choice in the way I live my
life. You know it. I have made peace with my fate. Do not tell
me that which would make me unhappy and discontent, I beg
you."

She did not see him, although he watched her as she walked
in his gardens in the company of either the Nasi or Oma. She
was, Karim thought to himself, more beautiful than ever. He
knew without a doubt that he had not stopped loving her, nor
would he ever cease to love his Zaynab of the golden hair.
Once he saw Hasdai ibn Shaprut stop and place a kiss upon her
lips. Anger surged through him, but then she looked up, and he
saw her face, smiling pleasantly at the Nasi but without any
sign of passion. The anger drained from him. Oma had not lied
to spare his feelings. Zaynab did not love her master! *But did
she still love him?*

Each day he grew better, and after a week he began to take
part in the training the captain of the caliph's Saqalibah was
giving to his own men. Another week passed, and Karim realized that he was much stronger physically. He was gaining his
weight back and sleeping soundly through the night. The men
began riding outside of the city in a first show of strength. He
was certain Ali Hassan's spies would be watching. They now
began to play a cat and mouse game with the vicious bandit.

Almost a month had passed when Hasdai told Zaynab, "We
are going to camp out in the hills now to see if we can draw Ali
Hassan out of hiding. He is constantly on the move, and our
spies cannot always find him. The prince thinks it is better if
we make him come to us."

"Is there any word of Iniga?" Zaynab asked him.

"I'm afraid not," the Nasi said. "She is probably dead by
now, and it is better if she is, my dear."

Zaynab clamped her jaws shut, silencing herself, but the
retort had almost flown from her lips. Iniga could not be dead!

When they found her, she would make everything all right. Karim might not have the rest of his family, but he would have his sister back. He would be glad of it no matter what they were all saying.

The men went off into the hills, leaving Zaynab and Oma to themselves in the palace. Every few days a messenger would come with a missive from Hasdai ibn Shaprut for Zaynab, informing her of their progress, which for now had come to naught. There was absolutely no sign of Ali Hassan, his encampment, or any of his men. Still, they meant to remain until the bandit came out of hiding, which they assumed he eventually would. When he did, they would be waiting for him.

One late summer's afternoon as the two young women walked at the far end of the gardens, half a dozen men rose up suddenly from the bushes to surprise them. Oma, with surprising foresight, pushed past them, running as fast as she could for the portico, screaming at the top of her lungs for Mustafa and the household guards. Zaynab, however, was not as quick. Surrounded, she was swiftly gagged and hustled through the little garden gate Karim had always used. One of her captors hauled her up onto a horse, and they galloped off down the street, escaping through the city gates before Oma's screams brought help.

Zaynab was no fool. She knew now, even if Karim and Hasdai did not, that their maneuvers in the hills had indeed attracted Ali Hassan's attention. This was his response to them. She didn't bother to struggle against her captor. She was already very uncomfortable as it was. If she fell from this moving beast, she could cause herself a most serious injury. She looked up into the rider's face, but it was veiled. "Who are you?" she asked him in Arabic, hoping that her words would not be swallowed up by the wind.

"Ali Hassan," he said shortly, but nothing more.

Zaynab almost had to admire the man's bravado. It had been a daring move to invade the Prince of Malina's garden and steal away the Love Slave of the caliph's representative. Now, however, she would learn if Iniga was alive. And the caliph's

Saqalibah would certainly be able to find Ali Hassan's encampment soon. She could see people in the fields along the very road they were traveling, gaping as they galloped by. Someone would report back to the authorities. She thought, perhaps, that she should be afraid, but she was not.

After several very discomforting hours during which Zaynab made certain to mark within her mind's eye the outstanding features of the changing landscape, they arrived at an encampment deep in the highest of the foothills of the mountains. The black tents were carefully set into the rocks, where they would be difficult to spot. Ali Hassan drew his horse to a stop beneath the awning of the largest tent. He dumped his captive most unceremoniously from her precarious perch atop his stallion.

To the relief of her dignity, she managed to land on her feet, although the jolt that slammed up her stiff legs almost buckled her knees. Zaynab forced herself to stand straight. Calmly, she smoothed down her windblown hair and shook the dust from the skirts of her lilac-colored caftan.

"Get into the tent!" he snarled, and leaping down from the horse, half dragged her inside.

She shook him off. "You are bruising me, Ali Hassan," she snapped back at him. "If you are to obtain a goodly ransom for me, I should not be mishandled. It will displease the Nasi greatly."

"Ransom you?" He roared with laughter as he removed the veil that had obscured his features. His black eyes mocked her. "I have no need of a ransom. You are Zaynab, the Love Slave, are you not?"

She nodded slowly. "I am." Her eyes went to the scar that ran from the corner of his right eye, across the right side of his mouth and down his chin. It was an old wound, but an ugly one. Despite it and a thin cruel mouth, however, he was an attractive man with strong features.

He saw her interest, and smiled. "Your beauty is renowned, lady. It pleases me to know that the talented sheath you possess, a sheath that has entertained the cock of the Prince of

Malina, Hasdai ibn Shaprut, and the Caliph of al-Andalus himself, will soon welcome my lance into its sweet precincts."

An icy chill of fear bubbled up in her, but Zaynab knew that to show any kind of fear before this man would only court disaster. "You may force me, of course," she told him calmly, "but you will know nothing of my talents if you do, Ali Hassan. I am not some common concubine to be terrorized into yielding to a man. Do you think that at your mere command I will spread myself for you?" She laughed at him, to his great surprise, then continued. "You have stolen me from the second most powerful man in all of al-Andalus. Do you not think he will hunt you down and destroy you? I was a gift to the Nasi from the caliph, whose child I bore."

"They did not come after the girl, Iniga," Ali Hassan replied.

Zaynab looked scornfully at him. He was not particularly intelligent, she decided. "When you kidnapped Iniga, you defiled her by that act itself. It would not have mattered if you raped her or not, although I suspect you did. She was the daughter of a prince; a wife, a mother. You took her virtue from her when you stole her away. I am a Love Slave, Ali Hassan. You cannot compromise my virtue in the same manner as you did Iniga's. By the way, is she still alive, or have your *gentle* attentions killed her?"

"She lives," he said shortly, nonplused by her lack of fear. He had never known a woman who didn't fear him, except perhaps Hatiba. She had loved him, so he had thought.

"I would see her before we discuss the terms by which you will return us to Alcazaba Malina," Zaynab said boldly. "I will even give you a single night of pleasure, such as you have never known, in exchange for your cooperation, Ali Hassan."

Ali Hassan laughed heartily, deciding now that she amused him. "By Allah, woman," he said to her, "you are as brave as a lion! If you truly please me, I will make you my wife. What sons I could get on a firebrand like you!"

"Do you honestly think I mean to end my days in a tent in the mountains?" she fenced with him. "I possess my own palace in Cordoba."

"Do not worry, my beauty," he told her. "I mean to eventually take Alcazaba Malina itself when I have destroyed Karim ibn Habib. He once took what was mine. Now I have destroyed or captured almost everything that was once his. And you will not have to live in that tiny dwelling they call a palace. I will build you a real palace of fine white marble with soaring towers, and hanging gardens to rival those of Madinat al-Zahra."

"How easily you brag," she said sarcastically, "but remember that I have both seen and lived in Madinat al-Zahra, Ali Hassan. They have been building it for years, and it is not yet finished. Do you perhaps possess a genie in a bottle who will help you build this palace of yours?"

"If you give me the pleasure they say a Love Slave can give a man, Zaynab, I shall give you anything you desire. I swear it by the beard of the prophet himself!" Ali Hassan declared vehemently.

"Take me to Iniga," she responded dryly.

"Very well," he said with an unpleasant little chuckle. He led her across the encampment to another, smaller tent.

Inside she saw that the shelter was divided by means of a dingy transparent curtain. As her eyes became accustomed to the murky gloom of the tent, she saw a figure on the other side of the hanging. It was a woman, and she was naked.

Ali Hassan put a restraining arm about Zaynab's waist and clapped his hand lightly over her mouth. "Be silent," he said low, "and watch," and he drew her back into the shadows where they might see but not be seen.

A man came into the tent, going through to where the woman stood waiting. Instantly she came alive, pouring water into a basin, drawing the man's male organ from his trousers, washing it thoroughly, then kneeling before him, taking it into her mouth to arouse him. When the man's member had burgeoned to its full size, the woman said in a piping singsong voice, "How will you have me, lord?"

"On your back, wench," the man growled, falling between the woman's outstretched legs even as she complied.

Zaynab drew a sharp breath. She barely recognized her friend, but the voice, for all its odd pitch, was Iniga's. Ali Hassan's hand removed itself from her mouth and fastened about one of her breasts.

"She has become a very amenable whore for the camp," he said.

The man finished his business and stood up, pushing his now flaccid manhood back into his trousers. Dropping a coin in a dish on the table with the basin, he exited the tent. As he did, a second man pushed by him and went through to where Iniga was washing herself off. Zaynab watched with a mixture of horror and pity as Iniga disposed of the dirty water and, refilling the basin with fresh water, began her ritual again. When she had bathed the new man's member and kindled it to a stand, she again asked, "How will you have me, sir?"

"I hear," the man said crudely, "that you have a fine ass."

Instantly Iniga was on her hands and knees. The man came quickly behind her, pulling apart the woman's bottom and pushing into her. She whimpered, but he paid little heed to any pain she might be experiencing, using her roughly until he was fully satisfied.

Zaynab wanted to weep for her friend, but once more she refrained from any show of emotion. She had to be strong if she was to save Iniga from this appalling life of cruel degradation to which Ali Hassan was subjecting her.

"I have seen enough, you pig," she murmured softly to her captor. "And if you do not cease squeezing my breast, I shall be bruised for a month. My skin is very fair, and I mark easily." She pulled away from him and walked from the tent, across the compound and back to the large tent that was obviously his.

He followed after her, his black eyes almost burning through her garment. Beneath his robes his own manhood was as hard as an iron rod, and he wanted very much to have this woman. He would turn her icy disdain into screams of pleasure before the night was half gone.

"Take off your caftan," he ordered her. "It is time you learned what a real man is like, my beauty."

Zaynab drew herself up to her full height and glared at Ali Hassan with utter disdain. "I am a Love Slave, you dog," she said coldly. "If all you wish to do is couple with me like some street prostitute, then do it, but you will learn nothing of the utter bliss I have been trained to give a man."

He was astounded by her words. Her lack of fear was beginning to unnerve him. To be faced with such a female of strong character was startling. "You are mine now," he blustered.

"So you have said, Ali Hassan," Zaynab replied, sounding very bored. "I am trying to instruct you in the proper possession of a Love Slave. Do you or do you not wish to be the envy of both your friends and your enemies? Do you or do you not desire to know paradise in my arms? Unless you do exactly as I tell you, none of these things will come to pass."

"What must I do?" he asked her curiously.

"First," she said, knowing now she had intrigued him, "you may not have possession of my full body for three days," and seeing the protest rising to his lips, she quickly continued, "because I must prepare myself properly for a new master. It is my custom to bathe twice daily."

"There is a stream nearby," he told her.

Zaynab laughed. "*A stream?* The water will be cold, Ali Hassan. No! No! No! No! Cold water roughens the skin. The water I bathe in must be warmed to just the proper temperature, *and* it must be scented delicately." Reaching out, she took his hand and brought it to her cheek. "Feel it," she invited him. "Is it not as soft as the finest silk? And the rest of my body, those parts not touched by the winds, are even softer." She smiled seductively at him, showing small white teeth.

"What else?" he growled. He could not take his eyes from her. She was the most beautiful woman he had ever seen. She was gold and ivory and aquamarines. He had never wanted any woman as much as he wanted this one. Patience was certainly not one of his virtues, but he would wait the three days for her because he wanted everything that she had to give. The erotic talents of Love Slaves were legendary, and he was in possession of one. He could scarcely contain himself.

"My servant, wretched girl, ran away when your men stole me from the prince's gardens. I need someone to serve me," Zaynab said.

"I will send a woman to you," he quickly answered, eager to please her.

"No! No! No! No!" Zaynab trilled again. "What do any of your peasant women know of how to serve a lady of rank like myself? No, give me Iniga as my servant. She will know just what to do, and will understand my orders. You can always find another whore for your men." Then she giggled. "Do you think it amusing, Ali Hassan, that the Prince of Malina's sister will be slave to the Love Slave he once trained?"

He guffawed loudly. "You're a clever bitch," he said. "Very well, my beauty, I will give you Iniga to serve you."

She favored him with a smile and then said, "Where are my quarters, Ali Hassan? I will need a bath, some food, and then sleep."

"You will remain here with me," he said slowly.

"No! No! No! No!" Zaynab said, but the remonstrance in her voice was of a gentler sort. "A Love Slave, Ali Hassan, *must* have her own quarters. My accommodations need not be large, but they *must* be private. Then when I am brought to you for your pleasure, or you visit me, all the camp will know, and your men will swell with envy, even as I will make you swell with your lust." She gazed seductively into his dark eyes, struggling to keep her amusement under control. He was positively drooling with his intense desire to possess her. She had begun this game with him in an effort to fend off his unwanted attentions, but she hadn't been certain how he would react. She was surprised to find such a vicious bandit so utterly gullible. She had not realized until now how powerful the reputation of the Love Slave really was.

"I will give you your own tent," he said. "It will be set up next to mine. I will have food brought to you now, and while you eat, it will be done. Three days? No more?"

"Three days, Ali Hassan, and then you shall enter paradise, I promise you," Zaynab said in sugary tones.

They brought her food, a bowl filled with a wheat cereal and chunks of lamb. It was a disgusting mixture, but she ate it all down, including the slab of round flat bread they gave her to use as a utensil. She washed the taste of it away with a sharp

wine. Then she sat and waited until finally Ali Hassan returned
and without a word drew her to her feet. He brought her out of
his tent and into the small tent that now stood next to it.

The little tent had been set up on a wooden platform covered
with a beautiful red and blue wool carpet. There was already a
charcoal brazier warming the space. There were two bed mats
with coverlets, a single low brass table with a lamp upon it, and
a second lamp of ruby glass that hung from the tent pole. There
was also a round wooden tub in the center of the floor that was
filled with steaming water.

He grinned at her, pleased with himself. "Well?"

"You have done well, Ali Hassan," she encouraged his
efforts. "Where did you find the tub for me?"

"I had my men saw a barrel in half, Zaynab," he told her.

"It will do for now," she answered him, "but where is
the soap? And my scent? It must be gardenia. I always use
gardenia."

"I do not know if any of the women in the encampment have
soap or scent," he admitted.

"I must have both, and they must be of the same fragrance,
but tonight I will settle for one or the other, Ali Hassan."

He stamped from the tent, and while he was gone she checked
the temperature of the water. When he returned, he handed her
a small cake of soap. She sniffed delicately.

"It's aloe," he said. "One of the women had it hidden away."

"Thank you," Zaynab said. "Where is Iniga?"

"Later," he said. "I want to watch you bathe."

"Are you capable of restraining your passions at the sight of
my naked body, Ali Hassan? Remember, I must prepare
myself properly for you, or you will never have the full joy I
can give you. Are you certain you wish to see me bathe?"

"Just what is it you must do?" he demanded, wondering suddenly if she were making a fool of him.

"A Love Slave's master generally uses her each day at least
once," Zaynab told him. "My sheath is used to the manhood of
the Nasi Hasdai. It takes three days of complete abstinence
for it to shrink back to its virgin state. And, of course, I do
certain other things that are secret. When I finally take you

into my body, Ali Hassan, you will find me as tight as a virgin, but without the boring impediment of a maidenhead. Then when my muscles caress your cock, it will have perfect enjoyment. If you entered me now, I should not be able to give you that pleasure for my sheath is not the correct size for your manhood."

"Ahhhhh," he said, as if he had actually understood her explanation. "Yes, of course."

"There is much more," she said with a little conspiratorial smile, "but those things must remain sacred to the Love Slave, Ali Hassan."

He nodded his agreement, but then said, "I am not some silly boy, Zaynab. I can watch you and not violate you."

"Very well," she answered him, not wishing to make him suspicious by too much resistance. She was amazed at how much he had actually believed. She would probably have to allow him some liberties with her body before she could escape him; or before Karim, Hasdai, and their Saqalibah found the encampment. By now they would have been alerted, however, and the trail left by Ali Hassan and his men would still be a fresh one. She drew off her caftan, slowly and with a very graceful motion. Carefully she laid it aside.

"Does my body please you, Ali Hassan?" she asked as she turned for him. "I have already had one child."

His burning gaze feasted on her breasts, her buttocks, her shapely legs, the triangle between her thighs. He licked his lips nervously as she pinned up her golden hair and stepped into the tub. "The three days will be an eternity," he told her. Then he sat cross-legged watching as she settled into the water and washed herself.

When she had finished, Zaynab arose and stepped from the tub. Beads of water sluiced down her lush form, and he could not take his eyes from her. "Your willpower is to be commended, Ali Hassan," she said. "I would like to reward you if you can exercise your self-discipline a tiny bit more. Do you think you can?"

"What would you have me do?" he asked, his heart hammering.

"Would you like to lick the water from my nipples, Ali Hassan? You may not touch me except with your mouth. You do not have to, but if it would please you, you may," Zaynab told him, as if she were bestowing some great honor upon him.

He put his hands behind his back. Leaning forward, he pushed his tongue from between his lips. A drop of liquid hung suspended from her right nipple, and he scooped it up with a quick motion. Then his tongue made several sweeps about the nipple before moving over to its mate. Finished, he raised his head up, looking at her triumphantly.

"Very good, Ali Hassan," she purred at him.

In answer he reached into his trousers and drew forth his manhood. It was the largest she had ever seen, long and quite thick. He presented it to her, cupping it in his hand. "It is eager to delve between your thighs, Zaynab, but I will wait the three days."

She ran her eyes down the length of him, then reaching out, caressed him with delicate fingers. "Find a woman tonight, and release its juices, Ali Hassan, for a man should never deny himself. You will be stronger with me for it. Restrain yourself altogether for three days, and you will be weakened gently. Now, put that big fellow away and send Iniga to me, Ali Hassan. I want to instruct her in her duties before I sleep."

Ali Hassan left Zaynab and walked across the encampment to Iniga's quarters. She was alone. "Hands and knees," he barked at her, and when she had obeyed, he knelt behind her, entering her female passage. She winced, but her discomfort was not his concern. He pumped her vigorously, closing his eyes and imagining she was Zaynab. His fingers dug into the flesh of her hips as he slammed himself into her again and again until finally his lust broke. He sighed, relieved, and stood up, yanking her to her feet.

"For the time being you will no longer be required to serve as the camp whore, Iniga," he told her. "Today I stole the Love Slave, Zaynab, possession of Hasdai ibn Shaprut. She is now mine, and wishes a serving woman. None of the females here in the camp would know how to serve her, but you should. Her tent is the small one next to mine. Put on your caftan and go to her immediately."

Wordless, Iniga grabbed up the dirty caftan that lay upon the floor, and pulling it over her thin frame, hurried from the tent. For weeks she had said little to anyone. Her throat still felt sore these months later from screaming when first Ali Hassan, and afterward several of his men, had raped her that day they had killed everyone.

Then Ali Hassan had decided that she should be his alone, but she had foiled him by showing no emotion at all each time he used her. He had retaliated by making her the camp whore. Now, he said she was to serve Zaynab. She remembered Zaynab, the beautiful girl who had been sent to the caliph. How had she come to this hell? Iniga entered the small tent next to Ali Hassan's.

"Iniga!" Zaynab's welcome was warm, but she was horrified by her friend's appearance. She was painfully thin and her lovely blond hair was dirty and matted.

"Zaynab." It is truly her, Iniga thought, but how could that be?

Zaynab saw the confusion in Iniga's eyes. "The bathwater is still warm, Iniga. Get into it and wash," she gently ordered her friend. Then she went to the opening of the tent, and handing Iniga's ragged garment to one of the two guardsmen outside, said in a commanding tone, "Take this to Ali Hassan. Tell him I want a clean caftan for my servant. She cannot wear this filthy torn rag. It is alive with vermin."

Returning inside, she knelt by the tub where Iniga now sat silently. Quietly she explained how she had returned to Malina and been captured by Ali Hassan. While she spoke she washed Iniga, who seemed unable to help herself. The girl's back was scarred with small raised weals. "What happened?" she asked Iniga quietly, running a finger along one of the welts.

"They beat me," Iniga responded dully. "There is this one man who enjoys whipping me, and afterward he uses me."

"You will not be whipped again," Zaynab said softly. "It is a secret, but soon Karim will come and rescue us, Iniga. Ali

Hassan thinks I am going to be his Love Slave, but he will never have me." She washed Iniga's hair thoroughly and rinsed it.

"They said they would kill my son if I did not give myself to them," Iniga said as her rescuer ministered to her. "Every day I see Malik, if I have been good and pleased them. The woman who cares for him holds him up across the encampment and he waves to me."

"Malik is not here!" Zaynab cried. "He is with your in-laws in Alcazaba Malina, Iniga."

"No," the girl said stubbornly. "I see him every day, Zaynab."

"Your mother gave Malik to the eunuch, Mustafa, when Ali Hassan and his men entered the harem. Mustafa hid in a cabinet with your son, Iniga. When the bandits had gone, he took Malik to Ahmed's parents for safekeeping. He is not here!" Zaynab told her.

"I see him!" Iniga replied heatedly.

"Across the camp? But never closer?" Zaynab queried her.

Iniga nodded slowly.

"They have tricked you, Iniga, into doing their will," Zaynab explained to the girl. "Malik is safe, my friend. You never have to serve them again as they have been forcing you to do."

"Then I can die," Iniga said, the relief in her voice plain.

"You do not have to die!" Zaynab told her. "Karim will soon be here to rescue us. You will go home to your little one, Iniga."

Iniga shook her head. "No," she said. "I am defiled, Zaynab. My husband has been killed, and I have been used as a whore by strangers. My life is over. I am not fit to raise my son. No decent man will have me to wife. My son must have a family for protection and influence. I am an outcast among outcasts. There is nothing for me but the blessed release of death."

"Would you leave me to the mercy of Ali Hassan?" Zaynab asked her. "You must help me fend him off until your brother comes. Do not leave me, Iniga. I have told you the truth. Do you not owe me a small loyalty, at least, for old times' sake?" Allah! She hadn't rescued Iniga to have her commit suicide. When Karim and Hasdai came, they would make the poor girl see reason.

"Very well," Iniga said. "I will remain with you for now, Zaynab. Had it not been for your kindness, I should still be the camp whore, unaware of the truth. To know that my child is safe is worth whatever I have had to endure at the hands of Ali Hassan." She arose from the tub, and taking the small damp towel Zaynab had used, mopped herself off. Her hair hung wet about her frail shoulders.

The guardsman pushed through into the tent, a fresh caftan in hand, his eyes sweeping admiringly over Iniga. "Here, wench," he said.

"If you ever enter this tent again without my permission," Zaynab said harshly, "I shall have Ali Hassan put your lustful eyes out with hot coals. Do you understand me?"

The guardsman recoiled, nodded, and fled.

"How do you dare speak to them like that?" Iniga asked admiringly.

"You cannot show fear with creatures like these, Iniga," Zaynab told her patiently. "If you show your fear, they will devour you. With Ali Hassan, I play the knowledgeable, superior courtesan. I scold him for his crudity and ignorance. But if I was with him and there were other men about, I should be the most biddable modest female Allah ever created. You see, Ali Hassan wants to possess all the pleasures a Love Slave can offer him; but he cannot be embarrassed before his peers, or his inferiors. Men are really quite simple, Iniga. What kind of a girl was your sister-in-law Hatiba that she gave herself to him? He is attractive enough except for his scar, but he seems to lack intellect."

"I do not know men except for the beasts they are," Iniga replied sadly, ignoring Zaynab's observations. "Ahmed was so good and gentle. All the men I knew before *that* day were. Now I know that those men were a rarity, that the majority of men are cruel, wicked beasts who care naught but for themselves. When . . . if, my brother comes to find you, Zaynab, do not leave him again. He loves you. He has always loved you. He did not love that bitch, Hatiba. I curse her name! Had it not been for her, my family would not have been murdered, nor I made into a whore!" Then Iniga began to cry as she had not cried in all the days since her capture.

Zaynab comforted her as best she could, but knew she could say little to Iniga that would ease her pain or take away her sorrow. All she could do now was to keep Iniga safe from Ali Hassan and his men. Karim and Hasdai would come in another day or two.

"Come," she said gently to Iniga. "Let us sleep."

In the morning they were brought food, and the tub was filled with warm water once again. Ali Hassan came to watch Zaynab lustfully as she bathed. When she stepped from the wooden tub, Iniga was there with a towel, but Ali Hassan stepped forward and took the cloth from the shrinking girl.

"Let me," he said in his deep voice.

"Can you suppress your desires, Ali Hassan?" she asked him as she had the day before. Her look was arch, but she was quick to note his black beard had been neatly barbered and was scented with almond oil.

His black eyes glittered beneath the bushy dark brows. "I am not a greedy lad, Zaynab," he said. "You will have the proper time to prepare yourself for me, but in the meantime I wish to enjoy the anticipation of possessing your lovely body." He mopped her back and shoulders. Then he moved the towel to her buttocks and dried each one in turn, fondling the firm flesh. Then he pushed a finger between the twin moons. "Do you know how to take a man here?" he asked her.

She felt the invading digit pressing against her rose hole. "Of course I do," she said, her voice sounding impatient.

The finger was removed, and he dried her legs. Drawing her back against him, he dried her breasts, fondling them enthusiastically, then moved on to her torso; but when his hand strayed lower, she snatched the towel from him, stepping away.

"I will freeze in this icy tent before you are done, Ali Hassan," she snapped at him. "Iniga, fetch my caftan."

He laughed at her, and noted, "Your skin is the softest I have ever felt where the wind has not touched it. You did not lie to me. Just touching you arouses me. *Look!*" He drew his manhood from his trousers again.

Iniga winced, turning away, but Zaynab laughed suggestively. "That randy fellow has no idea of the pleasure I shall give him, Ali Hassan. You must teach him to be more patient. Every time you look at me, he leaps eagerly up, ready for battle." Reaching out, she gave the fleshy peg a little tweak.

He roared with laughter. "Are you a woman who enjoys a wager, my beauty? I'll wager you a hundred gold dinars that I will have you shrieking with delight the first time I fuck you."

"Indeed?" she mocked him. "I will wager you five hundred gold dinars that I will make you howl with your pleasure the first time I make love to you, Ali Hassan."

"I'll take your wager, my beauty," he said with a raffish grin. Then he left her.

Iniga, her eyes wide with her fear, asked, "What will happen if my brother does not come, Zaynab? What will happen?"

"Do not fear for me, Iniga, my friend. If Karim and Hasdai do not arrive by the third day, they will arrive the day after, by which time I shall be five hundred dinars richer," Zaynab said grimly.

≋ *Chapter 17*

Ali Hassan came into Zaynab's tent on the morning of the third day. "Tonight," he said with a wide grin, "you are mine at last!"

"I regret I am not," Zaynab told him blandly. "My link with the moon broke last night and I am unclean."

His face grew black with his rage. *"You lie!"* he snarled.

"Iniga, do I lie?" Zaynab asked her friend.

"No, my lord, she does not lie," Iniga quavered. No matter what Zaynab told her, she could not help being afraid of Ali Hassan.

"Do you lie too?" he demanded of her menacingly, his face in hers, and Iniga grew pale.

"N-No, my lord! N-No!" she sobbed, trembling. "It is the truth."

"Iniga, fetch me something to eat," Zaynab told her. Iniga gratefully fled the tent. "She is too terrified of you to lie, Ali Hassan," Zaynab told him. "Can you not see it? Every time you glance her way she practically faints, the little coward." Zaynab laughed. "I am very sorry to disappoint you, but a woman's nature cannot be helped, now can it?" She moved so that she was standing directly in front of him. Sliding her arms about his neck, she nibbled on his lower lip. "Do you think men are the only ones who enjoy coupling, Ali Hassan? I burn to have that tent pole of yours deep inside me." She smiled winningly into his eyes, her full breasts pushing against his chest. "Another seven days, no more," she promised him, loosening her hold on him and moving away. "It will be even better for your enforced abstinence."

344

He groaned as if he were in pain; in truth, he was. Reaching out, he pulled her back against his body. "I am so hot for you, Zaynab," he admitted. He drew her hand down to his member.

"Ohhhhh," she trilled, knowing the exact response expected from her. "It's sooo *big*, Ali Hassan. Bigger, I swear, than the first time I saw it." Zaynab wrapped her fingers about him and gently squeezed.

"Seven days?" he half moaned. "No sooner?" He couldn't believe what this woman's touch was doing to him. The mere thought of her made him hard as a rock. Her hand on him brought him close to spilling his seed.

She sighed, sounding genuinely regretful as she released her hold on him. "No sooner, I fear, Ali Hassan," she told him. "I am filled with regret, but what can I do?"

He released her. "I will go raiding," he said. "I do not want to see you until the time is propitious. If I stay, I shall go mad with longing for you, my beautiful Zaynab." Then turning abruptly on his heel, he departed the tent. Several minutes later she heard the thunder of hooves as Ali Hassan and his men rode out from the camp.

Zaynab smiled, well pleased with herself. Her female nature had indeed been most cooperative. Surely within the week Karim and Hasdai would find them. She was amazed that they had not already come. Whatever Iniga might believe, Zaynab knew that neither of the men would desert the Love Slave.

Iniga crept back into the tent with food for them. "They have gone," she said. "There are only old men, women, and children in the camp now." She handed Zaynab a bowl. "Why did they go?"

"Ali Hassan did not feel he could control himself for the next seven days unless he was away from me," Zaynab said, laughing.

"You are so brave," Iniga said. "I wish I had been like you when they kidnapped me from Alcazaba Malina, but I was so afraid."

"You did what you did because you thought you were protecting your little son," Zaynab responded. "You were braver than I am, Iniga. You sacrificed yourself for your baby. I am merely playing a game with poor Ali Hassan until your brother and the Nasi come. The caliph's Saqalibah are excellent soldiers. I cannot understand why they have been unable to find this encampment. They must have scouts looking. Surely the light of the fires should draw them at night."

"There are no open fires," Iniga said slowly, wondering why she had not realized it before.

"What?" Zaynab was astounded, but then she realized that she had spent practically all her time here in this little tent. She had only had a brief glimpse of the encampment when she arrived.

"Ali Hassan knows fires could bring his enemies down on him. He allows no open fires. The tents all have braziers like this one for warmth. The cooking, however, is done in a single tent. Food is cooked for the entire camp there. It is done over braziers as well. There is one fire pit which is used only at night so the smoke cannot be seen. The tents are black, and the rocks in this canyon the same hue. Our shelters are set against them. We are easily overlooked, Zaynab."

"Then we must start a fire," her companion replied in practical tones.

"Zaynab, they will kill you!" Iniga said, frightened.

"They will not know how the fire started if we are clever," Zaynab said slowly, forming a plan. "It's no good doing it before Ali Hassan gets back. We want to help the Nasi to capture that villain so he may be punished for the attack on your family. It will have to be the night he possesses the Love Slave for the very first time.

"While I am entertaining our friend, you will creep behind several of the tents, carrying hot coals with you to set those tents afire. It will take a few minutes for the tents to begin to burn. You will have time to come back here. Who will suspect you? They believe you frightened and completely in their power. Be careful, and you will not be seen in the darkness, Iniga.

"When the alarm is raised and Ali Hassan rushes out to find mass confusion, I will set his tent afire by knocking over the brazier in his sleeping area. Then I will run out after him screaming that our tent is also afire. He will think it is some sort of attack. The flames should draw the Nasi and the Saqalibah to the encampment, for if Allah favors us, the fires will be almost impossible to put out in time to prevent our location from being discovered," Zaynab concluded triumphantly.

"I do not know if I can help you, Zaynab," Iniga said honestly.

"You must help me," Zaynab told her. "I have no one else to rely upon, Iniga. Once the sun sets on this camp, everyone shelters in his own tent. There is no fellowship among the people here, because any sounds of revelry would carry in the night and draw attackers down upon them. You will be perfectly safe. I promise you that on that night in particular, Ali Hassan will want perfect silence so his mastery of me— the cries he believes I will utter—will be heard by all his people. He is, I suspect, even now bragging to his men about his prowess and how I will howl with delight from his lusty attentions."

"I am so afraid." Iniga wept, clutching herself to still her trembling.

"While Ali Hassan is away, we will creep about the camp in the night together," Zaynab suggested, refusing to accept her friend's fears. "That way you will become familiar with what you must do and where you must go. You will see there is nothing to be afraid of, Iniga. My task is far more dangerous and onerous than yours. I must amuse that pig of a bandit long enough to give you the time you'll need. I will have to convince him of his great desirability, and that my lust matches his. You certainly would not like to do that."

"Nay," Iniga admitted, "I would not. Ohh, Zaynab, I am so afraid for you! He is a cruel monster when he couples with a woman! He is enormous! Far bigger than Ahmed was. He hurt me dreadfully. Ahmed never did the things to me that Ali Hassan did. He even forced himself into my fundament, laughing when I screamed. I am not brave enough, but I wish I could kill him. I hate him so!" Her pretty face was flushed.

"It's all right, Iniga," Zaynab comforted her friend, putting her arms about the terrified girl. "I was taught to accept a man

in more ways than you can even imagine. Ali Hassan cannot
hurt me because I know exactly how to prevent him from
doing me an injury. It is unlikely he will even get to breach me
at all if you do your part."

"I will try," Iniga promised Zaynab earnestly. "I want my
brother to find you. I want Karim to kill Ali Hassan!"

"You will succeed," Zaynab told her seriously. "Both of our
lives depend upon your succeeding, Iniga."

The encampment remained quiet for the next week. Each night,
the two young women slipped out in the pitch-darkness of the
night to move silently like wraiths about the camp until Iniga
was completely familiar with it.

"Why can we not simply flee this place?" Iniga asked Zaynab one evening as they waited to begin their nightly foray.

"Can you find your way out of these mountains?" Zaynab
asked her. "I tried to memorize the landscape as we came here
from the city, but once in these hills, I realized that it all looked
the same to me. There is no road or trail. We took many twists
and turns. Even if we tried to escape, we could as easily run into
Ali Hassan as find the Nasi and your brother. And if we were
fortunate enough to actually elude the bandits and show the
Saqalibah the way back here, Ali Hassan would be long gone.

"I want him punished, Iniga, for what happened to your
family. The caliph wants him punished so others will not emulate him or his bad behavior. It is far better for us to remain here
as bait. As long as Ali Hassan believes he may possess my
body, he will return to this camp," Zaynab concluded with
assurance.

The seven days passed far too quickly for Iniga. With a cool
demeanor that awed her, Zaynab went about the business of
preparing for Ali Hassan's return. Boldly, she marshaled the
women of the encampment to clean their leader's large tent,
which was a pigsty. She even had them wash all his garments
in the nearby stream. She cajoled them into making him a new
mattress, which they filled with fresh hay and sweet herbs.

"I do not need to be bitten by bedbugs,"she told Iniga.

She discovered a barrel maker amongst the old men. Giving

him one of the small rings she wore, she wheedled him sweetly into making her a large wooden tub, which she had placed in Ali Hassan's tent. Holding up another little gold ring with garnets on it, she offered to give it to the woman who could bring her matching soap and sweet oil. To Iniga's surprise, the Love Slave had a choice of fragrances from which to choose. Most of the women in camp had these items secreted away. She picked a heavy rose scent, knowing that it would appeal to her captor. Ali Hassan was not, she had already noted, a subtle man.

There were several young boys left behind in the camp. "I want the largest kettle you can find on the boil when your master returns," she told them. "As soon as he enters the camp, begin bringing buckets of hot water to his tent to fill the tub. I will see you are well rewarded," she promised.

"Ali Hassan is not known to be generous," one boy said daringly.

"He will be after he has spent a night with me," she said archly, and the boys laughed uproariously, poking at one another, their exchanged looks heavy with meaning.

She walked back into her own tent, where Iniga waited. "Now remember, this will be our only opportunity to help the Nasi to find us. Where is your container? Are the tongs with it?" she asked.

Iniga silently showed her the little brass dish they had made into a carrier for live coals. They had woven a handle for it from grass, reinforced with bits of wire they had taken from Iniga's earrings. She would use the tongs from the tent's brazier to transfer the coals into her basket, and remove the coals with them in order to start the fires. The previous night they had taken small piles of dried grass and set them partly beneath the rear flaps of the tents they meant to fire.

"Remember to begin on the far side of the encampment," Zaynab reminded her friend. "That way when the first fires break out, you'll be near enough to our tent to pop right back inside."

"I'm so afraid," Iniga said softly. "I pray I can do this for you, Zaynab. I want to be brave like you."

Zaynab grasped Iniga by her shoulders and stared hard into

her face. "If you do not help me, Iniga, I will have to sacrifice myself to Ali Hassan. I cannot hold him at bay any longer. Mind you, I do not fear coupling with this monster, but I should rather not do it if I can avoid it. Besides, unless we set the camp on fire, how can we guide your brother and the Nasi here to take their vengeance?

"Why are you still afraid, Iniga? What have you left to lose? Ali Hassan has taken everything from you that you held dear. Your family. Your husband. *Your little son.* You tell me that all that is left for you is a quick death. I do not understand you, but I will not argue with you on this point. However, before you depart this life, I would think you would want revenge on the man who is responsible for destroying you. If I were in your place, I would!"

Iniga's soft blue eyes filled with tears. "You are hard," she whispered, then wept softly.

Zaynab shook her head, her grip on Iniga loosening. "I am not hard," she said quietly, "but I am strong. I have had to be. Your mother was strong too. Listen to me, Iniga, you are no less staunch than the lady Alimah was. While I doubt your mother ever spoke of it, I am certain the Vikings who took her and her sisters from their family farm used them well before they sold them as slaves. To survive such harsh treatment, your mother had to be strong. You can be, too, Iniga. You must be, else they all died in vain."

Iniga shuddered. She was more a delicate Arab princess than she was a Viking girl's daughter. When this was finally over, she knew that she would die. She wanted to die, for there was nothing left for her to live for; but Zaynab was correct. She had to be strong now, if only for a brief time, if they were to succeed in punishing Ali Hassan. He must not escape or be allowed to continue disrupting the caliph's peace. "I will do what I must," she said low. "I will not fail you, Zaynab. *I swear it!*"

Her words were scarcely out of her mouth when they heard the rumble of horses' hooves as Ali Hassan and his men swept back into the encampment with a great shout.

"The sun is about to set," Zaynab said to Iniga. "The moon

is already in the skies. When it disappears behind the hills, go out from here and set the tents afire. Then come back and wait. I will return to you, and we will hide until the Nasi comes."

"What of Ali Hassan?" Iniga said.

"His passion should be cooled by the disaster," Zaynab answered. "He will be too busy trying to put out the fires to bother with either of us." She patted Iniga encouragingly, and then hurried from their tent to the large tent beside them. Ali Hassan was still swaggering about outside with his men, giving orders. The boys she had spoken with earlier were running in and out with buckets brimming with hot water, pouring them into the tub, which was just about filled. " 'Tis enough," she told them, waving them away. Then she began to pour the heavy rose fragrance into the water. The perfumed steam rose to fill the tent with its aromatic odor. The clump of boots outside alerted her, and she swung about as the bandit came into his tent.

"Welcome home, Ali Hassan," Zaynab said with a smile. She hurried to take his long cloak from him, laying it aside.

"It smells like a rose garden in here," he said, sniffing, not certain if he approved.

"I am going to bathe you," she said firmly. "Any man out raiding for a week reeks of himself and his horse, Ali Hassan. I'm not making love to you until you're as sweet as a flower."

He roared with laughter. His mood was very good suddenly. For a week he had been short-tempered and vicious with anyone in his vicinity. He could not get Zaynab from his mind, despite the fact that he had raped at least three women in that time to cool his ardor. It hadn't worked. He didn't want them. He wanted his Love Slave. So he had returned, determined to have her, to force her if he had to, but he wanted no more delays. *And here she was waiting for him.* He was absolutely delighted.

"So I'm to have a bath, am I?" He chuckled. "I can't remember the last time I had a real bath. Where did you get that fine tub?"

"I bribed one of the old men who is a barrel maker. And I bribed the women to bring forth their oils and soaps," Zaynab told him with a grin. Then she unlaced his shirt, pulling it off. "Whew, that stinks!" she said, dropping it to the floor.

"You're a resourceful woman," he growled at her.

"Aye," she agreed calmly, and taking his hand, led him over to a chair. "Sit down, Ali Hassan. We need to get your boots off." Turning about, she took one foot, lifted it up, put it between her own legs, then grasping it, commanded him, "Push my bottom with your other foot." With another chuckle he complied, and she removed the first boot. The process was repeated, and the second boot was withdrawn. Turning about, Zaynab said, "Stand up, and let's get those trousers off, Ali Hassan. Allah! They're filthy. These clothes of yours should be burned!" Her fingers moved to unfasten his belt buckle. Pulling the belt off, she yanked the trousers down with a swift motion. "Now into the tub with you, Ali Hassan," Zaynab commanded him.

"I am completely in your hands," he said as, kicking his pantaloons aside, he climbed into the bath, settling himself comfortably upon the bath stool. His dark eyes widened as she casually pulled off the lavender caftan she had been wearing since her capture. "What are you doing?" he asked her in a half-choked voice.

"You cannot expect me to bathe you from outside the tub, Ali Hassan," she told him impatiently. "I must get in with you. Unfortunately, this is the only garment I currently possess. Besides, it is not my custom, as you know, to bathe wearing a garment." Zaynab climbed into the tub with him. "Now, remember, Ali Hassan, that I must control our passion tonight. Later, when you have learned what possessing a Love Slave is really about, you may direct us, but not tonight. If you behave like some unruly beast, I cannot offer you the delights I was trained to give. Do you understand me, and will you comply? I am proud of my talents. I would tender you the greatest pleasure possible."

His dark eyes were excited. The thought of a woman dominating him was unfamiliar to him, but he nodded. "Whatever you desire, Zaynab. I am clay in your supple fingers. Do what you will, but give me that legendary pleasure only a Love

Slave can impart to a man! I have longed for you these seven days past!"

"Tonight," she promised him with a seductive purr, "will be like no other that you have ever experienced, Ali Hassan."

His eyes glazed over with her words.

"Open your mouth," she commanded him, and when he did, she scrubbed his teeth with a rough cloth. Then she handed him a small silver cup. "Take it all into your mouth, Ali Hassan, rinse well, and then spit it back into the cup. No lover would accost his lady with bad breath," she told him as he obeyed her simple instruction. "I have cleaned your teeth with a mixture of pumice and mint. What you are rinsing with is a combination of mint and ground clove, with wine."

He did as she bid him, returning the cup to her. Zaynab set it back on the tub's rim. His heart hammered in his chest when she gave him a warm kiss.

"Ahh, that's better," she approved, smacking her lips. "A lover should always taste good. Now, Ali Hassan, let us get the dust out of your hair." She quickly but expertly washed his short, dark hair. It had a curl to it, but it was rough in texture, unlike the hair of the other men she knew. Finished, she toweled his head damp dry. Taking up a fresh clean cloth, she now washed his face, amazed at the dirt she rinsed away. "Did you not wash the entire time you were gone?" she asked him, rubbing his neck and cleaning his ears.

The warm water was beginning to relax his muscles. He was enjoying all the attention she was giving him. "There is little time to wash or even sleep when a man's ahorse," he said. "Do you treat your lover like this every time he comes to you, Zaynab?"

"My former lovers were men of breeding and culture," she answered him bluntly. "They did not come to my bed with foul breath and dirty faces."

"We will bathe together every day from now on," he promised her. "And when I capture Alcazaba Malina, you will live in a palace, as I have already promised you. I will fill your bath with sweet oils of all fragrances, which we will enjoy together."

Zaynab said nothing, but she did favor him with a small smile.

She concentrated upon bathing him. She wanted to draw out
the process for as long as she could. Surely the moon must be
close to dropping behind the hills by now. Slowly, deliberately,
she took up her cloth, lavishly spread soap upon it, and washed
his barrel-like chest with its tangle of matted black hair. The
soap foamed amid the wiry growth, and his nipples seemed to
glow a deep rose. Carefully, she rinsed the soap away. She
washed an arm, a hand, and pared his nails. She laundered his
other arm and hand, trimming its nails. Turning him about, she
gently scrubbed his hairy back, rinsing the soap scum from him
with her cloth and generous amounts of water that she splashed
on him.

"You must stand upon the bath stool, Ali Hassan, for I must
wash what you now hide beneath the water in this tub."

With a deep chuckle he moved to obey her. She would get a
surprise when he climbed upon the stool. His member was
already well roused, and hard as a rock.

Zaynab ignored the obscene length of flesh as it bobbed out
of the water. She slathered soap up one leg, scrubbing dili-
gently, and pressed gently at a spot behind his knee, watching
with hidden amusement as his manhood shriveled away. This
was something Karim had taught her long ago; something she
had never thought she would have need for, until now. She
continued to work quietly, bathing his other leg, his buttocks,
his belly, his groin.

Boldly she cupped the twin orbs within his pouch. " 'Tis a
fine pair you possess, Ali Hassan," she told him. "They'll be
well milked by the time we're through." She had noted that he
enjoyed it when she spoke boldly to him. Her little hand
soaped his rod teasingly, holding him lightly, stroking him up
and down. She could feel him beginning to harden once more.
Quickly she rinsed him, managing to reach around and press
the secret spot again in order to deflate his lust.

"Now," she said, "you are clean, and must wash me, Ali
Hassan, before we exit our bath. Here is a clean cloth for you
to use."

He worked carefully to mimic her motions while she
instructed him gently. He could not tear his eyes from her

lovely breasts as he washed them. He couldn't help biting at her neck, nibbling on her earlobes. His hand could not restrain rubbing itself most suggestively between the twin halves of her bottom. His fingers found themselves pushing into her tight passage.

She scolded him with a mixture of amusement and scorn. "Are you a little boy that you cannot be patient, Ali Hassan?" She led him from the tub and handed him a piece of toweling. "Dry me quickly so I may attend properly to you," she said. "I will have no silliness, Ali Hassan, else I become angry with you. Then I shall be unable to concentrate upon all the delights that only a Love Slave may give to her lover."

Chastened, he dried her without further provocation.

Where in the name of the seven djinns was Iniga, Zaynab thought as she took up a fresh towel and began to dry him off. It seemed ages since she had entered Ali Hassan's tent. She had lingered over his bath, trying to make the time go by. If Iniga didn't fire the tents soon, Zaynab realized, she would have no choice but to couple with this man. Well, at least he was clean now, and dry. She could procrastinate no longer.

"Come," she said, taking his hand, leading him into his sleeping space. "I have had the women make you a new mattress, Ali Hassan. It is filled with fresh grass and sweet herbs. Lie down upon it, and I will administer to you."

He lay upon his back, and to his surprise, she stood over him, straddling him, looking down on his prostrate form. Reaching up, she pulled the pins from her magnificent hair, and it tumbled down about her like a shining golden cloak. She fluffed it, smiling. Seductively she drew her nether lips apart, saying, "Do you see my little jewel, Ali Hassan?" and when he nodded openmouthed and wide-eyed, she continued. "Tonight I will teach you how to make it glow with happiness, *and when I am happy,* I shall make you *very* happy." His heart hammered violently in his chest at the sight of the moist coral flesh, at her bold, suggestive words.

Now she squatted, crouching over him. He could scarcely breathe in his excitement. This was the most beautiful woman he had ever seen, and she was all his. A gasp ached in his burning throat as her pointed little tongue began to lick at his flesh. Fascinated, his eyes followed her as she carefully laved every inch of him from his straining throat down to his feet. When she commanded him to roll over, he immediately did so. The warm wetness of the tongue bath was extremely exciting.

A little moan escaped him as she first licked at his buttocks, then nipped them. Hatiba had never been such a lover. Oh, she had done whatever he had desired of her, but it had certainly not been like *this*. He couldn't even remember her face now. Hatiba had served her purpose even more than she realized. Had he not killed the unfaithful bitch, and all the others, the caliph would not have sent that ineffectual Hasdai ibn Shaprut to hunt him down, bringing Zaynab with him, Ali Hassan thought.

She sat upon his buttocks now, the weight of her peach-shaped bottom pressing suggestively into him. Her nails raked slowly down his back over and over again. It felt exciting, and at the same time irritating. Then she lay stretched out atop him. He could feel the tenderness of her belly and her breasts. She pushed his legs wide with her own.

"Do you know what I'm doing?" she whispered in his ear, licking the interior, blowing softly, and then biting gently upon the fleshy lobe. "My right hand is seeking between my nether lips, Ali Hassan. Ahh, it has found what it desires. Ummmm. As I lie with my body covering yours, I shall pleasure myself. You cannot see me doing it. You can only feel the movements and imagine what is happening. Ohh, yess! Ohhhh! Ohhhh!" Her movements were becoming more frenzied atop him, and then she moaned low, "Ahhhhhhh, yes!"

"Bitch!" he snarled. "I'm going to fuck you now!"

"If you should even attempt it," she shot back, "you will know nothing of the pleasures I can give you. You are behaving like a little child, Ali Hassan. Can you not be patient with me? I have had a whole seven days to plan the delights I shall share with you tonight. This is just the beginning." He felt her weight removed from him. "Turn over once more," she said.

When he had, she straddled him once again, but this time he could see her face, and her magnificent body. Leaning forward so that her breasts hung temptingly above his face, she reached out for something. His tongue snaked out to lick frantically at her nipples, and she giggled.

"You are a very naughty boy," she told him archly. "Raise your hands above your head, Ali Hassan. I am going to lightly bind you. I know you aren't afraid of me," she said, seeing his slightly startled look even as he raised his arms above his head in response to her request. She tied his wrists together first, and then turning about so that her buttocks were facing him, she had him open his knees, and bound his ankles together. "If you find yourself becoming apprehensive, Ali Hassan, just tell me, and I will loose you," she said, reversing herself again.

Her words touched his very masculinity. He was certainly not comfortable being so helpless, but he would have rather died than admitted it to anyone, let alone a woman. Instead he grinned up at her. "I eagerly await the special passion that only you can give me, Zaynab," he said, but his chest was suddenly tight with his nervousness, and drawing breath was difficult. He shifted himself slightly, relieved to find that his bonds were not really secure. If he struggled hard, they would release.

Where in the name of Allah was Iniga? Zaynab wondered even as she sat herself high on Ali Hassan's chest, leaning forward to slowly brush her full breasts across his face. "Inhale my special female scent," she commanded him in a husky voice. Then moving a little farther up, she pressed her mont directly over his mouth, even as her hand reached back to grasp his shaft.

He was absolutely frozen with his excitement. The feel of her fleshy mont pressing down so intimately upon him, the touch of her hand on his manhood. She was doing nothing more now than holding him firmly; yet it sent the blood roaring into his head, which throbbed. When she murmured the words *"Kiss me,"* he could scarcely contain himself. His lips pressed themselves against her moist flesh as she rewarded him with a little murmur of what he was positively certain was pleasure. Emboldened, he pushed his tongue from his mouth, trying desperately to lick at her. In response she turned herself again so that he might have full access to her mont while she began to stimulate his manhood.

She was kindling emotions in him such as he had never before felt. Each time he thought himself ready to explode with his lust, she would ease back, her fingers brushing him delicately. His tongue worked feverishly to rouse her to the same plateau, but although she plainly enjoyed these attentions—at least the sounds she made implied that she did—she did not for a single moment lose her mastery of their situation. He was filled with admiration for her even as his hot lust was rising to the boiling point. She had both his manhood and his mouth so occupied he could scarcely bear it, and yet she knew that he did. When her lips closed over his throbbing shaft, he moaned. Reaching back, she placed her palm over his mouth. Frantically he licked at it with his tongue, desperate to taste her again.

She had found her rhythm now, and she did not allow it to abate. Several times she forced his hunger back, easing off, tightening him up with her mouth and tongue when he began to falter. Then she grasped him firmly in her hand again, using several quick strokes which she alternated with slow, teasing strokes. She felt the man beneath her aching in sweet frustration. She knew she was going to have to put him out of his misery before he tired and lost his desire. That would only anger him. Zaynab knew that Ali Hassan's pride could be pushed just so far. Taking her hand from his mouth, she turned herself about. The man beneath her was pale, his face dappled with beads of perspiration.

Smiling down into his face, Zaynab lowered herself slowly upon his great shaft. His was the largest manhood she had ever taken in. He filled her full. When he was completely encased within her sheath, she pressed her muscles together, squeezing his shaft in her love grip. Ali Hassan's black eyes actually bulged from his head. He opened his mouth and howled with the violent pleasure she was giving him. It was certain everyone in camp heard him.

Then suddenly his eyes rolled back in his head, there was a rattle of sound from his open mouth, and he collapsed beneath her. Zaynab was astounded, but at that same moment she heard cries of *"Fire!"* echoing through the camp. Zaynab leapt from her victim, yanked the cords from his wrists and ankles, then straddled him once again.

One of Ali Hassan's men ran into the tent. Seeing his master thus, he flushed.

"Get out!" Zaynab commanded him. "My lord Ali Hassan says you should handle the situation, as he is otherwise engaged." Then she leaned forward, kissing the man beneath her, wriggling her body and moaning, waiting as she listened for the underling to leave. When she was satisfied he had, she arose again, staring down at Ali Hassan. He didn't appear to be breathing. Leaning over, she put her ear to his heart, and heard nothing. He was certainly dead. Carefully, she drew his arms down so that he would look more natural. Then she pulled a coverlet over him. Hopefully, with all the chaos outside, they would not discover him dead until the morning, by which point the Nasi and his Saqalibah would have arrived. She dared not fire this tent now, else the bandits come running to rescue their master. Zaynab pulled her caftan on, dimmed the lamps, and slipped from the tent.

Outside she discovered that half the camp was well afire. Ali Hassan's people were frantically running back and forth from the nearby stream in their desperate attempts to put out the flames. No one paid the least bit of attention to her as she sidled back into her own little tent.

"I did it!" Iniga's blue eyes were triumphant.

"And very well too," Zaynab responded, hugging her. "Ali Hassan is dead, Iniga. I think, perhaps, we had best put on our cloaks and slip away into the darkness while we can. The caliph's men should be here sometime soon, but if we must wait until dawn, it would be better if we were hidden away from here. Ali Hassan's men may discover him before the Nasi arrives, and hold me responsible."

"You killed him? How?" Iniga's eyes were wide with surprise.

"He killed himself with his overanticipation to possess me, I think," Zaynab said. "I played an innocent little game with him, keeping him well occupied until you had completed your mission, but you took so long, Iniga. Finally I had no choice but to sheathe him within my body. His excitement was so great at that point that his black heart gave out. It was far too easy a death for such a terrible man." She picked up her cloak. "Come, Iniga. We must flee now." But as Iniga reached for her own cape, noises of a different sort came from outside their tent.

They heard the sound of horses' hooves, the shouts of men, the screams of women, running feet, clanging weapons. The two young women looked at one another, and Iniga said fearfully, "What if the fire has attracted some other bandit, and not my brother?"

For a moment a band of fear wrapped itself about Zaynab's heart, but then her common sense prevailed. "I doubt there is another bandit in these hills right now, Iniga. Remember, the caliph's men have been searching for us almost two weeks." She took her friend's hand. "Let us step outside and see. We should welcome our rescuers."

Karim saw her as she stepped from the little tent. He saw his sister by her side. *Zaynab was safe!* He called to two of his men to ride across the camp to protect the women from further harm.

Within a very brief time the Saqalibah finished mopping up the little resistance attempted by Ali Hassan's men. The women and children in the camp were gathered together. They would be taken to Alcazaba Malina and sold in the slave market there. The remaining men would be publicly tortured and executed for the benefit of the citizens of Malina, so that the murder of Habib ibn Malik and his family could finally be put to rest.

The prince and the Nasi went into Ali Hassan's tent. Zaynab and Iniga were brought to them.

"Where is Ali Hassan?" Hasdai ibn Shaprut asked them.

"He is dead," Zaynab replied.

"How?" the Nasi said. "And when?"

"Just a short time ago, my lord. He died in the throes of passion, I regret to say. His lust killed him. It was too easy an end."

Karim walked across the tent to the sleeping area, and pulling the diaphanous curtain aside, looked upon the man who had murdered his wife and family. This was the man Hatiba had professed to love. He saw the bath with all its accoutrements. He pulled back the coverlet and spotted the silken cords, saw the angle of one leg, saw the pearlescent trickle oozing from the deflated manhood. He knew how the man had died, and while glad for his death, he agreed with Zaynab. It had been too easy, and too pleasurable a death.

"I did not mean to kill him thusly," Zaynab said quietly when he returned to where the others stood. "I merely wanted to keep him occupied while Iniga fired the camp. When we realized that Ali Hassan allowed no outdoor fires, we knew that was why you had not found us."

"My sister fired the camp?" Karim's gaze swung to Iniga, surprised. She stood silently, eyes lowered modestly.

"Iniga was very brave," Zaynab told them.

Hasdai ibn Shaprut said nothing, but he listened, and he watched the interaction between Zaynab and Karim. They spoke as old friends, and she was protective of his sister. What was between them really? What had been between them? It was the one thing that she had refused to discuss with him. "You had no doubts that I would find you," he finally said to her, and she smiled up at him.

"I am a Love Slave, my lord. I knew you would not leave me to Ali Hassan. How could you have explained my loss to the caliph who gave me to you?" Then she laughed, and touching his arm, looked into his face. "Can we please return to the city, my lord? I am ravenous for food that does not come in a wooden bowl, and I need a change of clothing. So does Iniga."

At the mention of her name, Iniga finally looked up. Her gaze rested first on Zaynab, and lastly, with love, upon her brother. Then, swiftly drawing a dagger from her robes, Iniga drove the weapon into her frail body. The others stared, surprised, as Iniga's legs gave way beneath her and she crumpled to the floor. Karim knelt, cradling his sister in his arms, tears sliding down his handsome face.

"Iniga, how can you leave me?" he pleaded with her. "If you go, my sister, I will have no one."

"I am defiled, Karim. Zaynab will tell you," Iniga said weakly.

Hasdai quickly knelt down and examined the wound, praying that it was superficial, but Iniga had struck herself a mortal blow. His sympathetic brown eyes met the prince's blue ones, and he slowly shook his head. Then the Nasi rose to his feet and put his arms about Zaynab. She was shaking with shock and weeping silently.

"D-Do not g-grieve," Iniga said to them, and then she sighed gustily, her gaze freezing.

"She is dead," Karim said tonelessly. "My little sister is dead." He arose, Iniga's body still in his arms. "She will be buried with her family," he said with finality.

In the camp they found a white burial shroud that someone had obviously put aside for themselves. They sewed the body of the young woman in it. By now dawn was already staining the skies. Karim, Hasdai, and their men fired the rest of Ali Hassan's camp, and then driving their prisoners before them, they rode from the foothills of the mountains down into the city.

The day was well under way when they finally reached Alcazaba Malina, but as word of their arrival spread, the bustle of commerce ceased. The citizens came from their houses and shops to see evidence of the victory their prince had wrested from Ali Hassan, whose severed head upon a pike led their way back into the town.

▓ *Chapter 18*

*I*t was amazing, Zaynab thought as they returned to the city, that she and Karim had looked on one another for the first time in several years, yet spoke to each other as if they had never been parted. She loved him. Did he love her? He had not loved Hatiba, Mustafa said, *but did he still love her?* And what good if he did? She belonged to the Nasi. Another wife would be found for Karim, she knew. The caliph wanted him remarried, wanted Karim to have heirs who would continue their loyalty to the Umayyads while ruling Malina for him. It is hopeless, she thought, and she wept silently in the closed litter.

Her tears returned when Iniga was buried between her mother and her husband. The girl's in-laws, dressed in white, came with their grandson to help mourn his mother. Zaynab praised her friend's bravery, and leapt to her defense when Iniga's father-in-law said, "I am surprised she was still alive when you arrived at the camp of Ali Hassan, my lady Zaynab." His voice, though kind, carried a faint tone of condemnation.

"She was alive," Zaynab replied quietly, "because she believed Ali Hassan had little Malik in his possession. Each day they would show her a small boy across the encampment who waved to her. They told her it was her son. In fear for the child, she did their bidding. Only a loving mother would have sacrificed herself so."

"Ahhh," Iniga's mother-in-law said, tears in her eyes, "she was always a good mother. We will see that Malik remembers her as such."

No one asked anything further until that evening, when Karim

363

came to the Nasi's quarters. "I wish to speak with Zaynab," he said, and Hasdai nodded his permission.

"Do you wish me to go?" he asked Karim politely.

"No, you may stay." He settled himself across from Zaynab and asked, "Now tell me exactly what happened to Iniga. I know that you know."

She sighed. "What difference does it make now, my lord Karim? Iniga is dead. Ali Hassan is dead. Nothing can change that, nor what went before it. Why do you wish to torture yourself?"

Her beautiful face, Hasdai noted, was concerned.

"Tell me what happened, Zaynab!" he said in a harsh voice. *"I must know!"*

"Why?" she demanded, but seeing there would be no arguing with him, Zaynab began her recitation in a flat voice. As she came to the end of her tale, tears began to slip down Zaynab's beautiful face. "I thought that if I could keep her alive until you came, Karim, she would want to continue living; but as soon as she knew I would escape unscathed . . ." Zaynab could not go on, her sorrow being too great. Hiding her face from the two men, she wept bitterly into her two hands. She would never understand why Iniga chose suicide over life. To Zaynab life was precious, and when it hurt or disappointed you, you got up and moved on to a better time.

Oma, who had been sitting silently, crept to her mistress's side, putting her arms about her. "There, there, lady, don't grieve," she murmured. "They have this code of honor here, and you couldn't save her from it, lady. 'Twas her fate, I fear."

"Are you satisfied now, my lord?" Hasdai coldly asked the prince. "I do not think Zaynab has anything else to say to you on the matter." He was furious with himself for allowing Karim al Malina to distress her so. Zaynab had a kind heart. She had cared deeply for her friend.

Karim, stricken, arose and left them. He thought he had known what Zaynab would say, but the depth of the brutality visited upon his sister was more than he could bear.

Finally, Zaynab's grief subsided a bit, and she said to the Nasi, "I tried to save her, Hasdai. There was no need for her to die, but she kept saying because she had been raped, she was defiled and no longer felt fit for decent society. Why should that be so, my lord? She was not at fault. It was the men who brutalized her who were at fault! I know several of them by sight. They are among your prisoners, and I want to see them die!" Her voice was shaking now. *"I must!"*

"Lady, Alaeddin said to me their deaths will be horrible," Oma whispered. "The prince burned for revenge before he heard your tale. Now he will be merciless. 'Tis too harsh a sight for our eyes."

The Nasi, however, disagreed. "If you wish to see these particular men tortured and executed, my dear, then you shall; but Oma is right. It will be a cruel and terrible sight."

"I would see it," she said fiercely, then turning to Oma, told her, "You need not accompany me."

"So be it," the Nasi told her.

Zaynab went with him and Karim to point out the two men she had seen using Iniga that day, and the man Iniga had pointed out as the one who liked to beat her before using her. The three of them were separated from the others, and brought to the main square of the city for public torture and execution. Each man was whipped hard, but not enough to either kill him or render him unconscious. It was a fine art that the whippers practiced. They made their victims suffer exquisite pain, and then they rubbed salt into the bloody wounds to intensify that pain. Each man was then stretched upon a rack. His fingernails and toenails were removed while he howled with agony. The air was heavy with the scent of blood, urine, vomit, and feces when finally all three prisoners were ready for the next stage of the torture.

Zaynab sat immobile upon the dais placed in the square for Hasdai, Karim, and herself. She was pale, but her eyes were hard and lacking pity. No one looking at those eyes would have known that beneath her veil she bit her lip to keep from crying out loud. She stared as a surgeon carefully removed the testes from each man's scrotum, numbing the area first, for the pain would have rendered him unconscious. The three would see themselves unmanned. The mental agony that caused was far,

far greater than any physical pain. A collective shriek arose from the three as their manhoods were sliced off in unison by three executioners, to then be fed to a pack of snarling, hungry dogs that had been rounded up for the occasion. The terrible wounds were stanched with hot pitch, causing further cries of pain. Zaynab swallowed back the urge to vomit.

The prince arose. "Come," he said to the Nasi and Zaynab.

They followed him up a flight of stairs to the top of the walls of Alcazaba Malina, which were some thirty feet in height. Ten feet down on the smooth white walls, great, curving black hooks were set to prevent any attacker from scaling the high barricades. The three half-dead men were carried up the stairs behind the prince and his party. At Karim's signal, each was carefully tossed from the wall, their descent stopped by the sharp hooks upon which they fell. Their screams were horrendous as their naked bodies were pierced through. They wriggled upon the hooks, crying out to Allah for a quick death, desperate to escape the all-enveloping pain.

"Depending upon their individual strengths," Karim said quietly, "they may live several hours to several days. The last to die will watch as the carrion birds pluck the sightless eyes from his companions."

"I hope it is the fat one," Zaynab said. "The one who beat Iniga. He is the worst of them all. I pray he suffers the most!"

Watching the three dying men somehow seemed to ease the pain in her heart. Zaynab knew she would always remember, but at least she felt justice had been done. Iniga had been revenged. Her honor would be cleansed by the death throes of the men who had maltreated her so terribly.

For the next few weeks Hasdai ibn Shaprut worked with Karim to set the government and its administration, unsettled by the death of Habib ibn Malik, back on an even keel. Zaynab spent her time regaining her strength and preparing for Oma's wedding to the vizier, Alaeddin ben Omar. In the days of Zaynab's captivity, Karim's former first mate had pressed his case with Oma. When Zaynab returned, Alaeddin came to her, pleading.

"You must convince her to wed with me," he said. "I love

her dearly. I have taken no other wife, in the hopes that she would change her mind and return to me, my lady Zaynab; but I am no longer a young man. I am past thirty. If I am to have sons, I must marry soon."

"I have told her I would free her, and I have advised her to marry you, my lord," Zaynab told him. "Last time, I know, she remained with me because I was going into a strange new world. Now, however, I have the Nasi, and I have the caliph's daughter. I should not want her to deny herself the happiness she could have as your wife. I will speak with her, but I can promise you nothing, my lord. Oma is every bit as independent in her thinking as I am. Are you certain you want such a wife? She will not change." Zaynab's eyes twinkled.

"I want only her!" he vowed earnestly.

"Do you love him?" Zaynab demanded of Oma later that day.

"Yes," Oma said, "but I love you too, lady."

"If you love him," Zaynab replied, "then you must marry him." She caught her friend's hands in hers. "Ohhh, Oma, do not be a little fool! I love you too. You are the best friend I ever had, but what you will have with Alaeddin ben Omar will be even better. You will have your freedom, and status as the wife of the vizier. You will have children of your own, and I know you want that. Best of all, you will have the love of a good man. Do not throw that away just to remain with me, Oma." Zaynab's eyes filled with tears. "Dearest Oma, if I could have what you have, I would be the happiest woman in the world!"

"You have the Nasi, and Moraima," Oma said slowly.

"The Nasi and I are friends, and of course I am grateful for that. I must live this life that fate has chosen for me, but you do not have to live it with me, my good Oma.

"I want you to live your own life as Alaeddin ben Omar's wife and the mother of his children. I would sell my soul for what is being offered to you, but I shall never know love again. The only man I have ever loved cannot love me. Fate has presented you with a golden opportunity, Oma. If you reject it this time, you will regret it all of your days, and I will think you the biggest fool ever born."

Oma burst into tears. "Ohh, lady, I am so torn! I want to be that black-bearded ruffian's wife, but I cannot bear the thought of leaving you all alone! You have no one but me to look after you."

"I shall have the Nasi give orders to comb the slave markets of al-Andalus for a girl from Alba," Zaynab said. "She will not be my dear Oma, but she will make her own place in my life. Marry the vizier, Oma. After all, you are not getting any younger either. You are sixteen, and I already had had Moraima when I was your age," Zaynab teased her friend. "If you wait much longer, the vizier will be forced to find a younger wife to wed."

"As if anyone would have him, the black-bearded villain," Oma said, and then she smiled tremulously. "Is it really all right? You will not mind if I marry him, and desert you?"

Zayab hugged her. "You are not deserting me, Oma," she reassured the girl. "Now, run along, and tell him of your decision. You will make him the happiest of men. I will dower you generously, and the Nasi will see to it that your bride price is also large."

"You are certain you are content to let Oma go?" Hasdai ibn Shaprut asked Zaynab that night as they lay abed.

"She loves him," came the quiet reply. "No one should throw away love, my lord, though there are those who would think me foolish for such sentiments. Will you negotiate her bride price for her? I should consider it a great favor, and I will need an imam to attend to the legalities of her freedom and the marriage contract."

"I will ask the prince to speak to the imam, and I will negotiate her bride price." He took a lock of Zaynab's golden hair between his fingers. "Tell me what you did to Ali Hassan. What pleasure was so lethal that it killed him?"

"Ali Hassan killed himself," Zaynab said impassively. "He boiled his heart in his own lust, my lord. I managed to keep him at bay until the night you found us. Finally I took him to the bed and made him lie upon it. I bound his arms and legs with silken cords. Then I began a sweet torture that between lovers is a delight, but for Ali Hassan was a death sentence, although I knew it not."

He reached up, and pulling her head down to his kissed her, and whispered against her lips, "Do to me what you did to Ali Hassan, my adorable little assassin."

"Are you not afraid of meeting the same end, my lord?" she teased him, but she was a little shocked by his request.

His brown eyes looked directly at her. "I am not afraid," he said softly.

If he had been another man, Zaynab would have found a way to avoid what he was proposing, but Hasdai was genuinely curious. She arose from the bed, and fetching her little golden basket, brought it back to the bedside. Reaching in, she drew forth two silken cords and bound him. She began by resting lightly upon his thighs and fondling her own breasts. He watched, fascinated, as she put a finger in her mouth, sucked upon it, and then withdrawing it, encircled her nipples.

Then she began his torture, and when he was well roused, and straining against his bonds, Zaynab sat back where he could see her, and teased at her little jewel until she was gasping and weak with pleasure. He struggled against the silken cords, wild with his desire to possess her, and at that point Zaynab lowered herself over his raging member, taking him into her body to slowly pleasure him. When the edge was off his hunger, she released him from his bonds, and rolling her over, he pistoned her again and again until they both found paradise.

Afterward he held her in his arms, saying, "What other little games have you kept from me, my dear? Next time I want to bind you and be the torturer. Would you object?"

"My lord, it is my duty to give you pleasure," she answered.

"Then so be it," he said, and promptly fell asleep, perfectly sated with the passion they had shared.

Zaynab lay awake for some time, and finally arose, pulling on a simple white silk caftan. Slipping through the diaphanous curtains, she walked out into the garden. The moon was full tonight, and it silvered the landscape below. She paced slowly, inhaling the fragrance of roses, nicotiana, and her own favorite, gardenias. The air was warm and the light breeze ruffled her long hair.

She needed to compose herself. Prepare herself for the voyage to al-Andalus; for the long years ahead of her that would be filled with passion while devoid of love. I don't want to be a Love Slave any longer, she thought silently, daring to let the words she could not voice blossom in her mind. I want to be Karim's wife, the mother of his children. I would give up everything I possess for that paradise! I would live in a black goat's-hair tent and eat from a wooden bowl the rest of my life if Allah would but grant me my desire. I hate the life I must live! She paced nervously through the garden.

I must control these mutinous thoughts, Zaynab thought, reminding herself that soon she would see her darling little daughter. Moraima was her life now. She would never again return here, nor see *him* again. It had been horrendous being so close to Karim, neither of them acknowledging the other except in the most formal of terms. It was worse being in the Nasi's arms, knowing Karim was in the same house. Why had she ever come back to Alcazaba Malina? *Oma.* She had come for Oma. *Or had she?* Suddenly she stopped, stiffening, sensing his presence before he even spoke her name.

"Zaynab!" He stood, silhouetted in the moonlight, wearing a caftan as white as hers, his hair pulled back so that she could clearly see his handsome face.

"Forgive me, my lord, I have intruded," she quickly said, and turned about to go. His hand fell lightly upon her shoulder.

"Do not leave," he said quietly. "We have had no real chance to speak together, you and I. Are you happy?"

She did not turn about, saying instead, "I am a wealthy woman, albeit a slave. I have a good master in the Nasi, a powerful friend in the caliph, and a child I love, my lord."

"But are you happy?" he asked her again.

She spun about, saying angrily, *"No!* I am not happy, Karim al Malina. I will never be really happy away from you! There! I have said it aloud to you. Do my words make you happy?"

"I have not been happy since the moment I left you," he replied.

"Oh, my lord," she cried furiously, "what good does this do either of us? I cannot have you, nor you me. Find another wife, and sire children upon her for the good of Malina, as your father would have wanted you to do. I will shortly return with my master to al-Andalus. I shall make certain that we never see each other again!"

"*Your master,*" he said sneeringly. "You make him very happy, Zaynab. His cries of pleasure could be heard throughout my garden this night. It pleases me that I trained you so well."

Her little hand flashed out, making hard contact with his smooth cheek. With equal speed he yanked her into his arms, his mouth descending to cover hers in a deep, burning kiss. His heart leapt at the familiar feeling of her body against his, at her lips softening against his lips in passionate response, but then she drew her head away from his. Tears rolled down her cheeks, and her eyes were like sea-washed jewels as she looked at him, anguished.

"*Zaynab,*" he whispered, his own heartache evident.

She pulled completely from his embrace. "You are far crueler to me than Ali Hassan was," she said low. "How could you, Karim? How could you break my heart again like this? *I will never forgive you!*" Then she ran from him, across the garden, through the diaphanous curtains, back to the chamber she shared with Hasdai ibn Shaprut. Trembling, she pulled her garment off and slipped into the bed again. The man beside her lay quietly, pretending that he yet slept, but he had seen the tableau in the garden and was troubled by it. Now the Love Slave lay by him, struggling to control her sobs. He had to know the truth, but he would not ask her until they were back in al-Andalus.

Oma's wedding to Alaeddin ben Omar was a quiet one. The vizier had no family but an ancient father. The bridal bath the day before was just between the two friends. Oma did not sit on a golden throne amid a wealth of gifts as Iniga once had, and perhaps it was better they were not reminded of that day. The vizier, his father, Karim, and the Nasi went to the mosque, where the imam, having been informed by the qadi that the marriage contracts were in order and agreed to by both parties, pronounced that they were man and wife. The four men returned to the palace. After a small traditional repast, Alaeddin ben Omar took his bride home to the fine new house that the prince had given them. His elderly father, Omar ben Tariq, would live with them, that he might enjoy his grandchildren in his remaining years. He had taken immediately to Oma.

"She is pretty enough, and has a sweet nature," he told his son, "*and* she is broad in the hips. She'll be a good breeder!"

"When do we return to Cordoba?" Zaynab asked Hasdai that same evening, after the bridal party had gone.

"Are you that anxious to leave?" he asked her thoughtfully.

"We have been gone over four months, my lord. The prince is restored to good health, and is fully capable of administering the government here for the caliph, or so you have said. Oma is settled. I miss my daughter. The Gulf of Cadiz is not an easy sea in autumn," she concluded.

"So the prince has told me," he said to her. "We are going to travel overland to Tanja, and sail the short distance across to Jabal-Taraq. We shall then travel to Cadiz, and meet our vessel at the mouth of the Guadalquivir. If you like, we will stop in Seville and see the city, my dear. I promised that to you on our voyage to Malina."

"I just want to go home," Zaynab said quietly.

"You cannot travel without a servant," he said to her.

"I want a slave girl from my own land, Hasdai. We will not find one here in Alcazaba Malina. Besides, I am perfectly capable of taking care of myself, even after my years in al-Andalus. I need no one to ride in the litter with me. I will be brought my meals, and when I can bathe, I am capable of doing it by myself if I must."

"Then we can leave tomorrow," he said. "The Saqalibah can be ready at a moment's notice, and so can I."

"I, however, cannot," she informed him. "My possessions must be packed. I will send to Oma tomorrow to come and help me. We can leave the day after, my lord."

"Give the bride a few days' respite, my dear," Hasdai said with a smile. "Although I know Oma will come to your call, remember she is no longer your servant. Why do we not plan our departure for a week from today. In the meantime I will want our host to ride about Malina with me to reassure his people that everything is all right now. Do you mind being alone? We will leave in the morning and be gone for several days."

"I am content with my own company," Zaynab said. "I shall visit the silver market and find something special for Moraima."

When Oma came to help her a few days later, however, Zaynab was delighted for her company. Together the two women packed the Love Slave's belongings for her return to al-Andalus. Oma was full of news.

"I have two sweet little serving girls in the harem," she told Zaynab. "One is from a place called Crete, and the other is a Rumi. They were a gift from my father-in-law. He is such a dear old man, Zaynab. When Alaeddin and I told him about the baby, he was simply delighted. Ohh, it is so wonderful to have a family of my own!"

"Baby?" Zaynab laughed. "You did not tell me about a baby."

Oma chuckled. "Well, you know that once we saw each other, Alaeddin and I couldn't keep our hands, and our other parts, quiet. I knew before you were kidnapped, lady."

"Yet you would have returned with me to Cordoba," Zaynab said softly. "Ohh, Oma! No woman ever had a better friend than I have had in you. I will miss you, but I will be content knowing you are so happy." Then seeing Oma's tears, she brushed them away, saying, "Tell me about your new home, and how many other servants do you have? Remember to be strict but fair with them. Is the house very big?"

"There is a eunuch who runs the household," Oma said, "but no eunuch in the harem. I told Alaeddin it was a waste of money to buy one just for me. There is a cook, and people to clean, and we have ten of the new Saqalibah to guard us. The prince gave them to us. He said we can never expect things to be as they once were, so we must be vigilant. The house has beautiful gardens with fountains. It is a lovely place, and I am so happy!" Her pretty face shone, confirming her words. Then she chuckled. "I cannot help but think how annoyed that horrid Mother Eubh would be to learn of our fates, lady. I'm certain she expected we would end up slaving for some Celtic chieftain in the hills of Eire. I'm sorry she cannot know of our happiness."

"Which is certainly far greater than hers, I suspect," Zaynab answered her friend. "We are the fortunate ones."

Hasdai and the prince returned late the following day, and ate together before retiring.

"I am informed that your caravan is packed and ready to depart at first light, my lord Nasi," the prince told him. "You will follow the coastal road connecting Alcazaba Malina with Tanja. The journey should take no more than three days. A vessel will be waiting in Tanja to ferry you across to Jabal-Taraq. Once there, you are again on the soil of al-Andalus proper. I will not save my good-byes for the morning, but rather now tell you of my deep gratitude. Had you not come to Malina, I do not think I should have survived, so deep was my sorrow. I know that the caliph sent you in response to a plea from my council, Hasdai, but once here, you truly felt my pain. You understood, but you did not allow me to wallow in self-pity. You made me remember my duty to my people, as my father would have wanted. For that, for your friendship, for so much more, I am very grateful."

"Now," Hasdai said with a smile, "your next duty is to find a young wife, and sire another generation of descendants of ibn Malik."

Karim shook his head. "I will not marry again," he said quietly. "My sister's son shall be my heir."

"But surely you want a wife, a harem of lovelies?" the Nasi pressed.

"I once fell in love with a woman that I could not have," Karim told him. "Then I married the girl my father chose because I wanted to please him and for once be a dutiful son. Hatiba had been promised to Ali Hassan. She loved him as I loved someone else. Even had my family's tragedy not occurred, I learned that a marriage without love is a hollow thing, Hasdai. No, I shall not marry again."

"What if you fell in love?" the Nasi asked.

Karim's eyes fastened onto Hasdai's. "I shall not love again," he said firmly. "How could I love another after my beloved . . ." Then he laughed ruefully. "Besides, Hasdai, I have certainly had my fill of women, have I not?"

The Nasi laughed. "Indeed, my lord, yes, yet a soft body beneath a man is truly paradise. I do not think I should want to be celibate."

"Obviously, Zaynab pleases you," Karim said abruptly, then wondered why on earth he had said it. Did he really want to know from the Nasi's mouth of the pleasure she could give a man? *He already knew.* Why did he continue to torment himself?

"She does," Hasdai said shortly, and then, "I should not have been so fortunate as to possess her for my own had not my lord, the caliph, had no way of putting the lady Zahra aside without causing confusion regarding the succession. The caliph adored Zaynab, and she him."

"A pity," Karim responded coolly, and then he said, "I think I shall retire, Hasdai. I shall see you in the morning before you depart."

Dismissed, the Nasi returned to his own quarters, where Zaynab was already asleep. He wanted to ask her about Karim, but he did not wake her. When the prince had said he loved a woman he could not have, Hasdai wondered if that woman was Zaynab. There was obviously something between them, although Zaynab had never given him any cause to doubt her loyalty. He had promised himself he would ask her, but not until they were back in Cordoba. He would keep that vow. She might be his property, but even so, Hasdai wondered if he had the right to question her about her innermost heart.

They departed in the early morning before the sun was too hot. Karim came to bid them farewell. Hasdai watched as he approached Zaynab, but the prince merely wished her a safe trip, and Zaynab thanked him in impersonal tones. Oma arrived with the vizier, and the two women hugged one another.

"I nae thought when we were taken from the convent that it would end like this," Oma said in their native tongue. "God, Allah, whatever ye want to call the deity, go wi' ye and keep ye safe, lady. I wish we dinna hae to part. I wish ye were remaining here. Could ye nae ask the Nasi? He would free ye if ye asked him, I know."

Zaynab hugged Oma. "Nay, lassie, he wouldna. He canna throw away the caliph's gift so lightly. Besides, he enjoys me." She smiled, and patted Oma's hand. "And there is Moraima. I canna leave my wee bairn, Oma. Ye'll understand when ye've borne yer own. Send word to me when it comes, lassie. I'll want to know yer safe." Then, after kissing her friend on both cheeks, Zaynab entered her litter.

Their caravan, accompanied by the caliph's one hundred Saqalibah, traveled a road that paralleled the ocean. It was a wide, well-kept road built hundreds of years ago by the Rumi. There were other travelers upon the road, some going the distance to Tanja, others merely moving from village to village. Every ten miles there were caravan stops: government-run inns with primitive but clean sleeping accommodations and food for both man and beast.

They traveled one-third of the distance they had to go the first day. Although they sheltered at a caravan stop, they had their own tents. Zaynab was irritated because she could not bathe until the following morning, before they left. The public bath belonging to the inn was, like all public baths in al-Andalus, open to women only until noon each day. After the noon hour it became the province of men.

Hasdai returned to their tent, refreshed from his ablutions. He was well fed, relaxed with good wine, and ready for love. "I have missed you," he said softly, reaching out for her. "It has been too long since we have been together, my dear."

Zaynab glared at him. "I am tired, my lord. My head aches from the heat and the dust of the road. I am filthy, and covered with grime." She moved away from him. "All I want to do is sleep. I do not like disappointing you, but I cannot be at my best under the circumstances. The innkeeper may have a whore for hire. If she is clean, I will not mind if you use her, my lord."

He looked at her, appalled. "I am capable of restraining my lust, Zaynab. I do not want a whore. I want you, but I will wait."

She flung herself on her mattress and slept. She was annoyed with him. He was always so reasonable. She wondered if he ever lost his temper. Certainly she had never seen him do so.

He shook her awake before dawn. "Go and bathe," he commanded her in a tight voice. "I have not had you in over a week, and I do not intend to wait until we return to Cordoba to do so."

Zaynab was astounded, but she obediently arose, and found her oils, soaps, and toweling. "What if the bath is not open yet?" she whispered to him. She drew on her all-enveloping cloak.

"It is open now," he said. "I asked the innkeeper last night."

She left the tent and hurried across the compound to the bathhouse. It was strange being without Oma. She paid the bath mistress her stipend and then stepped into the warm water. She debated about washing her hair, but she had done so before they left Alcazaba Malina. It could wait until Tanja as long as she kept the dust brushed out of it.

Returning to the tent, she slipped beneath the coverlet, and Hasdai immediately gathered her into his arms. "You are delicious," he murmured into her soft tresses, and his hand sought, found, and tenderly caressed a plump breast. "No games," he said. "I would simply be a man with you, my dear. Would another woman rouse me as you do, Zaynab? I wonder about it sometimes." He delicately pinched a nipple.

"You cannot know the answer to that question, my lord, unless you take another woman," she answered him. Her little hand stroked the back of his neck, and she felt the prickle of gooseflesh that her touch raised on his nape. "Would you like another woman?"

"No," he growled in her ear, and then the tip of his tongue insinuated itself into the shell of it, swirling about teasingly. He blew softly into her ear, sending a shiver down her spine. "I want only you, Zaynab." Then he was kissing her, his mouth pressing hard upon her mouth, his tongue infiltrating between her lips to play with her tongue. His lips traveled over her face and throat, working their way down to her breasts.

"Ummmmm," she purred with pleasure as he kissed her and fondled her. "Ahhhhh," she moaned as his mouth fastened upon first one nipple, then the other, drawing hard upon the flesh, stoking her rising excitement. He bit gently down on a nipple, sending a tiny jolt of sweet pain through her. Zaynab's fingers wrapped themselves in his dark hair, kneading his scalp as his hand moved down her belly to caress her mont.

"Unfortunately," he whispered to her, "there is no time for subtlety, my dear. If there were, I should pleasure you as you did me a few days back. When we get home," he told her as he mounted her, "I shall bind you to our bed, spread wide for my delight. Then I shall play with you until you beg for mercy, and your love juices will flow as copiously as they have ever flowed." He pushed himself slowly into her. "I will make you cry out with your happiness, Zaynab." Then he began to move energetically upon her, covering her mouth when she moaned with pleasure, for he did not want the entire place to hear her. She bit his palm, and he laughed, even as his own love juices exploded from his now satisfied manhood, filling her with his loving tribute.

Afterward he held her in his arms, the sounds of the caravan stop awakening in their ears. "We should start every day this way," he teased her, and then she laughed, snuggling against him.

"I shall look forward to our return to Cordoba, my lord," she told him. "I see now that you enjoy games, so we shall have to play some."

On the third day they reached Tanja. It was not a very impressive place, a clutter of low white buildings, and narrow winding alleys that passed for streets. There had, it seemed, always been some sort of settlement on the site since the time of the Ancients. It had even been there during the height of the Rumi empire. The city was set on a beautiful small bay of the Strait of Jabal-Taraq. Across the water the famed rock rose up from the sea. The view was utterly spectacular. The Nasi and his party were courteously welcomed by the caliph's governor, who housed them in his own small palace.

The following morning they were ferried across the strait, finally setting foot back upon the soil of al-Andalus that same day. Reorganized, their caravan wended its way to the mouth of the Guadalquivir, where their ship was awaiting them. They sailed up the river to Cordoba.

Zaynab did not choose to stop at Seville. She was too anxious now to see her child; but when at last they reached her home, it stood quiet. Hearing them in the courtyard, Naja ran from the house. His brown eyes were filled with tears. "Oh, lady!" he cried. "The princess is dead!"

▓ *Chapter 19*

Zaynab collapsed where she stood, crumbling into a heap as Naja's words pierced her to the heart. When she regained consciousness, which she fought strongly against doing, for she did not think she could bear any more pain, she was back in her own apartment. She moaned and closed her eyes, but Hasdai's voice forced her back.

"No, Zaynab, do not retreat from me," he commanded her sharply. "You must accept this terrible tragedy with the same strength with which you faced your friend Iniga's death. Open your eyes and look at me, Zaynab!"

"Tell me Naja lied," she begged him. "Tell me that I did not hear those terrible words I thought he spoke. Where is Moraima? *Bring me my daughter!*"

"Moraima is dead," he said quietly, "and Abra too, I fear."

"How?" Zaynab whimpered. *"How?"*

"There was an outbreak of spotted fever in Cordoba. Abra took Moraima to visit the caliph. Then, because it was growing late, she remained with the child at a cousin's house in the quarter. It was there, undoubtedly, that they became infected, although the disease was not in the cousin's home at the time. Several days later both of them came down with the sickness. Your servants fled. The caliph had his Saqalibah return to Madinat al-Zahra temporarily in order to protect their health. Only Naja and your cook, Aida, remained with Abra and the princess. Fortunately, neither of them caught the disease. Moraima and Abra died within hours of each other, my dear."

"Where is she?" Zaynab sobbed. "Where is my baby?"

"The caliph ordered her buried with Abra here in your garden," Hasdai said. "The house was then fumigated, and everything Moraima and Abra had was burned. Your servants were found and punished. They have been sold off. The caliph has sent new slaves to take their place."

"It does not matter," Zaynab said wearily. Nothing mattered anymore. She had been away with Hasdai, on a trip she need not have taken, and her baby had died, motherless, alone. What kind of a mother was she to have left her child while she traveled with her lover? Zaynab wept uncontrollably. Nothing Hasdai could do could make her cease, for her grief and her guilt were too deep. Finally, in desperation, he gave her a sleeping draught, that she might at least rest and regain her strength. Leaving Naja to watch over her, Hasdai departed for Madinat al-Zahra to render to the caliph his personal report on the state of affairs in Malina.

"You have done well, Hasdai," the caliph said when he had heard all the Nasi had to say. "I am astounded by Zaynab's bravery while captive to Ali Hassan, and while watching the torture and executions. It is a side of her I have never seen, nor could have even imagined." He paused, and then asked, "How is she? Moraima's death must have come as a terrible surprise to her. Is she all right?"

"She is in shock, my lord, and totally devastated. Before I left her, I gave her a sleeping draught, for she could not stop weeping. Naja is with her. She has no one else. It seems that Oma was in love with a man called Alaeddin ben Omar, who is now the prince's vizier. He had wanted to marry Oma before Zaynab was first brought to you. When they met again, their love for one another had not changed. This time Zaynab convinced Oma to marry. She freed her. The timing is unfortunate. She desperately needs Oma now."

"Could we not send for the woman?" Abd-al Rahman said, concerned.

"Oma is already breeding, my lord. It would not be advisable for a woman in her condition to travel so great a distance," the Nasi replied. "I will have the slave markets scoured for an Alban girl to replace Oma. It is the best we will be able to do."

* * *

Zaynab did not care. She had sunk into a deep depression from which there seemed no escape. There was nothing left to remind her of her child. Each day, she struggled to remember Moraima's dear little face, but eventually the memory began to fade away. She could not eat, nor was she sleeping well. Life had lost all meaning for her. She had no child, nor the hope of one. What was left for her? Her lover did not want offspring. Although he was fond of her, he did not love her, and she did not love him. Her black mood grew even darker.

Hasdai involved himself once again in the translation of *De Materia Medica*. He did not notice Zaynab's listlessness and ennui. The Greek translator from the court of the emperor in Constantinople had been working almost nonstop while they had been away. There was an enormous pile of pages that he had translated from Greek into Latin for Hasdai. Now Hasdai ibn Shaprut had to turn those Latin pages into Arabic. He was scarcely home, but Zaynab did not complain. He did not comprehend how serious the situation had become until Naja spoke frankly with him.

"She is dying, my lord," the eunuch said desperately. "She is slowly fading away like a perfect rose at summer's end. Do not let her die, my lord. Help her, I beg you!" His dark eyes were tear-filled.

"What can I do to help her, Naja?" the Nasi asked.

"Give her a child, my lord. Though she will never forget her dear little daughter, another child would give her an interest, would make her want to live again. Right now she has nothing, my lord. You are barely here. Oma is gone. There is absolutely nothing left for her, or so she believes. She does not even play her rebec, or sing any longer. Have you not noticed?"

Hasdai had not. He had been too involved in his work. He would always be too involved in his work. He was the caliph's loyal, efficient servant before he was anything else. It was what he wanted above all things. Still, he could not let Zaynab die, and suddenly he thought he knew how he might save her. He went to the caliph and told him of Zaynab's despondent condition.

"What can we do?" Abd-al Rahman was concerned. Deep in

his heart the caliph still harbored his affection for the beauteous Love Slave.

"I am not the proper master for Zaynab, my lord," Hasdai said. "My first love is in serving you. I will not have children with her, and children are what Zaynab needs. Moraima will always be in her heart, but she needs other little ones to love and cherish. I would like to give her to a new master, but before I do, I would ask your permission. I know that legally she is mine, but we both know why she came into my possession. So before I give her to another man, I would have your approval, my good lord."

"Who?" The caliph's mind and heart were troubled.

"I would give her to Karim al Malina as a bride, my lord," the Nasi told the caliph.

"Why?" Abd-al Rahman barked the word.

"There are several reasons, my lord. Firstly, the prince says he will not marry again, or sire children. He has told me that he will name his nephew Malik ibn Ahmed as his heir. I do not feel this solution is in the best interest of the Caliphate. The ibn Malik family have a tradition of loyalty to the Umayyad dynasty that goes back two hundred years. Malik ibn Ahmed's grandparents, who are raising him, have no history of governing. He would not be a good ruler. When I asked Karim why he would not remarry, he said he loved a woman whom he could not have. That he had learned a marriage without love was a hollow thing. I believe Zaynab is the woman he loves and cannot have. And I believe that she is in love with him too."

"She once told me she had loved someone before she came to me," the caliph said slowly. "Tell me, Hasdai, what makes you think it is the Prince of Malina whom Zaynab loves?"

"My lord, who else could it be? There was no one in her homeland. When she was brought to the merchant Donal Righ, she had been violated twice by strangers. Then Donal Righ gave her into the keeping of the Passion Master to train for your pleasure. I think they fell in love, but neither of them would behave dishonorably. We Jews have a saying, my lord: *Man plans. God laughs.*

"Karim al Malina educated Zaynab, as was his duty. Then he brought her to you as he had been instructed, but I suspect his heart broke to let her go. Zaynab understood her obligation to Donal Righ, who had given her such a fine opportunity instead of selling her to some primitive. Like the sensible woman she is, she put her past behind her, but deep in her heart she did not stop loving Karim al Malina.

"Now, my lord, both of these people have been grievously hurt by the vicissitudes that life has visited upon them. Zaynab is willing her life away. Unless we can do something to help her, she will die. Both of us have profited by possessing her. I believe that we each owe her a debt that can be repaid by sending her as a bride to the prince."

"I loved her once," the caliph said. "I thought she would be with me until I died. She gave me much joy, not just of a physical nature, but by her very existence. Do you love her, Hasdai?"

"Not as you did, my lord," the Nasi answered the caliph. "I have no time for that sort of love. If I did, I should marry, and make my father happy by siring a tribe of children for the house of ibn Shaprut. My greatest passion is in my service to you, my lord. Zaynab, however, is my friend. She has given me great physical pleasure. I have never known anyone like her. If she goes, I shall miss her, but I will quickly be involved in some mission or another for you, my lord, and it will not matter, particularly if I know she has gone to a man who will love her and get children on her. She is too intelligent a woman to sit idle. She needs a husband and little ones about her."

"Then send her to Karim al Malina," the caliph said quietly.

"No, my lord, I shall free her, but it is you who must send her back to the prince. He will not dare to refuse if the bride comes from Abd-al Rahman. Let me compose a letter to him in your name. You will say that on my recommendation you are sending him a bride that the line of ibn Malik, founder of Malina, not die, but live to serve the Umayyads forever." Hasdai chuckled. "The prince will be most put out, until he sees who you have sent him."

"Say also," the caliph replied, "that the lady is to be treated with the utmost courtesy and kindness; that she has my ear, and always will." Then he chuckled. "You will provide a generous dowry for her, Hasdai. After all, she is your property at the moment."

The Nasi smiled at his master. "She will be dowered like a princess," he promised the caliph. He could afford to be generous. He was a rich man, and Abd-al Rahman would be magnanimous to his devoted servant in return. He would lose nothing, but gain much in return for his generosity.

The matter decided, Hasdai ibn Shaprut put his plan swiftly into motion. There was no time to waste. A letter was drafted, and approved that same night for the caliph's signature. By morning the letter was on its way via royal messenger to Alcazaba Malina.

Next, the Nasi had his agents begin scouring the slave markets of al-Andalus. Within a few days they found a young girl they believed came from Alba, and she was brought to Zaynab's house.

Hasdai aroused the Love Slave from her lethargy, saying, "I may have found a servant for you, my dear, but since no one else can speak the girl's language, I am not certain. Will you see if you can communicate with her for me? If she suits you, I will buy her for you."

Zaynab looked at the girl. She was no beauty, with her freckles and carrot-red hair, but her amber eyes were intelligent, if a bit frightened. How had the poor creature ended up here? Zaynab remembered her own beginnings in al-Andalus, and had pity. "Are ye from Alba, lassie?" she asked the girl, whose eyes widened with relief.

"Praise be to God Almighty and the blessed Virgin Mary!" she cried, and fell to her knees before Zaynab. "Aye, lady, I am from Alba. How knew ye that? The tongue ye speak is nae quite my own, but I understand ye. I canna but hope ye understand me. Ye hae the sound of a northerner."

"Once I was known as Regan MacDuff," Zaynab told her. "This great lord, who is my master, would like to purchase ye to be my servant. I am called Zaynab, and I am a Love Slave. What is yer name, lassie?"

"Margaret, lady. I hae nae other," the girl told her.

"Ye must answer to the name Rabi from now on, lassie," Zaynab told her. "And ye must learn the tongue of these people, although we will speak our own tongue daily. It is a good thing to hae a language no one else understands when ye wish to speak in confidence. Ye will be safe wi' me, little Rabi. I am a good mistress."

Rabi kissed Zaynab's hem. "Bless ye, lady!" she said.

"This brown man is called Naja," Zaynab told her. "Go wi' him now. He will take ye to the bath, where ye must wash. We wash twice daily, lassie. He will help ye. Dinna be afraid. He is nae a real man, and will nae hurt ye." Then Zaynab turned to Naja and instructed him.

When they had departed, Hasdai said, "Then you are pleased?"

"If I die, take care of the poor creature," Zaynab said to him. Then she fell back upon the pillows of her bed once more.

"I will not let you die," he said quietly to her. "I have this day freed you, my dear, with the caliph's permission. You must regain your strength quickly, for in a few days' time you are to return to Alcazaba Malina as the bride of Prince Karim, Zaynab."

"What?" She sat up, astonished. Her heart was pounding. She could not have heard him right.

"How long have you loved Karim al Malina?" he asked her frankly.

The denial died in her throat as she looked into his eyes. "How did you know?" she said softly.

He smiled at her gently. "You never gave yourself away, Zaynab. You are probably one of the most perfect Love Slaves ever trained. It was the prince who first aroused my suspicions."

"Karim? How? He would not dishonor his trust," she defended him. "He is above all else an honorable man, Hasdai."

"I know he is," the Nasi agreed. "It was when we first came to Alcazaba Malina. I mentioned that you were with me. Weak from his ordeal, and still half in shock, he nonetheless roused himself from his stupor enough to ask after you with a degree of interest that I thought indicated more than simple curiosity.

When I asked Alaeddin ben Omar what had been between you, he said I must ask you. It implied that my suspicions were grounded in truth. When you were held captive, Karim alternately worried over it and reassured me that you could survive because you were clever and brave. The entire time we sought for the camp of Ali Hassan, his mind and his heart were filled with you, my dear. I could see you in his eyes, hear his concern in his voice. The final proof of his love for you came the night before we left Alcazaba Malina. I am afraid I witnessed that little scene between the two of you in the gardens."

"I did not leave our sleeping chamber to meet him," she said quickly. "I was restless and needed to walk. I did not know Karim would be there."

"I realize that," the Nasi said, and then he laughed softly. "I could not hear what was said between you, for I remained in the shadows of the curtains, but I could certainly hear the slap you gave him, even from across the gardens. But then he kissed you, Zaynab, and you did not struggle to escape him that I could see. Indeed, you melted into his embrace as if you had finally come home after a long and trying journey. It was at that moment I realized that not only did Karim al Malina love you, but that you, Zaynab, loved him. The scene was so poignant that my heart broke for you both."

"I never betrayed you, Hasdai," she told him.

"I am aware of that, my dear," he answered. "Indeed, both of you are filled with such a sense of decency and nobility that I cannot quite believe such goodness exists, despite the evidence of my own eyes. I have, I am afraid, become world-weary and cynical amid the superior civilization of al-Andalus and all its splendor, Zaynab. Such a simple thing as pure loyalty amazes me." He took her hand in his, rubbing it to put the circulation back into it, for she was so cold. It was no wonder, he thought, considering the shock she had suffered.

"I told you, Zaynab, that I would not allow you to will your life away, and I will not. If we had returned here to Cordoba, and all had been as we left it, I should have been content to leave things as they are, for frankly I enjoy not just your body, but your company. You are the perfect companion for me. Alas, fate has willed it otherwise.

"Unfortunately, I cannot give you the things that you truly desire, Zaynab. While I realize that you will never forget Moraima, you need other children, a house to run, a husband to share your life with, and I cannot be that man. No one, I think, knows better than you do, my dear, where my loyalties lie." When she smiled at his words, he felt hope for her again.

"A great deal of work has piled up for me in the four months we were away. I must devote myself to it, for the sooner it is done, the sooner we will have our medical school here in Cordoba. I do not have time to coax you from your sorrow, and if I did, what would remain for you? Oma is married, and has left you. Your child is dead. You are forced by the conventions of society to stay cloistered in your home without anything to do, without anyone to care for, waiting for an overworked civil servant to visit you occasionally. Neither the caliph nor I wish that kind of life for the woman who has brought us both so much pleasure and happiness.

"Since you love the Prince of Malina, and he loves you, the solution is quite simple. You are already a free woman, Zaynab, for I went to the chief rabbi of Cordoba before I returned to you today, and I signed the papers my secretary had prepared in his presence. As I am a Jew, and you belonged to me, the civil authority was Jewish in this case. The caliph has already sent a letter to Karim al Malina informing him that he has chosen a bride for him, who will be arriving shortly. I have dowered you quite generously, my dear. You had best take a firm grip upon life again, Zaynab, for you are quite obviously meant to live happily ever after, as the children's stories say."

She had sat listening to him quietly, taking in his words with amazement. Now he had ceased speaking, and her mind was awhirl. *Karim! She was going to be Karim's wife!* It was unbelievable! Zaynab burst into tears, to the astonishment of Hasdai ibn Shaprut.

"What is the matter?" he cried to her.

"I am so happy," she answered him, sniffling.

"Ahhh," he replied. He had seen his mother and sisters weep

in this irrational manner. "Then you are content with the fate the caliph and I have arranged for you, my dear?"

"Yes! Yes!" she told him, and then, "Ohh, Hasdai, how can I ever thank you for your unselfish kindness? I shall never be able to repay you, but I will always remember this wonderful thing you have done. I will never get over the blow of returning here to find my little daughter dead and buried, all trace of her gone from this house as if she had not ever existed. I miss Oma more than I had thought to miss her, even if I am happy she has her own life now. I tried to look forward, not backward, but all I could see stretching before me was years and years of loneliness, broken only by your visits. It is simply not enough for me, Hasdai! Thank you for understanding that."

"Do not make me into a hero, Zaynab, for I am not. I am a selfish man, wrapped in my work, and had your child survived her illness, I should have not let you go. You would have taught me pleasures of a sort I never thought to know. I shall miss you, and I shall miss them," he said with a smile.

"If you would let me, I could find you a beautiful slave girl, and educate her as to how to give you those pleasures," Zaynab said.

"No," he responded. "No matter how skilled she would become, she would not be you, my dear. Remember, you are no ordinary concubine. You are a Love Slave, a creature of sensuality and intellect, unique among women."

"You must not go back to what you were before you first came to my bed," Zaynab replied firmly. "You must not allow your love juices to be bottled up and fester. It is wrong, Hasdai!"

"I am skilled enough now, thanks to you, my dear," he said with a chuckle, "that I shall not be ashamed to visit Cordoba's most skilled courtesans when the need arises."

"At least once a week, and better twice," she said seriously.

"When I can find the time," he answered her.

"Which means practically never," she fumed. "You must have someone in your house, Hasdai, someone convenient, or you will never relax. If you do not want to own another slave girl, perhaps you could make an arrangement with some young courtesan to come to you twice weekly here in this house," Zaynab suggested.

"This house is yours," he told her.

"I give it to you," she said with a smile. "You prefer living outside of the quarter, and this house is very secluded. It suits you. You can work here when you choose, and entertain with the utmost privacy, my lord. Give me the deed. I will sign it over to you. You will have to find your own cook, however. I intend to take Aida with me. No! I will find you a cook. If I leave it to you, it will never get done. I must leave you with everything running smoothly, Hasdai." Her words tumbled out of her mouth one after another.

"You are beginning to sound like my mother," he grumbled at her, and then he laughed. "I told the caliph that you were really meant to be a wife, and a mother. I am happy to see my judgment proved correct."

Zaynab had a whole new lease on life. She sent Naja to the chief rabbi in the Jewish quarter with a polite note inquiring if he could recommend to her a respectable spinster or widow to housekeep and cook for a gentleman of the faith. Naja returned some time later in the company of a tall, spare woman who introduced herself as Maryam Ha-Levi. With her was her grandson, a boy of ten.

"I am all he has, my lady," Maryam Ha-Levi explained. "Would we be given house room here?"

"Of course," Zaynab told her, "the lad is welcome too. You must start immediately because I know you will want to set up the kitchens in a different manner than my own cook, Aida, has them. If this is not done before I go, and if you are not firmly established here, my lord will not know what to do. There will be confusion."

"I completely understand, my lady," Maryam Ha-Levi replied. "Men are not very practical or organized when it comes to the household. That is why the Lord God created women, I am certain. Is the master of this house to be its only occupant?"

"Yes," Zaynab replied, "although he may have guests from time to time. He will not always come home at proper mealtimes, I fear; or he will forget, and eat elsewhere. It will not be easy serving him, Maryam, but he is a good man. You must not scold him unless it is with kindness. His work absorbs him almost completely. Now, on each Wednesday and Saturday night, your master will be visited by a young courtesan from the city. He may forget that she is here, and be late; or possibly not come at all. Please see that the young woman is well fed no matter the circumstances."

"A courtesan?" Maryam Ha-Levi looked shocked. "Is this a respectable house, my lady? The reb said nothing about a courtesan. Whose house is this? I cannot bring my grandson into a house of ill repute."

"This is my house, and I am the lady Zaynab, once favorite to our gracious lord, Abd-al Rahman. Our daughter is buried in the garden of this house. Now I am to go to the kingdom of Malina in Ifriqiya to be married to its prince. I am giving the house to my friend, the Nasi Hasdai ibn Shaprut. He will be your employer, Maryam Ha-Levi. I think you will find him respectable enough. Like any unmarried man, he has needs that must be served.

"My eunuch, Naja, has visited the Street of the Courtesans and personally selected a fine young woman to pleasure the Nasi. If I did not do this for him, he would be too shy to seek out the comfort of a woman for himself," Zaynab concluded.

"He should find himself a good wife," Maryam sniffed.

"No wife would put up with him." Zaynab laughed. "He is wed to his work and his duty to the caliph. He will tell you that himself."

"Well," Maryam Ha-Levi considered, "a man like that needs to be taken care of, as you have said. The Nasi has a fine reputation for fairness. He will be a good master." She was already considering the prestige she was about to gain in the quarter by being housekeeper and cook to Hasdai ibn Shaprut. "How many other servants are there?" she asked.

"A kitchen helper for you, two maidservants who keep the house clean, the stableman, and a gardener," Zaynab replied. "It is not a big house, and its one lone occupant needs little. Any more servants would be frivolous."

Maryam Ha-Levi nodded in agreement. "It's enough to ensure that the food does not go to waste on the nights the master does not eat in his own house," she said practically.

"Naja will show you to your quarters, Maryam Ha-Levi. When your master asks you, tell him you have agreed to serve him for four gold dinars a month, plus food and housing for your grandson and yourself," Zaynab said with a twinkle in her eyes.

"Four dinars! It is too much, my lady," Maryam protested, her innate honesty coming to the forefront.

"The Nasi can well afford it," Zaynab told her. "Besides, you will earn it. Your master is fair, but not easy. Also, you have the boy to think of, Maryam Ha-Levi. He must be educated, and will need gold to start a business one day so he may attract a well-dowered wife. One thing I ask of you, however. Will you place fresh flowers on my daughter's grave each day? She is buried here in the arms of her nurse, Abra, one of your people. They died of the spotted fever several months ago. It is my one regret in leaving this house."

Maryam Ha-Levi was touched by Zaynab's request. She had obviously been a good mother. "I will honor your request, my lady," she promised. "What was your daughter's name?"

"The princess was called Moraima," Zaynab said softly, tears springing to her eyes. She could still not say her baby's name without weeping. Although she now realized that Moraima would have died whether she had been with her or not, she yet felt guilt for the child's unexpected death in her absence.

"I will take Maryam Ha-Levi and show her the kitchens," Naja interjected quickly. "And there are her new quarters to inspect as well, my lady." Beckoning the woman to follow, he hurried off, leaving his mistress to recover herself.

"She loved her child," Maryam Ha-Levi said, understanding.

"We all loved the little lady Moraima," Naja said quietly.

A brand-new wardrobe had to be made for the bride. As Zaynab had taken it upon herself to make certain that Hasdai's needs would be met after her departure, the Nasi, in turn, arranged for the bride's dowry, both financial and material. Several seamstresses were brought to the house, along with bolts and bolts of colorful, luxurious fabrics. There were blouses, coats, pantaloons, caftans, cloaks, and veils to be made. They were embroidered with silver and gold as well as jewels. They were lined, or quilted for cold days, or trimmed with fur. A female cobbler came and made patterns from Zaynab's feet. These she carried back to her husband's workshop so that slippers and boots could be made for the young woman who would soon be wife to Malina's prince. Everything was done within the space of half a month's time.

Hasdai brought Zaynab a wedding present, a magnificent necklace of sapphires and diamonds. "I have never given you a real gift before," he said. "I did not realize it until the caliph asked me what my final present to you would be."

She was stunned by his generosity. "I do not know what to say, my lord. It is a wonderful gift!"

"Abd-al Rahman has sent you a gift as well," he told her, and handed her a small velvet bag.

Opening the bag, Zaynab spilled its contents into her hand. Her cupped palm glittered with the sparkle of multicolored gems. She shook her head in wonderment. It was a fortune. "Thank him for me, but also say the best gift he ever gave me was the only one I ever asked of him. Tell him I regret I did not take better care of that gift." For a moment there was silence between them, and then Zaynab said, "I have a parting gift for you as well, Hasdai. Come and bathe with me."

Zaynab's new servant, Rabi, was struggling with learning both a new language and new customs. She wasn't certain which was harder: trying to wrap her tongue about impossible syllables, or helping a naked man and woman bathe. Her cheeks were constantly hot, and it was not from the steam. Still, in the short time in which she had been with Zaynab, she had come to adore her, and would do anything for her mistress, even if it meant standing naked herself while she performed her duties.

Rabi was excited about the trip they would soon be embarking upon. Zaynab had told her of her impending marriage. "And do they also wash naked in this place to which we're going, my lady?" she asked as she rinsed her mistress with warm, perfumed water.

Zaynab nodded, her eyes twinkling, and turning to Hasdai, said, "Poor Rabi is not yet used to our ways. Naja thought it very funny when he first brought her to the bath that she did not want to remove her garments to wash. He had a terrible time convincing her, particularly as she does not yet speak our language well enough. In an effort to show her what to do, he finally removed his own garments. Rabi ran shrieking out into the garden, and poor Naja, embarrassed, had to dress himself again and seek me out to find Rabi and tell her it was all right."

Hasdai laughed heartily. "Her poor flushed little cheeks do not add to her looks, particularly with all those freckles. I suppose I had better keep myself under control, else I frighten her."

Zaynab dismissed Rabi for the evening, and they returned alone to her bedchamber. There, to the Nasi's surprise, a beautiful young woman awaited them. She was as naked as they were. Her skin was milky white, her hair as black as ebony, and her eyes a vibrant violet color. Hasdai ibn Shaprut stared at her, fascinated, and to his surprise, he felt the beginnings of arousal. He looked to Zaynab.

She smiled softly. "This is Nilak. She is Persian, and lives on the Street of the Courtesans in the city. She will come each Wednesday and Saturday night to be with you. Try not to forget that she is here, Hasdai, and do come home," Zaynab teased him. Then she took his hand. "Come, my lord. Together, Nilak and I will offer you a bit of pleasure." She led him to the bed, and the three of them sheltered upon it. "Kiss her, my lord," Zaynab gently instructed him.

To his surprise, he was very curious. Reaching out, he pulled Nilak into his arms, his mouth finding hers. Her breath was sweet, and the kiss she gave him was delightfully passionate. The scent of lilacs clung to her skin. Releasing her, he asked, "Can you speak, Nilak?"

"Of course, my lord Hasdai," she said, laughing. Her laughter was like water running over stones in a brook, her voice sweet and exquisitely modulated. "I am honored that the lady Zaynab chose me for you."

The Nasi looked over at Zaynab. Then reaching out, he put his other arm about her. She lifted her mouth to his and kissed him sweetly. Hasdai was suddenly very aware that the situation in which he now found himself was one he had never imagined. Looking at one beautiful woman and then the other, he said, "I am overwhelmed, my dears, and I haven't the faintest idea of how to proceed. I have but two hands and one pair of lips."

Both of the women laughed, but it was Nilak who said, "Let us entertain you, my lord. You will soon see that it is possible to give us both incredible pleasure at the same time." Then slithering out of his arms, she wriggled down, her ebony hair spreading over his thighs as she took his manhood into her mouth and began to suckle upon it.

Meanwhile, Zaynab reached up, and drew his head to hers, her tongue running teasingly across his lips, daring his tongue to come out to play. He complied with her unspoken request, while his hands found her breasts and he began to fondle them. His head was whirling with the series of sweet sensations assaulting him. Zaynab twisted her body about, and immediately his fingers found her mont, insinuating themselves between her nether lips, tantalizing her little jewel, pushing into her sheath to mimic a manhood.

"He is ready," Nilak said, and while she lowered herself over him, slowly absorbing him into her sheath, Zaynab pulled away from her lover, drawing the pillows from beneath his shoulders so that he lay flat. Instinctively his hands reached up to caress Nilak's high, cone-shaped breasts, even as Zaynab squatted over him, offering herself to his tongue and lips. Reaching out with his tongue, he began to flick it back and forth over her little nub of swelling flesh. His heart was beating wildly. His senses were all afire. His mind was reeling with the waves of pleasure now rolling over him. His manhood exploded with a force he had never known. Both women were sobbing with their own satisfaction as the trio collapsed, limbs entwined, in a loving heap of fulfilled passion.

When finally her breathing had steadied and her heart had ceased pounding, Zaynab asked the Nasi, "You are content to have Nilak come to you, my lord?" She smiled down into his face.

"She may certainly come," he said enthusiastically, and reaching out, drew the girl back into his embrace, kissing her ripe lips. "You have given me pleasure tonight, Nilak. I will welcome your coming after the lady Zaynab has departed."

"Thank you, my lord," Nilak replied sweetly. Then rising from the bed, she left the chamber.

"Will she be back?" he asked Zaynab. "She is very lovely, and totally different from you. I know I told you no, but I thank you for finding her for me. We will have many enjoyable hours together, I am certain."

"She will not return tonight, my lord," Zaynab said. "I just wanted you to meet her while I was with you so you would not feel shy of a new woman. You did very well, my lord. I have taught you well."

The following morning, when Zaynab awoke, Hasdai was gone, but on the pillow where his head had lain was a perfect white gardenia. Zaynab smiled softly. It was really a shame that Hasdai would not marry. He was a very romantic man. She hoped that the young courtesan, Nilak, would appreciate the Nasi's gentler qualities; but perhaps Hasdai would not be as vulnerable with Nilak as he had been with her.

Zaynab did not see Hasdai again until her departure two days later. She would travel down the Guadalquivir to its mouth, then go overland to Jabal-Taraq, to be ferried across to Ifriqiya, where she would be met by the delegation from Malina and escorted to her new home. Her many trunks containing her dowry were loaded aboard a royal vessel called *The Abd-al Rahman*. Naja, Aida, and Rabi were almost sick with their excitement when the Nasi arrived with an honor guard to accompany her to the ship. He came in his official capacity, dressed in splendid robes of cloth-of-gold brocade embroidered with pearls and diamonds. Upon his head was a matching turban.

"We don't want to miss the tide, my lady," he said formally, and helped her into her litter.

At the docks he shepherded her aboard, taking her to her spacious cabin. "The caliph chose your route because of the late autumn. He feared storms. You will not sail from Jabal-Taraq unless the weather is fair, Zaynab. We both want you to reach your destination safely."

"Has there been any word from Karim?" she asked him anxiously.

He shook his head, and then told her, "The Prince of Malina has no idea who the bride is that the caliph is sending him, Zaynab. It was a small jest upon our parts, which I hope you will forgive. I am certain, knowing Karim, that he is angry and defiant regarding the caliph's order that he take this bride being sent to him. Imagine his surprise and delight when he learns his bride is the only woman he has ever loved." The Nasi took her by the shoulders and pressed a kiss upon her forehead. "May the God who watches over us all bless your journey and your new life, Zaynab. I will never forget you, my dear." Then stepping back a pace from her, Hasdai ibn Shaprut bowed low before departing the vessel.

Zaynab felt tears pricking behind her eyelids as she watched him go. He had been her lover; her good friend. She would miss him. His sympathetic insight was entirely responsible for this journey she was now embarking upon, which would take her back to the one man she had always loved. *"I will never forget you, Hasdai,"* Zaynab said softly after him. Then she heard the shouts upon the deck as the ropes binding the ship to its mooring were loosened, allowing the vessel to float free. Suddenly she was overwhelmed with excitement. She was going home. Home to Malina. *Home to Karim!*

Chapter 20

"*A* bride? The caliph is sending me a bride?" Karim ibn Habib, Prince of Malina, looked to his vizier Alaeddin ben Omar for corroboration.

"Yes, my lord," he said. "The caliph's letter states that he feels you should be married, and that you should start a family immediately, being the last male of the direct line of ibn Malik. The caliph says your family's loyalty to his family over the centuries is deserving of reward. So he has decided to send you a bride of his choosing. She will be arriving within the month, my lord."

"I distinctly remember telling Hasdai ibn Shaprut that I would not marry again," Karim said, his irritation beginning to grow as he sensed Hasdai's hand in all of this. "I also recall saying that I would appoint my sister's son as my heir. Why did he not tell the caliph that, Alaeddin?"

"Perhaps, my lord, he did," the vizier replied. He wasn't certain whether or not he should mention that although the caliph had signed this missive, it had been sealed with Hasdai ibn Shaprut's seal, not that of Abd-al Rahman. Deciding discretion was the better route, he said nothing to his old friend.

"I do not want a bride, Alaeddin," the prince said. "My experience with Hatiba was tragic. Like some animal, I got a child on her even though I did not care for her. I cannot do that again, Alaeddin. I will not!" There was a very determined look in his blue eyes.

"You cannot offend the caliph," the vizier counseled. "He is your overlord, Karim." Alaeddin ben Omar dropped formality for expediency's sake. He needed to appeal to his friend's

398

common sense. Karim was fully capable of being foolishly
stubborn. "Wait at least until you have met the girl. I know that
no woman can ever replace Zaynab in your heart, old friend,
but perhaps this bride will make her own place, if you will but
let her."

"I must accept this woman only because she comes from the
caliph," Karim replied. "I do not, however, have to bed with
her."

"Are you mad?" the vizier cried. "This letter specifically
states that your bride has the ear and the personal respect of
Abd-al Rahman himself! If you mistreat her, she will complain
to the caliph."

"She cannot complain to him if I do not let her," Karim said
ruthlessly. "She will live in the harem and its gardens, but
never be allowed out of them. There is nothing unusual in that.
The servants will not dare to intrigue with her, for fear of my
wrath, Alaeddin. She will want for nothing."

"You *are* mad," his friend answered.

"No, I am not! I am the Prince of Malina. I will not be told
that I must take a wife and then breed her like some stallion
being put to a mare. I cannot do it, Alaeddin. How can you
even consider such a thing? You are fortunate that you have
your beloved Oma. You may eventually have a little harem of
pretties, but you will not take another wife, old friend, will
you? Why must I? Because I am the prince here? Because my
family has served the Umayyads faithfully for over two hundred years? Those reasons are not good enough for me. I will
not do it!" His voice was strong, his handsome face
implacable. "I will marry the woman because I must, but that
is all I will do."

Later, in the security of his own home, the vizier fretted to his
wife about the situation. "He is obstinate, Oma. Allah pity this
poor woman the caliph is sending to be Karim's wife."

"You say the letter was sealed with the physician's seal, and
not the caliph's," Oma said thoughtfully. What motive had the
caliph's adviser in all of this? "Hasdai ibn Shaprut knew that

Karim did not want another wife. Yet he has obviously encouraged the caliph to send him one. Why? I wonder. Who is this
woman, and for what purpose is she being sent here? This
matter may not be as simple as it seems, Alaeddin."

Oma's words raised more questions in the vizier's mind
than they answered. Was there some hidden agenda on the part
of the caliph and his most trusted adviser? And if so, what was
it? Was it possible that Hasdai ibn Shaprut did not think Karim
capable of ruling, that this bride was in actuality a spy of Abd-
al Rahman? The vizier, however, kept these thoughts to himself. There was no cause for irrational suspicions yet. There
was no need to arouse the prince's ire any more than it was
already aroused. A good vizier assembled all the facts, found
the truth, and then presented it to his master.

Word was brought to Alcazaba Malina that the bride was
within two days of Jabal-Taraq.

"Will you meet her in Tanja?" Alaeddin ben Omar asked
Karim.

"No," Karim said with a thin smile. "I am going hunting in
the hills for a few days. I shall stay at Escape."

"Then do you want me to go to Tanja to greet her in your
name, and escort her back to Alcazaba Malina?" the vizier
asked.

"Yes," Karim said. "Do we have all the papers pertaining to
this marriage in hand?" And when his companion nodded in
the affirmative, the prince said, "Then let us take them to the
imam now, and have him perform the ceremony. Since the
woman is coming, she is obviously willing. You will witness
the event. Then, when my bride arrives, she will legally be my
wife. Shut her up in the harem. When I return, I will visit her
myself and explain to her the price she must pay for becoming
the wife of Malina's prince."

"Karim, I beg you to be kind to this maiden," his friend said.
"Remember, she is only a female. She has had no real say in
this matter. She may be some poor girl recently brought to the
caliph's harem, or mayhap the daughter of an official seeking
favor with Abd-al Rahman. She must do as she is told and

agree to be your wife because she has no other choice. Do not be cruel to her because of it."

"I will not be cruel, Alaeddin, but do you not understand? It is the same thing all over again. A woman I do not really want is being forced into marriage with me. How can I love any woman when Zaynab fills my whole heart, my very soul? Her memory sears me with such pain that I cannot even describe it properly to you. *I love her.* I will always love her. There can be no other woman for me ever. Do you not understand it, my old friend? You wanted none but Oma."

Alaeddin ben Omar sighed deeply. "That is true, Karim, but had Oma not come back into my life when she did, I should have found another woman to make my wife. I might not have loved her as I do my Oma, but I have an obligation to my father and my ancestors to create a new generation.

"We are friends of long standing, so I dare to speak my mind to you, Karim al Malina. You are the last of your line. It is your duty to sire sons so that the line of your great ancestor, ibn Malik, not die out. Life has mocked you, 'tis true, in taking the one woman you love from you. But what of Zaynab? Does she not suffer as well? Still, she did her duty as well as any woman when she went to the caliph, and then to Hasdai ibn Shaprut.

"Did Abd-al Rahman love her as you did? Does Hasdai ibn Shaprut love her as you did? Zaynab, however, does not cry out like a small child denied a favorite plaything. She does what she must, what she knows she has to do, and so, my lord of Malina, should you," the vizier said angrily. "It is past time you stopped feeling sorry for yourself, and started to behave as your father would have wanted you to; as a Prince of Malina should behave!"

Karim stared at his old friend, startled by the severity of his words and realizing that Alaeddin ben Omar was correct in all he said. "It is simply too soon," he said helplessly. "I am not ready for another wife."

The vizier nodded. "I will greet the bride, my lord, while you go to Escape and make peace with yourself," he told him. "Perhaps the caliph's timing is not the best, but that is not the fault of your bride, now is it, my lord? She comes to you filled

with hope, and with the same joyous expectations as any bride.
If she is very young, she may also be a little frightened. After
all she is being married to a virtual stranger, and sent far from
her home. With your permission, I will have Oma visit her in
the harem before you return."

"Yes," Karim said, "that would be kind."

The two men went with the qadi that evening to the head
imam of Malina. The wedding contracts were presented to him,
and having read them carefully, the imam then performed the
marriage ceremony. The bride was a wife before she even set
foot upon the shores of Ifriqiya, though she did not know it.
The following day Karim, in the company of half a dozen of
his personal guard, rode into the hills to hunt, while his vizier
rode to the city of Tanja to greet the royal wedding party. The
trip, a three-day one by caravan, took only a day and a half, as
Alaeddin ben Omar and his Saqalibah rode swiftly, without
encumbrance.

The caliph's governor in Tanja greeted them. He had been
informed of the pending arrival of the prince's bride, who
would be embarking from Jabal-Taraq the following morning,
weather permitting.

The next day dawned bright and sunny, unusual for late
autumn. The sea outside the city's bay was smooth and flawless. A watchman from atop Tanja's highest point, the minaret
of the main mosque, called out just before noon prayers
that the convoy was in sight. The vizier, in the company
of the governor, hurried down to the harbor to await the bride.

"You will stay another night, of course," the governor said
to Alaeddin ben Omar. "The lady will undoubtedly be exhausted
by her crossing and wish to rest. Do you know who she is, my
lord?"

The vizier shook his head. "It is strange," he told the governor, "but the caliph's letter mentioned everything but her
name and family. Nor was it present in the marriage contracts."

"Perhaps," the governor responded, "they were not certain
who they would choose until the very last moment. Such an
important decision is not to be made without careful thought.
The caliph is generous to send your prince a bride." He smiled

toothily. "Obviously Karim al Malina stands high in our gracious lord's esteem. What good fortune for him, and for Malina, but then Abd-al Rahman is always kind to those he favors." There was the faintest hint of envy in the governor's tone. As a royal governor, he thought himself more important than a mere provincial prince.

"I must accept your word in the matter, my lord," the vizier said smoothly. "Your knowledge is far greater than mine in such things. I am but a simple Malinean. I know my prince will want to thank you for your kindness." He smiled faintly and bowed to the governor. Alaeddin ben Omar had met men like this one before: civil servants with large egos. To handle such persons one had but to be gracious and just slightly self-effacing. The Governor of Tanja, believing himself superior to everyone but the caliph, was soothed.

The ship carrying Zaynab and her party, as well as those escorting it, sailed into the harbor of Tanja. Unobserved, Zaynab watched the shore from the window of her cabin as the vessel drew near the dock. Karim had not come. He was sulking because the caliph had sent him a bride he thought he did not want. She smiled to herself. What a surprise he had coming. She saw Alaeddin ben Omar in the company of the Governor of Tanja.

"Naja," she said to her eunuch, who stood next to her, "the large man with the black beard is Alaeddin ben Omar, the prince's vizier."

"Oma's husband," Naja replied. "He is a fine-looking man."

"Yes," she answered him, and then she smiled again. "If he asks you my name, make some excuse not to tell him. I am curious as to whether he will recognize me." She chuckled wickedly. "I am certainly the last person in the world Alaeddin ben Omar expects to see, Naja. He will, I imagine, be just a little intimidated by the arrival of the woman chosen by the caliph himself to be Karim's bride."

"You are like I have never known you to be, mistress," Naja said to her. "Why is this so?"

Zaynab put her hand on the eunuch's hand and said quietly,

"Because, Naja, I am free again, and I am going to the man I have always loved above all others." Then she called to Rabi. "Bring me the small sandalwood box with the silver banding." When the young servant had complied, Zaynab opened it, drawing forth three rolled parchments, each with a different colored seal upon it. "Gather around," she told her servants. She handed a parchment to each of them: the one with the dark green seal to Naja, the red seal to Aida, and the blue seal to Rabi. "Before we left Cordoba I went to the qadi and freed each of you," Zaynab told them. "These parchments are your proofs of manumission. I hope you will remain in my service, but if you choose not to, I will send you to any place you choose to go. It is important to me that those who have shared in my captivity now share in my freedom, and in my happiness."

The three were astounded. "Lady," Naja spoke for them all, "there is no way in which we can properly thank you, but I, for one, would remain in your service. I could have no better mistress."

"And I will always cook for you, mistress," Aida said, tears in her dark eyes.

"And I will remain also," Rabi said slowly in her new tongue before slipping back into her native speech. "Yer a good lady, and I couldna hae any better life than wi' ye back in Alba, where I should be poor again, and end up a whore to keep meself."

"Thank you all," Zaynab said simply. "Naja will give you your instructions before we disembark. We will probably remain the night here in Tanja before we start for Alcazaba Malina. It is a lovely place, and you will be happy there, I know. Now, Rabi, find my cloak. The vizier will be coming aboard shortly."

Naja instructed the others quickly, as Rabi helped Zaynab into a beautiful mauve silk cloak with a narrow hood that came down to just above her eyebrows. The young servant fastened a silk veil across her mistress's face so that only Zaynab's eyes were visible. The veil was not a diaphanous one, but rather made of a heavier fabric.

There was a knock at the door, and Naja went to answer it.

"I am Alaeddin ben Omar, Grand Vizier to the Prince of

Malina," the man standing before him said. "I have been sent to welcome the princess."

Naja bowed politely, and with an elegant wave of his hand ushered the vizier into the cabin. "Mistress," he said to Zaynab, who stood with her head modestly bowed, "this is the prince's representative."

She nodded graciously in acknowledgment.

"My gracious lady," the vizier said, bowing low, "I have been sent by my master to escort you to your new home. As we have a three-day journey ahead of us, we will stay in Tanja tonight so you may rest in comfort. May I take you to your litter now? It is large enough for your female servants as well."

"My lady thanks you," Naja quickly spoke up. "She begs your kind indulgence, my lord vizier. She is a modest woman. She has vowed that the sound of her voice and the sound of her name shall be first heard in Malina by her bridegroom, and not before then. She hopes everyone will understand."

"How charming," the vizier said, but he thought it odd. Still, the polite young eunuch was in deadly earnest. "Let us go ashore, then." Alaeddin ben Omar sighed, for there was obviously nothing else to say.

The governor had assigned the prince's bride an apartment outside of his own harem, much to Zaynab's relief. She was not certain that someone among the governor's women might not recognize her from her last brief stay. "Arrange to have the bath made private for me," she told Naja.

"There is no need, mistress," he replied. "This apartment has its own small bath." Naja had grown plump in Zaynab's service. Fair-skinned with rosy pink cheeks and intelligent brown eyes, he was beginning to cultivate a certain self-assurance that came from being the trusted servant of an important person.

"Your explanation to the vizier was most resourceful," Zaynab complimented him. "How romantic of you, Naja." She giggled. "I shall not speak until I greet my bridegroom, nor shall any learn my name before he does. Allah! If you could but design a poem, Naja, 'twould be an epic one!" Then she laughed again. "When he learns the truth, the vizier shall be very amused, for he appreciates a good jest, my faithful Naja.

Now, to the bath, for I am dying for perfumed water, and my hair is sticky with the salt air." She flung off her cloak, handing it to Rabi.

In the early morning, they departed Tanja for Alcazaba Malina. Zaynab's dowry and many belongings had been loaded upon a string of camels and into carts that were drawn by sturdy donkeys. The vizier was impressed in spite of himself.

"Your mistress's family is very generous," he remarked to Naja, who was overseeing the last-minute preparations.

"Yes, my lord," Naja said with a cheerful smile.

Zaynab walked from the governor's palace to the courtyard, and entered into her litter. She was once again muffled in all-enveloping silk cloak and veils, her head lowered as it should be. Alaeddin ben Omar could not even ascertain the color of her eyes, her form, or age. He wondered avidly what his new princess looked like. When they got to Alcazaba Malina, Oma would visit her in the royal harem, and return home to tell him.

The journey was an uneventful one. The night before they arrived, when they were once again on Malinean soil, the vizier came to Zaynab's tent and told Naja he would speak with his mistress. Naja ushered him into her presence. She sat upon a chair, dressed in a simple caftan, a veil covering her head, another her face.

Alaeddin ben Omar bowed politely. "I was instructed by my master to tell you when you enter the city tomorrow, you enter it as the wife of Karim ibn Habib, gracious lady. The marriage ceremony was performed several days ago by our chief imam, the contracts being in good order. He hopes this satisfies you."

Zaynab beckoned to Naja, who bent to hear her. Then straightening himself, the eunuch said, "My mistress is overjoyed by your words, my lord vizier. She wishes to know if the prince will be at the gates of the city to greet her."

Alaeddin ben Omar looked uncomfortable. "My master is hunting deer and pheasant in the hills, lady. I am not honestly certain if he will be there tomorrow. He is an enthusiastic sportsman, and the winter rains will soon begin. He hopes you will understand. I have been instructed to see that you are settled in the royal harem. My wife, the lady Oma, will be happy to keep you company until the prince returns. I am sure you have many questions about your new home. She can answer them."

"My mistress is most grateful, my lord vizier, for your words. She will welcome the lady Oma gladly," Naja told him.

Afterward, when the vizier had left, the eunuch said indignantly, "What manner of man is this prince, my lady, that he will not welcome his bride?"

"A proud and stubborn one, Naja," Zaynab said with a little laugh. "You see, he told the Nasi that he would never marry again because he loved a woman he was unable to have. You know that I am that woman. His mood will change when he learns the truth. In the meantime he hunts in the hills beyond the city, angry and resentful, determined to show this new bride he is the master of his own domain."

They entered the city the next day, and to Zaynab's surprise, the streets were lined with Alcazaba Malina's cheering citizenry, who had come to welcome their new princess.

"Ohh, lady, 'tis a grand reception," Rabi said, impressed.

Zaynab was touched, but she was also excited. Soon she would see her dear Oma again! Oma would be the only one to know her true identity until Karim came. Her friend knew well how to keep a secret. Remembering the vizier's devotion to Karim, Zaynab knew that poor Alaeddin would be unable to keep himself from riding out to find Karim, and bringing him the good news, should Oma tell him the truth. Zaynab was curious to see how long it would take her husband to come home on his own. *Her husband.* Karim was her husband now!

Their procession entered the courtyard of the little palace. "Allah!" Zaynab cried softly. "I have forgotten about Mustafa! He will know me if he sees me, and he is permitted free access to the harem. Aida, tell Naja to come to me as soon as we enter the harem."

Mustafa was indeed waiting to greet his new mistress. He stepped forward to hand her from the litter. Zaynab exited the vehicle, veiled, her head and eyes lowered.

"Welcome to Malina, Princess," the head eunuch said.

"My mistress thanks you," Naja said promptly, politely explaining why she would not speak for herself. He did not want to get on the bad side of Mustafa, who he knew was responsible for running the palace, and therefore an important man. They would have to work together.

Mustafa nodded at the younger man. Then he echoed what the vizier had said. "How charming."

They were led not to the harem, but to another part of the palace entirely. She whispered to Naja, and he then spoke to Mustafa.

"Is this the place where the prince's family was murdered, Mustafa? My mistress is afraid of ghosts."

Mustafa then turned to Zaynab and said, "No, gracious lady. The old harem is shut up, and that part of the building will soon be destroyed. Your apartment is next to that of the prince, your husband. My master thought you would be more comfortable here until he can build a new women's quarters."

So, Zaynab thought, Karim had been considerate of the unwanted bride after all. She whispered again to Naja, and he turned to Mustafa.

"My mistress would not offend you, Mustafa, but she asks that you not come to these rooms until after she has met the prince. When is he expected to return home? She is anxious to meet him."

"The prince has not yet sent word of his return," Mustafa replied. No, he has left us all to cope with this new wife, the head eunuch thought irritably. Then he politely took his leave of Zaynab.

"Do you think he is curious as to why you do not want him here, my lady?" Naja asked. "He seems an intelligent fellow."

"I do not think we have yet roused his suspicions," Zaynab answered. "Mustafa is the most circumspect of servants. I think he will attribute my request to shyness."

They settled themselves in the spacious apartments assigned to them. There was a charming small bath, tiled in green and white porcelain, with a bathing pool of green onyx. The day room was large and opened onto the garden, as did Zaynab's chamber. This room had an octagonal domed ceiling with carved wooden pendants that were ornately painted. The floor was of turquoise blue and white tiles. There was a wonderful bed set upon a dais of fragrant sandalwood, but the rest of the decor had obviously been left for the bride to complete. Rabi and Aida immediately set about unpacking Zaynab's belongings and hanging the sheer silk hangings, while their mistress, in Naja's company, explored the rest of her rooms. The two found several small bedchambers in addition to the other rooms, but these were totally void of furnishings.

"Go to Mustafa and tell him what we need," Zaynab said as they returned to the day room, which was prettily furnished with several upholstered divans, tables, and chairs. "I would have you all comfortable. And ask him when the vizier's wife is coming to see me. Tell him I wish to learn all I can about my adopted country before my husband returns home." Then she chuckled. "I cannot wait to see Oma's face!"

Oma arrived one rainy afternoon. As they had been expecting her, Rabi answered the knock at the door, for she was the only one of Zaynab's servants her friend did not know.

"Welcome, lady," Rabi said politely. "My mistress is expecting you and has looked forward to your arrival. She requests that you do not scream when you see her, as it might bring Mustafa or the guards."

What an odd request, Oma thought, and then her eyes widened as Zaynab came from another room, smiling. "Is it truly you? How . . . ?"

Zaynab put her arms about Oma and hugged her. "Yes, it is really me, dearest Oma, and in the two months I have been gone, you have gained a little bit of a belly. It is most becoming." She smiled. "The son of Alaeddin ben Omar thrives, I can see." She took her friend's hand and led her to a comfortable divan. "Sit, and we will talk."

"Why did not my husband tell me it was you?" Oma demanded, outraged.

"Because he does not know it is me," Zaynab told her mischievously. "He has seen nothing of me but a great muffled figure. I have kept my eyes lowered so he would not recognize me or grow suspicious. Naja has told everyone who will listen that I will not utter a word, or allow my name to be spoken until my husband comes," she finished with a laugh.

"No one knows? Not even old Mustafa?" Oma was amazed.

"Not even Mustafa," Zaynab assured her.

Oma shook her head. "How is it you are back in Malina, my lady Zaynab? Where is little Moraima?"

"Moraima died of the spotted fever while we were here last," Zaynab said softly, tears springing to her eyes, and she told the rest of the story to her friend. "May the God of Abraham, Jacob, and Isaac bless Hasdai ibn Shaprut for his kindness to me; and may Allah continue to smile on my dear Abd-al Rahman, that they returned me to Karim. When I found that my child was dead, Oma, I actually lost my will to live. I had no hope at all, but they saved me," Zaynab concluded. "They are wonderful men."

"The prince will be so happy," Oma said, honestly. "My husband has said how very unhappy he has been since his family was killed, even if he has done his duty by his country. He keeps no women, my lady Zaynab. He has become like a hermit, preferring his own company for the most part. He eats alone, hunts, and governs with a benign hand, but he has no real pleasures, and is so lonely. I have not really seen him smile in weeks."

"Yet he ran off into the hills to hunt, rather than meet his bride," Zaynab said tartly.

"He will regret his actions, I have not a doubt, when he learns that it is you," Oma said with a giggle. "How will you greet him?"

"I have not decided," Zaynab said, "but you will have to help me, Oma, by letting me know, as soon as your husband does, when Karim will return. When the vizier asks you what I look like, tell him that I am very fair, but no more than that. Tell him that I want nothing of my person known until my husband sees me. I have made myself quite, quite mysterious. If Alaeddin runs true to form, he will surely send word about it to Karim. My bridegroom will come home merely to satisfy his curiosity." She chuckled. "Men cannot abide a mystery, Oma."

* * *

When Oma reached her home her husband was eagerly waiting for her.

"Well?" he demanded. "What is she like?"

"She is charming; delightful, in fact," Oma said. "I have never met a lovelier lady than the princess. We are all most fortunate."

"But what does she look like?" the vizier asked his wife. "Is she fair, or dark? Slender, or full-figured?"

Oma smiled. "I cannot tell you, my lord. The princess has asked that I say nothing of her until she has met with her husband, but I will tell you this: She is not ugly."

Alaeddin ben Omar wanted to shout with his frustration. Karim had taken a wife. Malina had a new princess, and no one, not even the venerable Mustafa, had caught so much as a glimpse of her. It was intolerable! He had to find Karim! The prince must return home.

The following morning the vizier rode into the purple hills. He found Karim at Escape in the late afternoon. The prince looked more rested and relaxed than his friend had seen him look in weeks.

"Have you come to join me?" Karim grinned at his vizier. "The hunting is excellent. I cannot remember an autumn when it was better."

"Your bride has arrived," Alaeddin ben Omar said.

"Is she pretty?" Karim asked offhandedly. "What does Oma say? I know a proper maiden would not show her face to a man other than her husband, but I am certain Oma has already visited, and has reported everything to you. Is she dark, or fair? Plump, or slender?"

"I haven't the faintest idea," the vizier answered the prince. "You see, my good lord, your bride will show herself to no one outside the harem. Yes, Oma has visited, but she will say nothing of the princess's appearance except that she is not ugly. Your bride will not speak, nor will she allow her name to be spoken until her husband comes and hears it first. *Even Mustafa is forbidden the harem.* Your bride is served by her three servants, and no others. She walks within your gardens muffled like a mummy. She has vowed to reveal nothing of herself until you come to her."

Karim al Malina laughed. He was intrigued in spite of himself. Was this shyness deliberate on the part of his bride? Was she, Allah forfend, one of those coy creatures? "Does Oma say nothing at all about her?" he asked the vizier. "There must be something."

"Oma says the princess is charming and delightful, my lord," Alaeddin ben Omar answered dryly. "Nothing more."

"Hmmmm," Karim considered. Well, she certainly didn't sound like Hatiba. Oma was not a woman to demur when asked a question, nor would she lie to please anyone. If Oma had said his bride was charming and delightful, then she was indeed charming and delightful. He had to admit he was even more curious now. Still, it did not mean he would love this woman any more than he had been able to love Hatiba. He loved Zaynab, and he always would love her. But the girl was his wife. He wasn't a man who would deliberately make a woman unhappy. If the caliph wanted him to get sons on the girl, so be it! If he could not love her as he did Zaynab, at least he might be able to grow fond of her. It wasn't his bride's fault he felt as he did.

"I hope my wife is being clever, and not coy," Karim finally said to Alaeddin ben Omar. "We'll hunt in the morning and return to the city in the afternoon."

Oma had hurried to the palace as soon as her husband departed. "Alaeddin has gone into the hills to find Karim," she told Zaynab. "I have posted a messenger on the road outside the city gates. He will come directly to the palace to warn you when he sees them returning."

"They will not come tonight," Zaynab said with certainty. "Karim will not wish to appear too anxious to meet me. He will want to believe he still has the upper hand. But he will come tomorrow, for he will be curious about what the vizier tells him." Then she chuckled.

"I have never seen you so happy," Oma said. "Not since the

days when the prince was training you to be a Love Slave, my lady Zaynab."

"I haven't been so happy since those days," came the frank reply.

The next morning, Naja went to Mustafa and said, "The princess believes that the prince will come home today. She asks his indulgence in granting her a small favor. My mistress asks that the prince not visit her until the moon begins to rise over the gardens." He bowed.

"I will certainly pass on the princess's request, Naja. She is obviously a very romantic young woman, I can see," Mustafa replied with a small smile. "I feel this bodes well for the marriage of my prince and your mistress."

Zaynab spent the day with her three servants, preparing for Karim's arrival. Her long golden hair was washed and perfumed. She examined her body for any superfluous body hair, and removed what she found. The nails on her feet and hands were pared as short as possible. Zaynab's bedchamber was specially prepared, a decanter of sweet wine and her small golden basket set upon the octagonal tables by her bedside.

In late afternoon as she was eating her only meal of the day, she heard Oma's messenger come to tell Naja that the prince and the vizier had just entered the city through the western gates.

Zaynab finished her food and then bathed a final time. Rabi rubbed her mistress's body lavishly with sweet oils scented with almonds. The sky was growing dark. As it was almost winter, the days were shorter. Two lamps only were lit in Zaynab's day room. Mustafa came to tell Naja that his master had entered the palace and would honor his wife's request.

"Wake me just before the moon rises over the gardens," Zaynab told Rabi, and dismissed her servants. She then lay down and slept until her servant gently shook her shoulder, whispering, " 'Tis time, mistress." She heard Rabi scuttle from her bedchamber, the door closing behind her. Zaynab arose, stretched slowly, and walked to the windows to stare out. She watched as the full moon rose slowly over the gardens. Her ear caught the sound of the door to her apartments opening. She moved to her chosen position.

Karim entered his bride's rooms. Her servants were nowhere in sight, and the room was dimly lit in such a fashion as to point the way to her bedchamber door. He smiled. It was beautifully done. His new wife was clever, not coy, he immediately decided, leaving him more interested than he had been before. She would not bore him.

Walking across the floor, he put his hand on the handle of the door, turned it, and stepped into the room. It was dark, but for the moonlight filtering through the far window. He was at once assailed by the scent of roses, and to his surprise, realized that the floor beneath his bare feet was strewn with rose petals. He was almost ankle deep in them. As he crushed them with his feet, their perfume filled his nostrils. He grinned. They had not sent him some blushing, stammering maiden. Clever Hasdai! He had been sent a woman for a wife. *A woman of experience.*

And then two arms slipped about him from behind. "Welcome home, my lord," a smoky, whispery voice murmured tantalizingly to him. Slender fingers reached out to nimbly unfasten his caftan, drawing it over his head and dropping it to the floor. "Do not turn about, my lord," the shadowy voice breathed softly in his ear, sending a shiver of anticipation up his spine. "Not quite yet, I pray you."

He could feel her warm, silken nakedness against his own as her hands caressed him with sensuous little movements. Plump breasts, a rounded belly, firm thighs pressed into him. The hair on the nape of his neck rose at the touch of her lips as she kissed him, her hands fluttering over his taut belly. He was, to his great surprise, enjoying himself. Her bold yet sensual touch aroused him deeply.

"You are not at all what I expected," he said with understatement, and she laughed a husky laugh. "I thought that surely I had been sent some sweet little virgin to breed with, but you are not, I suspect, that girl. Who are you, and what is your name?" he asked her. He attempted to turn about.

"Not yet, my lord," came the mysterious, whispered reply. Zaynab was amused to feel him already hard as iron beneath her touch. Oma had not exaggerated. Karim had been abstaining from pleasure. She realized she would not be able to hold him at bay for a great deal longer. "Come," she said, taking his hand in hers, leading him to the bed, always keeping the dim light behind her, her face in shadow. Firmly she pushed him onto the bed, joining him to lie on her hip by his side, her hand gently caressing him still.

It was exciting, and yet frustrating, not to be able to see her face, he thought, but it did not prevent him reaching up to fondle one of her breasts, which hung like a tempting fruit above him. She purred with her own pleasure as he touched her. He was being seduced by a faceless woman. Oma had said she was charming and delightful, but what if she was ugly? His mouth closed over her nipple. Suddenly he didn't care. She had a body like a fertility goddess, and a manner that enticed him far more than any woman he had known in years. If he must be married to a woman who was not Zaynab, then let this be the woman.

Zaynab reached out with her hand to stroke his lean torso. She had almost forgotten how beautiful his body was, but now her fingers recalled every bump and crease of him as they slid over his flesh. His manhood was standing tall. She found that she was unable to prevent her fingers from closing about him, squeezing him tenderly. He was warm and throbbed with life. She could not stop herself from leaning down and taking him in her mouth. The familiar musk of him burgeoned on her tongue as she suckled him for a long moment, then slowly licked the length of him, encircling the ruby head of his member until she felt his hand, fastening itself in her hair, drawing her away.

"I have not had a woman in some time," he admitted to her. "Not since my first wife died. Ride me now, my sweet shadow lover. Once I have eased my pent-up lust, we will spend the night enjoying each other. You are skilled, I can see, but there is much I can teach you."

"Is there?" She laughed, even as she was mounting him,

and Karim thought the laughter had a strangely familiar ring to it.

She devoured his length within her sheath, closing it about the hard, hot flesh, her muscles squeezing him tightly several times. Then she began to ride him, slowly at first, finally with increasing vigor.

Reaching up, he grasped her two breasts and crushed them in his big hands. She was magnificent! She was incredible! Only once had he known such a woman. *Only once!* There could only be one such woman! It wasn't possible, and yet . . .

Her hair came loose and fell around her shoulders. The moon, reaching its zenith, suddenly filled the room with silvery light. Karim saw pale golden hair in his lust. He struggled with his passion, forcing his eyes to remain open, focusing on her face now fully visible in the moonlight.

"Zaynab!" he cried, and his desire exploded within her, rushing forth like a flood to water her secret garden.

Her aquamarine eyes met his, filling with tears of unashamed joy. She collapsed upon him, sated. "I have come home to you, Karim," she said happily. *"I have come home!"*

✤ _Epilogue_

Zaynab, Princess of Malina, sat in her summer garden watching the children at play. Six were her own. Seven belonged to her best friend, Oma. Her eldest son, Ja'far, was almost nine. Habib would soon be eight; Abd-al five; and Sulayman was just past two. Their two sisters, Qumar and Subh, were seven—identical twins, as their mother and her own sister had been. Oma's eldest, who was Alaeddin ben Omar's only daughter, had already cast her eyes upon Ja'far ibn Karim. Her name was Al-ula, and she told all who would listen that she intended to wed the heir of Malina one day.

"I think her far too bold in her speech," Al-ula's mother remarked to Zaynab. Oma had become the very model of the proper Malinean wife. Her husband had taken no other, although he kept two pretty women in his harem as concubines. They were both childless, and would remain so, if Oma could manage it.

"I find her amusing," Zaynab replied. "I do not want Ja'far to marry some obedient, boring girl one day. Al-ula would suit me well as a daughter-in-law, if she would suit my son. The choice, however, will be up to him when the time comes. He must fall in love even as we did."

"Aye," Oma agreed, nodding.

Zaynab grew silent for a time, contemplating back over the last ten years of her life. Smiling, she recalled the look upon Karim's face that first night when the moonlight had revealed her identity to him. His countenance had at first been unbelieving, and then when he was certain he was not imagining it, joyous beyond anything she had ever seen. They had wept with

417

happiness in each other's arms, vowing never to be separated ever again. She had indeed come home to him. Ja'far had been born nine months later to the very day, and Malina had rejoiced with its prince and princess in the birth of a son.

The other children had followed in their time, while Malina prospered as never before. In the marketplaces of the tiny country and in its single city, the people said that the prosperity of Malina was due to the happiness of its ruler and the fertility of his beautiful wife. Malinean silver and produce were in great demand in al-Andalus, and consequently commanded high prices.

In the hills, the mountain clans also thrived under Karim's rule, their herds growing fat in meadows of rich grass, and selling for premium tariffs at the yearly horse fair that the prince had commanded be held each autumn in Alcazaba Malina. Only a tenth of each sale was taken by the government. Content, the mountain clans were pleased to remain at peace.

The economic well-being of Malina was echoed all over al-Andalus under Abd-al Rahman's rule. Cordoba was Europe's most prosperous city, as well as its political and intellectual center, outshining both Baghdad and Constantinople. Missions from France, the German states, Ifriqiya, and the East came to the caliph's court to pay their respects, to learn, and to gawk. Abd-al Rahman enlarged the central mosque in Cordoba, giving it a magnificent minaret topped with three spheres shaped like pomegranates. Two were fashioned of gold and one of silver. Together they weighed three tons. *De Materia Medica*'s Arabic translation was completed, and the medical university in Cordoba was founded. Now students no longer had to go to Baghdad to become physicians.

The prince and his vizier entered into the gardens. Alaeddin ben Omar was beginning to show flecks of silver in his black beard. His face broke into a grin as Al-ula threw herself at her father, and he swept her up into his arms, kissing her rosy cheek. "Fit for a prince, she is!" he said, his laughter booming.

"Do not encourage her bad behavior," Oma scolded her husband.

"Oh, I will marry her one day," young Ja'far ibn Karim said

with a twinkle in his blue eyes, "but she will have to grow a fine pair of breasts before I do, my lady Oma."

"Ja'far!" his mother said sternly, but then she laughed.

"Just like his father," Karim murmured, seating himself next to his wife, his arm slipping about her waist, kissing her ear.

Zaynab smiled, turning to look lovingly at him. If anything, she loved him more today than when they had first been reunited. "I would," she said, "that it could go on forever like this, Karim."

"Aye, my jewel," he answered her. "If there be paradise on earth, then here we have surely found it!"

And about the four adults the children ran back and forth laughing and playing, their young faces alight with their innocent happiness, their minds unclouded, thinking about nothing more important than whether their parents would allow them to stay up after dark to catch lightning bugs in crystal jars so they might watch them until they fell asleep.

"They are the future," Karim said to his wife.

"In the spring," she responded, "I shall give you another bit of the future, another tiny piece of immortality, my darling."

"I love you, Zaynab," he said. "Always and forever it has and will be you, no other, my jewel."

Zaynab reached up, touching Karim's cheek tenderly. "How extravagant you are, my dear lord. *Always and forever?* I shall hold you to it!"

⁂ A Note from the Author

I hope you have enjoyed *The Love Slave*. The Moors of Spain have a rich and varied history, of which I have only touched a tiny part. For those of you who like the history in particular, I suggest the following reading list:

Muslim Spain: Its History and Culture, Anwar G. Chejne. University of Minnesota Press, 1974.

The Moors in Spain and Portugal, Jan Read. Rowman & Littlefield, 1975.

Moorish Spain, Richard Fletcher. Henry Holt & Co., 1992.

The Rise and Fall of Paradise: When the Arabs and Jews Built a Kingdom in Spain, Elmer Bendiner. G.P. Putman's Sons, 1983.

The Moors: Islam in the West, Brett & Foreman. Echoes of the Ancient World, Golden Press, 1980, 1985.

Andalus: Spain Under the Muslims, Edwyn Hole. Robert Hale Ltd., London, 1958.

The Jews of Spain: A History of the Sephardic Experience, Jane S. Gerber. Macmillan Co., The Free Press, 1992.

And as always, I invite you to write me about my books at P.O. Box 765, Southold, NY 11971-0765.

Love Letters

Ballantine romances are on the Web!

Read about your favorite Ballantine authors and upcoming books on our Web site, LOVE LETTERS, at **www.randomhouse.com/BB/loveletters**, including:

♥ What's new in the stores
♥ Previews of upcoming books
♥ In-depth interviews with romance authors and
  publishing insiders
♥ Sample chapters from new romances
♥ And more . . .

Want to keep in touch? To subscribe to Love Notes, the monthly what's-new update for the Love Letters Web site, send an e-mail message to **loveletters@cruises.randomhouse.com** with "subscribe" as the subject of the message. You will receive a monthly announcement of the latest news and features on our site.

So follow your heart and visit us at
www.randomhouse.com/BB/loveletters!